BLOWING IN THE WIND

About the Author . . .

BERNICE M. CHAPPEL was associated with the field of education in Michigan for twenty-nine years. During this time she was a classroom teacher for nineteen years, followed by ten years as a school social worker. She holds a Bachelor of Science degree from Eastern Michigan University and a Master's degree in Education from the University of Michigan.

Since her retirement, Bernice M. Chappel has visited nearly every country in North and Central America, several in South America, most of the Asian countries and a few European nations.

Blowing In The Wind

The Fury of Frontier War

Bernice M. Chappel

Library of Congress Catalog Card Number 89–040634

ISBN: 0–923568–06–9

Cover art by Patricia von Strohe

PUBLISHED BY

Wilderness Adventure Books
320 Garden Lane
Box 968
Fowlerville, Michigan 48836

Typesetting by LaserText Services

Manufactured in the United States of America

CONTENTS

Also by Bernice M. Chappel

In the Palm of the Mitten

Bittersweet Trail

Lure of the Arctic

Reap the Whirlwind

FORT RIDGELY 1862

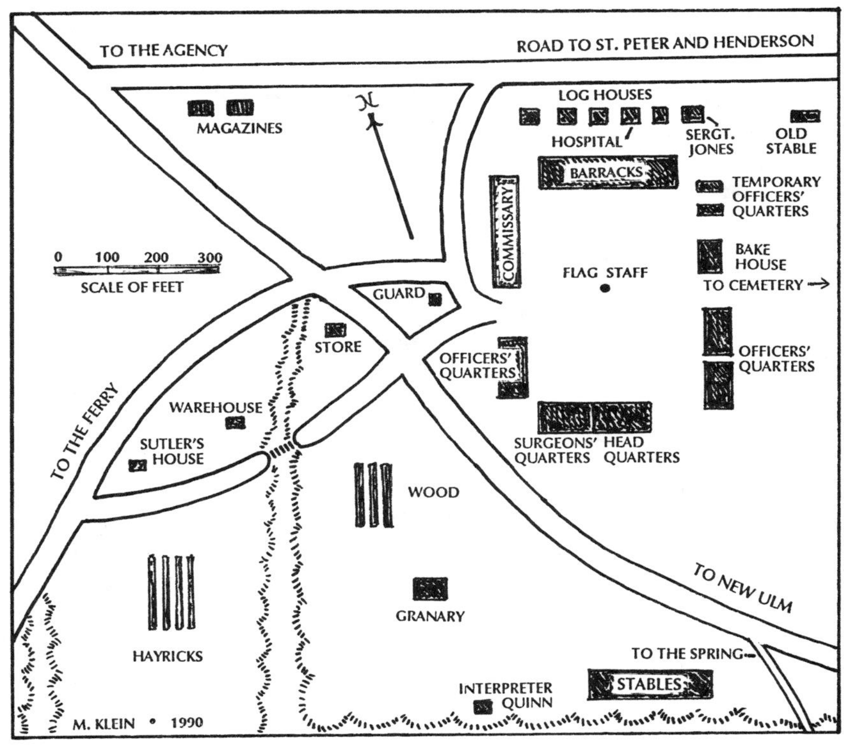

FROM A SKETCH MAP BY BENJAMIN H. RANDALL

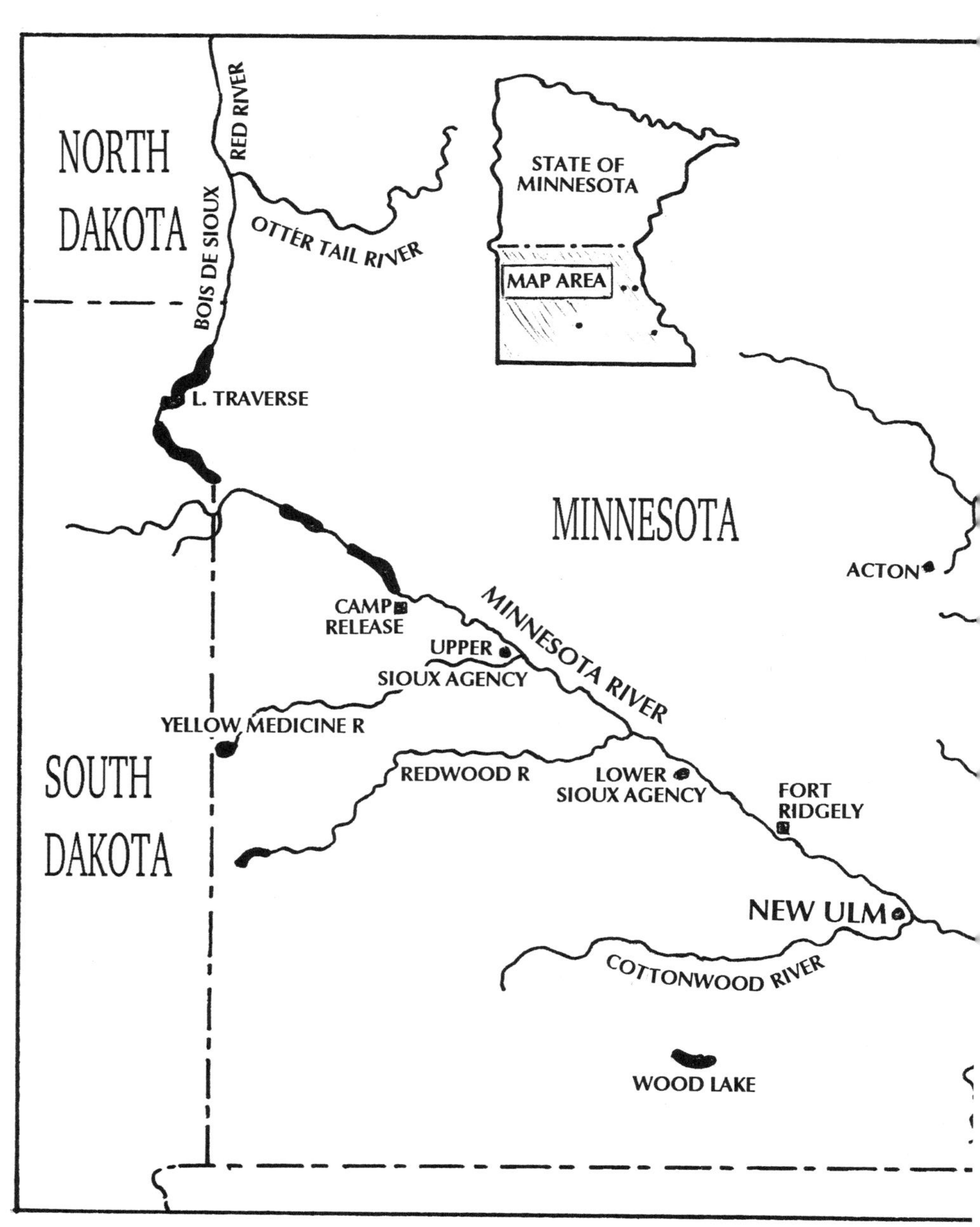
NORTH DAKOTA
RED RIVER
BOIS DE SIOUX
OTTER TAIL RIVER
STATE OF MINNESOTA
MAP AREA
L. TRAVERSE
MINNESOTA
ACTON
CAMP RELEASE
MINNESOTA RIVER
UPPER SIOUX AGENCY
YELLOW MEDICINE R
SOUTH DAKOTA
REDWOOD R
LOWER SIOUX AGENCY
FORT RIDGELY
NEW ULM
COTTONWOOD RIVER
WOOD LAKE

MISSISSIPPI RIVER
ST. CROIX RIVER
WISCONSIN
FOREST CITY
HUTCHINSON
MINNEAPOLIS
ST. PAUL
FORT SNELLING
MINNESOTA R
MISSISSIPPI RIVER
HENDERSON
ST. PETER
MANKATO
WINONA
WINNEBAGO AGENCY
MAP OF SOUTHERN MINNESOTA
SIOUX OUTBREAK AND WAR — 1862
M. KLEIN • 1990
IOWA

BOOK 1

The Crossing

1.

AMELIA SLOWLY SLID HER ARMS into her dark gray wadmal coat. She turned. Her glance took in every detail of the cottage which had been her home for two years. There was the tiny bedroom where she and Wilhelm had spent every night since their wedding, and the room where she had given birth to year-old Eduard. The fire still smoldered in the fireplace where she had cooked and baked for her family.

Now the little home was bare of all furnishings. Nothing remained to indicate they had lived here—nothing was left except her memories. She brushed away a tear and stooped to pick up her sleeping baby. He whimpered.

"There, there," she crooned. "We have to go, Eddie. We are going to America."

Almost as though he understood her emotion, the baby wakened screaming. She rocked him in her arms. "I feel like screaming too," she murmured.

The door burst open. "Amelia! Everyone's waiting!" Wilhelm seized her shawl and draped it over his wife's head. He tucked the long ends snugly about the screaming baby. "It's raining and cold," he said as he snuffed out the candle.

Silently they walked down the path to a flat-rack-wagon piled high with the Winters family members and all that was left of their possessions.

Grandmother Mary Winters complained shrilly. "Hurry up, child! We're getting wet while you putter around, and we still have to stop at Ketchums!"

Amelia's mother-in-law, Elizabeth, called, "I've saved a corner here on a big chest for you and Eddie." Silently the young wife climbed up and took the crying baby from her husband.

Amelia glanced around in the early morning light. "Good morning." She spoke to her father-in-law, Ernst, and his father, old Jacob. They nodded.

A neighbor, Johan Weber, the driver and owner of the pair of oxen, joked. "Thought you'd made up your mind to stay here, Amelia." The wagon started.

"We should have all stayed here!" Old Mary complained. "America!" She spat out the word as she pulled her shawl over a leather bag on her lap.

Though there were seven people and the driver, the group was silent as the oxen made their way three miles to the former home of the Ketchum family.

Ernst, Wilhelm's father, called, "If they're ready we'll soon be on our way to Hamburg!"

When they stopped before the Ketchum cottage the family came out to the waiting wagon. Grandfather Adolph, walking unsteadily, made his way across the yard followed by his youngest son, August. The old man's elder son, Frederick, his wife Harriet and their five-year-old boy, Lewis, and three-year-old Anna proceeded to settle themselves on top of the second wagon loaded with the Ketchum possessions.

The men were jubilant. "At last we are on our way to a better life!" Wilhelm shouted to the Ketchum family. "No more grubbing this worn out soil! No more hungry winters because our crops failed! They say the soil is rich in America, and that it grows beautiful wheat and rye!"

Ernst shared his son's enthusiasm. "We should have made this move long ago. I'm forty-five—almost too old to change, but I've still got some good years left."

The old men of the two families, Jacob and Adolph, both were sixty-five. Jacob said, “I’m old but I want to see America. We won’t be a burden, will we, Adolph?”

“I won’t bother nobody,” the old man hiccupped, “not as long as I have my beer.”

Great-grandmother Mary Winters snorted. Elizabeth whispered to Amelia, “He’s disgusting.”

“Let’s go!” August shouted to the driver of the oxen. “We want to reach Hamburg tonight. Can you believe we’ll be sailing toward America tomorrow?”

Lewis and Anna sat on a clothes-filled canvas bag at their mother’s feet. Lewis said, “Mama, can we get a dog when we are in America? I wish we didn’t have to leave Gretchen. She’s a nice dog.”

Harriet pulled her shawl together across her ample bosom. “I know. We’ve all had to leave things we love. Maybe we can get you and Anna a puppy when we’re settled at our new home.”

For a long time the only sounds were the driver’s voices speaking to their oxen. The two children huddled together at their mother’s feet and the baby slept in Amelia’s arms.

The young mother swallowed the lump in her throat. She had not cried last night when she said good-bye to her parents at the old home, but returning to the cottage she had been unable to hold back the tears at the thought of her mother’s last words: “Remember, ’Melia, my only child, someday I will meet you in heaven.” And both of her parents had held Eddie as they kissed him good-bye. Her mother had said, “May God protect you, you helpless little baby.” It was unlikely she ever would see her parents again in this life. But where Wilhelm went, she and Eddie must follow.

A sharp penetrating wind blew from the north. April weather in Germany was unpredictable. This day was wet, cold and unpleasant. Perhaps it was an omen of things to come. Amelia cuddled the baby. She had another reason for dreading this trip, one she hadn't yet mentioned to Wilhelm. She suspected she again was with child, but—she would wait to be sure before she told him. She was committed no matter what the circumstances were.

Wilhelm and his father had been silent. Finally Wilhelm said, "Pa, remember the picture I showed you of the wheat field in America?"

"Yah. Big field, no fences. Shocks of wheat so close they almost touched."

"In America, Pa, we'll have big farms instead of a few acres of worn out soil. At forty-five you are young enough to make a good life for you and Ma. It's too late for Grandpa and Grandma—and Adolph."

"Yah," Ernst shook his head. "It's a long road to the days when we'll be, as you say, making it good. We have no oxen or cows or pigs. We have no house. We don't even know where we are going in America." He glanced around at the loaded wagon. "Everything we own is on this wagon."

"I've read about America. There's land for the taking—fine rich land. We have money in our money belts from the sale of the farm and animals. And our fare is paid to New York."

"Yah." Ernst hesitated before he continued, almost in a whisper. "I hope we've done the right thing by the family."

The rain had stopped. They rode silently until August shouted from the Ketchum wagon, "We're hungry. Want to open the food baskets?"

"We're ready!" Wilhelm replied.

The wagons stopped near a wooded area. Men and children went behind trees and bushes to relieve themselves while women unpacked bread and sausage for the noonday meal. They moved about to stretch cramped muscles as they ate while Lewis and Anna raced around releasing pent-up energy.

Soon the wagons again were on the road headed toward Hamburg. The afternoon seemed endless to the women and children. Repeatedly Grandmother Mary asked, "When will we get there?" Often she voiced her opinion of the trip in no uncertain terms. At last, in late afternoon, they reached the harbor town.

Fishermen were mooring their boats at the pier where housewives with baskets waited to buy fresh herring. A sharp penetrating wind blew over the harbor. The men turned up coat collars and the women pulled their woolen shawls closer about themselves and the children.

"We never have wind like this at home," Elizabeth complained. "It cuts through skin and bones."

Residents of Hamburg stared at the strangers with their high loads and whining children. Professional men, dressed in the fashion of gentlemen, walked by and looked at the little group with amusement: evidently peasants in gray wadmal clothes with their shawl-wrapped wives and runny-nosed crying children. And they had two wagon loads of old chests, trunks, canvas bags, homemade boxes, baskets and bundles. They were going across the ocean. What got into these people to undertake such a journey? And every day there were more of them arriving at the harbor.

Wilhelm called to a fisherman. "Do you know where the *Herman Reiter* is anchored?"

The man stared at him a moment. "Yah. She's an old brig. She arrived two days ago. She's anchored over there." He pointed. "She sails tomorrow."

All eyes turned toward the old brig where the fisherman had pointed. Frederick's voice revealed disbelief. "Is *that* our ship?"

The rest of the group stared in silence which spoke of wonder, disappointment and anxiety.

Amelia said softly, "Our ship is so little."

All of them had thought an ocean-going vessel would be much larger. The ocean was huge, and in comparison this ship was small and—and *puny*.

August said, "Maybe it looks small because it's not near us. The boat must be larger than we think." But though he wanted to encourage the group, his voice showed his disappointment.

Two masts stretched toward the sky. They were as tall as the ship was long. Silently they studied the old sailing vessel, the *Herman Reiter* which would be their home for several weeks.

Wilhelm said, "We must get things on board for soon it will be dark." The drivers guided the oxen to the pier beside the old ship.

2.

THE *HERMAN REITER* WAS AN EMIGRANT SHIP that made regular trips between Hamburg, Germany and New York City. On this trip she carried eighty-five passengers, all emigrants to North America, and a crew of sixteen. She carried a cargo of pig iron in her hold.

The passengers, farmers and their families, had spent their entire lives on solid ground. Life on shipboard was a new and alien existence to them. Their movements were awkward and clumsy as they walked for the first time on the ship's plank floor deck. Moving about was difficult for the planks were laid in such a way that they were lower at the rail and higher toward the center of the deck.

The water beneath the ship moved constantly—a wave rose, a wave fell. The people were unable to walk naturally. On this April day in 1850 the German emigrants wandered about the deck of the *Herman Reiter* insecure and bewildered. They felt helpless against their unknown antagonist, the sea, which they would first view when the Elbe River entered the North Sea. From there it would be four hundred miles to the English Channel, and after that, the ocean—miles and miles of ocean before they reached New York City.

The next afternoon when they sailed there was mist and fog blanketing the harbor. The ship moved slowly with a weak, slow roll. Wilhelm, his father and August were at the stern. Other male passengers in gray wadmal jackets and sturdy peasant boots stood on the deck and watched. The fog horn sounded constantly, a weird, threatening warning. They could scarcely see the shore. All were silent as the homeland was swallowed up in gray mist.

Finally Ernst said, "The old life is over. We have made our choice. I'll miss the old place and relatives and friends but—I have nothing to lose. I'm tired of the drudgery. Poor crops, worn-out soil—" Again he was silent.

Back on the poop deck Captain Miller stood near the wheel where he watched as the ship eased out of the harbor. The wind was light and the little vessel moved slowly. He glanced up at the sails.

The Captain was German, about fifty-five with iron gray hair and beard, watery blue eyes and weather beaten skin. He had spent many years at sea, the last twelve as commander of the *Herman Reiter*. He loved the sea and could not imagine why his countrymen would want to leave the homeland to go to America. Why couldn't they be as contented poking in the soil of Germany as America? These damned peasants were becoming a nuisance. Twelve trips he had made, and each time he had packed a larger number of them into the hold. They came dragging chests, heavy boxes, huge canvas sacks, baskets and small tools. Junk. And on this trip there were more women and children and old people. Now there were entire families from babies to old white-haired grandparents and great-grandparents.

Captain Miller loved the *Herman Reiter*. She was ancient, but seaworthy. She had one fault, however. She always was damp. She sweated. And the passengers would complain. They always did, but why hadn't they stayed home? The city of New York. He had never been inland in America, but no decent person could like New York City. Twelve years ago when he first touched at that port, he had seen hogs poking in the filth of the town's streets. Pigpens, the streets were then. Cholera was raging with hundreds dying daily. To him, the town itself had looked dead and stinking of corpses. But things were better there now, for it was lively and had wealthy people in beautiful clothes. He had seen them riding in shiny carriages through the streets.

The second mate, an Englishman, approached the captain. In broken German he reported on the passengers who were his responsibility. He said everyone finally had found their assigned bunks. There were complaints that they were crowded and uncomfortable and they pushed and shoved each other until they realized there was no more room to be had. Then they settled down. One of the young married men and his father—Winters was their name—had created an uproar because they were crowded. The young fellow said they were cheated, that they had paid for better quarters. The mate had told both of them to quiet down and pull in their big feet if they wished to remain on board. He hoped those two wouldn't cause trouble by stirring up the others.

Captain Miller puffed on his pipe as he listened to the second mate. Peasants crawled over the ship like the grasshoppers of North America. He hoped they could be controlled. Perhaps he should not have allowed so many aboard, but they would thin out in the weeks ahead.

Silently the captain went to his small cabin below the poop deck. He poured himself a large mug of beer and sighed as he sat at the table. Long days of open water lay ahead for the entire spring would be spent at sea. And then, the slimy Hudson River, the entrance to New York Harbor—he'd not think about it until he was there.

In front of Captain Miller was his book, *Medical Adviser for Seamen.* No doctor was aboard, so this book was the only authority he could turn to in case of a medical emergency. He rubbed his forehead. The crowded conditions in the hold below could lead to health problems. He recalled trips in the past when he had cholera aboard. Often during those voyages, he performed a repulsive duty of the captain—burying those who died. Always, before a voyage was over, he had read funeral prayers for several emigrants; then the corpses were lowered into the sea. There was no doubt about it—he was the ship's master to the unhealthiest cargo possible—human beings.

In the hold huge pieces of canvas were hung to divide the space into three compartments; one for married people with children, one for unmarried men and one for unmarried women. The family bunks were located near the stern and divided from one another by rough boards nailed together. The small compartments looked like horses' stalls or cattle pens. Mattresses were cases filled with straw and laid on the deck of the hold. For unmarried passengers bunks were strung between the stanchions. There were upper and lower berths, one-man and two-man bunks.

Dust escaped from the old unaired mattresses as the people made up their bunks—beds for eighty-five persons. Family belongings, clothing and personal items, were kept at the foot of the beds. With knapsacks, food baskets, bundles and bedding, the family compartments seemed unbelievably crowded. Each one wondered where they would find room to sleep.

Here and there were rough little tables where people could sit and eat, and around them were tubs and baskets which had to be piled somewhere. There was hardly room left for people to move about.

August bunked with his Grandfather Adolph. The old man muttered, "We'll have to sleep on our sides. There's not room to sleep on our backs." He sniffed. "And the whole place smells like piss and puke."

August scratched his head. "Yah, but we do have a lower berth. How would you like to climb up there to go to bed?" He pointed.

Old Mary interrupted. "Shut up, Adolph. Soon the whole place will smell like beer from your breath." She sat on the edge of Jacob's and her compartment, the strap of her ever present padlocked leather bag over her shoulder.

Adolph growled, "That old witch. Don't know how Jacob stands her."

Amelia sat in her compartment with Eddie on her lap. She wished Wilhelm would return. Adolph was right. The hold stank of urine and vomit. And even in mid-afternoon it was dark as a cellar. She felt she was a prisoner in this horrible place where they would live for many weeks. Why—it was like a grave—dark, damp and smelly. Even with most of the men above on deck, the air was thick and stifling. At night the passengers would be piled like kindling in a wood pile. How would they breathe? She stared at the hatch. Their only air came from that small opening, and when there was rain, it would be closed. She felt panic at the thought of smothering.

Eddie whined and she cuddled the baby to comfort him. For weeks he would be confined to this compartment. He was learning to walk and should have room to run and explore, but the floor was damp and dirty. She couldn't allow him to get down. She reached into a food basket and gave the child a small piece of bread. He nibbled on it, his blue eyes staring as people walked past.

Adolph and August climbed to the deck. They looked closely at the hatch covering which had a few small holes through which air could enter.

On deck they breathed deeply of the cool spring air. The ship rocked gently. Other men were walking about and talking as they became acquainted with the sailing vessel and its passengers.

Old Mary's husband, Jacob, silently studied the coils of ropes which reminded him of giant snakes. The old man glanced up toward the eleven sails which were filled and tightened by the gentle breeze. He gently rubbed his left shoulder. "Yah," he murmured, "The masts are pine."

Up in the masts hung nets of heavy rope. A few seamen climbed about up there and shouted to one another in English. Jacob looked far out to sea to relieve the dizziness he felt from watching the climbing sailors.

Wilhelm, Ernst and Frederick came from behind him. "Want to go up there, Grandpa?" Wilhelm asked.

Adolph muttered, "That would be a way to get away

from Mary's nagging."

Frederick ignored the old man's remark. "I'm still surprised at the small size of this ship. I paced it off. She's forty paces long and eight wide. The floor of our old house was as large as the deck, and close to a hundred people will eat, sleep and live in this space!"

Wilhelm mused, "I expect if everyone on board was up here it would be so crowded some of them might fall overboard."

"Yah," August replied. "If something happens out on the ocean, look, there's only a few rowboats here on deck."

Ernst nodded. "Don't mention it to the women. They're already complaining about being crowded—don't add fear to their misery."

Frederick grinned as he pointed to a small square shanty just aft of the port bow. "Harriet says that outhouse is about big enough for one family. There's only five or six holes. She wonders what we're to do when the place is filled and there's no place to go."

Adolph chuckled, "Tell her to use the pail that sets beside her bunk." The men grinned at the thought of Harriet's wide buttocks fitting over the small wooden pail.

Wilhelm said, "Amelia hasn't said much, but one of these times she'll let loose. I know she is upset that our quarters are so poor. And I don't blame her. We paid good money for passage to New York, and look what we got! A stinking hog pen to live in!"

They were silent for a time. The water purred softly against the hull. Finally August said, "Will, your mother said you complained to the second mate. Think he'll make any change?"

Wilhelm shook his head. "I made an enemy of the man. He won't do me any favors. Besides, what can he do? There's just so much room."

Jacob pointed. "Is that a man on the front of the ship?" The group walked up to investigate.

"I read in a book about ships that a wooden person or bird at the front is called a figurehead," Wilhelm explained.

"H-m-m-m. This one's a good-looking woman," August remarked. "She looks as though she's leaning ahead and staring for the first sight of America."

"Can't see it too soon for me," Adolph snorted.

The men continued inspecting the ship. They preferred staying on deck as long as possible for no one looked forward to going below into the dark hold filled with the stinking smell of urine and vomit.

3.

THE SHIP'S BELL CLANGED. Passengers of the *Herman Reiter* learned that continual ringing of the bell was a summons for everyone to appear on deck. They poured up from the hold through the hatch where they gathered around the bell-ringing second mate. Soon the deck was packed with men, women and children.

"What does it mean? Why are we called here?" The questions were repeated over and over. Finally the tall young man put aside the hand bell and in broken German he shouted, "I will soon pass out the first week's provisions."

Three seamen rolled tubs and barrels from the storage hold and after removing covers they arranged the containers near the second mate. The smell of food tantalized everyone and several children murmured, "I'm hungry."

The ship's officer announced, "We will pass out food once each week. There will be no more until next week, so use it carefully. You must understand that the food you get today is a week's supply for your family. Each one of you will share alike. The provisions will be measured so all will get the same allotment.

"You are allowed to prepare your food in the galley here on deck, and if you don't have cooking pots, you can use the ship's. You must agree among yourselves on the time you are to cook, and take turns so everyone gets their chance.

"Garbage and dishwater must be thrown overboard —always leeward. You must not throw anything windward.

"You will get fresh water once each day, half a gallon for drinking, cooking and washing for each person—no more. We expect you to keep the hold clean. Every morning before the water is issued the hold must be cleaned of vomit and other dirt."

The second mate paused. There was dead silence among the passengers as they strained their ears to understand the broken German speech of the Englishman. Finally he continued. "You must handle fire with great care. It is forbidden to smoke below deck or to use unprotected lights. These are orders of the captain. We are on a long voyage and everyone must realize our rules are for the protection of all of us. On board ship the law of the sea is in effect and the captain will punish anyone who does not obey instructions." The stern blue eyes of the ship's officer glanced around the group coming to rest with a challenging stare into Wilhelm's face.

The man continued. "Only one member of a family needs to stay as I pass out provisions. Go below and get your containers. When the head of the family is in line we will pass out the food. The rest of the family should stay below until we are finished."

There was talking and commotion as the passengers descended into the hold. Soon a representative from each family returned with various types of containers. The second mate, with his scales, was waiting to weigh the provisions.

As he worked the ship's officer frequently repeated, "Remember, use your provisions sparingly. There will be no more until next week."

Many types of food were distributed; among them were flour, sugar, mustard, salt, pepper, sauerkraut, syrup, bread and biscuits, salted meat, rice, butter, salt herring, peas and barley. The people crowded around the man to receive their allotments in crocks and pans. The ones who didn't have containers tied their salt pork, peas or salt fish in their aprons. Others carried food in their bare hands.

Distributing the allotment was a time-consuming duty for the second mate which caused him endless figuring; six ounces of sugar and butter, four ounces of coffee and salt, a tenth of an ounce of pepper and thirteen ounces of flour. Even vinegar was measured, two ounces per passenger. It took several hours before the provisions were distributed. The smell of cooking drifted through the ship. It would be a long time before everyone had a turn at the galley.

The second mate was relieved that he was finished with the chore of dispensing food and arguing with passengers who thought he was cheating them.

Hungry people who had been unable to get in to cook stood about on deck munching on ship's biscuits which were hard and dry. Some of them crushed the biscuits in their hands before eating the small pieces.

Silently they looked into the evening twilight. The first day of their ocean voyage was ending.

4.

AMELIA TURNED RESTLESSLY in the family bunk. Their big food box and a canvas bag of clothing were at the foot of the bed. With Eduard and Wilhelm beside her there was little room on the outer edge of the bunk. Each time she went to sleep, Eduard turned, kicking her in the stomach. He was fourteen months old, still a baby in diapers. She had continued to nurse him in the belief that nursing mothers did not become pregnant. Now she wondered.

Her mind dwelt on her first pregnancy. Morning sickness, flares of temper over minor things—she felt nausea at the memory. It had even been hard in their airy clean cottage in Germany. Here, in this hell hole it would be unbearable. Before she was married she had occasionally missed a period. But at the back of her mind a thought lurked. She now had missed two periods. She must not think about it. Her head ached.

She sat up on the edge of the bunk. The ship creaked as it moved ahead toward the North Sea Channel. Though the hatch was open, the air was bad from being breathed by more than eighty people. All of the passengers in the family compartments were jammed together in a room the size of her living-room-kitchen in their cottage in Germany.

Amelia rubbed her forehead. The sounds of sleeping people, the snoring, mumbling in their sleep and coughing annoyed her. How was she going to exist in this damp, dark, stinking hole for weeks to come? Anger surged through her—anger and resentment toward her husband. This American trip had been his idea. He had talked about it for months until his parents and grandparents were convinced—that is, the men were convinced; the women's protests had not been considered. Old Grandmother Mary had protested loudly but they had brushed aside her objections as one brushes away an annoying fly.

The Ketchum family also had caught the "America fever" from Wilhelm. They, too, were trapped.

Eddie whimpered. Amelia patted his shoulder. "Sh-sh-sh," she whispered, but he continued whining. Unbuttoning her nightgown she lay down and gave the child her breast. He quieted immediately.

Thoughts continued to plague her. She was a shy person. She didn't like all these strangers crowding about her. She couldn't step outside their bunk without bumping into someone. Everything she did must be done in full view of people. Yesterday when she had nursed Eddie she had crawled to the far corner of the bunk and turned her back. She couldn't open her dress and expose her breasts to strange men. It was dreadful that she must dress and undress among all these people. Finally, toward morning she dropped into a period of restless sleep.

At daylight Wilhelm wakened her. He was fully dressed and standing beside the bunk. "Get up," he whispered. "There's no one in the galley. You can cook breakfast while I stay with Eddie."

Silently Amelia threw on her clothes, and taking a cooking pot and some salt pork, she hurried to the galley. Breathing deeply of the crisp morning air she sliced the fat pork and set it over the fire. Wilhelm liked potatoes three times a day. When the food rations were passed out, there were no potatoes. Perhaps they wouldn't keep in the damp hold.

Reluctantly she flipped the slices of salt pork, turning her head to avoid the odor of hot grease. A wave of nausea swept over her.

"You 'most done?" A woman with straggly dark hair stood behind her with food and cooking utensils in hand. And behind her four other women waited.

Amelia swallowed. "I'm done." Carrying everything was difficult. She almost collapsed as she entered the hold. Evil smells streamed up at her; the foul air, sweaty bodies and the sight of the fat salt pork she carried were too much.

Rushing to their bunk she gasped, "Take this. I'm sick." Dashing to the deck above she stood by the rail and retched. Wilhelm, carrying Eddie, followed.

"What's—what's wrong?" he asked.

She straightened and wiped her mouth. "I'm sick, can't you see? Go eat your breakfast and get biscuits out of the food basket and feed Eddie."

"Is there anything I can do for you?"

"Just go—and leave me alone." She gagged and returned to bend over the rail. Puzzled, Wilhelm stared at his wife. "Go! Go! Let me alone!" she exclaimed.

Shaking his head Wilhelm made his way to the hold through the ascending and descending people. What was wrong with Amelia? She seldom was short-tempered. Perhaps she was ill from the motion of the ship, but the water had been calm—no one else was seasick.

Still carrying Eddie he descended into the hold. The air was bad. The people were breathing the air from each other's mouths down here.

Eddie squirmed, his hunger aroused at the sight of people eating breakfast on beds and at the small tables.

Frederick and Harriet Ketchum and their children were at a far table.

"Where's Amelia?" Harriet asked as she munched on a ship's biscuit and salt pork.

"On deck. This stinking air got to her. She's throwing up."

Frederick nodded. "We should stay on deck when the weather is good."

"There's not room for everyone up there," Harriet argued. She glanced at Lewis. "Eat slowly. That is all you'll get until noon."

Eddie wiggled. "Bread," he said. Wilhelm carried him to the family bunk and gave the child his breakfast. They ate slowly as they watched people come and go.

A seaman approached. He appeared friendly as he nodded and smiled at the passengers. He appeared to be inspecting the hold.

"Hardly room to get through," Wilhelm remarked.

"Yah. Ship's overloaded," he hesitated before he added, "but in a few weeks it usually thins out." He was gone.

Wilhelm scratched his head. How could the passengers thin out in the middle of the ocean?

"My God!" he muttered when the meaning of the man's words hit him.

The bell on deck rang insistently. People left their breakfast and went above. Wilhelm stood behind Amelia who sat on a coil of rope.

When the group was silent the second mate announced, "Each morning at this time I will issue water for the day. You will get your two quarts per person after you have cleaned the hold. The report this morning is good. Not much sickness last night. Get your water vessels and line up."

"You look better," Wilhelm said softly to Amelia.

"The fresh air smells good. I'll take Eddie while you get our water." She rubbed her head. "I don't see how I'm going to get along with only six quarts of water a day."

"Do we drink that much?"

"Six quarts is all we get for drinking, cooking, keeping ourselves clean and washing our clothes."

Wilhelm shook his head as he descended into the hold. An hour later, the last in line, he approached the second mate. He held the kettle as the ship's officer silently measured out exactly six quarts of water; Wilhelm lingered, uneasily shuffling his large boots.

"You want something?" the second mate asked as he replaced the cover on the water barrel.

"Er—can something be done to get fresh air into the hold?" he blurted.

"*Herr* Winters, your quarters are the same as the rest of the passengers—no better, no worse. There is no way to get more air into the hold. If you wanted fresh air, you should have stayed in Germany." He turned.

"Wait!" Wilhelm ordered, his eyes flashing. "We're living like pigs in a pen! We've been cheated! You're only interested in getting our money. We paid forty-three dollars and fifty cents in American money for you to take us to New York, and what do we get? We're treated like animals in a cage!"

"Winters, if you don't shut up I will call the captain!"

Amelia pulled on her husband's arm. "Please. Don't say anymore," she begged.

"You'd do well to listen to your wife. Life in the brig is not as comfortable as in the hold, and *Herr* Winters, the captain has the authority to confine you there!" The second mate turned on his heel and strode away.

"You shouldn't have said anything," Amelia said softly.

"Damn it! We paid good money to sail to America. We didn't expect to be treated like animals living in a dark unhealthy stinking hole!'

Ernst came up from below. "You'd better quiet down, Son," he said softly. "I've heard stories about the brig on ships. Things they do to prisoners are shocking. Don't make conditions worse for yourself."

"Yah, you're right. But we were cheated."

Ernst nodded. "But nothing can be done about it now. We can live through it for a few weeks."

Wilhelm glanced at Amelia's pale, drawn face. "I hope so," he said softly.

5.

THE TIME PASSED SLOWLY as the ship sailed through days of April mist and drizzle which confined passengers to the hold. Then for several days the weather was cloudy. The heavy body of the ship was deep in the sea as she plowed her way slowly through the soft, blue-green waves. The figurehead on the bow seemed to scan the sea with her piercing eyes.

Captain Miller was unable to take their position by the sun in the cloudy weather. He measured distances and figured his course by dead reckoning. The speed was slow and the passengers were restless. He glanced up at the sails. They hung limp and lifeless in the light wind.

Adolph Ketchum approached. His walk was unsteady. The old man smiled as he remarked, "Fine calm weather we're having, Sir. We hope God gives us many quiet days." He continued, "I have yet to be seasick."

Captain Miller snorted, "If God wished us well He would give us stronger wind." He turned leaving old Adolph staring at his back.

Damned peasants. They didn't realize how many weeks the crossing would take if they had only quiet winds. They had no idea of anything at sea. They had only traveled on manure wagons. And they were happy with the calm weather because they had escaped seasickness. But what difference did it make? They would reach America soon enough and they could again poke in the dirt on the other side of the ocean.

And so for days on end the first mate wrote in the ship's log: Wind light southeast. Cloudy. At times rain and fog.

Then suddenly, the weather changed. The wind kicked up and the temperature dropped. In the daytime the people went on deck wearing coats, shawls, sheepskins and blankets. They were more comfortable there, away from the fetid air of the hold.

On deck Amelia leaned against a barrel. She held a short rope attached to Eddie's waist. "He's like a calf staked out to pasture," she thought as the child took three or four uncertain steps before sitting down hard on the plank deck.

Grandmother Mary Winters pulled her shawl about her shoulders. Her leather bag hung from one arm. Her sharp eyes searched Amelia's face. "What's wrong, child? You don't look good."

"I'm all right. I don't like the sea."

"Me neither, nor do any of the other women, but we don't look pale as ghosts and we eat our meals, though the food's bad, and we don't throw up night and day like you do."

Amelia stared out to sea without answering.

"You're in the family way."

The blood rushed to Amelia's face, a tell-tale flush that convinced the old woman she was right in her suspicions.

"Have you told Wilhelm?"

"No."

"Have you told Elizabeth?"

"No."

"I'd think your husband and mother-in-law should know."

Amelia glanced at Wilhelm who was in conversation with a group of men near the rail. He turned.

"Grandson, your wife has something to tell you." The old woman tucked her scrawny hands under her black shawl. "Tell him," she whispered as she joined a chattering group of women.

Eddie tugged on his leash as Wilhelm came near. "What is Grandmother talking about?" he asked.

Amelia's face flushed beet-red. He waited. Finally she blurted out, "I'm in the family way."

He stared at her. "Of all the bad luck! You couldn't have picked a worse time!"

Amelia's blue eyes flashed fire. "What are you saying?"

"I mean it's a bad time."

She flared. "I can't be pregnant to suit you! Is it all my fault that I'm with child?"

"Keep your voice down." He glanced about. "I haven't said that." Eddie tugged at his father's trouser legs.

"You said it's a bad time! But isn't it your fault, too? Didn't you have a part in it? Didn't you put me in this condition? Perhaps you also picked a bad time!"

"Sh-sh. People can hear you." His wife's anger convinced him she was pregnant. She had been like this the first time, too. "Don't be so upset."

Her face was fire red. "You make it sound as though I alone were to blame! I'm to blame less than you! I'd like you to go through it! The sickness all the time—all the time—" Her voice trailed off and she burst out crying. Holding her hands over her face she stumbled toward the hatch, rushed down the steps and threw herself on the quilt-covered bunk.

Wilhelm felt helpless. Elizabeth came to look after Eddie. "She'll be all right, Son. Mother Winters told me what's wrong."

They stood silently for a time as Eddie tugged at his leash. At last Wilhelm said, "Damn it, it is a bad time. The first few months when she was pregnant before, it was impossible to please her. Now that time falls during the crossing. I shouldn't have spoken my thoughts, however."

Elizabeth agreed. "It's hard for everyone on this awful ship. It must be nigh unbearable if a woman is in the early months of pregnancy. I'll help all I can with Eddie, and you be kind to her, Son, when she has these flare-ups."

Wilhelm nodded. "I'd better go see how she is." The ship lurched, nearly throwing the passengers off their feet. He grasped the rail. " 'Twouldn't take too much of this to make me seasick," he grinned as he went down the hatch.

Amelia was in bed with the covers over her head. Gently he pulled the quilt from her face. "I'm sorry," he began.

She yanked the quilt back over her head. "Leave me alone! Just get out and leave me alone!" she demanded.

Reluctantly he returned to the deck. As he went above he heard Amelia retching as she dragged the wooden bucket from beneath the bunk.

6.

THE DAYS DRAGGED ON. Now the passengers were accustomed to the schedule. During the day they spent most of the time on deck but nights were almost unbearable for seasickness was rampant. Lights were not allowed after ten in the evening, and at times people could not find the bucket in time. Then the first dim light of day revealed the night's happenings.

People were up early. The first chore of the day was to clean the hold. Men carried sea water in big buckets and women scrubbed the floor and washed a few clothes and hung them on deck to dry.

There was dissatisfaction among the women about doing laundry in salt sea water. Grandmother Mary complained shrilly from her seat on the edge of her compartment. "Our clothes are a disgrace! Look at the woolen jackets! The soap won't suds—might's well wear them dirty!"

The woman in the next compartment agreed. "I have so much washing with Louise sick. She sweats something awful and she coughs and vomits until we're almost frantic."

Harriet asked, "What's wrong with her?"

"She's coughed for a long time, but now the vomiting is killing her. She can't keep anything down, and sometimes she throws up blood." She lowered her voice. "She's only fifteen but she has had a bad cough for three years. I'm afraid it's consumption."

Harriet combed and braided Anna's hair. "Maybe the captain has something that would help. He has medicine in his cabin."

The woman sloshed her daughter's nightgown up and down in the bucket. "Whenever my husband asks the second mate, he says the captain is resting and cannot be disturbed." She grimaced. "He needs a lot of sleep."

Amelia sat at one of the small tables with Eddie on her lap. The hem of her skirt was tucked beneath her thighs to prevent having it touch the wet plank floor. She seldom talked to anyone other than her family or the Ketchums. The woman with the ill child spoke to her. "You're sick often. I hear you at night."

"I'm sorry if I disturb you." She wiped Eddie's nose.

"You don't. There are so many sick people that I wonder what it would be like if this place was quiet."

Soon the second mate came to inspect the hold. A little later he rang the bell on deck to call people for the rationing of water. As they stood in line there again was grumbling about the limited water supply. When Mary Winters stood before the ship's officer she complained, "Half a gallon a day is not enough for a person to live decently." Her shrill voice carried to the others and several joined in the complaint.

"We need more fresh water! Sick people need water! Talk to the captain!" The clamor increased down the entire line. Some of the men banged their water pitchers to emphasize their demands.

The second mate glared at Mary. "You're to blame for this! They were all right until you started complaining!" He eyed her sternly. "You're the grandmother of that troublemaker, Winters. I won't forget this. He measured out Mary's water and shoved her aside.

"Now listen!" the second mate shouted. "We are on a long voyage! There have been voyages when there was not much wind and we were on the water for three months! Three months! We hope to reach New York in eight or ten weeks, but we don't know. There may be a day when you have to manage with less than two quarts a day. Learn to save the drops!"

The passengers silently filed before the ship's officer as the words "three months" rang in their ears. Mary hung her leather bag over her shoulder and descended into the hold.

Wilhelm, Frederick and August sat at a table with another passenger. Mary listened as she went about her work. Wilhelm asked, "Where are you going to settle in America?"

The man, Charles Weber, ran his hand through his hair. "I've heard of a place called Minnesota where land is good. Think I'll go there."

"Is it far from New York?"

Weber nodded. "Several hundred miles, but I'm going most of the way by water.

"How is that?"

"I'll go west from New York City by steam train, then across Lake Erie by steamship to a place in Michigan called Detroit."

"I've wondered about taking land in Michigan."

Weber shook his head. "Twenty years ago it would have been all right, but the good land is in the southern part of the state and most of it is sold. It costs more, too, and I've read the Minnesota land is richer. And you can settle anywhere you want if no one else is on the land. They call the people "squatters." You pay a small amount of money to the government after you've lived on the land for a period of time."

"Squatter. I don't like that word," Wilhelm said. "How do you get to Minnesota from Detroit?"

"I'll take a steamship north on Lake Huron to the top of Michigan, then down Lake Michigan on the west side of the state to Chicago. From there we'll go on river boats to Minnesota. Are you interested?"

"I might be. I'll talk to my father and grandfather about it." Wilhelm paused. "Seems like a long ways.

Aren't you afraid you'll get there too late to plant crops?"

"I hope not," Weber replied. "Maybe we'll get good winds and arrive early in New York."

Mary snorted. "If we go all that ways it will be fall before we get there. Know what that means? No house or food for winter. We'll either freeze or starve to death. Men! You're never satisfied—you have to search for something better. And you drag your women along with you!" She glanced at Amelia. "My time on this earth is short, but Wilhelm, I feel sorry for your poor wife. All she has to look forward to is a life of drudgery in a strange country—if this trip across the ocean doesn't kill her first."

Wilhelm grinned. "Now Grandma, you like excitement as much as any of us." After a moment he asked, "Where is Grandfather?"

"Resting. He has that old pain in his chest and shoulder."

Wilhelm nodded and resumed his conversation with Charles Weber. "I'd like to know more about this Minnesota state."

"It's not a state yet. It's a territory. I have a book about it that I'll loan you." He lowered his voice to a whisper. "There's not many whites there yet, but Indians are everywhere. Better not mention that to the women."

Wilhelm nodded. "Are they friendly?" he whispered.

"Not really. They don't like whites moving into their hunting grounds. But the United States government is behind new settlers, so we would be safe."

Amelia came to stand beside Wilhelm. "Will you look after Eddie while I cook dinner?"

Wilhelm smiled as he reached for his son. "Come here, Eddie. We'll go for a walk on deck." The baby squealed with delight as his father carried him toward the hatchway.

Amelia took a kettle containing water-soaked beans from beneath the bunk. From the food basket she removed a small piece of salt pork. Her stomach twisted at the familiar rancid odor of the meat. Though they were less than two weeks at sea her stomach rebelled at the monotonous diet of salted meat and dried foods—rice, beans, and peas with bread or ship's biscuits, and water as a beverage.

She carried her food up to the galley and joined the line of waiting women. Finally she reached the door. Soon she'd be inside. Suddenly the sails snapped and the ship lurched as a gust of wind sent the *Herman Reiter* scudding over the water.

The woman at the cookstove screamed. Boiling liquid from her cookpot had splashed on her hand resulting in scalded skin. Her kettle danced while peas and water hissed on the hot stove.

Amelia rushed to help. Seizing a towel she grasped the handle of the pot and lifted it from the rocking cookstove.

The woman gasped as she studied her scalded hand. "I'll take it," she said reaching for the kettle. "They'll have to eat the peas half-cooked."

"You'd better put your hand in cold water," Amelia suggested.

The woman snorted. "There's no fresh water to waste on burns!"

Amelia placed her tightly covered kettle on the red-hot cookstove. The beans would cook in a short time for she had soaked them since the previous day. Standing by the cookstove she daydreamed of the time when she could cook and fry over her own fire, and when she could take as long as she wished to prepare a meal. It was impossible to fix good food on a rocking cookstove on a ship. And she craved a change of diet—something fresh. Milk. What wouldn't she give for a cup of milk? And Eddie should have milk. Her breasts were drying up and he needed milk.

"You 'bout finished?" the woman at the door inquired.

"Just a few minutes longer."

The ship leaped forward again. Amelia struggled to keep from falling while water from the pot of beans hissed on the hot stove.

"Don't let it kill the fire," the woman warned.

When the beans were done she carefully carried the hot food to the hold where Wilhelm and Eddie waited. She sat at the little table with her family and munched on a piece of dry bread as they ate.

Wilhelm remarked, "These beans are good. Better have some."

"I keep thinking of milk," she murmured, "And fresh cabbage and potatoes and apples—all the good things we had at home."

"Yah. It's worse for you when you're with child. I wish I could do something for you."

She got up suddenly. "I'm going to lie down. I can't stand the smell of beans and pork."

"You have to eat," Wilhelm said softly. "You don't eat enough to keep a bird alive."

"Don't tell me what I have to do!" She threw herself on their bunk and turned her face to the wall. After tossing for an hour she sat up in bed and rummaged in their luggage and brought out yarn and knitting needles which she carried to the airy deck above where she joined several women.

Harriet called, "Over here, Amelia! There's room on this box for you!"

Silently she sat beside her friend as she unrolled gray yarn.

"What are you knitting?" Harriet asked.

"Socks for Wilhelm and—" She stopped speaking as she inspected a small grayish-yellow speck on the light-colored yarn. What was it? She pulled it from the wool and placed it on her hand. Staring silently, she was horrified to see it move. She knew what it was—a body louse!

As she watched the small, wingless, flat-bodied insect move across her hand, anger rose within her. Big, fat body lice! Now she remembered—Eddie had been scratching himself the last few days, and she too had an itching about her neck. She shuddered and quietly killed the crawling insect between her thumb and forefinger.

Harriet asked, "What's wrong?"

Without answering she rushed down to her bunk. Ignoring the other women she stripped to the skin. Her clothes were full of lice. In every seam of her woolen clothing there were gray-yellow specks crawling in the soft cloth. Every pleat and crease was filled with nits. There were nests of them in the armholes. As she crouched naked she could see red spots on her stomach and chest. She had felt some itching, but in the half-light when she dressed and undressed she had not seen the disgusting spots. She covered her face and burst out crying.

Wilhelm found his wife lying naked on the bed. He tossed Eddie to the back of the bunk and grasped Amelia's shoulder. "What's wrong with you?" he demanded as he pulled a quilt over her. "Have you lost your senses?"

She turned away, still sobbing. "I'm full of lice! My God, what can I do? We're all full of lice!"

He shuffled his feet uncomfortably and stared at her.

"Er—uh—we've never had lice. Where did they come from?"

She sobbed quietly. No, she never had body lice. She had come from a clean family and she had kept Eddie and Wilhelm clean. Her mother always said it was a disgrace to have lice and that only dirty people—tramps and whores—had body lice. Her mother said body lice were a sign of a person's disposition and that the insects nested on lazy, dishonest people and that the lack of them was an indication of a clean upright person. She was dishonored.

Wilhelm patted her shoulder. "Don't feel so bad. We'll get rid of them. But where did they come from?"

"This filthy ship." She wiped her eyes and blew her nose. "They must be in the mattresses."

"Hm-m-m. 'Tis not your fault. You got them from someone else," Wilhelm said softly. He remembered an old saying about how fast body lice multiply. Elizabeth, his mother, once said, "A night-old louse already is a grandmother." He pulled the quilt high about Amelia's shoulders. "We have to tell the others." Eddie squealed and held out his arms.

The news spread like wildfire. The men went to one side of the hold to undress and the women went to the opposite side. They found what they were looking for. All the passengers were infected.

Disgust, disbelief and anger raged through the adults who sat picking lice from their clothes and killing them one at a time with thumbnails pressed together. An angry murmur like the sound of an approaching storm surged ever louder through the hold.

Finally Mary Winters exploded. "We have to do something or they'll eat us alive! Somebody has to go to the captain!"

Old Adolph hiccuped as he squashed a louse. "You go and give him a good tongue-lashing, Mary."

"Shut up, you old drunk! I'm surprised lice would

suck your beer-soaked blood!" She turned. "The captain won't listen to a woman. This calls for a man." She glanced at Amelia who was retching uncontrollably. "You go, Wilhelm."

Reluctantly he went above and toward the Captain's quarters on the poop-deck. He met the second mate.

"Where are you going?" the man demanded.

"I want to see Captain Miller."

"He's resting."

"I need to see him. The people in the hold asked me to speak for them."

"I'll take care of any problems."

"I want to see the captain!"

"Winters, get back where you belong! The captain is resting!"

Angrily Wilhelm shoved the second mate aside and strode toward the captain's quarters just as the door opened.

Captain Miller looked from one man to the other. "What's wrong?" he asked.

The second mate apologized. "I'm sorry but *Herr* Winters insists on seeing you." He grasped Wilhelm's arm. "I'll take care of everything."

Wilhelm twisted away from the officer. "Sir, the people sent me to talk to you."

The captain gestured impatiently. "Come in."

Briefly, in German, Wilhelm explained the problem of the body lice. "The women are frantic," he said. "Do you have soap we can buy so we can scrub our clothes and beds?"

"Yah, yah. There is soap. But Herr Winters, when you have problems you must have the second mate help you."

Wilhelm nodded. "Thank you, Captain, for seeing me."

"Yah, yah. Send someone to the second mate for soap." He turned away dismissing Wilhelm.

He passed the ship's officer at the open hatch and the man glared angrily as he muttered, "You'll regret going to the captain over my head, Winters."

The women began at once the extermination of the small crawling creatures. In the galley they boiled underwear and other clothing in strong lye. They emptied straw from the mattresses into the sea, washed the mattress casings and scrubbed the bed boards and plank floor with hot soap-lye sea water. The captain sent down a quicksilver salve which they rubbed on their bodies. They scrubbed their scalps and combed hair and beards with fine-toothed combs so vigorously that their scalps and faces bled from the brass teeth. Finally, after several days of intensive extermination, they were satisfied.

"We will have to sleep on hard beds with no straw mattress for the rest of the trip," Amelia whispered to Wilhelm, "But I feel clean again."

Louise, the girl in the next bunk hacked violently ending with a searing, tearing cough. Her misery continued hour after hour.

7.

WITH LIGHT WINDS AND SUNSHINE and little activity to occupy the passengers of the *Herman Reiter*, the days passed with a monotonous sameness. The men explored the ship and talked with some of the German seamen. They learned the ship carried her cargo of pig iron in her bottom to make her lie deep in the sea. They were told they should eat all the sauerkraut and peas they could get to avoid scurvy which was a dangerous and often fatal disease for people whose diet did not include fresh fruit and vegetables.

The Winters and Ketchum men spent many hours in conversation with Charles Weber discussing the advantages of settling in Minnesota Territory. They read the book he loaned them and were impressed. But they could see disadvantages; they might arrive at their destination too late in the season for crops to mature before frost, and the Indians were believed to be unfriendly. Still, they felt the advantages of settling in the territory were outweighed by the disadvantages.

Another problem they would be forced to meet in America was their inability to speak English. On the *Herman Reiter* the passengers and many of the ship's crew spoke German, but in America they would be unable to communicate.

August Ketchum owned a small book designed for the average German peasant titled *Guidance For Immigrants In The English Language*. Even before he left Germany he had spent hours reading and practicing the words and expressions. As a result, the Winters and Ketchum men looked to August for instruction as they practiced English hour after hour.

Early in the voyage August had noticed an attractive young daughter of a German family among the passengers. Her beauty was enhanced by a fair complexion, blue eyes and blonde curly hair. By inquiring of friends and family, he learned her name was Gretchen Meyer and that her family planned to settle in Ohio where relatives already were located.

Gretchen was shy, and to August it seemed she was constantly in the company of her aggressive, buxom mother. Finally one morning while Mrs. Meyer was cooking in the galley, he found Gretchen standing at the rail looking westward.

"Good morning," he said in his best English.

She turned, smiled shyly, and shook her head, indicating that she did not understand.

"Guten Morgen," he replied. He continued speaking in German. "Have you learned any English?"

She shook her head and turned to look into his eyes. "No one will understand me in America. Can you speak English?"

August studied her face and his heart skipped a beat. He swallowed. "Yah, some." He continued. "I have an English book. We could study together. I'd help you—if you'd like."

Her eyes danced in anticipation. "Would you, please?"

After their first meeting Gretchen and August sat on the deck practicing English expressions several times each day. The second mate smiled to himself when he passed them, but he did not offer to correct their faulty pronunciation, and they were too proud to request assistance from the arrogant ship's officer.

After they left the North Sea the sailing vessel entered the Strait of Dover and the English Channel, that arm of the sea which separates France and England. The water had been calm but the evening they entered the English Channel they encountered their first rough weather. The *Herman Reiter's* topsails were bottom-reeved and the first mate wrote "Storm" in the log.

At dusk Wilhelm, his father and grandfather stood on the afterdeck. High, white-topped waves slammed against the ship. Suddenly a wave broke over the deck soaking them to their knees.

Wilhelm laughed and grasped the old man's arm to keep him from falling. "You all right, Grandfather?" he asked.

Jacob grabbed his left side. “Yah.” A tortured expression crossed his face.

Ernst took his other arm. “We’ll take you to the hold, Pa. Ma will be looking for you.”

“Yah. Yah.”

The three staggered across the rolling deck as the first mate shouted, “Batten down the main hatch!”

Suddenly the whole deck became a slippery incline. The ship listed to one side. Old Jacob stumbled and was wrenched free from the helping hands. Wilhelm grabbed the rail with one hand and his grandfather’s arm with the other. Ernst crawled to the rail and hung there waiting for the *Herman Reiter* to get back on an even keel—which she did, only to roll over on the other side.

The first mate bellowed, “Everyone get below!”

The three men and a couple other passengers staggered over the heaving deck toward the seaman who was waiting to close the hatch.

When old Jacob was in the hold he went to his bunk. Mary was waiting. “You old fool, don’t you know better than to stay out in a storm? You could have been washed overboard!” The old man silently grasped his side and turned his face to the wall.

Nearby Louise gasped for breath after a coughing spell. Her mother gave her a spoonful of sweet syrup but the coughing continued.

Inside the hold the light was dim so the passengers retired early. The ship lurched constantly. Some people already were seasick and the sounds of retching came from all sides of the hold. The Ketchum children cried softly. Harriet was busy holding the wooden pail for first one child and then the other as she struggled to control her own heaving stomach.

Amelia lay quietly beside Wilhelm who held Eduard

on his arm. In spite of the roughness of the sea and the myriad sounds, the father and son slept.

Then it was night. Inside the hold the darkness was impenetrable. The ship lurched and Amelia's body rolled over her husband's. He slept on as she crawled back to the edge of the bunk. She could hear people snoring, groaning, talking in their sleep, vomiting, praying, swearing and cursing.

She gasped as their bunk seemed to sink. She grabbed Wilhelm's shoulder as she cried out, "We're sinking!"

"Be quiet," Wilhelm whispered. "It's only the storm."

The ship pitched and rolled. A loud roar came from the sea which was like that of a wild beast trying to throw the *Herman Reiter* from its back.

Amelia bit her tongue in an attempt to be silent. She had to throw up. There was no air. She couldn't breathe. The bunk rocked up and down. Any minute she expected the planks of the hull to splinter and the sea to rush in and drown them.

"I can't breathe," she gasped.

"It is stifling," Wilhelm agreed as he turned over on his other side. Eduard slept on.

She swallowed. When the crew had battened down the hatch they had closed the small holes which let air in. The air they breathed had been breathed by others through filthy mouths and throats. There no longer was air—not enough for another breath. She took tiny breaths—they would all smother in this hole in the bottom of the ship. She felt faint.

She gasped for breath in weak, short jerks. "Will—I'm choking to death—"

"You're all right." He patted her shoulder.

Someone lit a candle. Mary Winters shouted, "Don't start a fire, you fools!"

The candle was snuffed out. The sounds of wooden pails being moved and vomiting came from all directions.

"I can't see the bucket," Amelia panted. She threw up on the floor.

They continued breathing the putrid air while passengers swore, moaned, groaned, vomited, puffed, prayed and cried. Eduard wakened and joined other crying children in adding to the confusion. A baby on the other side of the ship sounded like a cat mewing.

Amelia listened to the storm. Waves roared as they splashed and broke over the deck above. When waves struck the ship the sound was like thunder. Thud, roar, and then the sound of running water. How long before the old *Herman Reiter* would be pounded to pieces?

Perspiration clung to Amelia's body. She grasped Wilhelm's shoulder. "I'm afraid," she whispered.

"The storm will blow over."

"I'm going to die—I have to get out of here."

"There's nothing we can do. No one can help us. We'll be all right."

No one could help them. Wilhelm was right. The near hundred people in the old hulk could only lie and wait. The ship would sink with all of them and tomorrow there wouldn't be a trace left on the surface. In the space of a few minutes they would all be dead. Her parents never would know how she had died.

Amelia lay flat on her back, her mouth open as she gasped for air. Suddenly something came down from the bunk above. A slimy fluid covered her face and filled her mouth. She shuddered and gagged as the smell told her what it was. Vomit.

The stench of vomit, urine and feces was overwhelming. She had to get out or she would surely die. She felt her way in the darkness between the bunks. The floor rose and fell as she skidded on the slime-covered planks. She fought her way toward the hatch. She had to get into the open air. The foul stench filled her throat. She choked as she crawled up the hatchway. Soon she would breathe fresh air.

But the hatch was fastened. She pushed and pounded to no avail. She could not get out. They would all choke to death down here.

Vomiting and sobbing she clung to the side of the hatchway until Wilhelm carried her back to their bunk. "You'll feel better when the storm is over," he whispered.

"We'll all be dead by then." She lay down and resigned herself to death by smothering if she didn't drown first.

All night the *Herman Reiter* plowed on over a hissing sea with violent waves licking at her sides.

8.

DURING THE STORM most of the passengers remained in their bunks, ill with seasickness. Day and night they retched. Unable to eat, they consumed nothing but water. Wilhelm and Eduard ate lightly and Amelia not at all. Because she remained in bed Wilhelm tried to cook on the rocking cookstove in the galley. After two attempts during which he was forced to hold the handles of the pans to keep them on the stove he was resigned to eating the ship's hard biscuits and drinking water.

For two full days the storm raged. Wilhelm had given up trying to get Amelia to eat. She gagged and was seized by convulsions at the mere mention of food. In the early morning light he held a cup of the ship's stale water to her mouth.

She shook her head. "It's slimy and there's stuff floating in it. It stinks."

Wilhelm poured a few drops of their supply of vinegar into the cup and stirred it. He sniffed. "Try this. I think it will taste better."

She drank. Wilhelm said, "The storm will soon be over. Then the seasickness will stop."

She cried out, "Will! The bucket!"

The water she had drunk came up mixed with a greenish slime. Wilhelm silently wiped her face. He was concerned that she was unable to keep down either food or water and that she vomited night and day. She was becoming weak. Her pregnancy made her increasingly uncomfortable. He was concerned—she couldn't stand this sickness much longer.

He hadn't realized how miserable a voyage across the ocean could be. He almost wished they hadn't started. But surely, when the sea calmed she would be better.

Suddenly old Mary's shrill voice rose above the sounds in the hold. "Jacob! Jacob! Wake up!"

Wilhelm and his father rushed to the old people's bunk where Mary was shaking her husband. "He's dead! He's dead!" she repeated over and over.

Ernst seized his father's left wrist and felt for the pulse. There was none. He dropped the already stiff arm. "He's gone," he said softly.

The Winters and Ketchum families gathered around Mary who muttered about the fate that had befallen Jacob. "We shouldn't have come on this awful voyage. If we'd stayed home Jacob would be alive." She put her hand on Elizabeth's arm. "Why do the Winters men do these things? They have to try new things, even if it kills them." She glanced at Wilhelm. "And your poor wife—you may lose her, too."

Soon the second mate came down to the family compartments carrying a piece of canvas. The passengers watched as the body of Jacob Winters was shrouded in canvas.

Mary dabbed at her eyes. "What—what will you do with him?"

"When the storm dies down we'll have a funeral service on deck," the second mate replied. He carried the lifeless old body from the hold.

The people pondered the uncertainty of life. A dead person had been lying among them. There would be more. Each one wondered if they would be next.

Amelia questioned her husband. "Do people die of seasickness?"

"I don't think so. Grandpa has been having pains in his chest and shoulders. It's likely his heart gave out."

"But the seasickness made it worse."

"Maybe."

That day the storm spent its force and the northwest winds began to die down. The waves sank and the water became smoother. By evening it was calm.

Wilhelm stayed with Amelia and Eduard until the funeral hour arrived. "I'll be back as soon as I can," he said. "They soon will have the service on the afterdeck.

She nodded. "What will they do with Grandfather's body?"

"He will be buried at sea."

Amelia shuddered. "It's awful."

"They can't have corpses lying on the ship."

"I guess not. The dead sink to the bottom of the sea." She paused. "Down there he can rest, don't you think so?"

"Yah. He can rest. But don't think about it. Think of getting well."

"It would be nice to rest and not to be sick." There was a note of envy in her voice.

"Don't, Amelia. Don't think about it."

"Wilhelm—I'll—I'll never reach America."

"Stop it! Seasickness doesn't kill people!

"I've known it for a long time. Ever since I came into this awful hold I've known I'd never get out alive."

"Your mind's playing tricks on you. Put those thoughts away—Eddie and I couldn't get along without you." He patted her hand and stooped to kiss her clammy forehead.

"Don't you remember? I was afraid before—?"

He remembered. He was responsible for this voyage. Now his grandfather was dead and Amelia— "Listen to me," he began. "The seasick always feel they are going to die, but as soon as they reach land, they are well again. You'll be all right. We'll reach America together."

Silently she turned her face to the wall. He patted her shoulder. "Eddie and I will be back when the funeral is over."

A few days later another death occurred. Louise, the ill girl in the next compartment, was found dead by her bereaved mother when she wakened in the morning. Refusing to believe the girl was dead, her mother screamed, "Louise! Louise!" as she shook the stiffening corpse.

The father tried to quiet his wife. "She's gone," he said quietly. "The consumption killed her." He spread a blanket over the blood-stained body and bed. "Poor child. She bled to death."

"No! No! She can't be gone! Only a little while ago she was coughing!" The bereaved woman threw her body on the bunk beside her dead child and sobbed.

The second mate came down with his piece of canvas. "Wait. Please wait," the child's mother begged. "She might wake up."

The man lifted the eyelids of the young girl. "She is dead," he said.

"Wait. Just a little while. Wait."

"I can't. We can't leave the dead lying here in the hold."

"Only an hour. Please."

But the officer paid no attention to the mother's pleas. He pulled the corpse from the blood-soaked bed. The woman screamed as she grabbed hold of the body of her dead child. Her husband pulled her hands away and August helped the Englishman with the body.

They carried Louise to the afterdeck where the second mate laid a weight in the canvas. Soon the sounds of hymns being sung drifted down to Amelia in the hold. Again, the funeral took place on the afterdeck. The poor girl was out of her misery. Perhaps, at times, death was better than life.

Wilhelm watched as the body slid into the sea. Suddenly he remembered a statement he had heard days before on the *Herman Reiter*. "There's always more room in the hold the farther we are out at sea."

9.

AUGUST AND GRETCHEN leaned against a coil of rope as they read the English textbook which August had bought in Germany.

It was a pleasant, sunny May afternoon with a moderate wind. Passengers sat in small groups putting in the time until their next meal. The odor of boiling beans and rancid pork drifted from the galley as the young couple struggled with the unfamiliar words. Another difficulty was the fact that the words were printed in two ways; first, they were spelled as they should be, then the same words, within brackets, were spelled differently to simplify pronunciation. The young people did not understand this arrangement and it caused them much confusion.

Gretchen declared, "I'll never learn to speak English!"

August studied her downcast eyes. "Of course you will. Learning English takes much practice. Don't be discouraged. I'll help you."

"But August," she lifted her eyes to his. "How do you know you are saying the words right? Maybe Americans won't understand you."

He had thought of that, but he shoved doubts from his mind. "Of course they will," he said confidently.

Wilhelm, deep in thought with Eduard nearby on his leash, sat on the afterdeck. In memory he again saw his grandfather's shrouded body as it slid into the sea. And that young girl, Louise—how many more passengers would meet the same fate before they reached New York? Grandmother Mary was bearing up well. She was seen all over the ship with her ever-present leather bag. What on earth did she carry in that bag?

Wilhelm was physically healthy but being forced to live in cramped quarters was depressing. Never before had he worried about the future. Now the fear that he had been wrong in convincing his family to go to America constantly gnawed at his mind.

And Amelia. She had not had a well day since they had been on the sea. He needed her physically but there was no way of telling how soon they could live together as a healthy couple should. Eddie came to sit on his father's lap. Soon he napped in Wilhelm's arms. The sun was warm. He closed his eyes against the glare on the water and his thoughts returned to Amelia. Now she complained of new ailments. Her legs, arms and joints ached; her back hurt. He couldn't understand. Her ailments were those of an old person, not those of a twenty year old woman. She often had chills and she said she was always cold, even when she sat in warm sunshine. It was as though her blood no longer warmed her. And something bothered her breathing—a pressure in her chest. She constantly felt tired and weak. What was wrong with her? Never before had she been sick in bed, except at the time of Eddie's birth. But she was sick now.

Every day she had less energy. It was an effort for her to move and she had no interest in preparing meals or in dressing and undressing herself and Eddie. More and more of the work was left to him. He knew she wasn't lazy. She truly was sick. This sea voyage had sapped the energy from her body.

He had bought medicine from the captain but it hadn't helped. "I'm sorry, Will," she said, "I'm afraid I'll be a hindrance to you in America. And when the baby comes—" Tears filled her eyes.

"You'll get well when we're on land and you have good food again. You can't live on stale water and ship's biscuits. It's no wonder you're sick." He paused before he continued. "Can't you force yourself to eat beans and peas and salt pork?"

She's shuddered. "They start the vomiting again. If only we had good fresh milk—and some apples. What I'd give for an apple!"

Eddie whimpered and changed his position. Then he slept. Wilhelm's thoughts returned to their diet; stale salted meat that smelled of sour wooden tubs; never anything fresh; no potatoes or carrots or cabbage; no milk or apples. It was no wonder most people complained of not feeling well. Several of them looked like walking ghosts. He was sure their diet was at fault. And Amelia was dangerously ill because she was unable to eat the rotten food. None of them would feel really well until they landed and ate as people should.

One thing Wilhelm knew. Never again would he cross the Atlantic Ocean. For the rest of his life he would live on land.

Though the sun was shining and the day was warm, Amelia remained in the bunk. She was sure she had some dangerous disease which threatened her life. Her mouth and gums were sore and two of her teeth were loose. Her joints ached and she was depressed, restless and tired. There were bruises on her arms and legs though she couldn't recall having bumped them. This was not seasickness. This illness attacked her life. Others spoke of "ship-sickness," and someone had said it was scurvy, but they had not taken to their bed as she had. They did not have to lie day and night in this musty hold which was like a horrible grave. Her grave. Some day the second mate would come down with a piece of canvas for her—like Grandfather and Louise, they would carry her out in a piece of canvas and bury her at sea.

She sighed. She had been warned. God had warned her those last days at home, but she hadn't obeyed. She had felt from the first time she entered this place that it would be her grave. There was nothing more she could do but to wait for death.

10.

FOR SIX WEEKS THE *HERMAN REITER* had been at sea. It was May, and at home in Germany flowers were blooming. Here on the sea there seemed to be no seasons but only changes in the wind, which was mostly from the west. Even the wind was against them as though it tried to push the immigrants back toward Germany.

Now there were days when gentle breezes flowed across the deck. They talked of home. What were the farmers doing? Were the oats planted? Had the winter manure been spread on the fields? Had the animals been turned out to pasture?

They all were weary of the sameness of life on the ship and of continually being surrounded by water. The sea seemed endless. They longed for the sight of a living plant—a green tree or bush, or even a weed. They sat on the rough plank deck of the ship and dreamed of May in Germany. The green fields, the fragrance of flowers, the odor of freshly-baked bread, the smell of warm milk fresh from the cow—all the longed-for smells they had left behind.

The people were tired. Though they did almost no physical labor, everyone was exhausted and their bodies were filled with aches and pains. Two more corpses were buried at sea. There had been four deaths and there likely would be more. Depression gripped them. They no longer joked or told amusing stories. No laughter was heard and children whined endlessly. There was no enjoyment in the food they consumed for they ate only to stay alive until they reached America. Often during the month of May the beautiful days suddenly were shrouded in thick fog. Beneath a heavy gray shawl of mist their vision was confined to a few yards and it seemed the whole earth consisted of the ship's worn old deck. They no longer could see the sails above them. The fog irritated them and caused them to be short-tempered. They were easily angered and men and women argued over small matters. The women fought over the use of pots and pans in the galley, and on a few occasions, the pans were used as weapons.

With soft gray fog on all sides they seemed to be standing still. Did the *Herman Reiter* move at all? Concern spread among the passengers. Were they lost?

The weeks passed until they had been on the ocean almost eight weeks. They asked the seamen when they would reach America and answers varied from: we're about halfway to a little over halfway. They had once been told it would require eight weeks for the crossing. But no one could tell them where they were or how far they had sailed. Had they already passed New York? Would they ever arrive? Were they lost?

Doubts arose about Captain Miller. Could he find his way over the water with no signs? He might be able to steer by the sun in daytime and the stars at night in clear weather, but what could he do when it was foggy? Perhaps even the captain didn't know where they were.

There were many things the passengers would have liked to ask the captain but he was rarely on deck. He spent most of his time in his cabin and no one was encouraged to speak to him.

On one of the rare occasions when Captain Miller appeared on deck, Ernst Winters approached him. "Herr Captain, when do we land in America?"

The captain turned to stare into Ernst's eyes. "What day do we arrive? I would tell you if you'll give me a little information about the weather. Tell me, will the days be cloudy or clear? calm or windy? rainy or foggy? And could you tell me which direction the wind will blow from day to day for the next few weeks? If you can tell me these things, Herr Winters, I'll tell you when we'll land."

After this encounter no one was willing to approach the man with questions.

The captain was glad he had squelched the ignorant peasants. He might have tried to explain latitudes and prevailing winds and the compass, but they wouldn't have understood. They were longing for land, but what was their hurry? Soon enough they would be poking about in the earth again. Of course, if the winds had been favorable they would already have landed in America.

Suspicion was rampant among the passengers. It must be farther to America than they were told. Everything was against them—the winds, the fog. They grew bitter and some repeated the thoughts of all of them: If I ever put my feet on land I will never again cross the ocean.

The *Herman Reiter* sailed on over the seemingly endless Atlantic Ocean through rain and sunshine, through fog and storms. Usually the wind blew against her bow and rigging which hindered her progress.

The passengers' thoughts traveled back over the immense water they had sailed on for almost two months. It seemed the sea was without end.

11.

WILHELM, DEEP IN SLEEP, rolled with the motion of the old *Herman Reiter*. After weeks of ocean travel he no longer was disturbed by rough water.

Amelia whispered, "Will. Will. Wake up." She pulled his arm.

"Huh? What is it?"

"I'm bleeding."

"You're what?"

"I'm bleeding."

Wilhelm climbed over his wife and felt on the floor for the bottle with a piece of candle in its neck. He lit it and held it above his wife's face. He gasped. Her cheeks and neck were covered with blood and cotton wads stuffed in her nostrils were saturated red balls. "My God! What has happened?"

"I have a nosebleed."

"Why didn't you wake me before?"

Her voice was weak. "I thought it would stop. I stayed on my back without a pillow, but the blood still comes. I stuffed cotton in my nostrils, but it soaks right through. I don't know what else to do. I'm so tired."

She was a ghastly white. Her eyes were frightened and glassy. Wilhelm stared at the streaks of blood on her neck and nightgown and at the saturated cotton wads floating in the pan on the floor. He never had been able to stand the sight of blood. His knees felt weak.

Thoughts rushed through his mind. Amelia had been so weak that for several days she had remained in bed, eating almost nothing. Now she was losing her life's blood. Her gray-white face was the color of a corpse's. He had to do something—his wife was dying.

"Are—are you in pain?"

"No. Just so tired."

"We have to stop the bleeding."

She turned her head. "Eddie is sleeping?" The slight motion caused blood to drain from her nostrils.

"Yah. But lie still."

"If it doesn't stop I'll bleed to death."

"It will slow down soon."

"But if it doesn't?"

"I'll get help."

There had been a storm early in the evening and now the wind again blew as it tossed the ship around. Many people slept through the rough weather, some snoring noisily.

As the ship rolled, Amelia rolled in her bunk and Wilhelm staggered to stay on his feet.

An angry voice came from nearby. "Put out that candle! You want to start a fire?"

Wilhelm was aware of nothing but the desperate condition of Amelia. He bent over her and wiped her face with a towel. She could not stand such bleeding much longer. What could he do? At home in Germany there were remedies to stop bleeding, but here on the ship there were none. The captain!

"I'm going to call the captain!"

"No. Not in the middle of the night."

"He has to help us. He has to."

Wilhelm knew the captain had a medicine cabinet and that he was expected to act as a doctor. He also knew that on two previous occasions when he had approached the man, he had been brusque. Most passengers were afraid of him. Even the seamen held him in consternation. He had never shown feelings of sympathy for the unfortunate people in the hold. He dispensed medicine for the sick and when they died he performed funeral services and lowered the bodies into the sea. The passengers considered him an unfeeling man, but Wilhelm was desperate. Surely he couldn't refuse help to a dying woman.

Amelia murmured, "Don't go. There's no use."

Wilhelm snuffed out the candle. "I'll be back soon."

Feeling his way in the darkness he reached the

hatch. For a time he struggled with the door. Finally it opened. Heavy waves broke against the deck. He hardly noticed that he was soaking wet. He felt his way toward the afterdeck where the ship's officers were quartered.

He skidded and fell against a closed door which immediately was yanked open. He faced the second mate.

"Winters! Get below!" the man bellowed.

"Please. I have to see the captain."

"Get inside, you fool! My quarters are getting wet!" The door closed and they stood glaring at one another. "What do you want that couldn't wait until morning?"

"I want to see the captain! My wife is dying!"

"You peasants are my responsibility. The captain must not be bothered with your little problems."

Wilhelm grasped the door knob. "You can't stop me! I *will* see the captain!"

The second mate's hand shot out and landed squarely on Wilhelm's chin. Surprised and off guard, he staggered momentarily. Automatically his fist struck back hitting the second mate on the side of the head. The man staggered backward and went down. Without a backward glance Wilhelm was out of the door and stumbling toward the captain's cabin.

He knocked heavily on the door. There was no answer. He continued pounding, expecting the second mate to appear behind him at any second. Finally an angry voice came from inside.

"What in hell's going on?"

Wilhelm tried the door and it swung open. Captain Miller apparently had been asleep for he sat on the edge of the bunk, half dressed. His hair was rumpled and his puzzled eyes stared at Wilhelm. The expression changed to anger as he recognized his intruder.

"What do you mean by disturbing me? Haven't you got it through your thick head yet that you take your problems to the second mate?"

The captain had thought that one of the crew was calling him because of an emergency with the ship—no one else would dare to disturb him in the middle of the night. He glared at Wilhelm.

"It's my wife! She's bleeding to death! We can't stop it and I think she's dying!"

Captain Miller yawned. He needed his sleep. Because of the weather he had been awake for many hours. He ought to tell his nervy visitor to go to hell—but he didn't. The man kept repeating that his wife was dying and the captain couldn't answer that he needed sleep. He wondered—perhaps he should turn this fellow over to the second mate—after all, the peasants' problems were not his responsibility.

This was the farmer, Winters, who previously had had trouble with the second mate. He was likely one of the smarter peasants. The captain felt a little sorry for the man. If his wife was lying at death's door, he would do what he could.

"How long has your wife been bleeding?"

Wilhelm quickly related the details of what had happened. The captain nodded. "Scurvy. This bleeding from scurvy happens occasionally."

"She's also with child."

The captain shook his head as he pulled on his boots. "We'll see what we can do." He took his *Medical Advisor* from a shelf and flipped the pages to "scurvy." He stopped and read aloud: "Bleeding from the mouth and nose may be excessive, and may last so long as to be dangerous to life. Treatment: If the person becomes weak remove the patient to cool, fresh air and make packs from cold water and place them on the forehead, nose and back of the neck. In severe cases, bind a towel around each of the four limbs, above elbows and knees, so as to stop blood in these parts."

The captain took clean towels from a chest and gave them to Wilhelm. He lit a lantern and beckoned Wilhelm to follow. The deck rose and fell causing the farmer to stumble. The captain who walked as though his feet were nailed to the deck grabbed Wilhelm's shoulder to steady him.

When they reached the hold Amelia lay with closed eyes. "The captain's here," Wilhelm said. She opened her eyes.

Captain Miller glanced at her face and at the amount of blood in the pan. It's gone too far, he thought. This woman has lost so much blood that the end is near. She must have had scurvy for several weeks. He felt sorry for her. She was still young. It would be hard for the husband in America with the child over there motherless. It would have been better for this young couple if they had stayed in Germany. His glance went from Amelia's face to the farmer's. Poor fellow.

Wilhelm studied the captain's expression. It was hard. The man had no pity, he thought.

"We will try to stop the bleeding. We'll do what we can."

He sent Wilhelm for a pail of sea water and soaked the towels. He then packed them about Amelia's head and knotted other towels which he tied tightly above her elbows and knees. She groaned.

"It hurts, Frau Winters, but the towels must be tight to keep the blood in your limbs."

Before he left the captain told Wilhelm that Amelia must remain on her back and that the wet towels should be changed often to keep them cool.

The instructions were brusque, given as they would have been to one of the seamen. Captain Miller returned to his cabin. The farmer and his dying wife remained in his memory. The man was young and he seemed bright. He would remarry. If he had been near the sea in Germany, instead of inland, he likely would have made a good seaman.

The captain sat on the edge of his bunk. They were nearing the end of the voyage. It had been a pleasant crossing with fewer storms than usual. There had been deaths and by tomorrow he likely would conduct another funeral and burial. People were the most unhealthy cargo a ship could carry. He envied captains who carried other cargo. They might get to sleep even on stormy nights. He lay down and closed his eyes.

12.

DURING THE NIGHT WILHELM changed the cold packs two times but the bleeding from Amelia's nostrils continued. High waves slammed against the *Herman Reiter*. Amelia's body rocked with the motion of the ship and her husband grabbed the edge of the bunk to keep from falling from his stool.

There was commotion on the other side of the hold. Someone was ill and a child cried. From nearby bunks came the sounds of groans and snoring. Now and then Wilhelm briefly lit the candle and looked at Amelia. She was unconscious. Time passed and the next time he changed the cold pack the bleeding had slowed.

Wilhelm wondered if he should wake his parents. He decided against it. There was nothing they could do. He thought of the second mate and was surprised that the man hadn't been down to the hold to punish him for the brief fight. He was glad he had struck the officer no matter what punishment was meted out. Soon it would be morning. Then he would have to face the music.

A heavy boom from above was followed by a splintering of boards. A wave must have smashed something on deck. Amelia opened her eyes.

"Will—take care of Eduard."

"Of course. But you're better. You're not bleeding."

She sighed. "Your mother will help."

"Yah. Yah. But you're going to get better. Is there anything you want?"

"No." She closed her eyes. "I'm so tired, and I'm cold."

He pulled the blood-streaked quilt about her neck. Her face felt cold. He dropped heavily on the stool. "Amelia, I'm sorry we left Germany. Can you forgive me?"

"For what?"

"I forced you to come. You didn't want to leave home."

"You thought it was best for us—for all of us. Don't blame yourself."

"But I am to blame."

Again Amelia slept. With daylight the storm quieted. The passengers began to crawl from their bunks. The talking ceased as the second mate descended the hatchway. He strode to Wilhelm's side with a determined step. Even in the dim light it could be seen that a large lump protruded from his forehead above a purplish-black eye.

"Winters, come with me!" he ordered.

"My wife is ill. I must stay with her."

"You refuse to come with me?"

"Yah. I refuse."

"I have orders from Captain Miller!" The tall English officer turned on his heel and strode toward the hatchway. "I'll be back!" he shouted.

"What's wrong?" Amelia whispered.

"I had a little trouble with him last night. I may have to go with him." Wilhelm went to his parents' bunk where he told them of the events of the past night.

Ernst asked, "What will they do with you?"

"I don't know, but if they lock me up, Ma, will you look after Amelia and Eddie?"

"Of course."

"She's awful sick, Ma. I didn't think she'd live until morning."

"We'll take care of her and Eddie, whatever happens."

Five minutes later the second mate and two husky seamen came to the Winters' compartment. The Englishman said, "Are you coming quietly or do we have to drag you?"

"Where are you taking me?"

"I'm going to throw you in the brig. That's too good for the likes of you!"

"How long will I be there?"

"You can rot in the brig for all I care, but you'll be there until we dock in New York. You'll find quarters in the brig are not as fancy as here in the hold." He pushed Wilhelm toward the hatchway. "Get going!" the man shouted. The two seamen followed.

Amelia's eyes were wide and frightened. Wilhelm had kissed her. "Ma will look after you and Eddie."

"I'm scared, Will."

"I'll be all right. Just get well."

There was much conversation among the passengers that morning as they cleaned the hold and prepared breakfast. "We are treated like animals," a woman complained, "and most everyone is half sick. They say it's scurvy."

Sobbing broke out from one of the family compartments. An elderly woman had breathed her last. Half an hour later the second mate returned with his canvas to remove the corpse.

In his cabin Captain Miller recorded the death: Leah Wagner from Hamburg, Germany. Mother of Anna Schmidt also of Hamburg, Germany. Born December 2, 1785. Died June 5, 1850 on board the *Herman Reiter* on voyage to New York. Certified, Charles Miller, captain.

The little ship sailed along through a calm sea on a beautiful June morning. The storm of the previous night was forgotten. A small group of passengers had gathered on the afterdeck for the funeral of Leah Wagner. The people stood in a half circle around the rough plank bier which had been placed on two sawhorses; the corpse, wrapped in canvas, lay on the planks.

The passengers were dressed in their best clothes; women and girls wore silk scarves over their heads and the bareheaded men in dark wadmal jackets, stood behind the women. Before them the bier leaned toward the water. The feet of the canvas-wrapped corpse nearly touched the rail.

As the captain came from his cabin the flag was lowered to half-mast. He, too, had dressed for the funeral in a dark, double-breasted coat with wide flat cuffs. His head was bare and his iron-gray hair was neatly combed. In his hands he held a prayerbook.

August Ketchum stood beside Gretchen. The two had become almost inseparable in recent days. As the captain opened the prayerbook some of the people folded their hands. All stared somberly at the wrapped body on the bier.

The captain flipped through the book as he searched for the proper page. His thoughts were of Amelia. Apparently she still was alive. Her hot-headed young husband could cool off in the brig. He located the page he wanted.

His voice was loud and clear as he began to read. He wondered how many times he had read the same words at a funeral. He began: "O Lord God! Thou who for the sake of sin lettest people die and return to earth again, teach us to remember that we must die . . . "

The people, their heads bowed in reverence and their hands clasped, listened to the words from the prayerbook. Gentle waves lapped softly against the *Herman Reiter*. The dead woman's daughter sobbed.

Captain Miller haltingly started a hymn. Gradually the people joined in to sing two stanzas. He closed the book and stepped back from the bier. He motioned and two seamen stepped forward and as he gave the sign the canvas-wrapped body slid into the sea.

The ship's flag was raised and lowered three times in respect to the deceased.

The passengers began to scatter when the raucous call of a flock of seagulls caused everyone to stare into the western sky. The seagulls were coming to meet them! The birds swarmed in large flocks through the rigging. Once again there was life on the sea. Smiles wreathed the formerly somber faces.

August squeezed Gretchen's arm. "We're going to make it!" he exclaimed.

The rough bare bier was dismantled by two crew men who carried away the planks and saw-horses. And the *Herman Reiter* sailed on with one less passenger.

13.

AUGUST AND GRETCHEN leaned against the rail of the ship. Sunlight glistened on the gentle waves. Porpoises frolicked along the ship.

"I've never seen such big fish," August commented. "They must be five or six feet long."

Gretchen shaded her eyes. "I wonder if they're good to eat? Fresh fish would taste good."

"Yah. Everyone is tired of salt meat. Amelia gets sick at the thought of it."

"She's feeling better," Gretchen commented. "She is sitting up again, but she's white as a ghost. She needs good food."

"Yah. She's worried, too, about Wilhelm locked up in the brig. I heard two seamen talking. He's in solitary confinement. It must be bad down there if it's worse than the hold."

"Do you think we'll be in New York soon?"

"I think so. We're seeing birds now and this is the first time we've seen these big fish." The porpoises swam ahead of the ship, then jumped and played around the bow as they came back along the side. He hesitated. "In a way I'm going to be sorry to reach New York."

"Sorry! Why?"

"Because in a few days you'll be leaving us when your family gets off the lake steamer in Ohio." He squeezed her hand. "I wish you were going to Minnesota with us."

She seized his arm. "So do I," she whispered.

He took both of her hands and looked into her eyes. "Will you marry me and go to Minnesota with us?"

She blushed. "Yah. I was afraid you wouldn't ask me."

August pulled her to him and planted a long kiss on

her upturned lips. She responded, then pulled away. "They're watching us," she whispered.

The passengers on deck were observing every action of the romantic couple with approving smiles. "Don't mind us," a man called. "It's good to see someone happy."

August waved and turned back to Gretchen. "I must tell you that life won't be easy in Minnesota. We will have to build a cabin before winter."

Gretchen squeezed his arm. "I won't mind if we're together." In a moment she asked, "Where will we be married?"

"Captain Miller can perform the marriage ceremony just as he does the one for funerals."

For a time they were quiet, each one deep in thought. Finally he asked, "Will your parents be willing for us to marry?"

"They won't like for me to be so far away from them, but I think they realize we are falling in love."

August grinned. "Your mother is a controlling woman. I'm a little afraid of her, but I'll get my courage up and ask your parents for your hand." He hesitated. "Suppose they say 'No.' "

"I have some of my mother's disposition. I hope they will approve, but if they don't, we will go ahead with our plans. Will you speak with the captain?"

"As soon as I talk with your parents."

They turned as Ernst and Elizabeth Winters came from the hatchway with Amelia between them. She was too weak to stand. Her father-in-law supported her as Elizabeth spread a blanket on the deck. Together they eased her down where she leaned against a coil of rope.

"This fresh air and the sunshine are so good," she said. "I have to get my strength back so I can walk off the ship in New York. When do you think we'll be there?"

"In a few days," Elizabeth said as she pulled the blanket over Amelia's legs. "The breeze is cool and you've not been outside for a long time. Keep covered."

Old Mary Winters, her leather bag over her shoulder, emerged from the hatchway leading Eduard. "We're like moles," she grumbled. "We've lived in that dark hole so long we can't see in the sunshine."

"Come, Eddie," Amelia said. "Come to Ma."

The little fellow toddled to his mother and sat on her lap. She tickled him under the chin. "You're walking so well now. You and I and Pa will walk off the ship together in a few days."

Eddie squealed. "Pa!" he shouted.

"We'll see him in a few days," Amelia replied. She turned to Ernst. "Have you been able to learn anything about how he is?"

"Not a thing. The seamen have orders not to talk about anyone in the brig."

Amelia stared with unseeing eyes at August's and Gretchen's backs. What was happening to Wilhelm? How could conditions be worse than they were below in the hold?

14.

WILHELM LEANED HIS HEAD against the damp wall of the tiny brig. It was dark. He saw no light except twice daily when a crew member with a lantern brought his food and water. He estimated the room might be five by six feet and perhaps five feet high.

How long had he been confined? To him it seemed many days, but he had no way to determine night from day. When he attempted to stand he must crouch because of the low ceiling.

The room was bare of furniture. His days and nights were spent sitting or lying on the damp planks of the floor without a covering. Only one item for his convenience was left in the brig, a wooden pail in which he relieved himself, and which was not emptied until it was nearly full. The only air in the brig came from a four inch opening below the door. The lack of ventilation and the stench were overpowering.

Wilhelm thought constantly of Amelia. Did she survive the terrible bleeding? Had she recovered? And if she had, what of the baby she carried? This trip had been a disaster from the first day, and it was all his fault. For months he had argued and coaxed until she agreed to go with him to the new land. It had sounded so good—rich, fertile land in America, almost free for the taking. Bountiful crops which would lead to prosperity that he never could achieve in Germany.

When he got out of this hole, he would make right all the wrongs, the suffering he had caused her on this trip—if she recovered. If she died—he wouldn't allow himself those thoughts. And Grandfather Winters likely would have still been alive if they hadn't made this trip. Wilhelm constantly was tortured by feelings of guilt.

Grandmother Mary, his mother and Amelia all were critical of the Winters men's tendency to forever seek greener pastures. Perhaps they were right—but he couldn't help it, he wanted life to be better for his family than it would have been in Germany.

Wilhelm scratched continually. He knew he was covered with body lice, and he hadn't had a bath since they had thrown him into this filthy hole. The place likely hadn't been scrubbed in years.

A glimmer of light told him someone was coming. A moment later a shallow dish was shoved beneath the door. He crawled over to it on all fours.

"Here's your grub," the crew member said as he shoved a hard ship's biscuit under the door beside the dish. Better eat it fast unless you want to share it."

Wilhelm grunted. He knew only too well what the man meant. "How long before we reach New York?" he asked as he steadied the dish of luke warm bean soup and took the biscuit.

"I'm not supposed to answer questions," the man said loudly. Then he whispered, "A few more days."

William said softly, "Do you know anything about my family? Is my wife all right?"

"I don't know. I'm not allowed in the passengers' hold. I have to go."

As soon as the man was gone Wilhelm squatted on the floor and lifted the bowl of soup to his lips. In spite of his discomfort, he was hungry. The soup tasted good. He reached for the biscuit which he had stuffed into his pocket. An angry squeal and a sharp bite on the finger told him one of the rats in the pig iron hold was making away with half of his meal.

Wilhelm swore. He had learned that if he ate his biscuit first, he must fight the rats away from his dish of food. If he ate his dish of food first, the starving rats always managed to steal his biscuit.

Slowly he finished the soup as the rats—he couldn't tell how many—fought over the biscuit in the corner of the brig. He drank the last of the soup, slid the dish under the door and crawled to lean against a corner wall. Still hungry, he dreamed of the good meals Amelia used to prepare, while snarling rats fought over the remaining biscuit crumbs.

15.

THE *HERMAN REITER* SAILED ON through balmy June sunshine. The shapely woman figurehead leaned toward the west, her eyes gleaming and her curvaceous body washed clean by the spray. The passengers now saw other vessels daily for the ship frequently met steamers and sailing vessels. Constant swarms of raucous sea birds screeched from the rigging. The water which had been clear and blue, now contained slime, and discarded objects floated on the surface; these signs indicated that land was near.

The mood of the peasants had changed from depression to one of hope. And on this day, June 12, 1850, a happy event was to take place, one of the few that had occurred in the past ten weeks of the sea journey. August Ketchum and Gretchen Meyer were to be married at high noon.

Women's laughter, a rare sound on the old ship, came from the hold and galley as the ladies prepared the best meal they could put together with the remaining supplies. They pooled sugar for a wedding cake and the baked beans and pork were sweetened with a supply of honey which Adolph Ketchum had hoarded along with his German brew.

The old man staggered on deck with his great-grandchildren, five-year-old Lewis and three-year-old Anna in tow. The children's pale faces were scrubbed and they were dressed in their best clothes.

The people on deck smiled as Adolph stumbled and muttered, "Darn ship. It never holds still."

Mary Winters replied, "You're drunk! You should have given away your brew instead of your honey!" She shifted her leather bag to the opposite shoulder.

"Humph!" the old man snorted. "Maybe I will! Yah!

We'll have a celebration!"

Frederick shouted, "Fine, Pa! But wait until after the wedding ceremony!"

"Yah! Yah!" He grasped the rail to steady himself.

Amelia, on the arm of her father-in-law, and Elizabeth, leading Eduard, emerged from the hold. A man gave Amelia his seat on a coil of rope. "What a beautiful day for a wedding," she said. "I wish Wilhelm could be with us."

Elizabeth nodded. "When they let him out he is going to be happy to see you are better. You have a little color in your face now, and you're stronger every day."

The peasants, dressed in their finest clothes, chatted as they waited for the arrival of the captain and August and Gretchen.

At last Captain Miller, dressed in his black redingote and with his hair smoothly combed, strode on deck carrying a prayerbook. He took his place near the rail, turned a few pages, then flipped them back again until he located "How to Conduct a Wedding Ceremony." While he was waiting for the young people to appear his eyes fell on Amelia. Poor woman, she had been close to death a few days ago. He was glad he had saved her life. He thought of Wilhelm and hoped he had learned from his experience in the brig.

Soon August came forward and stood facing the captain. Then, near the hatchway a woman's soprano voice sang a German hymn. Everyone turned to watch Gretchen on her father's arm as she advanced to stand beside August. Dressed in a white summer dress with a borrowed lace curtain for a veil, she was radiant.

The captain waited for the music to end before he read a short sermon on the sacredness of married life. Then, following the text in his prayerbook he conducted the ceremony as the bride and groom exchanged promises to love and honor one another "as long as they both shall live." Finally the captain declared the couple to be man and wife and concluded the civil ceremony by saying, "Those whom God hath joined together, let not man put asunder."

August and Gretchen stood waiting, not knowing the ceremony was over. The captain chuckled. "You can kiss your bride now," he said softly to the groom.

Then pandemonium broke loose. Men cheered, whistled and stamped the deck as they lined up with their wives to offer congratulations and to kiss the bride.

Amelia remained seated until Captain Miller stood alone near the rail. Her knees felt weak as she approached him. "I am Amelia Winters," she began.

"Yah, I know. I'm glad you are better."

"Captain Miller, I want to thank you for saving my life."

"Yah. Yah I—"

She broke in. "Sir, when will you let my husband go free?"

He hesitated. "Soon. I hope he has learned that passengers don't strike ship's officers."

Amelia nodded. "He was worried about me."

"Yah. Yah."

Adolph Ketchum's voice rose above the confusion of sounds. "Folks! I don't have a son get married every day! I saved some German beer from the old country. Get your cups and we'll have a little snort to celebrate the wedding of August and Gretchen! Who-oo-o-o!"

Mary blustered, "The old sot!" She turned to Elizabeth. "I hope they drink all of his brew so for once we can see him sober."

Gretchen's mother dabbed at her eyes. She made her way to Harriet Ketchum's side. "It's hard," she began. "Going to a new land is not easy, and now we've lost our only daughter." She sobbed.

Harriet replied, "August is my husband's brother and he's a fine young man. Gretchen has a good husband, Mrs. Meyer."

The lady wiped her eyes and blew her nose. "That's good to hear." She eyed Adolph who was cavorting about in a ridiculous manner. "Does he drink like his father?"

"He seldom drinks and neither does my husband. When they were growing up they saw too much of what liquor does to a man."

While the festivities continued a group of ladies carried the wedding cake and other food from the galley to a make-shift table made from rough planks.

A woman with a strong voice announced, "Get your dishes and silverware! We'll eat here in the fresh air! Sit or stand wherever you can find room! After dinner Herr Charles Weber will play his accordion and we'll dance."

Shouts of approval came from the sea-weary peasants as they made their way to the hold to get their dishes.

During the afternoon as the healthier passengers continued the celebration, Ernst circulated among the men collecting money to present to the young couple in lieu of the usual wedding gifts. When he passed Amelia, he bent to whisper, "I'll put in some for you and Wilhelm. He can pay me back later." She smiled her thanks.

For Amelia the day was marred by only one cold fact—the absence of Wilhelm. She returned to the hold that afternoon wondering. What did the captain mean by "soon"?

16.

THE NEXT MORNING PROMISED another balmy day. People lounged about the deck in the warm sunshine. Amelia, still weak, relaxed with Eduard by her side, his short leash about her wrist.

Some of the women had begun cleaning up and preparing for landing. Many were doing laundry. Clothing must be washed and mended. Many of the garments which were in shreds were thrown into the sea. Everything had a repulsive, musty odor from the dark, damp hold where they had spent so many hours.

In the afternoon while Grandmother Mary watched Eduard, Elizabeth helped Amelia sort the family's clothing. Many blankets and some garments were thrown overboard. Amelia felt they were discarding too much but she could not stand the sight of the stinking rags which were a reminder of the nightmare voyage.

When she hesitated about discarding something, Elizabeth said, "We don't want to feel ashamed when we meet Americans. If they saw us wearing these musty rags they would wonder what kind of people we were."

When the clothing had been laundered and repacked, the women scrubbed the hold. Harriet sniffed. "It still smells musty," she remarked.

That night after lights were out, Captain Miller ordered the second mate to bring Wilhelm to his cabin. The prisoner, dozing in a corner, was roused by the sound of a key in the lock. Then a glimmer of light from the lantern caused him to shield his eyes.

"Get up!" the officer commanded.

Wilhelm slowly rose to stand in a crouched position, blinking in the unaccustomed light.

"Move smart, Winters! Or maybe you don't want to leave your cozy little room."

Wilhelm hesitated, his hands over his eyes. "Are you letting me out?"

"You don't deserve it, but I'm following the captain's orders." He kicked at a rat that scurried down the narrow hall. "Guess you'll miss your little pets." The officer turned. "Follow me."

Wilhelm staggered. His muscles were weak and sore. How long had it been since he walked? Painful involuntary spasms seized the muscles in both legs. The sudden contractions caused the tissues to knot in hard masses in the calves of his legs. He hobbled after the second mate.

The man turned, holding the lantern before Wilhelm's face. He covered his eyes. "I can't see," he said softly.

The officer sneered. "What a specimen of humanity you are, Winters. Feel like a fight?" He stuck a fist under Wilhelm's nose. "You are the first passenger who ever struck me, Herr Winters, and you'd better be the last. Straighten up! Walk like a man!"

Wilhelm gritted his teeth to stifle the moan from the pain in his legs. He hobbled behind the officer on the way to the ladder which led to the afterdeck two levels above. Finally they stopped in the darkness before the Captain's door; it opened at the second mate's knock.

"Sir. Here is Winters."

"Thank you. That is all." Captain Miller stared at the man before him. Filthy clothes and hands, the odor of an unwashed body, pasty-white face—how could a man deteriorate to this condition in less than three weeks?

"Come in, Winters. Sit there." The captain pointed.

Wilhelm still covered his eyes against the light as he hobbled inside and dropped into a straight chair.

"What's wrong with your legs?"

"Cramps." He massaged the knots in the calves of each leg while avoiding looking toward the light. "Sir."

"Yes, Winters."

"How is my wife?"

"She recovered, though she still is weak."

"Thank you. You saved her life."

They sat silently for several seconds. Then the captain remarked, "I can see the brig was hard on you. As captain, when a passenger becomes unruly and strikes a ship's officer, I have only one recourse. Severe punishment—otherwise the problem could escalate to mutiny. You'll remember the people had been grumbling about conditions for days, and the second mate suspected you were the ringleader. Then you struck him. Such behavior demands severe punishment."

Wilhelm nodded, a wry grin on his face. "I've paid in full for my misconduct, Sir."

The captain got up. "You're free to go, Winters."

Slowly he got to his feet. "Sir, my body and clothes are filthy. I have lice. I don't want to go to my family this way. If the galley is empty, I'd like to wash up there. And these filthy clothes—I'll throw them overboard."

"Yah. Yah." Captain Miller took an oilskin from a hook. "When you're cleaned up, wear this to get to your bunk in the hold."

"Thank you, Sir." Wilhelm limped out the door into the June night. He glanced up at the stars. He thought they had never been so beautiful.

17.

ERNST SHOOK WILHELM'S SHOULDER. "We're almost there!" he exclaimed. "I saw America!"

Clumsily Wilhelm climbed from the bunk as fast as his sore muscles would allow. "You're sure, Pa?"

"Yah. Hurry. A seaman is telling us about New York." Ernst returned to the deck followed by Elizabeth.

Many passengers already were gathered at the rail, their eyes straining to see through the misty half-daylight. In the distance grayish-appearing land could be seen. Amelia and Wilhelm stared into the mist. Slowly the rising sun drove away the fog and the people glimpsed the roofs of houses with church steeples rising above them. They saw a large town, larger than any they had seen at home. This was New York.

The ship's bell clanged calling all passengers on deck. The weak and elderly were carried or supported by those more able. Captain Miller came from the afterdeck. He waited for quiet as he surveyed his passengers. As always, at the end of the voyage, the people were pale, thin and puny-looking. A few days of fresh food and exercise and they would recover. It had been a good voyage—only seven deaths. He recalled a trip when cholera struck his passengers and half of them had been buried at sea. But now he must instruct his countrymen about life in America. Poor devils, many hardships lay ahead of them.

He began: "Today we will dock at New York City. Listen carefully as I give you instructions. After we dock at the East River Pier near Battery Park, you can bring your possessions on deck. I will go to a bank and change your money to American dollars. Everyone must pay a $2.50 landing fee which I will collect when I get your American money. However, the American authorities will not allow us to leave the ship for three days."

Voices were raised in protest, a great swelling of guttural, angry sounds. The captain lifted his hand for silence. He continued. "The Americans must be sure we do not have cholera aboard. We will have to wait."

The June sun beat down on the deck of the *Herman Reiter*. Weak and aged people now sat on the deck. Wilhelm squinted into the sun while Amelia leaned against his knees holding Eduard.

The captain continued. "We will be free to go in three days. I know the symptoms and there is no cholera on the ship—only scurvy, and that's not catching.

"In America, as in Germany, there are shysters who will take your money unless you are careful. Don't trust anyone who makes an offer that sounds too good to be true. There are interpreter-guides who are reliable. I'll allow them to talk with you and I'll do my best to keep shysters away—but you must always be cautious. How many know where they are going from New York?"

Hands were raised as various places were called out; Ohio, Pennsylvania, Michigan, Illinois, Minnesota Territory.

"There will be plenty of reliable interpreter-guides. Of course you will have to pay them a reasonable fee to make arrangements and to go with you.

"You have three days now to prepare to disembark. If you have questions, the second mate will help you." His eyes scanned the passengers—pale, gaunt children, bedraggled, tired-looking young people and tottering, weak old ones. His responsibility to the group would soon be finished. He strode to the comfort of his cabin, glad to leave the sorry sight of his passengers behind.

Wilhelm helped Amelia to stand. They studied the New York skyline. Suddenly Amelia gasped. "What's—what's wrong?" Wilhelm asked. "Are you sick?"

Tears streaked her face as she laughed. "I'm so happy! Will, the baby just moved for the first time! I hadn't told you, but I've been afraid it was dead. Oh, Will, it's a good sign! The baby lets us know it's alive just when we see the new land!"

He squeezed her arm. "We'll forget the crossing. Things are going to be better for us now. You'll see."

BOOK 2

The New Land

1.

THE *HERMAN REITER* HAD ANCHORED at the pier, the gangplank was lowered and the German immigrants started going ashore. A warm June sun greeted them to the new land.

The Winters and Ketchum families, a group of thirteen, waited their turn at the gangplank. Wilhelm led Eduard while he supported Amelia with an arm about her waist. A few passengers were so weak that relatives carried them ashore. The Ketchum children and Eduard were pale and thin. As Mary Winters hung her leather bag about her neck she muttered, "Our grandchildren look as though they had been under a board all winter." She paused, then continued as she thought aloud. "Poor Jacob. He wanted to see America, but he lies out there at the bottom of the ocean."

Wilhelm was in high spirits. Now Amelia would recover and once again they soon would be on solid ground. Charles Weber joined the group. "We're a sorry-looking crowd." He grinned. "We look like a ragged flock of molting hens or plucked geese."

"Yah," Wilhelm laughed. "Our feathers are pretty well plucked, but we're in America!"

Slowly they started down the gangplank. Then, puzzled, one and all stopped after a few steps on solid ground.

Amelia said softly, "Will, I'm dizzy. The ground in America rolls like the ship."

Wilhelm stumbled. His legs were wobbly. He glanced

at the others. They, too, were giddy and unable to walk straight. He took a deep breath. He couldn't understand what was wrong. He turned at Charles Weber's laugh.

"Guess we've still got our sea legs," Charlie shouted as he staggered about.

Eduard screamed. His eyes were wide and frightened. Accustomed to the smallness of the deck and hold, he was unable to comprehend the vastness of the land about him. Even Lewis and Anna seemed to have forgotten what it was like to walk on dry land.

After ten weeks at sea the German immigrants were emotionally insecure and physically unstable as they took their first steps on American soil. Puzzled, they stood in a group a short distance from the gangplank. Karl Schmidt, an interpreter-guide recommended by Captain Miller had been hired while they still were aboard the *Herman Reiter*. Where was he?

Mary grumbled, "Lord knows we paid him enough to guide us. You'd think he'd be here. He's likely run off with our money."

Adolph staggered over to Mary. "Hold your tongue, old woman! He has things to 'tend to!"

"He's coming," Ernst remarked. "He looks worried."

A stout, short man with a red face puffed down the gangplank toward the waiting peasants. He carried a bell-shaped horn which he put to his lips. "All of you who have hired me as your guide, come to this group!" Karl Schmidt shouted in perfect German. He pointed to the Winters—Ketchum people and several other families.

The weak and elderly were supported by friends and relatives as the large group congregated in the hot sun. The guide mopped his sweaty face as he shouted, "Anyone here who has not paid the $2.50 landing fee?" No one responded.

He continued. "Do all of you have your American

money from Captain Miller?"

The men nodded and Mary patted her leather bag. Again Karl Schmidt shouted into the horn. "I have made arrangements for us to go up the Hudson River on the river boat, *Henry Hudson* as far as Albany. From there we will take a steam train to Buffalo, where we will board a lake steamship to Detroit and Chicago." He paused. "Some of you will get off along the way. Raise your hands if you don't plan to go as far as Chicago." More than half the group responded.

"Yah," Schmidt murmured. He motioned toward the *Herman Reiter*. We have to get your possessions off the ship. I have a man who will guard them. Pile them here." He indicated a large vacant spot. "The *Henry Hudson* will dock and we'll load this afternoon and start up the Hudson River tonight. Anyone unable to help with unloading can sit over there under the trees in Battery Park. Let's get started."

The elderly, sick, women and children slowly made their way to the inviting shade of nearby elm and linden trees where Old World peasants from many countries rested. They were surrounded by chests, bundles, baskets and prized possessions. A babble of foreign tongues filled the air.

The German people sat apart from the chattering Italian, Irish and Scandinavian immigrants who clutched knapsacks and bundles as though they feared hustling foreigners would snatch their belongings.

Harriet, with a child on either side, rested near Amelia and Eduard. They studied the people. Rough, broad-shouldered farmers stood with hands behind their backs as they appraised the new land. Their heavy clothing was wrinkled and baggy and much too warm for the 75-degree June weather. Sweat poured from flushed faces.

Women leaned against tree trunks nursing hungry babies from their scrawny breasts. The babies fretted with frustration for they were uncomfortable from the heat and heavy blankets.

Eduard cried and Amelia gave him her nearly dry breast. A small boy wrapped in a coat that hung almost to the ground chewed on a crust of coarse rye bread which was covered with spots of mold. Amelia thought the bread must have come from the old country. She wished Wilhelm would bring their food basket. Eduard would eat the dry bread, too, if she scraped away the mold.

They watched as a stream of people moved along the dusty road. These were the folks who lived in New York, the largest city in North America. There were gentlemen in tall black hats and long-tailed coats with skin-tight trousers, and ladies in bonnets with tiny laced waists above full, bright-colored skirts which hung to the ground.

Gretchen whispered to Amelia, "How do they make their skirts stand out so wide?"

"They must have many stiff petticoats under them. They're pretty—there's 'most every color."

"Yah. And notice their parasols. They match the skirts." Gretchen giggled. "The men carry fancy canes. Do you think August and Wilhelm will dress like these men?"

Amelia laughed aloud. "And carry canes and wear high black hats?"

Grandmother Mary and Elizabeth smiled. It was good to hear Amelia laugh again. For a time they watched silently. Then Mary remarked, "They act like they don't see us. They look past us as though we aren't even here."

Amelia laughed. "We do look funny wearing wrinkled winter clothing on a hot day." Eduard stopped nursing to stare at his mother. It had been a long time since he had heard her laugh.

The men continued unloading their possessions under the direction of Karl Schmidt. From where she sat, Amelia could see the harbor and the long row of ships at the piers. Over there was a tall yellow house and above the entrance were two words in large black letters: Castle Garden. What did the words say? Suddenly anxiety overwhelmed her. She was in a land where she could neither understand nor read the language. She was like a deaf mute in America.

The heat was unmerciful and the air oppressive, but even though she was uncomfortable she was glad they were on land. She said a silent prayer of thanks to God for delivering her family from the nightmare of the ocean crossing.

Eduard whined. Like her, he was hot, thirsty and hungry. He toddled over to sit with the Ketchum children. For the first time in weeks Amelia felt hunger. She must eat well now for the sake of the baby that should arrive in November. She put her hand on her abdomen as the fetus stirred. Resting her head against a tree trunk, she dozed.

"Are you sleeping?" Wilhelm stood over her, a paper bag in one hand and their water pitcher in the other. "I've brought you something." He held out the bag.

Eagerly she looked inside. "Strawberries! And fresh bread!" Quickly she hulled a berry and reveled in the delicious aroma and taste of the fresh fruit. Eddie came and she gave him a huge strawberry. As he tasted the strange fruit his puzzled expression changed to one of pleasure.

"More!" he exclaimed.

Wilhelm laughed and held the pitcher out to Amelia.

"Try this."

"Milk! Fresh milk!" Tears came to her eyes as she sipped the rich milk. "It's so good." She held the pitcher for Eddie to drink. "He doesn't remember the good milk we had in Germany," she said as he smacked his lips.

Other men also had brought treats to their families. Laughter spread through the group as they picnicked under the trees. Everything was a treat—the fresh bread, fruit, milk and sausage.

"Do they have plenty of food where you bought this?" Amelia asked.

"Yah. I saw loaves and loaves of bread and whole tubs of milk. I'll buy more before we start up the Hudson River."

Wilhelm looked toward the harbor. "The guide told me that one of those ships is ready to sail for California. He said it's a fast clipper and that the men on board are going to California to dig for gold. The men were laughing and singing noisy songs. They likely were drunk."

"Where is California?"

"Many miles west and south of Minnesota." Wilhelm stared out over the harbor. "Maybe California is where we should be going. They say out there you can pick lumps of gold out of the rivers or dig them from the ground. It would be easier than farming."

"You're a farmer," Amelia said softly.

He brushed back a lock of hair. "Yah, but digging for gold would be exciting." He grinned. "Karl Schmidt said there are hardly any women in California so a ship load of white and colored ones soon will sail for the gold fields."

"Humph! They're likely whores."

"Yah. But those men are having fun." There was a note of envy in his voice. In a moment he went on. "Karl

Schmidt says there are two thousand whorehouses that are open day and night, seven days a week in New York City. I guess they won't miss the shipload that are going to the gold fields."

"Humph! It's disgusting!"

They munched on the delicious food as the parade of people passed; whites, beautifully dressed, an occasional Indian with a blanket around his shoulders and Negroes in bright colors sauntered past them.

Amelia mused, "I thought Negroes were slaves in America and that they were chained and led around by guards. These colored people are laughing. They have pretty white teeth." She pushed her tongue against her scurvy-loosened teeth and sore gums.

"Yah. I guess the slaves are all in the south."

"When do we go on the river boat?"

"We leave at five o'clock. I will get food to take with us. 'Melia, you should have seen the market—barrels of vegetables and baskets of eggs, tubs of butter, all kinds of cheese and bread and meat. I've never seen anything like it."

"People must live well in America. Before we leave, take our food basket and buy only things that won't spoil." Eduard slept between them on the ground. Amelia brushed a fly from his face.

Wilhelm wiped his sweaty forehead. The day was nearing its warmest hour in mid-afternoon. The immigrants, their stomachs full, rested with closed eyes. Women leaned against trees with sleeping children beside them.

"Karl Schmidt is getting our tickets for the whole trip to Chicago," Wilhelm said. "It costs $8.00, and children under three are free."

"Sixteen dollars. That's a lot. It must be very far."

"Yah. We go up the Hudson River to a place called

Albany. Then we take a steam train to Buffalo where we get on a lake steamer and go all the way to Chicago."

"Another ship! I hate ships. After we get to Minnesota I'll never go on another ship!" She paused. "How do we get to Minnesota from Chicago?"

Wilhelm grinned. "Guess."

"No! Not another ship!"

"Yah. A river boat."

"We won't get there before winter."

"Yah, we will. And I'll build you a nice cabin, and we'll have good land. By a year from now you'll like our new home."

She clamped her lips in silent resignation. Wilhelm got up. "Pa and Ma and Grandma Mary are sleeping. You rest while I fill our food basket at the market." Amelia nodded.

The *Henry Hudson* was late leaving New York. It was not until eight in the evening that she steamed away loaded to capacity with passengers and baggage. The people were crowded together on the lower deck while the upper deck was piled high with their possessions.

"Where do we sleep?" Grandmother Mary called to Wilhelm.

He grinned sheepishly. "Right here, Grandmother."

The old lady shifted her leather bag to the other shoulder as she shouted, "Here? There's not even room to stand without stepping on someone! Where's that guide? Is this what we paid eight dollars for?"

Other voices joined in the clamor to complain until Karl Schmidt, red-faced and puffing, came from the upper deck. He put his megaphone to his lips and looked over the crowd. People were crowded together in the late afternoon heat. Parents held their children in their arms. "Friends," he began, "I know you are uncomfortable but fortunately we will be on the *Henry Hudson* only one night. There are no sleeping accommodations but by using every inch of space you'll be able to sit on the deck. The night will be pleasant and warm. This is quite different from ocean travel. We will have steady, easy passage on a calm river. You'll see small islands and always there will be land on both sides of the Hudson River. You are practically on solid ground.

"Find yourself a place to sit, and sleep when you can. We will be in Albany tomorrow morning."

After eating a light supper from lunch baskets, the immigrants settled down for the night. Soon mist rose from the water and towered over the land.

The *Henry Hudson* was driven by a large stern wheel which plowed deep into the water stirring up whirls of foam, leaving a wheel track in the white foaming water which evened out and was gone as soon as the wake passed. Behind the ship the river flowed calm and even on its way to the Atlantic.

Shortly after daybreak the *Henry Hudson* docked in Albany. Tired and exhausted from lack of sleep, the people left the boat and gathered around their guides who marched them on a dusty road along the river to the railroad station. Ernst carried Eduard while Wilhelm supported Amelia with an arm about her waist. At the station they were directed to a large room or hall where they waited.

There were groups of English, Irish, Italians, Germans and Swedes. They were told by guides in their own languages to remain in one place and that no one should move from where he was.

"What are they doing?" Grandmother Mary asked in her shrill voice.

Ernst replied, "I don't know, Ma, but we'd better do what they tell us to."

Two American inspectors circulated through the

crowd as they pointed at each one, counting them. The men came back, pointed, mumbled and counted again.

Karl Schmidt shouted, "You must stand still so they can count you!"

"We're like sheep in a pen," Grandfather Adolph muttered.

Finally the numbers checked with the numbers in the passenger contracts and they were directed to board the train.

2.

KARL SCHMIDT PUFFED AHEAD OF HIS GROUP as he led them to the train. The German country people had never seen a steam train. To them, the twenty cars looked like high-roofed wagons which were tied together in a long row. They stared at them, curious yet fearful. Each enclosed car sat on eight iron wheels and had windows. The locomotive, they thought, must be the car that pulled the train. It had only four wheels but they were three times as large as the ones on the other cars. There were two small wheels in the front. A smokestack belched thick black smoke and sent red sparks whirling into the air so they knew there was a fire inside. This worried the rural people who handled fire cautiously.

Mary sputtered, "We're fools to ride in a string of wagons pulled by a contraption with a fire burning inside. Sparks are flying and those roofs look mighty dry. We could be roasted alive!"

"Yah, old woman," Adolph replied. "I've heard steam trains sometimes blow up and pieces fly into the air.

Maybe you'd better stay here."

Mary snorted, "I wasn't talking to you!"

Karl Schmidt stopped beside the fourth car and motioned for them to climb a small ladder. Inside, the car was about fifteen feet long and seven feet wide. Rough board benches lined both sides leaving a narrow aisle in the center. Another German group shared the car with them.

Food baskets, boxes, bundles and knapsacks took up most of the room so they were crowded. Some of the men who were unable to find space on the benches sat or lay down on the floor.

On the end of one bench a place was made for Mary and Amelia. Wilhelm sat on the floor holding Eduard on his lap. Near the door there was a sign in black letters. WATCH YOUR STEP. Wilhelm wondered what it said. He had seen this same sign near the pier in New York. He could see other words on signposts outside the window and it was annoying not to be able to read them. He was a grown man as unable to read this language as a five-year-old.

Their guide was talking in English to a man in a blue suit with brass buttons. He must work for the railroad. Wilhelm was sure they were talking about the travelers. He listened, but he couldn't hear a word that sounded like the English he and August had studied on shipboard. The sounds were mixed-up and crazy. He felt depressed. He would never be able to speak this language. Here in America one could insult you to your face and you couldn't answer—you could only stand there and stare, awkward and dumb.

The official left the train and closed the doors. Schmidt spoke in German. "Stay in your seats, people. Our train will soon start."

The instructions were followed by a long piercing

whistle from the locomotive. Eduard, Anna, Lewis and the other young children screamed, long terrifying screams. They had never heard such a horrible sound. When it stopped the children became quiet. Their hands clutched parents, benches or anything within reach. The adults smiled apprehensively.

The train was moving. They could hear the wheels rumbling along the iron rails, and they could see through the windows that they were moving. The car jolted and creaked. As they gained speed the car leaned a little to one side. Again the children shrieked. "It's tipping over!" Lewis screamed.

Frederick spoke softly to his son. "Be quiet."

"I'm scared."

"Everything is all right," the father whispered.

Eduard climbed on Amelia's lap and looked into her face. She forced a smile and pointed out of the window at the houses and trees which seemed to be moving backward. Suddenly she felt dizzy and sick. She closed her eyes. Perhaps the dizziness would pass. Finally Eduard slept.

Still Amelia sat with her eyes closed. The train increased its speed. The engine belched smoke and sputtered as the wheels creaked and the cars rocked and jerked. The people sat silent, rigid and tense, each moment expecting the cars to leave the rails or catch fire. But nothing happened.

Amelia opened her eyes. Again she saw trees, houses and farms rushing past with incredible speed.

Mary whispered, "Are you all right?"

She closed her eyes. "I'm a little dizzy."

Pale and silent the passengers sped on, each one looking hopefully toward their arrival in Buffalo. They felt as though they were moving with the speed of the wind.

Gradually they relaxed and began to talk. The heat inside the car grew uncomfortable. The woolen clothing stuck to their perspiring skin. No fresh air was coming in and it grew more oppressive until breathing became difficult. The children whined.

August Ketchum stood near the guide. "Couldn't we open the windows?"

"*Nein.* They're nailed shut."

"Could we open the door?"

"No. It's locked and won't be opened until we stop." The portly man mopped his brow. "It's hot, but I'll look after you. There are reasons why the windows and doors are locked. Once some Swedish immigrants became frightened and were killed when they jumped from the train. The railroad men locked the doors after that. Then, last year on a hot day, a horrible accident happened. When the train arrived in Buffalo and the doors of a windowless car were opened, seven people were dead of suffocation. Three of them were from Germany. Some of the others were unconscious. These people had no interpreter. They had cried and begged to have air, but there was no interpreter to look after them. Since that terrible tragedy the railroad company has opened the doors whenever the train stops." He smiled and his perspiring face wrinkled. "I will look after you. No one will suffocate in my car."

The passengers relaxed for a time but the train slowed and the sound of the wheels changed from clackety-clack, clackety-clack, to a strange, hollow rumble. They looked out and saw water on either side. They were crossing a wide river on a railroad bridge.

Old Adolph exclaimed, "*Mein* God! Iron rails across the water! We'll drown! I need a stein of beer!"

Mary snorted. Karl Schmidt explained, "The Americans are brave people. They risk their lives to try new things. This bridge is safe." Soon they again were on land.

The children were hungry. Food baskets were opened and bread, sausage and cheese were distributed. People who had not bought food in New York went hungry for they could not buy food on the train.

The day passed slowly. The passengers eagerly looked forward to each stop when the doors were opened and a breeze flushed out the stale air. The journey continued through the day and night as the locomotive puffed across New York state. Everyone looked forward to the end of the trip. Mary had said many times, "I'll be glad when we're there. Any minute something could happen on this new-fangled contraption."

In the forenoon of the next day they arrived at Buffalo.

3.

AFTER A DAY OF CONFUSION the German immigrants and their possessions were transferred to the lake steamer, the *Antoine Cadillac*. The ship was of medium size with a water wheel on either side, and like the *Herman Reiter* she was crowded with people and cargo. The quarters in steerage on the middle deck were only slightly more comfortable than those on the sailing vessel.

Amelia and Wilhelm sat on the edge of their four-foot-wide bunk while Eduard frolicked behind them. Amelia stared at her fellow passengers. They, too, were immigrants from countries in the Old World. The remainder of the Winters and Ketchum group were scattered throughout the steerage area.

The passengers' possessions were stacked together helter-skelter on the lower deck and the owners had to watch that nothing was stolen or fell overboard. On the *Herman Reiter,* they were allowed the freedom of the upper deck, but here they were confined to their own level. Amelia resented the fact that though there was plenty of room on the deck above where there were only a few first class passengers with individual cabins, steerage people were crowded into airless, dark quarters.

Karl Schmidt explained that first class cost much more than steerage berths and that only wealthy people were able to travel first class.

Amelia silently pondered her observations of the people on the upper deck. The women were dressed in silk skirts and velvet shoes and the men in tall hats and long coats of expensive cloth. Like the women she had seen in New York, these ladies carried open parasols. They were not traveling to find new homes; they had homes. Why would anyone travel if they were not forced to? Why would anyone sail these huge lakes for pleasure? If she ever was settled in her own home, she certainly would stay there.

Food on the *Antoine Cadillac* was plentiful, but to the Old World passengers it seemed to be strangely prepared. The fare consisted of things mixed together so that they were unsure what they were eating. Though the food was not to her liking, Amelia ate that she might regain her strength and thus provide nourishment for the active, developing fetus.

While Wilhelm walked about carrying Eduard, Amelia sat on the side of the bunk watching the steerage people. Even to her inexperienced eyes, they were an odd lot. Dressed in outlandish clothes, they laughed and sang in Irish, Swedish and Italian, and they behaved in strange ways. While the German immigrants were loaded down with possessions, tools of all kinds such as axes, spades, hoes, saws, barrels, clocks, and many beer kegs, the Swedish immigrants seemed to have relatively few possessions.

With Eduard riding astride his father's shoulders, Wilhelm came to sit beside Amelia.

She asked, "What kind of men are those in leather jackets with knives in their belts?"

"Karl Schmidt says they are fur hunters on their way to the West for fall hunting." He paused. "I wonder if they'll go as far as California?"

"Where?"

"California. Where the gold is."

"Humph. We're farmers." Amelia studied three strangely dressed men. Red, striped, woolen blankets which they held closely about themselves covered them from their heads to their knees. Trousers with legs reaching halfway to their knees were held in place with string belts. Low, soft moccasins covered their feet while fire-red bands of cloth hung from their ears. Their skin was a dusty brown and deep-set black eyes lurked under dark brows.

Amelia whispered, "Will, who are those people?"

"Indians."

"Will there be Indians in Minnesota?"

"Yah."

"They don't talk to anyone, and no one talks to them. Sometimes they grunt a little to each other. They look at us, but I don't think they like us. I think they could be cruel."

"Yah. But these Indians aren't wild or they wouldn't be on this ship."

"Are the ones in Minnesota wild?"

Wilhelm lifted the squirming Eduard to the berth. "I

don't know. We won't bother them, and I don't believe they'll give us trouble."

As they watched, a man dressed in the suit of a business man approached the Indian men. He spoke to them in guttural speech. "You think he's Indian?" Amelia asked.

"I don't know. He's dressed like a white man, but his skin is brown like an Indian's." Wilhelm shrugged.

For a time, while Eduard napped behind them, they watched the passengers. Amelia whispered, "Did you see the two Negroes back there with their feet chained to the berth?"

"Yah. They are slaves that were caught in New York state. They ran away from their master and were trying to get to Canada."

"What will they do with them?"

"They'll be taken back to their owners and punished for running away."

"Whipped?"

"Beaten. Karl Schmidt told me some of the owners are kind but others beat the slaves so bad they sometimes die."

"That's terrible. No wonder they look so worried. I saw some Negroes working on the ship. They seemed to be part of the crew."

"Yah. They are free men. Those two over there are shackled and in foot chains because they have savage tempers."

Amelia nodded. "I don't blame them. It must be terrible to be a slave."

Silently Amelia studied her neighbors. Most of them seemed to need a thorough scrubbing and their children were filthy. She hoped her family would not again become lice infected. Most of the men chewed tobacco, and since no spittoons were provided, the deck was slimy with men's spittle.

Eduard wakened and climbed into his mother's lap. "Down," he said pointing to children crawling on the filthy deck.

"No." Amelia reached into her food basket and gave him half a slice of bread. She knew they should wash their hands, but water in the washing buckets used by steerage passengers was not often changed and after many people had washed in it, it was thick and black and the few towels were wet and grimy. She would ask Karl Schmidt if he could get them fresh water; then she would use her own towels.

Even though Amelia was annoyed by their lack of cleanliness, she liked these foreign people, for though they were dirty, they appeared friendly. They smiled at her and murmured words she couldn't understand, but she knew they wished her well. All she could do was to return the smiles of those who could have been true friends.

Amelia worried about life in the new land. How could she make herself understood? Among the Americans she would be like a deaf-mute. Her eyes met those of one of the Indians. She sensed his dislike. Why? Why was he annoyed with them? She looked away.

Eduard squealed, "Down!"

Wilhelm set the child on his shoulders. "We're stopping to take on wood for the steam engines," he said. "Eddie and I will watch."

Shortly old Mary and Gretchen joined Amelia. "You're looking better," the old woman remarked. "There's a bit of color in your face now." She sat beside Amelia and pulled her ever-present leather bag to her lap.

"I feel better every day. The food is helping me to get stronger." She paused. "When do your parents leave the boat, Gretchen?"

"Tomorrow or the next day. The ship stops at a place called 'Toledo'." She brushed back a lock of blonde hair. "My parents are sad, and so am I." She hesitated. "We may never see one another again."

Amelia nodded. "At least your parents will be in the new land. Mine are across that horrible Atlantic Ocean."

Mary snorted, "Men! It's not enough to drag us from our homes in Germany and across the ocean, now we have to cross three big lakes," she rubbed her forehead, "I can't remember the names."

Gretchen nodded. "Erie, Huron and Michigan."

"Humph!" Mary exclaimed. "I'm tired of boats! Why can't our men be content to settle in Ohio or Michigan? But no, they have to go to the ends of the earth!"

"Yah. And we are to go on river boats from Chicago to Minnesota." Amelia shook her head. "Will's never satisfied. He even said he'd like to go to California to look for gold."

"Yah," Mary scolded. "Men are all alike. They're always looking for greener pastures, they can never let well enough alone. And my grandson, Wilhelm is the worst of the lot!" She pounded her leather bag with a gnarled fist. "And the others look to him for suggestions."

"All the women are tired to death of this journey. It's the middle of June and we've been sailing since the first of April. Eleven weeks!" Amelia's eyes again met those of a nearby Indian. She quickly looked away. "But we will survive, I guess."

Gretchen and Mary nodded.

4.

IN MORNING SUNSHINE the *Antoine Cadillac* steamed from Lake Erie into the mouth of the Detroit River. The Ketchum and Winters families stood by the rail. They passed Grosse Ile and took delight in the forested shores on either side.

"Looks like good land," Ernst commented.

"Yah," Frederick answered. "Level and nice." Silently he appraised Gretchen's trim figure as she leaned over the rail.

Mary said, "We should stop here. Michigan looks good."

Wilhelm interrupted. "Grandma, our fare is paid to Chicago, and besides the best land is already taken here."

Mary tossed her head. "You're not always right, Grandson! The women are for stopping in Detroit. We've had enough of ships!"

Wilhelm glanced at his mother, Amelia and the Ketchum women. They nodded. "Hm-m-m." The men's eyes were not meeting his. "Pa, do you want to stay in Michigan?"

Ernst shook his head. "It will be too late when we get to Minnesota to plant crops—but I guess the land is better."

"By the time we found land here, it would also be too late to plant."

August asked, "Do we have enough money to carry us through the winter?"

"There's plenty of wild game and fish in Minnesota," Wilhelm argued. "I don't think we should change our plans."

Adolph hiccuped, "Hell! Let's go to Minnesota! Might's well starve in one place as the other!"

Mary snorted, "Shut up, you old sot! You don't have a brain in your head!"

Wilhelm ignored the old peoples' jangling. "How many of you men want to stay in Michigan?" No one answered. "Then you all want to go on?" They nodded silently.

Mary bristled. "How about the women? You drag us along to God-forsaken places! You almost killed your wife taking her on that ocean trip! Us women are no better than those slaves they took off the ship in chains. Yah! German women are slaves to their men!"

Wilhelm grinned. "Grandma, you'll like Minnesota."

The old lady snorted, tossed her bag over her shoulder and strode away leading Eduard by the hand.

Karl Schmidt approached the group. "Soon we'll dock," he announced. "Detroit is an old town. It has streets and stores and churches like cities in Germany. You have noticed apple and cherry trees along the shore. Farmers sell their fruit and vegetables at the street market. It's a pretty good place to live if cholera doesn't strike in the summer."

Wilhelm broke in. "Who owns those little white cabins that are back from the river?"

"French farmers are there. Their narrow farms go from their buildings to the river. Most of them sell their crops at the market in Detroit." The guide paused. "We will dock in a short time. It will take several hours to unload and to take on supplies and more passengers. We'll sail about seven o'clock tonight, so you'll have the day to visit the city."

There was noise, confusion and shouts in several languages as families prepared to disembark. Suddenly Mary's shrill scream silenced the confusion. "Eddie! Eddie's overboard!"

Her shriek brought people running to the bow of the

ship. Wilhelm arrived to see the man who had been speaking to the Indians spring over the rail and vigorously swim toward Eddie whose head suddenly bobbed above the water before he disappeared beneath the waves.

Amelia, her hand over her mouth, smothered a scream. Silently she prayed, "Please God, don't let him drown."

The chaos was deafening. Women's screams, men's shouts and children's terrified cries created pandemonium aboard the ship. All eyes followed the dark swimmer who slowly made his way to the spot where Eddie last had been seen.

"Go! Go! Go!" Karl Schmidt shouted in English. "A little to your right!"

Again Eddie's blonde head appeared. The shouts were deafening as suggestions in many languages were yelled to the rescuer. Desperately he plunged toward the child, seizing him by the hair as he again started to sink.

Bedlam reigned as the swimmer grasped Eddie, spitting and coughing, and swam toward the ship where a crew member threw a rope to the man who was holding the boy's head above water.

As the dripping rescuer and child were pulled aboard, "Thank God," was murmured in many tongues. The Winters family surrounded the man as Amelia hugged her coughing, sobbing child.

"Thank you, thank you," each one murmured as they shook the man's hand. Wilhelm spoke to the interpreter. "Find out who this man is. We want to know the name of the man who saved our child."

Karl Schmidt spoke in English to the man while water dripped from the rescuer's clothing. After several minutes of rapid conversation, Karl replied, "His name is Simon Pokagon. He is a Potawatomi Indian who has taken up the ways of white men. His tribe lives on the west side of the state on the shore of Lake Michigan not far from Chicago. He will travel with us on the *Antoine Cadillac*. He is glad he could rescue your little boy."

Again the family murmured their appreciation to the Indian who nodded his acceptance. Soon they were docked and wagons were rolling ashore. People, boxes, and bundles spilled from the hold, along with babies, older children, axes, shovels, and pieces of cherished furniture and cooking utensils.

There was pandemonium. Crying children were separated from parents. Lost baggage caused problems until it was located. A steady stream of people with luggage and boxes left the ship. Eventually Amelia returned with Eddie now clad in dry clothing.

Great-grandmother Mary was repentant. "I'm sorry, Amelia. Eddie just pulled away from me and he was overboard."

"He is fine, Grandma. It could have happened if he had been with any of us."

"But I was furious with Wilhelm and the men because they wouldn't stay in Michigan. If I hadn't been so angry I'd have been more careful with him." She hesitated. "I know I'm a disagreeable old woman, but I wouldn't do anything to hurt that child."

Amelia patted Mary's arm. "I know that."

Hawkers drumming up business circulated through the milling people at the bottom of the gangplank as they called out names of local inns and hotels. Cries of "Mansion House," "Eagle Hotel," "American" and "Steamboat Hotel" were heard.

Elizabeth commented, "It would be nice if we had our animals with us. We don't have anything to start our life in Minnesota."

Wilhelm glanced at his silent father and wondered

what his thoughts were. He turned to answer Elizabeth. "Ma, these people have not come across the ocean. They're bringing their animals from farms in the east—New York state where we landed and other states, too. We'll get along fine. We'll buy animals in Minnesota."

"Humph!" Mary snorted. "Michigan looks good to me!"

"Shut up, Mary!" Adolph hiccuped. "It's been decided we're going to Minnesota!"

When the last departing passengers had gone down the gangplank with wagons, horses, oxen and cows, Karl Schmidt suggested that the German group might enjoy exploring the city. August and his bride, Gretchen, already were halfway down the gangplank. The interpreter warned Wilhelm, Ernst, Frederick and Adolph. "Like cities in Germany, you may find dishonest people here. Watch your money. There likely are pickpockets in that crowd down there."

With Eddie riding on his father's shoulders the Winters and Ketchum group separated at the foot of the gangplank. Amelia walked beside Wilhelm, thankful that Eddie was safe, that her strength and vitality had returned and that the baby she carried was active. "Where are we going?" she asked as they separated from the milling crowd of people, wagons and farm animals.

"We'll try to find the market and stores," Wilhelm replied.

Silently they wandered through the streets with strange names. Randolph, Jefferson, Woodward. Supply-filled wagons rolled past, the wide-rimmed wheels clattering on the bricks. Horses and oxen strained to keep the wagons moving, ever fearful of a cut from the driver's whip. Families peered from the wagons as they stared at the people on the boardwalks.

Dozens of persons hurried about their business;

bearded men in rough work clothes, women carrying baskets of vegetables, society ladies with exquisite hats and outer wraps, children following their mothers or holding to their skirts, business men and government officials with white shirts and wide-brimmed hats. Numerous Indian and French people mingled with the frontier men who dressed in shirts and knicker-type pantaloons above knee-high knitted socks and heavy shoes.

People stopped to chat with friends on the sidewalk. For a long time Amelia had been silent. Finally she said, "I can't understand a word these people are saying. I feel lost in this strange land."

"We'll learn fast, and August taught us some English on the *Herman Reiter*. We'll manage."

They paused at the corner of Woodward and Jefferson. "There's the market," Wilhelm said. "I'll buy some fruit."

French speaking farmers shouted out their prices in broken English.

"Will. There are cherries and strawberries."

"Yah." He pointed to the cherries.

The man asked, "How many you want a' ze cherry?"

Wilhelm shook his head, still pointing.

"You no speak ze English?"

Silently Wilhelm pointed and shook his head. He pulled two American coins from his pocket and extended his hand. The Frenchman shook his head in disbelief as he spoke to a nearby farmer. "Two dollar for ze cherry? Ze man must be reech."

"Take it. He don't know no better."

The farmer's dark eyes sparkled. "Zank you! Zank you! Zanks for ze business." He shoved a bushel of cherries toward Wilhelm and took the coins.

Amelia gasped. "What will we do with a bushel of cherries?"

Wilhelm scratched his head. "I don't know. Eat 'em, I guess." He carried the basket to the front of a dry goods store and leaned against the wall. They silently munched on the sweet, juicy fruit as people passed them.

"They act like they can't see us," Amelia whispered. "They look right past us."

"Yah."

"These people don't like us."

"They can't talk to us. When we learn English it will be better."

Through cherry-stained lips, Eddie squealed and pointed. Wilhelm said, "It's the Indians from the ship with Simon Pokagon."

Simon stopped and put his hand on Eddie's head. "Nice boy," he said. He glanced questioningly at the basket of cherries, then at Wilhelm who shrugged. The two Indian men stared at the little family.

Simon strode a few feet to the French farmer. "Did you sell cherries to this man?"

The Frenchman chuckled. "For two dollar."

"He's from Germany and doesn't know our ways. You should give him back part of the money."

"No. He want ze cherry. I want ze money. I no give it back." He turned to wait on a customer.

Simon motioned to Wilhelm. "We'll take you with your cherries back to the *Antoine Cadillac*. Perhaps we can find Karl Schmidt. Come." He spoke in their language to the two Indians. One of them hoisted the basket to his shoulder and the little procession headed for the Detroit River.

5.

FOR SIX DAYS THE *ANTOINE CADILLAC* sailed two of the Great Lakes, Huron and Michigan. Time was spent with Karl Schmidt mastering a few often-used English expressions and in learning the value of American money. With the help of the interpreter they learned from Simon Pokagon that Michigan Indians were displeased with whites who had claimed their land and killed or driven away the game. They also were informed that most of the Indians had been removed by the United States government from their Michigan homes and sent to reservations west of the Mississippi River.

Through the interpreter Simon Pokagon said, "By 1840 most of the Michigan Indians had been taken west."

August asked, "Did they want to go?"

Simon was emphatic. "No! They were driven like animals from their homes and forced to walk hundreds of miles to a strange land. Many died of disease and exhaustion." His dark eyes flashed. "Mrs. Winters asked why Indians are unfriendly. The government made treaties with us—treaties my people didn't understand. They took our homes and drove us away!"

"Why wasn't your tribe sent west of the Mississippi?" Ernst asked.

Simon gazed over the sparkling waters of Lake Huron. "My father, Leon Pokagon, had signed a treaty which gave our band of 250 Potawatomi some land in western Michigan. My father died in 1840 and I have tried to keep our people together. We are of the Roman Catholic religion."

"Your people believe in God?" Harriet smoothed her dress over her obese abdomen.

Simon nodded. His two Indian companions seemingly paid no attention to the discussion. The Germans believed they did not understand the language—or perhaps they were scornful and aloof because of resentment toward all whites.

Simon continued as Schmidt interpreted. "Many years before I was born, Roman Catholic missionaries visited Indian camps in Michigan, and some of our people accepted the white man's religion. Are you Catholic?"

Ernst shook his head. "Lutheran. But we don't go to church often."

Frederick shifted his three-year-old daughter, Anna, to his right knee. "Will the Indians in Minnesota be unfriendly?" He twisted a curl of Anna's blonde hair about his finger.

Simon shook his head. "They won't be happy to see you settle on their hunting grounds. They are of the Sioux tribe." He hesitated, then continued softly, "The Sioux are more warlike than the Potawatomi."

"But we won't bother them," Wilhelm said. "We will be friendly, if they will."

Simon shrugged and quickly changed the subject as he noticed the fear in the eyes of the German women.

The six days required to reach Chicago passed quickly. Pleasant weather, good food and plans for the future occupied the time. Karl Schmidt hurried to find lodging for the group for the two days they must wait for a river steamer. He accompanied the men on shopping trips and continued to advise them about the English language.

On July 8 Schmidt took the two families with their possessions to a steamer on the Chicago River which, with a connecting canal and the Illinois River, would carry them to the upper Mississippi.

When they were loaded the guide and interpreter

had finished his obligations. Farewells and best wishes for the future were said and he departed.

Amelia stood at the rail of the new ship holding Eddie's hand. Her heart was heavy. Now they were alone—entirely alone in the new land on a new steamer. The river flowed through flat land and the shores were close to the rail on either side.

Harriet waddled over to stand beside Amelia. "I'm tired of ships," she puffed, "but this is better than that awful ocean. Here we can see land."

"Yah, but it's strange, flat land with miles and miles of grass. No trees, no hills—just grass." The wind caused long ripples in the dark green grass which traveled as far as they could see.

"It's kind of pretty." Almost mesmerized, the two women watched the rippling billows rise and fall to the horizon.

Finally Harriet said, "Yah, it's pretty, but it's not home. I feel lost. I don't know where I am or where I'm going."

Lewis came to stand beside his mother. "Pa says that grass would be good for cows."

The grassy hummock swayed and sank and came up again with a monotonous sameness. "I know some new words," Lewis exclaimed. He motioned. "This is 'prairie land'."

Amelia patted the boy's head. "You're very smart. I'm afraid I'll never learn English."

Lewis beamed. "I'll help you."

"Yah, the children will learn it fast. They will teach us," Harriet murmured.

Elizabeth joined the women. "This is nice—quiet and peaceful—not noisy like New York City and Detroit and Chicago."

"Yah," Harriet repeated, "but it's not home. Here

there's nothing but grass, grass, grass."

"Yah," Wilhelm's mother continued, "but this is beautiful hay. A farmer could cut enough hay to fill his barns and there still would be miles of it left."

"Left to go to waste," Amelia added. "There are no people here, or animals or trees or bushes or woods, no roads or paths, nothing to show that people ever have been here. Why, if a person was out there without a guide, he could wander over this flat land—until—he died. How could anyone find their way in that grass when one mile is just like all the others?"

Suddenly the wind picked up, sweeping through the grass and stirring up endless waves. A sudden gust flattened and rolled over the vegetation pressing it down so that it lay flat on the fertile land. Then the wind lessened and the rich grass straightened to billow back and forth in rolling ripples.

The men came from the bow of the ship. They were silent and sober. Amelia asked, "Will Minnesota be all grass and no trees?"

"We hope not," Wilhelm said slowly. "This is rich land—you can tell by the grass—but it's not what we want."

Gretchen who had been silent, added, "It's almost like the land is not finished—like God forgot the trees and woods. This land is—is *empty*. I feel closed in on all sides by this grass. I feel little and helpless like I'm nothing more than a grain of sand on this vast prairie."

August grinned. "You're homesick for your Ma and Pa."

Mary swung her leather bag to her right shoulder. "I told you," she chided. "I told all of you in the beginning that we should stay in Germany!"

Adolph snorted. "Humph! Was you ever wrong, old woman?"

"Once! When we were young I thought you were something special! But you turned out to be a disgusting old drunkard! I'm thankful I married Jacob, God rest his soul, instead of you!"

"So am I!" Adolph retorted.

Ernst shook his head. "None of us like this prairie. It's not what we're looking for."

Wilhelm said slowly, "This land would grow great crops, but we'd never feel at home here. We have to have trees for shade in summer and for fuel in winter and to cook with. There's no timber here to build houses. Karl Schmidt said people who live on the prairie dig holes in the earth and live like gophers. We couldn't stand that." He gazed out over the waving grass. "Yah, I'll be glad when we see the last of the prairie."

But as the river journey continued more great stretches of prairie opened before them and the more they saw of its vastness, the more insignificant they felt. It was as though they had wandered into a lost world.

6.

NIGHTS ON THE RIVER STEAMER were quiet and restful after the wind died down. The monotonous grass was cloaked in darkness which comforted the travel-weary Germans.

One evening as they sat on deck watching the approach of night Lewis pointed and shouted, "What's that red in the sky?"

"Looks like a fire," Frederick replied as he shifted Anna to his other knee.

"It is a fire," Wilhelm said slowly. "There aren't any people here. What would start a fire like that when there aren't any buildings or trees?"

Gretchen mused, "Those gold-red flames against the dark blue sky are kind of pretty."

Fascinated, they lingered on deck far into the night. Ahead of the steamer a wall of flames shot into the air and heavy clouds of smoke drifted toward the east.

"It's scary," Amelia whispered to Wilhelm. "The smoke's so thick we can't see the stars."

"I wish we could ask the captain what's going on," Wilhelm said, "but Karl didn't teach us English words for this."

Mary declared, "It's the last day, the end of the world! We'll all die in this cursed land."

They were silent, pondering her words. In retrospect they recalled the German pastor's words about doomsday, the last day of the world. "The heavens will tremble, God will descend from His throne to judge the world and the burning skies will light His way to earth."

Hopefully, Ernst said, "Maybe the captain will moor the steamer before we are up to the fire."

August exclaimed, "It's a wild fire and it's spreading fast!" He pointed. "See how it grows wider and wider! It spreads faster than a man could walk!"

"Yah," Adolph commented. "We'll all roast alive like chickens in an oven when the ship runs into the flames." He shuffled away. "I need a beer."

"How do you think the fire started?" Frederick asked.

Mary cackled, "God did it to end the world."

Wilhelm ignored the remark. "Remember that little thunder storm we had about five o'clock? Maybe lightning started it."

"Naw. Wet, green grass wouldn't burn," his father argued.

"But there's dead grass on the ground from last year and hundreds of years before. *That* would burn."

"Hm-m-m. Maybe."

Mary stood up. "We know we can't pass through that burning wall and live. We all had better read our Bibles and pray." She walked away.

No one slept that night and few went to bed. Prayers were heard as the passengers prepared for Judgment Day, always with eyes on the burning skies.

Toward morning Wilhelm shouted, "We've turned! The fire is to the left of the steamer! There was a turn in the river! Yah, we're pulling away from the fire!"

In daylight the flames seemed less terrifying. During the day they grew more distant and by evening they no longer could be seen. Again, all around them the flat prairie was green and endless.

Adolph staggered up to Mary. "Well, old woman. You didn't go to meet your maker after all. Too bad!"

"Humph!" she snorted tossing her bag over her shoulder and missing Adolph's nose by an eyelash.

Like a furrow through the grass, the river continued westward. The steamer's drivewheel churned, throwing glistening drops of water into the sunlight.

Among passengers of Swedish, Finnish, Norwegian and Italian descent, the German families kept to themselves. Though the other immigrants smiled and nodded, because of the language barrier, they were unable to communicate.

Silently the Germans brooded about their homeland, the long trip and the uncertain life they faced in Minnesota. They had ridden in an ox-drawn wagon, been blown across the Atlantic by the wind, traveled on a steam train, and then across three Great Lakes by steamship. Now they were on a river ship traveling night and day through a new land that seemed endless. Their old home grew farther away with every turn of the drivewheel. The distance was incomprehensible.

Now in each mind one thought was uppermost; they never could return to their homeland; never again would they see Germany.

7.

THE DAYS PASSED SLOWLY. Now the grasslands were left behind and once again wooded country bordered the river. Still, people were short-tempered and frustrated. Inactivity, heat, insects and poor food fostered irritability. Several who were nauseous spent hours in the sick bay.

Suddenly a bell rang on the upper deck and the river steamer turned toward shore and moored deep in the forest. The German families, puzzled, watched the proceedings.

"Why are we stopping, Pa?" Lewis asked.

"I don't know. They're putting out the gangplank, but there are no buildings here."

"Maybe they're taking on wood," Wilhelm suggested.

"No, two crewmen are carrying something—a bundle—and two more men with shovels are behind them. Hm-m-m." He glanced at Amelia.

The four crewmen with the bundle disappeared into the forest. After a time they returned without the bundle.

Harriet announced, "That was a burial. Someone has died on this boat."

"We're not sure," Elizabeth said softly.

The bell rang again, the gangplank was pulled in and the steamer slowly backed away from the shore.

After this occurrence such stops were frequent. They happened quietly and were over so quickly that at first most passengers hardly noticed them. The Winters and Ketchums, however, were sure such stops were made for burials.

After several of these delays, Gretchen whispered to Amelia, "There's death on this steamer. They stop but no freight is unloaded or no firewood taken aboard and they always carry a bundle off but they don't bring it back."

"Yah. The men with shovels have time to dig a shallow grave and to have a short funeral. But what is killing people?"

"It has to be a disease that kills fast," Gretchen said.

"I'm almost afraid to say it," Harriet whispered as she waddled close to Amelia and Gretchen, "But I think it's cholera."

"No!" Both women exclaimed. Elizabeth and Mary joined Amelia and Gretchen.

Mary demanded, "What are you two whispering about?"

Amelia hesitated. "We—we think these stops are to bury people who have died of cholera."

There was a long pause. Then Mary muttered, "I knew something bad would happen. We've suffered three months to get this far and now we'll all die of cholera in this God-forsaken land!"

The women were right. Cholera was on board the river steamer. Hurriedly the corpses were removed and buried in the mid-summer heat for death was breathing down the neck of everyone on board. Cholera and fear haunted them night and day.

The Germans knew about cholera. It raged in the

heat of summer. On the steamer the July air was burning hot. It was worse than anything they had ever experienced in Germany. The melting heat dulled appetites for the ship's food which sometimes smelled bad. Fresh food would not keep and large black flies buzzed about. Soon maggots were discovered in the meat.

And the cholera—how did it spread? Was it through food or drink or on unclean dishes? Every person on board felt that death hovered nearby, for now the steamer stopped several times a day to perform a hurried burial.

After one such delay Adolph announced, "I won't eat another bite of the rotten food on this steamer! I'll drink my beer. That will keep me healthy!"

As the old man staggered away Wilhelm said, "He may be right. It could be the food. I think we'd better starve until we get to Minnesota."

Amelia nodded. "We can go many days without food, but we will have to drink the water. But—maybe that will give us cholera, too."

Wilhelm replied, "We'll leave the steamer in a few days. And we'll try to stay by ourselves as much as we can. But we will have to drink the water."

Gretchen watched the wake behind the steamer. "I'm going to drink water from the river, and I've heard that vinegar put in water makes it pure."

"Yah," Elizabeth added. "We have vinegar left from the ocean trip. We'll use that to kill the poisons and hope for the best." She glanced about at the others. "We're all healthy now."

Harriet silently shifted her ponderous weight and leaned on the railing. She hadn't felt well for several hours. Lewis clung fearfully to his mother's hand. The conversation had frightened him. "Will we die, Mama?" he whispered.

Forcing a smile his mother replied, "Of course not. We'll be all right when we get to Minnesota."

Mary cackled, "Adolph's beer might be good for something. I remember hearing that a spoonful of salt gulped down with beer would keep one from getting cholera." She laughed shrilly. "Adolph the old guzzler won't get cholera!"

Suddenly Harriet bent over the rail and retched. I'm sorry," she gasped. "I'll be all right soon." She continued vomiting and retching as the rest of the group looked on in horror.

Two crewmen appeared. One gave the ill woman a towel as they each grabbed a fleshy arm. "Come. You must go to the sick room," one man said guiding her away from the railing.

Frederick, with Anna in his arms, followed. In German he demanded to know where they were taking his wife. The crewmen shook their heads and motioned for him to remain on deck.

Lewis, screaming, clung to his mother's skirts. Frederick forcefully removed him. "She'll die!" the child screamed. "Mama will die!"

Sitting astride Wilhelm's neck, Eddie whimpered as he stared at Lewis. He was frightened by the screaming and the horrified expressions on the faces of relatives and friends.

Frederick spoke soothingly to Lewis. "Soon she'll be better."

"She'll die!" the child screamed again and again as he clung to his father's hand.

Amelia pulled Lewis to a bench beside her where she talked to him in a soothing voice until he quieted except for an occasional sob.

Lewis, a farm child, knew about death. He had seen pigs slaughtered. He had seen the squealing animals suffer as they lay helpless, their throats slashed with the life blood gushing out. Again he remembered their helpless struggling and kicking as long as they could move, until at last they were still. And all the while Grandfather Adolph had stood over the pig catching the blood in a bucket. " 'Twill make good blood sausage," he had explained to Lewis.

Elizabeth stared into the woods beside the river. "Someone should be with Harriet." When no one replied she started toward the sick bay. A moment later she returned. "They won't let me in," she said softly.

A flock of half-grown mallard ducklings lifted from among the cat-tails at the edge of the river. The green iridescent feathers of their heads changed to a beautiful greenish-blue in the sunlight. They flew in a noisy circle around the steamer, alighting a short distance behind in the sparkling blue water.

That evening the bell rang on deck and the steamer moored in a small cove. Again two men went on shore carrying shovels followed by two others with a gray-wrapped bundle. Soon they returned with only the shovels.

The passengers were silent. Another member had died. Who would be next? Lewis still whimpered at Amelia's side. Finally he gagged, his stomach heaved and vomit spewed down his shirt and onto the deck.

Gretchen and Elizabeth, their eyes wide and frightened, stood as though rooted to the deck. Frederick rushed to comfort his son, but almost immediately a crewman came to quarantine the child in the sick bay. Crying hysterically, he calmed somewhat as Frederick said, "They'll take you to Mama."

Amelia sighed. "We're so helpless. If only we knew what to do."

Mary murmured, "This is God's punishment for our

being dissatisfied with our homeland. The Swedes and Norwegians over there, and the Italians like us, they all were dissatisfied with their homeland. Now we'll all die and be thrown into a grave along side of this cursed river!"

She set her leather bag at her feet. Suddenly she picked up the bag and shuffled to Wilhelm. "If I die, you and your father are to have what is in this bag."

"Yah, Grandmother," Wilhelm replied absently.

Adolph snorted, "You won't die old woman! You're too mean to die! The devil wouldn't know what to do with you so he'll leave you here to pester us!"

During the night most of the passengers remained on deck in the open air. Filled with foreboding of events to come, they seldom spoke for each one was engrossed with the horror that faced them.

Amelia feared for the life of her unborn child; if she contracted cholera it would take the life of both her and her baby; and suppose Wilhelm died and she and Eddie remained; how could they exist in this strange land?

Frederick cuddled Anna. If Harriet and Lewis were taken, he and his little daughter would have to face life alone. He rubbed his aching forehead. They never should have left Germany.

Gretchen sighed and swallowed repeatedly. She must not vomit or they would put her in the sick room with cholera patients. She believed she was pregnant—but then it might be cholera. She prayed she and August would be spared to share their life in the new land.

Elizabeth held Ernst's hand. So far, none of her family were ill. It was almost too much to expect that all of them could be spared.

Even Adolph and Mary were silent, their minds occupied with the possible fate of their little group.

When morning came, no one left for breakfast. Eddie

and Anna whined from hunger but they were given only a cup of river water with a dash of vinegar.

Inside the sick bay two male attendants did their best to help the five cholera victims. All were immigrants and the English speaking attendants were unable to communicate with the ill people who were Harriet and Lewis, two Italian women and a Swedish man.

Harriet's body was wracked with convulsions, her arms and legs contorted and her ponderous body twisted from side to side. She moaned, and at times lay still. When the masked attendants tried to make her more comfortable, she screamed. Her face was a greenish-blue color. Time after time she repeated the cycle—convulsions, cramps, diarrhea and a period of restless sleep. She grew weaker with each cycle.

Finally Harriet's moaning died down and she became unconscious. Her raucous breathing could be heard above the moans and cries of the other ill ones.

On the bunk near his mother Lewis retched and cried intermittently. He also was convulsing, though not as violently as Harriet. An attendant lifted him to remove the diarrhea soiled sheet. The stench of vomit and fecal matter was overpowering. Beads of perspiration hung quivering from the eyebrows of the overworked men.

"It's useless," one of the attendants murmured. "The best you can wish for them is that it soon will be over."

A few hours later Harriet's body shuddered, she gasped and was silent. Almost immediately the shrouding cloth was placed about her as Lewis screamed, "Mama! Mama!"

"Hush, little one," the attendant said. "Soon now you will join your mama."

The deck bell rang, the ship moored and four husky men carried Harriet's remains to a lonely grave in the wilderness.

8.

HARRIET AND LEWIS LAY a few miles apart in graves near the river. Two deaths in one family. Who would be next?

Ernst asked, "You think bleeding them might help the sick ones? I have a bleeding iron. Getting rid of the bad blood might help."

Amelia remarked, "I lost enough blood on the *Herman Reiter* when I had scurvy. I don't have any to spare. Besides we don't know what the attendants do for the sick ones. Maybe they bleed them." There was a long period of silence.

Eduard and Anna constantly begged for food. Hungry and short-tempered they no longer would be quieted with vinegar water.

Later that day the steamer docked at a clearing to take on firewood. A few rough huts were nearby. Amelia said, "There are people here and I see a cow in the woods. Perhaps we could buy a little milk for the children."

Wilhelm nodded. "Yah. I'll try." Taking a tin pitcher from their supply pile, he descended the gangplank. Groves of evergreen and leaf trees grew on either side of the clearing. Long-haired bearded men emerged from the forest carrying axes which they leaned against tall piles of firewood.

Wilhelm shouted, *"Guten tag!"* (Good day) Ragged children and a few tired-looking women came from the huts to stare at him. The men shook their heads indicating that they did not understand.

Wilhelm tried again, holding out the pitcher. *"Bitte, milch."* (Please, milk.) He reached in his pocket and held out a few coins. *"Geld."* (Money.)

Suddenly the captain dashed down the gangplank and ran toward Wilhelm. "Cholera!" he shouted. "This ship has cholera aboard!" He pulled Wilhelm back to the gangplank while settlement men, women and children scattered as though they were pursued by the devil.

The captain shouted, "If you'll let us have firewood, my men will load it and I'll pay you on the trip back if we're free from cholera!"

A fierce-looking woodcutter yelled from a safe distance, "Take it and get out of here!"

Back on deck Wilhelm was met by Anna and Eduard. "Milk," they begged.

He shook his head and held the pitcher upside down. "No milk. Soon now, when we reach the Mississippi River, we'll get on another boat. We'll find milk there."

Tears of disappointment trembled in Amelia's eyes. The children didn't understand why they were denied food. Poor babies.

Anna climbed on her father's lap, sobbing. "I'm hungry, Papa."

Frederick rubbed his head. "Yah. Yah. Soon, maybe tomorrow we will get on another boat. Then we can eat."

The next day they saw *The Chief*. She was a beautiful ship about one hundred fifty feet in length and had been in use on the Mississippi for only a few months. Captain Weber took pride in the newly-painted side-wheeler. To the immigrants *The Chief* looked like a clean, white, narrow floating house. On each side of the prow a picture had been painted of an Indian chief with a red-feathered headdress. For centuries Indian warriors and their families had paddled canoes where *The Chief* now traveled. She was but one of a fleet of eight hundred steamboats that moved throngs of people to the northern wilderness.

Loaded with passengers, *The Chief* plowed her way upstream over sometimes smooth and sometimes choppy waters. On either side of the Mississippi a variety of trees rose from a variety of terrain, from swampland to grassy meadows or high cliffs. Cedars, willows, sycamores, alders, maples and oaks were but a few of the kinds of trees the passengers saw.

The crewmen on *The Chief* were both white and negro, and some were of tan-colored skin, the sons of white fathers and negro mothers. All were dirty and half-naked for they worked deep down in the steamer's bowels where they stoked the engines. They had a deck separate from the passengers where they gathered in the evening, sitting in groups and singing monotonous songs over and over again.

Before they left the steamer the Germans learned the half-breeds and negroes were singing about freedom for the slaves of the South. Over and over they sang and chanted, "We will be free, we will be free."

The Germans now were on the most beautiful ship of their journey to the new land. When they boarded and showed their tickets they were overjoyed to find Captain Weber spoke German.

"Yah, yah," he beamed. "My countrymen from the old land!"

Had it not been for the memory of Harriet's and Lewis' deaths, the Winters and Ketchums could have been content. They were nearing the end of their journey, they were on a clean ship with good food where cholera had not appeared, and they had found a German captain who welcomed them warmly. However within each mind there still was anxiety—suppose some of them still carried the cholera poison within them?

It now was near the end of July. The passengers sought relief from the intense heat by spending most of the time on the covered deck, some even sleeping there. Thunderstorms with fiery daggers of lightning brought only brief relief from the humid atmosphere. Travelers from the cooler climates of Norway and Sweden sat exhausted and listless as they stared at the green forests. After the first day on *The Chief*, time dragged.

Mary complained. "We'll never get there. Minnesota must be at the end of the earth!" She placed her leather bag between her feet.

Adolph snorted. "What's your hurry, old woman? Are you in a hurry to lose your scalp to an Indian?"

August saw fear in Gretchen's eyes. "Stop it, Pa," he urged. "We will treat the Indians well, and they won't hurt us."

"Time will tell," Adolph replied. He chuckled. "Mary will treat the Indians well? She never treats anyone well. Might be a good thing for the rest of us if the Indians carried her off."

Mary jumped to her feet, her face red with anger. She seized her leather bag and as she swung it wildly the heavy pouch hit Adolph in the chest knocking him backward from the bench.

Ernst grabbed Mary's arm. "Sit down, Ma!" he commanded. "We're all tired of hearing you and Adolph bicker!"

August, grinning, helped his sputtering father to his feet as the old man muttered, "The old witch. I hope the Indians get her."

Amused, the Italians, Norwegians and Swedes watched the scene. The little incident provided an opportunity to laugh, though they could not understand the exchange of words.

Every day August and Wilhelm sought Captain Weber's help with English. He gave them a written list of expressions such as: My name is ____, I want to buy ____ (tools, cows, pigs, food, etc.)

The German men asked the captain's advice about a

suitable place to settle. Without hesitation he replied, "Up the Minnesota River about one hundred miles you will find very good unclaimed land. Last spring a few German families settled there as squatters. Squatters are people who settle on the land that they have not paid for. Of course, they have no proof that they own it."

Ernst remonstrated, "I don't like the sound of that. Someday the government might claim it."

"Yah, but usually in a few years you can get a title to the land. The United States government passed a law in 1841 that anyone who lives on government land has the right to buy it before anyone else. When it is offered for sale you can buy up to 160 acres at $1.25 an acre."

"Then we wouldn't have to pay now," August said.

"No. It likely will be several years before the land is surveyed."

Wilhelm said, "We could buy more tools and animals with our money if we didn't have to pay for the land now."

"Yah."

Frederick asked, "How will we get up the Minnesota River to this German settlement?"

"There is a lumber company that owns several barges that bring lumber down to the Mississippi. Because they return empty, they would be glad to take you and any tools and animals you buy, for a small fee."

Wilhelm asked, "How does it sound?" The German men smiled and nodded.

"I like it," August replied. "How about you, Fred and Ernst?"

"Sounds good," they agreed as one voice.

"Nobody asked me," Adolph pouted.

"You're too old to work, Pa," August said. "You and Mary can pick berries and chase away wild Indians."

The old man growled, "I'd throw the old witch into

the river—or give her to the Indians."

Anna sat on her father's knee. Since Harriet's and Lewis' death she had not allowed him out of her sight. "Where can we buy supplies and food?" Frederick asked as he twisted one of Anna's blonde curls about his finger.

"You'll get off the steamer at St. Paul. We have oxen and a few cows aboard *The Chief*, as well as carts and tools you'll need. A man in St. Paul ordered them for he buys and sells supplies and animals needed by settlers."

"Things are looking brighter," Wilhelm remarked.

From the deck of *The Chief* the passengers saw a constant change of scenery. Many steamers passed. There were floating objects such as boxes, barrels and small trees that had been uprooted by recent storms.

Suddenly Gretchen shouted, "There's a body!"

She was right. Floating in the muddy water entangled in green branches, a head with a brown face and long black hair was plainly visible.

With horror in her voice Elizabeth asked, "Who is it? A settler's wife?"

"Likely an Indian woman," Ernst replied.

Later that day as *The Chief* rounded a bend in the river, on a high cliff overlooking the Mississippi a group of silent Indians watched. Only a few hundred yards away they stood as still as statues. With feathers in their hair and bows in hand they stared at the steamer as it rolled through the water, its smokestack spewing black smoke.

Captain Weber came to stand with the Germans. "They're strange people," he remarked.

"How do they feel about settlers coming here?" Wilhelm asked.

"They're not pleased," the captain replied. "They live by hunting and fishing and settlers drive away the game."

"Are—are they savage?" Amelia asked.

"I haven't heard of any serious problems where you're going, but they are silent and rather unfriendly. Just leave them alone."

Suddenly the gentle sound of the waves splashing against the sides of the steamer was broken by *The Chief's* piercing steam whistle; the sound echoed from the cliffs. The Indians shrieked with surprise and terror and disappeared behind bushes causing the passengers to laugh hilariously.

Adolph followed the captain as he walked away. "In Germany I heard stories about the Indians. Do they shoot poisoned arrows and kill people with wooden spears?"

Captain Weber spoke softly. "Yah. They're horrible people. They tie captives to poles and burn them to death, but there's no need to frighten the women. You're here and we hope things will go well with you." He walked away.

Adolph muttered to himself, "I need a beer."

The nights were dark, so black that the passengers could see neither shore. As they slept on deck they often saw campfires from Indian camps.

Adolph, through an alcoholic daze, now was convinced the natives lurked out there in the darkness waiting for settlers to be captured and burned at the stake. As he watched the fires he knew they were close and that he would die here among the heathens. He felt a great fear.

Finally on August 1, 1850, the German group arrived at St. Paul at the confluence of the Minnesota and Mississippi Rivers. The summer was so far advanced that it was too late to plant crops. They realized the seriousness of the situation. They faced a long winter with no supply of flour, meat or vegetables.

9.

IT WAS HIGH NOON when the Germans arrived in St. Paul. After their belongings were off-loaded from *The Chief* and piled beside the dock, Captain Weber introduced them to Hans Sachs, the local merchant who had come to claim his order of animals and supplies.

The August sun was unmercifully hot. The obese store owner, his clothing drenched with perspiration, welcomed his countrymen as he attempted to lead four oxen toward the barn behind the store.

"Auf Wiedersehn," (goodbye) the German group shouted as Captain Weber returned to his ship. He waved, the steam whistle shattered the noonday stillness, and the steamer continued its northward journey.

Wilhelm hurried after Hans Sachs to help with the oxen and Ernst and August pushed a four-wheel cart containing a crate of squealing shoats.

Frederick, leading Anna, sat under the nearest tree. "Might as well get out of the sun," he said to the child.

Mary grumbled as she mopped her perspiring face. "This place is hotter than Hades."

"Better get used to it," Adolph replied. "One of these days you'll be goin' there."

A few minutes later Wilhelm and August returned. Wilhelm exclaimed, "Herr Sachs has invited us to his store for lunch. Coffee, bread, milk and sausage—a good German lunch!"

"Yah," August added, "and he said we could sleep on the floor of his house tonight and that tomorrow an empty lumber barge will start up the Minnesota River!"

"It's about time our luck changed," Frederick said.

"Luck!" Mary spat out the word. "Herr Sachs is softening you up so he can rob you when you buy oxen, cows, pigs, tools and food!"

"I like the man, Grandma," Wilhelm replied. Ernst and August nodded their agreement.

"He's a fat slob! Likely drinks beer all the time!"

Adolph bristled. "I drink beer and I'm skinny as a rail!"

Wilhelm ignored the old people's jangling. "We can leave our things here by the river, Herr Sachs said. It will save time loading when the barge comes tomorrow."

"Somebody will steal us blind," Mary sputtered as she tightly grasped her leather bag.

Ernst winked at August behind his mother's back. Still grinning, he said, "Let's go get that German lunch. Sausage! We haven't had any good German sausage since we ate the last of our food from Germany on the *Herman Reiter*."

St. Paul was a small outpost village with few stores. The largest was the establishment of Hans Sachs. After a bountiful lunch the men purchased two pair of oxen, two six-month-old pigs, and two cows. They also bought plows, a few panes of glass to be used for windows in the cabins they would build and shovels and pitchforks to add to the small supply of tools they had brought from Germany.

While the men bargained with the merchant in the barn behind the store, the women made purchases inside. The clerk, who was Hans Sachs' son, made suggestions. "You'll not have a store near you," he said, "so try to think of things you'll need."

Amelia and Elizabeth had lists: sugar, flour, salt, tea, coffee, rice, beans, dried apples—the list seemed endless. The pile of staple foods grew larger and larger.

Frederick, followed by Anna and Adolph, wandered inside. He spoke to Gretchen. "Will you buy for Pa and Anna and me?" he asked. "I'll pay you."

She smiled. "Yah, Frederick."

Like a lost soul he wandered outside to stand beside the river staring downstream in the direction where Harriet and Lewis were buried.

Amelia, now in her sixth month of pregnancy, was becoming clumsy and short of breath. She dropped down on a keg of nails to rest. Eduard amused himself by wandering about the store.

Gretchen brushed aside a lock of blonde hair. "Are you buying cloth for baby clothes?" she whispered.

"Yah. After I sit a minute."

Gretchen hesitated. "I—I think I'd better get some too."

"Really?" Amelia giggled. "Are you glad?"

"Yah, and so is August."

"Are you sick in the morning?"

"No. I had a few bad times when we were on the riverboat. I didn't say anything or they would have put me in sick bay with the cholera patients. I'm fine now—healthy as a horse."

Mary came from the opposite side of the store. "What are you two whispering about?" she demanded loudly.

The women giggled. "She's in the family way, too," Amelia whispered.

Mary flipped her leather pouch over her shoulder. "Well—I feel sorry for both of you. This wilderness is no place for babies." She shuffled away as though the very thought of having children there exhausted her.

The next morning after the crew of the Minnesota Barge Company had off-loaded, the empty steam raft docked near the Sachs Store.

Finally, several hours later, the Germans, their animals and possessions were loaded. Carrying baskets of food, each of the party of eleven found a place to sit on the open barge amid boxes, barrels, bawling cattle, squealing pigs and a dog which had been purchased for

Eduard.

Wilhelm, Ernst and August enjoyed the adventure. Laughing, shouting and telling jokes, their voices rose above those of the noisy animals and the chug of the steam engine.

August shouted, "While we were in the barn yesterday Father bumped into fat Herr Sachs. He looked at tall skinny Father and said, "There must have been a famine around the Mississippi."

"Father, quick as a wink, said, "From the looks of you, you caused it."

Everyone except Frederick laughed. He sat moodily staring into the forest as he absently stroked Anna's blonde hair.

Eduard ran to take an apple from a nearby basket. "Good apple, Mama," he said as he munched.

"Yah. The apples taste so good. I'll never forget how much I wanted apples when we were on the *Herman Reiter*."

Wilhelm grinned. "Did you know that the animals in Noah's ark came in pairs?"

Adolph stared at his half-eaten apple with disgust. "Not the worms. They came in apples."

Again everyone laughed. After a time Gretchen said, "Herr and Frau Sachs were really nice to us. It seemed good to have a tub of warm water last night and to take a real bath."

"Yah," Wilhelm said. "Frau Sachs was playing with Eddie and she said, 'I'll bet he's spoiled'."

"No," I said. "He just needs a bath."

"Wilhelm," Amelia chided. "That's not very nice."

The English-speaking crew kept to themselves in the engine house. Arrangements had been made to stop the barge a few hours before night each evening so the animals could pasture and drink. The crew had been instructed by Hans Sachs that the passengers were to be let off near the homes of the four German families they had transported the previous year.

The barge was under way shortly after daybreak each morning as the steam engine pushed it up the river. Sleeping on the raft was not easy. Mosquitoes were kept away with the use of half a dozen smoking smudge pots, but howling wolves, screaming loons and shrieking owls wakened the group many times each night, and the dog, named Chief by Wilhelm, kept up a constant yammer of whines, growls and barks.

"What does he see out there in the darkness?" Amelia whispered to Wilhelm.

"Deer, 'most likely, and he hears wolves."

"Are there bears in Minnesota?"

"Yah, I guess there are."

"I won't let Eduard outside alone. A bear might carry him off." For a moment she was quiet, then she said, "Maybe Chief is barking at Indians."

"I doubt it." Wilhelm turned over. "Go to sleep."

But Amelia didn't sleep. Her mind was in turmoil about the future. They would have to build a cabin and a barn before winter; most of their money had been spent at Hans Sachs' store; her baby would be born in November; the Minnesota wilderness was not a safe place for small children; they might run out of flour and other staples during the winter. She sighed. But her greatest worry was one she tried to put from her mind. Indians.

In the morning they passed a few buildings on the shore but the barge did not stop. The Germans heard the word 'Mankato' as the crew waved to a few people on shore.

The next day they saw an Indian camp, a Santee Sioux encampment on the riverbank with braves standing before their teepees. The men, like the squaws, wore their coarse, black hair parted in the middle in braids over each shoulder. Breechcloths covered their loins and feathers decorated their hair. Scrawny dogs dashed about answering Chief's frantic barks.

The men all assumed the same position. Standing straight and tall, they cupped one hand over the other before the chest as the barge puffed past the camp.

"I wonder what they mean by that sign?" August said softly.

"Hm-m-m," Wilhelm mused. "The barge crew are making the same sign. "Maybe it means 'we're friendly' or something like that."

Behind the braves, squaws and black-eyed children stared at the people on the barge. Cooking pots steamed over campfires.

"Whatever they're cooking smells good," Elizabeth said. "It smells like beef."

Ernst sniffed. "It's likely venison. I don't think they have cattle."

A short distance upstream from the camp corn grew in a small field. In early August the rich green plants had tassels and ears were forming.

"They'll have a good crop," Adolph prophesied. "Must be rich land to grow corn like that."

"And there's been plenty of rain. Remember how dry it is in Germany in August? We should have great crops here. I can hardly wait until next year!" Wilhelm answered.

"Hold your horses, Grandson," Mary snapped. "There's many a river to cross before you harvest corn next year. Those heathen back there may have finished us off before you have a corn crop."

No one answered. Each one was busy with his own hopes or fears for the future. As they neared the end of the river journey, silent, watching Indians were often seen in the forest.

"There must be many camps around here," Wilhelm observed. "They seem friendly."

Adolph hiccuped, "We'll soon know."

That evening as the animals pastured, August and Wilhelm followed a path a short distance into the woods. The lumber company had cut most of the timber near the river. Stumps three to four feet high remained.

Wilhelm exclaimed, "It's terrible waste!"

"Yah, they're lazy. Want to cut the trees without bending over," August replied.

"The Indians are smart, though. They've planted crops around the stumps. That's easier than clearing the land."

August pointed. "There are deer tracks. We should have plenty of meat this winter."

"Yah. I expect Indians and deer have made this path."

There were sharp twists and bends around fallen tree trunks and places where the ground was so soft it sank underfoot.

"Do you suppose this path goes to an Indian camp?" August asked.

"Could be. They creep through the woods so quietly they could be watching us now."

"Yah." In a moment August said, "We'd better go back. The women will be worried."

They returned to a cold supper of bread, sausage and cheese.

"Tomorrow we'll reach the promised land," Ernst announced.

Mary laughed harshly. "Yah, it only promises more misery!"

The following day about noon the barge docked. Through the trees they saw several log buildings. Almost immediately people came running toward the river.

Wilhelm shouted in German, "We are new settlers!"

Several men whooped a welcome and summoned the rest of the adults.

For a time all was confusion. The shouts of the English-speaking crewmen unloading trunks, boxes and crates, combined with the pandemonium of German expressions of welcome and bawling cattle, squealing pigs and Chief's sharp yips at dogs on shore, all together created a cacophony of noise that was deafening.

On the north bank of the Minnesota River a short distance from where they had landed Frederick glimpsed a sudden movement in the brush where several Indian braves crouched to watch the arrival of the newcomers.

The crew members arranged the supplies in two piles, the ones ordered by the four families already settled in the wilderness, and the second pile for the newcomers. They led the animals down the gangplank as Chief and the other dogs yipped at the heels of the oxen.

The remainder of the day was spent in getting acquainted and in feasting on German food; sauerkraut, sausage, new potatoes, apple dessert and strong coffee seemed like a banquet to the newcomers.

Charles and Sarah Schling and their year-old-daughter Louise welcomed Wilhelm and Amelia warmly. Both families felt they had common interests.

John and Justina Wagner, like August and Gretchen Ketchum, had been married but a short time. Justina, a vivacious young woman of about twenty years, proudly showed Gretchen her two-room log cabin. "You'll have one like this in no time," she chattered, "and I'll help you get it ready for winter."

Otto and Phidelia Hess, the newcomers found, were an interesting couple. Otto, about age forty, was a doctor and a farmer. Phidelia in her mid-twenties, had eagerly accepted Otto's proposal of marriage before they came to America because she loved adventure and had despaired of escaping the hum-drum existence of a housewife in Germany.

Herman and Magdelene Moltke were a middle-aged couple with Amos, a twenty-one-year-old son. Herman, a Lutheran minister, and Otto Hess, the doctor, had been friends when they were children in Germany. Herman came to the area ten years before. Like Otto, Herman's profession in Minnesota did not require many hours of work, so he, also farmed.

It was a day to be remembered. Even Mary and Adolph called a truce and entered into the celebration with anticipation for the future. Eduard and Louise played on the floor with six tin plates which Sarah had ordered from St. Paul.

The adults talked and circulated between the four farms which were located, two on each side of a narrow trail, about one-fourth mile apart.

"How many acres do you have?" Wilhelm asked Charles Schling.

"About eight. But part of the land is taken up by stumps. It's slow work plowing and working around these stumps. I've taken out some of them." He paused. "Corn looks good and we had a fine wheat crop."

"Guess you're all set," Wilhelm remarked.

Charles nodded. "Herman Moltke's son, Amos, says we would do better if we moved west to the prairies where there are no trees."

"Yah. But our people wouldn't like that. We Germans like trees." Wilhelm peered inside Charles' barn. "How many cows do you have?"

"Two, and two calves. Next year Sarah will make butter to sell. The men on the lumber barge will sell it for us in Mankato or St. Paul. Mankato isn't much of a place yet, but it will grow."

Wilhelm scratched his head. "I had to pay one hundred American dollars for a yoke of oxen, and thirty dollars for a cow. My money is going fast. Everything is sky-high here."

"Yah. Hens are expensive, too. Laying hens cost five dollars apiece, and the foxes or wolves kill many of them."

Wilhelm went on. "We thought we had plenty of money when we left Germany. Now I don't have much left, and it's a year until I'll have crops to sell."

The men leaned against a manger in the little log barn. Charles ran his fingers through his beard. "It helps that we don't have to pay for the land now. Each settler can claim one hundred sixty acres after it is surveyed."

Wilhelm shook his head. "I don't understand how we can build on land we don't own."

"We're squatters. We live on government land that has not been surveyed or sold. After it is surveyed, it will be put up at auction, and because we were here first, we will be given the first chance to buy it."

"How long before it will be surveyed?"

"Might be several years before we have to pay for the land."

Wilhelm nodded. "Is the weather usually like this in summer? Is there plenty of rain for the crops?"

Charles shook his head. "I may as well tell you what I've been told. 'Course I've only been here one year, but Herman and Amos Moltke—they can talk to the Indians —they say that there are years when crops are a failure."

"Why?"

"Drought, forest fires, or grasshoppers."

"Grasshoppers?"

"Yah. Hear 'em singing out there? They never stop, day or night."

"They eat the crops?"

"Yah. The Indians say about every fifth year they come in swarms that blot out the sun. They eat every green thing and leave only bare ground behind. They say they'll even eat clothes when they're left outside."

Wilhelm shook his head. "Like the plague of locusts in the Bible."

"Yah. But we can stand a bad year now and then if we have more good ones. The first year you're here is the hardest."

They strolled outside. Wilhelm looked toward the west. "Will you go with me to help me pick out land?"

"Sure. Your pa and August and Frederick will want land, too. We could all go together."

"Yah. How far does this trail go?"

"It runs along the river for many miles. It's an old Indian trail."

"They give you much trouble?"

Charles scratched his head. "They stay over there most of the time." He pointed toward the west. "Sometimes, though, they hunt near here, and they've come to our cabin to beg for bread a few times." He hesitated. "Herman and Amos say that the Indians don't like it that we've settled here."

"When we were on the barge the Indians on shore and the crew men made a sign to one another. They cupped one hand over the other. Do you know what it means?"

"Yah. It's the Indian peace sign."

Wilhelm nodded. "How did the Moltkes learn to speak the Indian language?"

"They're educated people. Herman and Magdelene came to Fort Snelling as missionaries. Amos was about ten years old. He went with his father to visit Indian camps. Before long they both could speak the language of the Sioux. Mrs. Moltke has learned the language, too. In fact, they also speak English."

"H-m-m-m. Three languages—German, Sioux and English."

As they started back to the cabin Charles said, "Tomorrow we'll choose your land."

10.

AFTER BREAKFAST the settlement men went with the Winters and Ketchum men to select their farmland. Grasshoppers and locusts buzzed on every side. Deer and rabbits bounded away at their approach. Ducks quacked on a nearby pond. Squirrels scampered up trees and a flock of wild geese honked above them. Amos pointed out a raccoon in a tree, an animal unknown to the newcomers.

In high spirits they walked along the trail. The path was winding for it followed the course of the Minnesota River. High stumps left by the lumber company marred the beauty of the wilderness.

Leaving the path, the men wandered through lush forests of tall straight trees—oaks, birches, aspens, elms, maples and ash. They also recognized willows rising above blackberry and hazelnut thickets.

"After the first frost I'll gather hazelnuts," Wilhelm commented. "Amelia can use them in baking."

August observed, "Everything we need is here in the forest; trees for all our needs; for cabin timbers, floor planks and roof, for tables, benches and for firewood."

Adolph said, "There's plenty of dead trees, too. The

wood is dry and will make a hot fire to warm my old bones."

John Wagner said, "When you see the land you want, we will mark it with stakes."

After a time Wilhelm exclaimed, "Right here is where I want to live! Oaks to make my buildings, maples to give us sugar and wild crab apple and plum trees. Look at those branches, they're bending down with fruit! And there are thickets of berry and currant bushes. Amelia can pick raspberries, currants and blueberries next summer. And down there by the river where the trees are cleared there is waist-high grass that I can cut for fodder! Yah. This is the land I want!"

"It is good land," Charles agreed, "but it is quite far from the settlement."

"But it has everything I want!"

"Then it's yours!" With his axe Otto Hess chopped two stakes and drove them into the ground beside the path about one-fourth of a mile apart. On each stake he tied a white rag. He also cut marks in trees near each stake. "Your land starts at the river between the stakes and goes back for 160 acres," Otto explained.

Wilhelm's eyes shone. "It's beautiful land—not like that worn-out soil in Germany. I'll clear it as fast as I can. And next year I'll have wheat where the trees are cut—and—and I want the cabin and barn close to the river so there'll always be water. I'm moving here as soon as I can."

His enthusiasm was catching. However, Ernst, August and Frederick chose land closer to the settlement. By afternoon the group returned with glowing reports of the land they had chosen.

11.

AMELIA AND MARY washed the breakfast dishes at the Schling cabin while Sarah bustled about making the bed and folding blankets that had been used by overnight guests who had slept on the floor.

"It seemed good to sleep on dry land last night," Amelia remarked. "I never want to be on another ship."

"Yah," Mary said, "But with that grandson of mine for a husband, you can never be sure what he'll want to do next." She banged a frying pan down on the hearth for emphasis.

"This will be our home," Amelia declared. She lowered her voice so Eduard wouldn't hear, "Only with small children, I'm worried about wild animals and—and Indians."

Sarah glanced at Louise and Eddie. "I know. Charles says I'm a killjoy because those things bother me, too, but in a year we haven't had serious problems, though bears have carried off some small pigs."

"Do you think the men will be gone all day?" Amelia asked.

"They'll likely be back by afternoon," Sarah said confidently. But at the back of her mind a nagging foreboding of trouble alarmed her. This was the first time since they had been here that there wasn't a man in the settlement. She had whispered her concern to Charles before he left, but he had smiled and made light of her anxiety. But the Indians were always watching. They likely knew all the men were gone.

"I'll make a big pot of venison stew," she announced, "with lots of vegetables." Taking a basket from the corner she said, "I'm going to the garden to get potatoes, carrots and onions."

"I'll help you." Amelia clumsily stepped over the

threshold and followed Sarah. Mary was left with the two children.

While Sarah dug a few hills of potatoes, Amelia picked them up. Next they pulled and topped carrots and onions.

"How did you get along last winter without fresh vegetables?" Amelia asked.

"We ate a lot of wild game and bread. But we did miss potatoes, cabbage and other fresh things." She paused. "Our gardens are good this year. We'll share with you."

Amelia's eyes filled with tears. "Thanks. You're so good to us."

As they walked back toward the cabin Sarah asked, "Where was your home in Germany?"

"Between Bremen and Hamburg. Where did you live?"

"Near Ulm on the Danube River. I get homesick sometimes, but I know we can never go back. I'm trying to learn to speak English. Magdelene and Amos Moltke often hold a class. They're teaching us. Herman and Magdelene are missionaries to the Indians, but so far they haven't converted many around here." She said softly, "Amelia, the Indians don't like us."

"Do they come to the settlement?"

"Sometimes they stop to beg for bread. They haven't harmed anyone—yet."

Amelia shivered. She quickened her pace, slapping at mosquitoes as she went. The women walked silently the rest of the way to the cabin.

An hour later Sarah stirred her pot of stew. The room was sweltering hot from the August heat and the fireplace fire. Amelia bent across her ponderous stomach to scrub the family's clothes in a tub of steaming water, while in the bedroom, Grandmother Mary entertained the children with old German nursery rhymes.

Suddenly something blocked out the light from the window. Brushing back a sweaty lock of hair, Amelia glanced up. Her heart leaped, then almost stopped as she stared into the faces of two Indians with beady black eyes set deep under low foreheads. Unable to make a sound, she backed against the wall, her whole body trembling.

Sarah, unaware of the visitors, replaced the kettle cover and threw more wood on the fire. Amelia watched in horror as two tall Indians dressed in brown-red deer-skin clothing with deerskin moccasins on their feet silently stepped over the threshold.

Their faces were beardless but on their cheekbones were blood-like streaks of red paint; coarse black hair hung in tufts from their head, shining as if it was greased. From the backs of their necks red animal tails dangled. They looked shaggy and hardly human. And they had sneaked into the cabin as silently as wild beasts.

Petrified with fear, Amelia could not take her eyes off the cruel and treacherous-looking red-streaked faces. Long knives hung at the men's sides. They might stick these knives into all of them! She gasped.

Sarah turned and silently crumpled to the floor in a faint. In the bedroom Mary's voice droned on as the children squealed with delight at the nursery rhyme nonsense.

The Indians looked around the cabin, stepping over Sarah to look in the simmering kettle, and to raise the cover of a trunk containing the Winters family's clothing. The younger Indian picked up a long butcher knife from the table and ran a finger lightly along the blade.

"No!" Amelia croaked. "No! No!"

Mary, her old eyes flashing fire, dashed from the

bedroom towards the Indians. "Get out! Get out!" she screamed.

Still holding the knife, the young Indian stared at the angry old woman as the older man picked up Mary's leather bag and started toward the door.

Charging at him, she seized Wilhelm's rifle which stood in the corner. She pointed the gun at his head. "Drop that bag!" she hissed.

Thwarted, the man tossed the bag on the floor and slowly started toward the door followed by the younger brave who still held the butcher knife. Mary poked him in the chest with the barrel of the rifle.

"Drop it! Drop it, you thief!" she yelled.

Angrily he threw the knife across the room and strode outside to follow the older man toward the river.

The children clung to Amelia screaming in terror. "We're all right," she soothed them. "Grandma saved us. We're fine now." Her heart pounded, and in spite of the heat in the cabin, her trembling body felt as though it had been drenched with ice water.

Mary knelt beside Sarah. "Bring me some cold water," she ordered.

The water revived Sarah almost at once. "Where are they?" she gasped.

"Gone," Mary said. "I should have shot the red devils."

Suddenly Amelia dropped into a chair and laughed hysterically until tears ran down her face. Gasping, she exclaimed, "The gun wasn't loaded! Wilhelm never leaves it loaded in the house!"

Mary cackled raucously, her wrinkled face contorted with a wide grin. After she caught her breath she declared, "Them red devils might's well learn they'd better not fool with this old woman. Next time the gun will be loaded!"

12.

FOR FOUR DAYS Wilhelm, Adolph and Ernst worked to build a shanty at the location Wilhelm had chosen. Finally they stood back and appraised their work.

"It's not much of a shelter," Wilhelm said, "but Charles says we have two months before winter. By that time I'll have a cabin built, and then we'll use the shanty for a barn."

Adolph chuckled. "Wait 'til Mary sees this. She'll have plenty to grumble about. Can't you hear her? 'This is a house? This—this hut that's no more than nine feet square? And the roof— 'tisn't even wood! Bark and sod! 'Twill leak like a sieve! And no floor—only hay on the ground. What a hovel. It's not even fit for a pig sty!' "

Ernst and Wilhelm grinned. "Yah," Wilhelm admitted. "I hope Amelia won't mind that she'll have to cook over an outside campfire until I get the cabin finished. It's a shelter for only a short time, then the animals can have it this winter."

The following day Wilhelm moved the family's possessions to their new home. Several trips were required. Besides their things from Germany, there was the supply of foodstuffs which had been bought in St. Paul: One barrel of rye flour for bread, a few pounds of sugar, a sack of salt and other household necessities. Also included were boards for the door of the cabin, glass for two windows and the tools he had purchased in St. Paul.

Wilhelm was pleased with his yoke of oxen. Their powerful bodies gave promise of energy to pull heavy loads. Slow and good-natured, they contentedly chewed their cuds, refusing to quicken their pace in spite of Wilhelm's urging.

Finally when everything had been moved to the new

site, Wilhelm returned to the settlement for Amelia, Eduard and Mary.

The trail was rough and the springless wagon jolted with teeth-jarring bumps. The wheels of the oxcart were made of four rounds sawed from a large oak log. The axles fitted into the holes in the rounds with wooden pegs on their ends. The back wheels were slightly larger than the front ones. The dry wooden axles groaned as the solid wheels turned and they squeaked from the friction of wood against wood.

Eduard squealed with delight as they pitched and jolted over hollows and bumps in the trail. Amelia and Mary were silent, but their stoical facial expressions revealed their feelings.

Wilhelm joked. "Don't stand stiff-legged. Bend your knees and let them act like springs!"

Mary exploded. "If you don't get Amelia out of this contraption you'll be to blame if she loses her baby!"

Wilhelm stopped the oxen. "Are you all right?" He studied his wife's drawn face.

"More! More!" Eduard giggled. "Let's ride more!"

Amelia held her hands tightly against her abdomen. "I can't stand any more of that jouncing wagon. I'll walk." Wilhelm helped her down to the grass-covered trail.

Mary's mouth was set in a tight line. "I'll walk, too."

Chief barked and jumped at the oxen's noses. They shook their heads and threatened the dog with curved horns. The wagon groaned and squeaked and Eduard squealed with joy as the procession started. Finally they reached their new home.

"We're here!" Wilhelm shouted. The oxen chewed their cuds and stood patiently switching flies from their flanks with long bushy tails. Occasionally they turned their heads to see what the humans were doing behind them.

"Where's the house?" Amelia asked. She pointed. "Is it far from the barn?"

Wilhelm stammered. "Er—er—that's the house for now."

There was dead silence. Even Chief was quiet as though he sensed the women's feelings.

"More ride! More ride!" Eduard squealed as he ran back and forth in the wagon.

Mary stooped to go inside the dark little hut. Under her breath she muttered, "No floor, no fireplace, no decent roof. It will leak like a sieve. It's not fit for a pig sty."

Sick at heart, Amelia silently inspected the hut. The child she carried kicked violently. Only eleven or twelve weeks before its birth. She hoped the jouncing, jolting wagon wouldn't cause a miscarriage. Their trunks and winter food supply were piled in one corner of the little shelter.

"Where will I cook?" Her voice was so low that Wilhelm could hardly hear her.

He took her arm. They stooped and went outside. "I've made a little cooking place out here. It's close to the door. It's makeshift, but we couldn't have one inside because we couldn't get rid of the smoke. It will be warm for a few more weeks and by the time it's cold, I'll have a log house built for you with a big fireplace in one end."

"We'll sleep on the ground?" she whispered.

"Yah, until our house is built."

"It's hard for Grandmother and for me—to get up off the floor."

"I'll help you. You weren't this big before Eduard was born."

"I know. And it's still more than two months. Maybe I'll have twins," she whispered.

13.

THE MONTH OF AUGUST passed slowly for Amelia. Cooking at the outdoor campfire was difficult, for she must reckon with rain and wind. Many meals consisted mainly of cold venison, bannock and milk with wild plums or crab apples for dessert. When the weather was good she made a form of rye skillet bread, or bannocks, and stored it in a box in the shanty to keep it away from field mice which were everywhere. She also cooked up hearty venison soup.

Amelia longed for her comfortable cottage in Germany. It seemed to her that there she'd had everything a woman could want. In the Minnesota wilderness she had nothing, not even a chair to sit in. She struggled clumsily to her feet from her seat on a block of wood to add more fuel to the cooking fire.

She was resentful. She knew full well that Wilhelm had chosen the land farthest from the settlement. He said it was better soil, but she doubted it. He had to be different, able to conquer a more difficult situation than the others. His father and August already had their cabins built because the close neighbors had helped one another. Wilhelm said several men would come to help erect their cabin when he had the logs cut. She could hear him chopping a short distance away.

Amelia continually scanned the brush along the riverbank. She had seen Indians nearly every day, but none had approached the shanty.

Mary and Eddie emerged from a nearby thicket flushing the sow from her meal of acorns beneath the oaks. The cowbell tinkled softly as their cow pastured near the river.

Eddie ran to his mother. "Snake!" he squealed. "We see snake! Big snake!" he spread his arms wide.

"Yah," Mary sighed.

Eddie went on. "He opened his mouth like this!" The boy demonstrated, "and he shook his tail at us. It made a noise."

"Yah. Another thing to watch for. Rattlesnakes." Mary dropped down on a log.

Amelia bit her lip. Finally she said, "Grandmother, there isn't any need for you to stay with us. You'd be more comfortable at Father Ernst's and Mother Elizabeth's. This is no way for you to live—rattlesnakes." She shuddered. "They could be in the shanty in our beds. At least, at Father Ernst's you'd live in a house!"

Mary snapped, "I'm here because I want to be! Don't you want me?"

"Of course. I don't know what I'd do without you. But—but—at your age, life should be easier."

"*My* age? I can do anything you can, except have babies!" She got up and shuffled into the shanty.

Amelia's eyes appraised the little hut. Her family were squatters—she hated the word. They were living on land they hadn't paid for in a miserable little shanty. She could hear Eddie laughing as he played in the hay inside the hut. At least, he was happy. And Wilhelm was happy. He had great hopes for the future. She was grateful that he was satisfied, but deep down she was grateful too—she was grateful that no one at home, neither her parents nor relatives nor friends need ever see this shanty they lived in.

For days Wilhelm worked felling oaks for cabin timbers. He chose only the straightest trees, stripping them of bark so they would dry more quickly. For roof and floor boards he rough-hewed young lindens. He dug sod for the roof and gathered birch and pine bark to hold the sod in place. With his oxen he transported the building materials to the spot they had chosen for the cabin.

While Wilhelm worked, Mary watched Eddie and helped with the cooking. Amelia unpacked their clothes from the big trunk. They smelled musty. She carried armloads to the riverbank where she washed them in a soft-soap mixture made from boiled deer and rabbit fat and ashes.

Bending over her huge abdomen to scrub the clothes was exhausting. Finally Amelia hiked up her skirts and waded into the water to a large rock against which she scrubbed the soap-laden clothing. When the rinsing and wringing was completed, she spread the garments on bushes to dry.

After each washing session in the river Amelia found she must perform a disgusting act. The warm water was alive with bloodsuckers which burrowed through her skin in search of blood. Shuddering, she grasped the dozen or more slimy, inch-long black worms and pulled them from her legs and feet.

At last Wilhelm announced he was ready to go to the settlement to ask for help in erecting the cabin. When Amelia objected to his being gone, leaving them with no protection, Wilhelm laughed. "My rifle is in the shanty. Grandma will run off any Indian that bothers you, won't you Grandma?"

The old woman cackled, "The red devils better keep their distance or I'll fix them so they won't bother anyone else!"

Wilhelm chuckled. "Better hide your leather bag or they might get it next time."

"Yah. It's under the hay in the shanty. They won't find it. Now get going, Grandson. Amelia's nervous and it's bad for her."

Wilhelm nodded. "If the weather's good probably we'll have a gang here tomorrow to help put up the cabin. They'll come early and women will bring food.

There's plenty of venison from the buck I dressed last night."

"Have you found more plum and crab apple trees nearby?" Amelia asked.

"I've gone up the river half a mile or so. There are some up there—in fact there are several. It almost looks like an orchard."

Amelia brushed a fly away from her face. "We'll need a lot of food to feed all those people."

"Go along, Grandson," Mary said. "We'll get some fruit and we'll have everything done by night."

Amelia studied the forest. "Did you see Indians up there?"

Wilhelm laughed. "No, but Grandma can take the rifle. Then no Indian would dare ruffle your feathers. I'm sure they have all heard about you, Grandma."

"There must be a camp nearby," Amelia worried, "because we see them on the trail or in canoes on the river 'most every day." She sighed. "Well, they haven't hurt us—yet."

That afternoon the two women with Eddie and Chief tagging behind them walked along the trail. There was a hint of fall in the air and an occasional maple showed traces of red. Ducks rose splashing from the river as Chief barked furiously at their ascent. Eddie squealed with glee. Mary's leather bag swung from one shoulder and she carried the rifle over the other. Baskets hung from Amelia's arms. As she walked her eyes constantly searched the bushes for Indians.

"That tall grass will make good fodder for the animals." Mary motioned toward a clearing.

Amelia sighed. "There's so much to do before winter. The cabin and furniture to be built, hay to be cut and stacked—that's Wilhelm's work. I have to dry apples, fish and venison, gather nuts and sew for the baby."

Mary shifted the rifle to her other shoulder. "I'll watch Eddie and help all I can."

Amelia pointed. "There are apple and plum trees. They look like a fruit orchard. Do you suppose the Indians planted them?"

"Maybe—and maybe not." Mary leaned the rifle against a plum tree and tossed her bag on the ground beside it. "We'll soon have our baskets filled."

Eddie munched on juicy plums as the women gathered fruit. Suddenly Chief barked and the boy shouted, "Man! I see man!"

Mary seized the rifle. "Where? Where?"

"There!" the boy pointed to a spot where the underbrush was thick.

Amelia's heart pounded as tales of scalping raced through her mind. She stood frozen to the spot. Mary stumbled over the rough ground in the direction where Chief barked and Eddie had pointed. The dog's ferocious barks ended with angry growls followed by yips and howls of pain.

"The devils!" Mary muttered. "They've hurt the dog!"

"Come back, Grandma!" Amelia shouted. "They've gone!" Eddie, screaming, clung to her skirts.

Chief came slinking back, his tail between his legs. Like Eddie, he hid behind Amelia.

Mary stopped to stare at something high in an apple tree. She pointed the rifle. "Come down out of there!" she yelled. Amelia and Eddie peeped from behind the trunk of a large tree.

The wind sighed softly through the forest. There was no other sound. It was as though humans, animals and insects were waiting for an answer.

After a time Mary moved closer. Shading her eyes, she shrieked, "I see you! Come down or I'll shoot!" Still there was no reply or movement from the figure in the tree.

"Hm-m-m," Mary breathed, lowering the rifle. Puzzled, she walked closer. "Come here, Amelia," she called.

Together the women stared at a prone figure in the tree.

"He can't be asleep," Amelia whispered. "I think he's dead."

A full grown Indian, tightly wrapped in a bright blanket with only his face visible, lay on a wooden platform about ten feet from the ground.

"Hm-m-m," Mary muttered again. "They're strange critters. You suppose he died up there and they just left him? Don't the heathens bury their dead?"

Amelia glanced around nervously. "Let's get out of here. There was a live one out there a few minutes ago."

With backward glances over their shoulders the little group gathered their possessions and slowly made their way back to the hut as the women silently pondered the strange customs of their neighbors, the Santee Sioux.

14.

BY NINE O'CLOCK THE FOLLOWING DAY people from the settlement arrived at the Winters' place in squeaking oxcarts. Wilhelm's parents, the Ketchums, the Moltkes, the Hesses and Schlings, thirteen people in all, descended from the crude vehicles. The seven men who had brought their tools immediately set to work under the direction of Herman Moltke.

Amelia and Wilhelm had chosen the site for their home among some large sugar maples a few hundred feet from the river. Their house would face the water and it would be twenty feet long and fourteen feet wide. The back of the cabin was toward the forest. The narrow trail ran between the river and the house.

Herman Moltke assigned Charles Schling and Amos the job of peeling bark from the heavy foundation logs for the footing. When they were ready the oxen dragged the logs to the building site. Work progressed rapidly under the direction of Herman and soon the eight men had the walls three feet high. There was much laughter and joking as the work progressed.

A short distance away the six women chattered as they unpacked the food they had brought and placed near the campfire. There were loaves of bread, cold venison, pots of sauerkraut and sausage and rabbit stew. There was sauce made from plums, wild cranberries and apples.

Eddie and Louise Schling played with Chief under Mary's watchful eye. The women sat about on logs and blocks of wood watching the progress of the builders.

"Are you going to have a dirt floor?" Sarah asked Amelia.

"Wilhelm said they would split small logs and lay them with the flat side up. He can hew and smooth them this winter. She sighed. "Everything made of iron is so expensive. Wilhelm paid a dollar for hinges for the door. He didn't buy many nails for he said they will use wooden pegs to take the place of nails.

"Yah, and you'll need a good fireplace. Minnesota winters are very cold, and with a new baby you'll have to have good heat," Magdelene Moltke remarked.

Phidelia Hess, an attractive dark young woman, watched the men at work. "Do the wolves bother you?" she asked.

Amelia shook her head. "We hear them howling at

night, but they haven't been near the hut."

"Wait until winter when they get hungry! They can be vicious then!"

"Don't frighten Amelia," Magdelene objected. "Wolves carry off chickens, but they've never given us much trouble at the settlement."

Phidelia continued. "I don't like them. I've heard stories about how they attack when they're hungry."

Elizabeth Winters asked, "Have you seen any bears out here?"

Amelia shook her head and replied drily, "I only watch for Indians, and Grandmother Mary will run them off." The women laughed.

"They'd better keep their distance," Mary cackled.

Phidelia went on. "You know your land is next to a large camp, don't you?"

"No!" Amelia's heart pounded. No wonder she saw them lurking around most every day.

"I wouldn't want to live out here with them right next door."

"Phidelia," Magdelene sputtered. "Herman and Amos and I have worked with the Indians for many years. They have never harmed us. You don't understand their ways." She turned to Amelia. "Don't be afraid, dear."

Sarah stood up. "They frighten me, too. They act so —so unfriendly. They never smile."

Phidelia smirked. "Maybe I should try to get acquainted with them. Some of the young braves are quite handsome."

Magdelene shook her finger at Phidelia. "You'd better not let Otto hear you say that, young woman!"

"Otto! All he's interested in are his medical books and his farm. I thought that when we came to America interesting things would happen. We've been here a year and I'm sick of Minnesota. I wish I'd stayed in Germany!"

Mary sputtered. "You're not the only one."

Amelia threw more wood on the fire. "How far away is the Indian camp?"

Magdelene smoothed the apron over her broad thighs. "Don't let Phidelia worry you. There are many camps along the river. You saw them when you came on the lumber barge."

"But how far is the first one?"

"Less than a mile. They have a fruit orchard not far from here."

Amelia's and Mary's eyes met. "I'm—I'm afraid we took some of their fruit yesterday," Amelia stammered.

Mary grumbled. "How could we know it belonged to them? And there was a dead Indian in the tree—maybe he was supposed to scare us away. The heathen! That's no way to leave a dead person! Why don't they bury him?"

Everyone looked at Magdelene for an answer. She began. "The Sioux want to keep the remains of their loved ones near them. They place their dead on scaffolds where the corpse finally dries out. When nothing but bones is left, they are carefully gathered and placed in rock crevices where the dead person once lived."

"It's weird," Elizabeth declared.

"They want to keep their dead near them. It's like continuing to have the company of the departed," Magdelene said. "Some tribes place the scaffolds of their dead near the edge of the camp, while others place them in the forest. Perhaps the dead Indian in the orchard especially loved that spot."

"How high are the scaffolds?" Gretchen asked.

"Ten or twelve feet from the ground. They're rough platforms built of sticks that are held up by four poles driven into the ground. If the person is a man who had a favorite horse, some tribes kill the horse and tie the head and tail to his scaffold."

Gretchen shuddered. Magdelene patted her shoulder. "Their ways seem strange to us, but our ways are just as strange to them. We have to try to understand one another."

"Have you and Herman had much success in converting the Indians to the Lutheran religion?" Elizabeth asked.

The broad, plump face clouded. "A few of them welcome us, but most of them don't. Several miles up the river a chief, Little Crow, allows us to talk to his people. Right now, he's the most friendly of any of the chiefs."

The men continued working with many trips to Adolph's barrel of beer. As the day passed, the walls grew higher and the men's voices became louder. By mid-afternoon they were placing linden poles across the top of the building for roof boards. Cut sod was tightly packed on the poles.

Herman said, "Sod doesn't make as good a roof as split shakes, but it should get you through the winter."

"Yah," Wilhelm agreed. "Next year I'll put on shakes. In a year or two I'd like to build a better house."

By late afternoon the cabin was completed except for the fireplace. About four o'clock the group departed for the settlement as Wilhelm and Amelia shouted their thanks.

By the end of the next week the fireplace was completed, two rough beds with hay mattresses were built in the corners and a wobbly table made from split logs set beneath a window with blocks to serve as chairs. When the winter food supply and the clothing trunks were brought in from the hut, there was little living space left in the cabin.

Amelia was pleased with the big fireplace. It drew nicely and it seemed like a luxury after cooking on the temperamental campfire. Clumsy and awkward, she tired quickly, and it seemed she never would finish all that was to be done before the birth of the baby. She and Mary chinked the cracks between logs in the cabin with sod and mud; they dried apples, plums and cranberries in the warm September sun; they smoked fish and venison over the old outside cooking place, and on rainy days, they sewed for the new baby.

"We're lucky there's plenty of wild game and fish," Wilhelm remarked as he brought a string of whitefish to be cleaned and dried.

Amelia said, "If there's plenty, why are we smoking and drying so much meat?"

"Herman and Charles say that in bad weather they sometimes can't find game. Then, we'd go hungry if we didn't have this."

The days sped by, the weeks flew and only a month remained before they could expect winter weather. Mary's sharp tongue often lashed out at Wilhelm, but with Amelia and Eddie, she was gentle. Every day the young mother thanked the old woman for her support.

It seemed to Amelia that this pregnancy was longer than her first one. Perhaps it was because of the hard journey from Germany while she carried the child within her. And she was so big that she wondered if she would have twins. She hoped it was only one, for twins would be inconvenient.

Every day she felt heavier. When she stood, she no longer could see her feet over her ponderous abdomen. She now could walk only a short distance so that she stayed near the cabin with Eddie. They watched dozens of fat, gray-brown gophers playing around the buildings as the animals' heads popped up from the grass while they observed the humans. There were furry flying squirrels sailing about in the trees, their long tails waving; some were so tame they ate from Eddie's hand. In the warm autumn sun the crickets sang their last summer songs.

Rats and mice were a constant nuisance. Their holes seemed to be everywhere, for they would appear in the grass and suddenly disappear down a hole. It was an unending battle to keep them out of the cabin and away from the food.

Wilhelm spent several days cutting and stacking wild grass which would provide winter feed for the cattle. The haystack grew until it was taller than the shanty which now was used as a barn.

Amelia was lonely. As she watched Eddie at play she dreamed of her relatives and friends in Germany. Though the settlement was not far away, she had seen the women only once since their arrival. Because of her condition, she could not risk riding in the bouncing oxcart to visit them, and besides, there was work to be done before winter. When the wind blew from the west they could smell smoke from the Indian campfire. The Sioux were their only neighbors.

Amelia tried to put from her mind rumors she had heard from the women at the settlement. Though she had lived there only a few days she recalled that Sarah Schling feared the Sioux so much that she had fainted when they appeared at her cabin. Phidelia Hess had said they were a treacherous and unreliable people always watching their chance to scalp and kill whites—but on the other hand, on the day when they'd built the cabin, Phidelia had joked about the handsomeness of the young Indian men. Amelia had her suspicions about Phidelia; she had seen the way she looked at Wilhelm and August. Of course, Dr. Hess was much older than Phidelia, but he seemed a nice person.

Amelia recalled varying reports she had heard about

the Indians. Magdelene Moltke and her husband and son had worked with the Sioux for many years. She said they were kind and that when settlers were in need, they gave them food. She declared they were as innocent as children. But the Moltkes could speak the Indian language and the Sioux accepted them.

Amelia's scalp crawled at the recollection of some of Phidelia's stories. She said the Sioux were bloodthirsty and cruel and that they blinded prisoners with spears before burning them alive. If they were "innocent as children" how could they torture and murder settlers' wives and children? She didn't know what to believe. Though they saw them on the trail nearly every day, the Indians had not molested them. Wilhelm said they were harmless.

Still, from time to time, they had heard ear-splitting yells from the Indian camp. These were human sounds, not wild animal calls. At night, lying beside Wilhelm, Amelia had been terrified. At such times she had inclined to believe Phidelia's stories. Restless and uncomfortable from the activeness of her unborn baby she thought that after the dangers they had escaped on their journey to the new land, she could hardly imagine anything worse. Yet, she could vividly visualize a scalping or a prisoner being burned at the stake. The wild neighbors filled her with insecurity.

Then, one Indian summer day in October, some of the squaws approached the cabin. Mary had taken the rifle when she went to collect hazelnuts and Wilhelm was nowhere in sight. Amelia, her heart pounding, was thankful there were no men in the group. They stood in the yard staring at Eddie, who silently stared back at the strange people. One of the women who carried a baby on her back reached out toward Eddie.

Amelia screamed. "No, Eddie! Come here!" Looking

over his shoulder he ran to her.

The women turned and went inside the empty shanty. In a minute they returned and slowly walked toward the cabin. Several of them carried small children in pouches. All of them looked undernourished and scrawny. A wizened old woman with a wrinkled, haggard face that looked like cracked red clay hobbled toward the cabin. The others followed.

When they were at the door, Amelia stepped back. Her heart pounded. What were they going to do?

Talking among themselves they pushed past her and went into the cabin. Clinging to Eddie's hand, Amelia backed against the wall. What should she do? In her condition, she couldn't run. She must stand her ground as though she was unafraid.

The women, still conversing in low guttural sounds, explored the cabin. They looked into the flour barrel, in the makeshift cupboards and even in the kettle of rabbit stew that simmered over the fire. One of them opened the box where Amelia kept loaves of rye bread. She called to the others.

Bread! They wanted bread! There were three loaves in the breadbox. She would divide them among the nine women.

Clumsily making her way to the table Amelia cut the loaves into thirds, giving each woman a piece which they accepted silently. Taking a last look around the cabin, the group filed out led by the decrepit old matriarch, and slowly made their way up the trail toward camp.

Amelia, her legs weak from fright, dropped on the bed. They hadn't hurt her or Eddie. Perhaps they were just curious about their new neighbors. She felt sorry for them. They looked underfed and wretched. Maybe the Indian men beat them. Wilhelm had seen their camp. He said they lived in hovels of bark and matting hung over a few poles. How could they survive winters in such flimsy shacks?

That evening as they sat around the supper table, the family talked. Wilhelm said, "I think they're harmless, but we can't be sure. We'd better not try making friends of them by giving them food. We'll need every bit of flour we have for ourselves this winter."

"Yah, but I was half scared to death, and they left after I gave them bread."

Mary sputtered, "The men are a lazy bunch. The women do all the work in the fields and around the camp. No wonder they look as though they're half-dead. I can't stand a lazy man!"

"They hunt and fish, Grandma."

"Yah. And the heathens scalp people, too! They'd better not bother us when I've got the rifle!"

Wilhelm scratched his head. "I don't know about them. I don't think they can be trusted. Though they don't want to farm much of the land, it's too bad to let it grow nothing but wild grass. The settlers will produce crops—but maybe the Indians feel we don't belong here in their country. They were here first." He hesitated. "It's best if we don't become too friendly with them."

That night as Amelia lay sleepless, she was puzzled. No one knew for sure what was in the mind of the Sioux. She felt sorry for them, yet they frightened her. They were heathen who did not know the difference between good and evil. As she listened to the yells from the camp she felt no one could condemn them. She only hoped the Moltkes could bring them the message of Christianity.

Amelia sighed. She was fortunate. Compared to the Indian women, she lived in a castle and she was thankful she had not been born a Santee Sioux Indian.

15.

PEOPLE IN THE LITTLE GERMAN SETTLEMENT were preparing for winter. Old Adolph, Frederick and Anna lived with August and Gretchen in a large cabin. Gretchen, four months pregnant and inexperienced at housekeeping, found it difficult to keep up with the task of preparing meals for six people besides doing the washing and mending.

Ernst and Elizabeth's cabin was a short distance from the Ketchums. She often went to Gretchen's home to give her advice and to help with the work. One afternoon as they were mending socks Elizabeth asked, "Is Frederick getting over Harriet's and Lewis' deaths?"

Gretchen glanced outside at the father and daughter who were sitting on the ground beneath an elm tree. "I don't know. Frederick doesn't talk much to anyone but Anna. They're always together, night and day. He cuddles her and strokes her hair and won't let her out of his sight."

"It's not good for the child," Elizabeth remarked.

"He says he is going to build a cabin so they can live by themselves next spring," Gretchen said. She lowered her voice. "He hasn't done much work here. He's left everything to August and his father.

"Hm-m-m. What does he do all day?"

"Holds Anna and sits and stares into the woods."

Elizabeth shook her head. "It's natural for him to grieve, but Anna should have other things to think about." She paused.

"They're only interested in each other. We've tried to get them to go to the Moltkes' English sessions, but Frederick won't go and he says Anna can't go without him."

Elizabeth smiled. "I've learned quite a few English words. I wish Wilhelm and Amelia lived nearer so they could attend."

"Maybe next spring they can come in the wagon."

"Yah."

"By spring Amelia and I will have our babies."

"Yah." Elizabeth tossed a mended sock onto the table. "There will be other babies next year, too. Sarah Schling and Justina Wagner are expecting. That will make four new ones."

"I'm glad Otto Hess is a doctor."

"Uh-huh. Phidelia should have a child, too. She needs something to keep her busy."

Gretchen nodded. "She and Otto shouldn't have married. They don't get along."

"He's old enough to be her father. I think she married him so she could come to America, and now she finds life here is dull."

"Phidelia says somehow she will get through the winter because next year new people will be coming from her old home in Ulm to settle here. She's hoping for more excitement then."

"Oh?"

Gretchen smiled knowingly. "There will be younger men in the group."

Elizabeth clipped the yarn from her needle in a sock she was mending and slammed the shears down on the table. "Humph!"

"She's made friends with some of the Indian men. They often stop at her place for bread. She says they don't frighten her."

Elizabeth shook her head. In a moment she said, "I worry about Amelia. She almost died on the way across the Atlantic and I'm afraid something will be wrong with the baby. And she's so big! I've never seen a pregnant woman so huge."

"Yah. It's strange. I'm healthy as a horse."

Elizabeth mused. "I'm glad Mother Winters is with her, but I wish Wilhelm had chosen land closer to the settlement so I could have helped."

"Her baby should be born next month. August says we shouldn't have winter weather that early. One of us will get out to help."

Elizabeth nodded. "I hope we can."

BOOK 3

Frontier Life

1.

IN EARLY NOVEMBER there was a sudden change in the weather. One morning an icy northwest wind awakened the shivering family for the wind found every unsealed crack and crevice in the rough little cabin. Eddie whimpered in his trundle bed until Wilhelm placed him next to Amelia while he hurriedly dressed and started a fire.

Mary's shrill old voice followed him in a tirade. "You dragged us to this miserable place, now I hope you're satisfied. We're freezing in this shack, and 'tain't even winter! We'll likely all die of lung fever before spring. And with a new baby coming! Tell me, how can a new baby live in this—this Eskimo house?"

"Hush, Grandma. Eskimos live in snow houses." A blast of wind struck the cabin causing the newly laid fire in the fireplace to flicker. "Indian babies live in rickety lodges and they get through the winters quite well."

"Humph!" Mary turned over and pulled a quilt over her head. "I ain't gettin' up until it's warm in here!"

"Yah, Grandma. I'll see you next spring!"

The old woman snorted and burrowed deeply into her bed. Wilhelm put on his heavy woolen coat. "I'm going to the barn to milk and feed the animals," he said to Amelia. "You stay in bed until it warms up out here."

She didn't answer. He opened the door. A blast of wind from the northwest slammed the door against the cabin wall. Hastily stepping outside, he struggled to close the door. He stood a moment to look around. The grass lay flat on the ground. At the edge of the forest trees were blown down, the roots extending upward. Two of his hay stacks had blown over. He was surprised that the little shanty-barn still stood.

Wilhelm stepped away from the cabin and started toward the barn. With the unrelenting northwest wind to his back, he was swept along so that he struggled to stay upright. His woodpile had blown down and three-foot blocks rolled toward the southeast. The wind swept away anything not tied down.

When he reached the barn, the door was torn from his hand. It splintered as it struck the side of the shanty.

"Damn!" he muttered. He hurried to his tool box in the corner. The animals complained loudly. The squeals of the pig blended with Chief's high pitched yips and the bawling of the cattle.

"Yah, yah. I'm hurrying to close it up," he muttered as he searched for the few remaining nails in the bottom of the chest. At last the opening was closed against the icy blast.

The merciless wind had penetrated his woolen coat and pierced his flesh. His hands were blue-red from the cold and his feet felt numb. He had never seen a wind like this in Germany; but he remembered hearing Otto Hess say that temperatures in Minnesota could fall forty degrees in a few minutes.

As he fed the animals and milked the cow, he planned. There was still much to do before they were ready for winter. And Amelia—maybe he should take her to his parents' home in the settlement until after the baby was born. There she would be near Otto Hess, the doctor. They'd better talk about it soon.

After breakfast Wilhelm tightened the cabin as best he could by closing the cracks with moss and wet clay. After many trips inside to warm up, he worked on the barn.

During the second night Wilhelm got up several times to keep the fire alive. By morning the wind died down a little, but in late afternoon it increased again accompanied by showers of hail. Pieces of ice as large as walnuts and hard as stones pounded against the cabin. In a short time the wind piled the hail in drifts along the sides of the buildings.

Finally by the third morning the storm was over, the sun came out, the hail melted and warm, late fall weather returned.

Amelia stood in the open door of the cabin watching Wilhelm gather the scattered firewood. "I wonder if we'll often have storms like this one?" she said.

"They tell me there are many windy days here," Wilhelm replied. "I want to get everything shipshape while this warm spell lasts. I need to box in the spring at the edge of the river so it will be easier to get water, and I want to build a small shelter against the side of the cabin where we can store venison and other wild game during the winter."

Amelia stepped outside and sat on a stump. "We'll have to eat a lot of meat. I wish we had more vegetables. I'll be nursing the baby and I'm not sure so much meat is good."

"Yah." Wilhelm thought a moment before he asked, "How long do you figger you have?"

"Before the baby comes? Three or four weeks, I think."

Mary shouted, " 'Twon't be that long!"

Ignoring his grandmother's remark, Wilhelm continued, "I figger I can have everything caught up in ten days. When it is cold enough I'd like to get two or three deer to hang in the shelter. When that's done, I'll take you to Ma's and Pa's until you and the baby are ready to come home."

Amelia nodded. “I’d like that.”

Mary cackled, “That’s the first sensible thing you’ve decided since we left home!”

“Grandma,” Amelia said, “Can you take care of Eddie and cook for him and Wilhelm while I’m gone?”

Mary snorted. “ ’Course I can! You think I’m a doddering old woman?”

Amelia struggled to her feet and planted a kiss on the wrinkled old cheek. “I think you’re the finest woman I’ve ever known.”

Tears glistened in Mary’s eyes. Abruptly she turned to blot them with her apron.

2.

AMELIA TURNED RESTLESSLY on the marsh hay mattress. There was no way she could get comfortable. Her back ached, but her ponderous abdomen prevented her lying comfortably on her side. She could hear the wind howling around the corner of the cabin. Two or three days and then Wilhelm would take her to his parents home.

Because she was unable to sleep, she reminisced about home. She thought of her parents. It had been more than seven months since she had seen them. Her heart ached as she realized she likely would never see them again. She would be in the wilderness the rest of her life. This cabin wasn’t home; home was the little cottage in Germany. She had written a letter to her parents shortly after they had arrived in Minnesota, but home was so far away. She hoped by spring she might have a letter from them.

Amelia tried to lie still so she wouldn't disturb Wilhelm. She could hear the wind blowing hard. She hoped they weren't going to have another storm. Grandmother Mary snored loudly in the next room.

The dull ache in her back continued. She wondered how long it was until morning. Maybe when she stood on her feet the ache would go away.

Her heart leaped! Was this low back pain the beginning of labor? No! No! It wasn't time. She tried to relax. At last morning came.

Wilhelm pulled on his clothes and went to start the fire. He glanced outside. "Damn!" he exploded.

"What's wrong?" Amelia called.

"Snow! Two feet of snow and the wind's blowing! Damn!"

Amelia bit her lip. She wouldn't tell them yet, but she was certain she was in the first stages of labor.

Half an hour later, his clothing snow-covered, Wilhelm returned from the barn with a pail of milk. Silently he hung his coat and removed his boots.

"It's bad?" Amelia asked softly.

"Yah."

Mary continued dressing Eduard. "You can't take Amelia to Ernst's in this weather."

"No." He rubbed his forehead. "Maybe the storm will be over soon." But he knew this was hopeful thinking. Already great drifts were everywhere. The trail was blocked. There was no way the oxen could pull the wagon through these snowdrifts. Unless the weather changed rapidly, Amelia would have to give birth here.

Eddie shouted, "I'm hungry!" He stamped across the rough floor to his high wooden block seat beside the table.

While they ate steaming bowls of cornmeal mush, the adults were silent as each one contemplated what the immediate future held for the family. Eddie chattered, “Can I have Chief inside?”

“When Pa goes to the barn again.” Amelia’s face was pale.

“Can I play outdoors in the snow?”

“Not today. You’d get lost in the storm.” Wilhelm recalled that for a moment as he returned from the barn, he had lost sight of the cabin in the swirling snow.

Mary was unusually quiet. Her sharp old eyes studied Amelia’s face. She observed the paleness, the strained look, and the occasional wince of pain. She knew. Amelia was in labor.

The candle flickered on the table. “It’s ’most as dark as night,” Amelia said.

“Yah. I never saw it snow this hard in Germany,” Wilhelm replied. “And the wind keeps it stirred up.” He wondered why his grandmother was so quiet. She hadn’t made a cutting remark all morning. Eddie climbed on his lap.

Amelia staggered to her feet. “I’ll put some venison cooking.” While Mary cleared the table and washed dishes, Amelia cut a large roast into small pieces. As she grasped the knife she felt a sudden jerking convulsion and severe pain began in the small of her back. It slowly spread through her lower body. She gasped.

Wilhelm asked, “Something wrong?”

“Not much. The baby’s kicking hard.”

“You have pain?”

“It will go away.”

She continued cutting up venison. She had told the truth—the pain would go away, but she knew it would return, again and again and again, always increasing in intensity. She remembered. A blast of wind slammed snow against the window.

By noon when they sat around the table the pain had

grown more intense as it radiated from her back and cut through her lower body. Pains were lasting longer now, too. She hadn't told them, but she was sure Mary knew. Though she wasn't hungry she forced herself to swallow a few spoonfuls of broth.

Eddie chattered, "Good meat, Mama."

Wilhelm watched Amelia. "Are you all right?"

"I don't feel so good." The pain eased, but in a short time it returned so violently that a low moan came from her lips.

Mary and Wilhelm jumped up. "It's the baby. It's time," Amelia said softly.

Wilhelm stared at her drawn face. "But—but—it's too soon!"

"Shut up, Grandson!" Mary exclaimed. "Amelia and I will handle this. You keep the fire going, heat lots of water and look after Eddie."

The old woman guided Amelia to the bedroom. "Has the birth-water come?" she asked.

Amelia panted, "Yah. This morning."

Mary said calmly, "I know what to do. I've been a midwife before. Get undressed and into bed." After a time she asked, "When did the pains start?"

"In the night."

"How long did it take when Eddie was born?"

"About twelve hours."

"Yah."

"I'm so large this time. The baby must be big."

" 'Twill take time. You had any pushing pains yet?"

"No. Only the warning ones, but they're getting harder and closer together."

Mary shouted, "Grandson, get water heating! And we need a roaring fire. This place is too cold for a new baby! Men," she muttered. "They're useless when you need them most."

The hours wore on. It was night and Amelia's pains had increased in intensity. She bit her lip stifling moans until the contractions passed. Mary shuffled about between the bedroom and fireplace. Wilhelm stared into the blazing fire.

"How much longer?" he asked.

"This baby's slow in coming. Must be a big one, but it's not time yet. You might's well rest beside Eddie in my bed."

The hours crept by. The only sounds in the cabin were the snapping of the fire, the howling of the wind and soft moans from the bedroom. When the contractions were five minutes apart, Mary twisted a sheet into a rope and tied it to the foot of the bed.

"Now," she directed Amelia, "when the next hard pain starts you pull on the sheet and push down with your belly muscles. That should hurry things along."

Hours later beads of perspiration stood on Amelia's forehead. She panted, "I'm so tired. I can't push anymore."

"You have to."

"It's taking so long. Something must be wrong. When will it be morning?"

"Soon now." Mary went to sit at the table with Wilhelm. The wind howled down the chimney and snow slashed against the kitchen window. A sudden piercing scream came from the bedroom. Eddie cried out and rushed to Wilhelm who ran to Amelia's side.

"I'm sorry," she gasped. "I push and push but nothing happens."

Eddie sobbed. Mary shoved Wilhelm aside. "Take Eddie and get out of here! Wrap him up and go to the barn and do the chores! You're in the way! Get out of here!"

Wilhelm grasped Mary's arm and pulled her from the

room. "She looks terrible. Why is it taking so long?"

"I don't know. Sometimes it does."

"If the baby hasn't come by the time I'm back from the barn, I'm going to the settlement for Otto Hess. He'll know what to do."

Mary agreed. "We need a doctor."

The door closed behind Wilhelm on a blast of wind and snow. Mary returned to the bedroom.

Amelia gasped, "I'm so tired. It wasn't like this with Eddie."

"Yah. Yah." Mary straightened the folded sheet beneath the restless woman.

The violent contractions were getting closer together. Amelia gasped in agony with each pain as she moaned, bit her lip and pulled on the knotted sheet. "Why doesn't that baby come?" she panted, too fatigued to speak clearly. "It's been thirty hours."

"Yah. Yah." Mary stroked Amelia's forehead.

The tortured woman grasped the rough old hands. "I'm glad you're with me."

"Yah, I know."

Another contraction began, building in intensity until Amelia screamed with agony and frustration. As the pain diminished she whispered, "I can't push anymore. I don't have the strength."

The door burst open and a flurry of snow sailed in on a blast of wind. Wilhelm and Eddie hurried inside to be greeted by a scream from the bedroom. A frightened look swept over Wilhelm's face.

"She can't stand this much longer," he said. "I'm going to get Otto."

"Yah. Hurry."

"I'll follow the river. Otto can ride his horse and maybe I can borrow one. We'll be back as soon as we can." He went to the bedroom to explain his plan to

Amelia.

She nodded. "Please hurry." He kissed her and left.

Mary stood at the kitchen window as Wilhelm started along the riverbank. She saw him only briefly before he was hidden from view by the swirling snow.

Another piercing scream from the bedroom told of the awful force of the contractions. Eddie clung to Mary's skirts for security. The old woman's mind was in turmoil. She couldn't help Amelia. She had never faced a childbirth like this. The poor child, she couldn't live through many more hours of this agony.

Slowly Mary made her way to the bedroom.

3.

As HE HEADED EAST a blast of wind struck Wilhelm's back. He turned up his coat collar and stared into the swirling snow. He could see the river to his left, but the trail was obliterated by drifts. I'm all right, he thought, as long as I keep the river in sight.

Though it was early in the day, the clouds and heavy snowfall created the impression of late afternoon twilight. He repeatedly brushed the snow from his eyelashes and strode on.

Just my luck, Wilhelm thought. The timing was all wrong—Amelia going into labor early and a roaring blizzard before they were ready. He didn't know what to expect of the weather in Minnesota. Perhaps he should have chosen land closer to the settlement, but he hadn't known then that they were near the big Indian camp, and that they could expect this kind of weather. He recalled reading in Charles Weber's book about Minnesota on the *Herman Reiter* that there sometimes were blizzards but it hadn't said they came this early in the season. He wondered about Charles Weber and how he was getting along. He had chosen to settle north of St. Paul.

He plodded on, detouring around deep snowdrifts as he kept an eye on the river to his left. The gusts of wind increased in velocity; they penetrated his clothing. In the air high above the trees a heavy roar could be heard. The trees swayed and creaked. Everything was enveloped in snow—hurling, whipping, smarting snow.

"Damn," he murmured as he protected his face with mittened hands, "I've got to move faster. I have to get the doctor for Amelia." The dreaded thought returned to plague him—she might not survive this childbirth. He shivered. His legs ached from stepping high in the deep snow. The river—yes, it was there to his left. He couldn't miss the settlement if he followed the river.

Suddenly a heavy crashing sound cut through the roar of the blizzard, followed by the noise of splintering wood and another crash. He brushed the snow from his eyes. Several big trees lay entangled across the trail. Detouring to the right he paused to rest against the upturned roots of a giant pine. Breathing heavily, he removed a mitten and felt in his pocket for his pipe, tobacco and matches. After five minutes of unsuccessful attempts at lighting the pipe, he gave up in disgust.

He started on, surprised at the number of fallen trees around which he must detour. When at last he was in the clear, he glanced to the left. The river was not there! His heart lurched.

Stumbling on, he turned to the left. Five minutes later he knew. He was lost. He leaned against a swaying tree to collect his thoughts. The wind, which should be at his back, was blowing straight into his face. He turned to retrace his footsteps, but already they were nearly obliterated. Within a few minutes not a trace of his tracks remained. Wandering aimlessly, he searched in vain for the fallen trees where he had detoured away from the river. Nothing looked familiar.

His mind was in turmoil as he leaned against a swaying tree trunk to collect his thoughts. The northwest wind penetrated his clothing and flesh. He shivered. The snow beat into his eyes so that he could not see. Everything around him was whirling snow. He was like a blind person fumbling about in the storm. Though he had lost all sense of direction, he must keep moving else he would freeze to death. He staggered on.

Amelia—Eduard—Grandmother Mary. What would become of them if he didn't return? He stumbled and instinctively glanced upward to grasp a tree branch for support. Through the bare swaying branches he could see something a few feet above. Puzzled, he walked a short distance, staring at the object in the swaying tree. Suddenly he knew. A snow-covered, wrapped body, a dead Indian!

Could this be the corpse Amelia and Grandmother Mary had seen in the Indian fruit orchard? No. Impossible. The fruit orchard and Indian camp were west of his land, and he was east of there on the way to the settlement. He plodded on, plagued by the thought that Amelia might die if he didn't get help. Forcefully he put the frightening possibilities from his mind and breathed a silent prayer for guidance.

It was strange that he hadn't seen a living creature since leaving the cabin. No rabbits, or deer, or birds—it was as though he was alone in this vast wilderness—except for a dead, frozen Indian.

His thoughts returned to Germany. At home the snowflakes fell soft as wool on your face, but in Minnesota they were sharp and hard and pricked like pins when driven in your face by a strong wind.

Wilhelm's heart pounded. The wind shouldn't be blowing in his face! Not if he was traveling east. He was heading directly into a northwest wind! Desperately he turned and walked in the opposite direction. This has happened twice, he thought. I must be walking in a circle.

The trees bent and swayed, the tops bending lower as the motion of the trunks increased. Now snow mixed with hail whipped against his back. Though it was daytime, the dark clouds and the dense snow-filled air made the vast wilderness appear to be in the twilight of evening.

Wilhelm breathed deeply. He was freezing. If only he could find shelter. He couldn't survive this weather many hours. His hands and feet were numb. He squatted beneath the low branches of a towering pine. Scraping away the snow he found dead twigs and needles which he placed in a small pile. He pulled off a mitten and with numb fingers he felt in his pocket for matches. Still squatting, with his body shielding the tiny heap of branches, he crouched and struck a match. The flame sputtered and went out. He felt in his pocket for another match. It also went out before the needles caught fire. Several more times he failed to ignite the twigs. It was hopeless. No tiny match could start a fire with damp twigs in this howling blizzard. Stiffly, he got to his feet.

Wilhelm wondered what time it was. It seemed he had been wandering for hours. He doubted he could survive a night in this weather, but he had to go on. He beat his hands together and stamped his feet to restore circulation. He heard a sound. As he listened, the howl of an animal seemed to come from nearby. A wolf, perhaps.

He walked on. Now there were several animal voices howling in unison. Just my luck, he thought, to run into a hungry pack of wolves. He broke small twigs from a dead branch and carried the remaining stick for protection.

Suddenly the howls of the animals changed into excited barks. He didn't know wolves barked like dogs. They seemed very close. All at once one of the beasts lunged out of the curtain of whiteness to stand at his feet, barking furiously, his tail wagging. Immediately, three more scrawny dogs joined the first to jump against him as they yipped sharply.

Overjoyed, Wilhelm tossed the stick away and patted the excited animals who turned to bound away through the snow. Though his legs were stiff, he bolted after them. Breathing hard to keep up he stopped suddenly at the sound of a human voice shouting to the dogs.

"Help!" he yelled. Through the swirling snow he could see a small building with a blanket-covered man standing outside the door. There were several bark shanties nearby. The Indian camp!

"Help!" he shouted as he staggered toward the Indian lodge. "Help me!"

The blanket-clad man ran to Wilhelm's side and grasped his arm. "Come," he said gruffly. Together they went into the semi-darkness of the bark lodge.

Shaking with cold and exhaustion Wilhelm allowed himself to be led to a small fire in the center of the lodge. The Indian removed the wet coat and draped a blanket about Wilhelm's shoulders. From somewhere in a dark corner, a squaw appeared with a wooden bowl filled with stew.

"Eat," the Indian commanded.

"Thank you, thank you," Wilhelm murmured as he tasted the hot food. "Good."

The squaw threw more wood on the fire in the stone ring. As he ate, Wilhelm's mind was busy. Who was this Indian who spoke English words? And was this the camp near his land? It was fortunate that for the past month he, Amelia and Mary had spent a few minutes each day studying a book of English phrases which August had loaned them. He was unsure of his pronunciation, but perhaps the Indian could understand him.

When he had finished eating, the Indian said, "Me, Little Crow." He pointed to himself.

Wilhelm nodded. "Me, Wilhelm Winters."

"You are lost?"

Wilhelm did not understand. He shook his head. "Where—where my house?"

The Indian pointed. "By river."

"Yah." A noise behind him caused Wilhelm to turn. In the semi-darkness he saw another blanket-covered man who silently came to stand beside the fire.

"You say English?" Wilhelm asked Little Crow.

"Yes. Meester Prescott say Sioux talk and Little Crow say English talk. He learn us."

Wilhelm shook his head. He had never heard of anyone named Prescott. He thought of the English expressions he knew. "You will take me to my house?"

Little Crow pointed outside. "Storm. Can't go."

Wilhelm rubbed his forehead. "In my house sick woman."

"We sleep. Next day we go your house."

Shadows from the fire danced on the walls of the lodge. Outside the wind howled and snow hissed against the rickety door. Pointed piles of white streaked inward from the entrance where snow had been driven inside by the force of the wind.

Reluctantly Wilhelm accepted Little Crow's decision to remain in camp until the storm was over. That night as the Indians snored in their bunks, he turned restlessly on the dirt floor near the smoldering fire. If Amelia still was alive, she and Mary would be frantic with worry about him. And what of his animals in the barn? If Mary tried to care for them she surely would be lost in the storm between the cabin and barn. He still didn't know if this Indian camp was the one near his land. It seemed to him that he had wandered miles through the storm. At last morning came.

Still the storm continued. Little Crow and the other man went outside for a time. When they returned Little Crow said, "Storm soon stop. Then we go your house."

About noon the sun came out and the wind quieted. Little Crow strapped snowshoes made from deerskin thongs and flexible willow branches to his and Wilhelm's feet.

Outside Indians were moving about between fifteen or twenty bark lodges. Little Crow and Wilhelm headed east through a sparkling fairyland of huge drifts. Before long Wilhelm mastered the knack of walking on snowshoes. They came to the river but nothing looked familiar until he saw his cabin in the distance. Smoke rose from the chimney. His pace quickened.

Barking, Chief came bounding over the snowbanks to greet him. Wilhelm tried to run but the unfamiliar snowshoes tripped him and he fell face first in the snow. Chief nuzzled his neck. Swearing softly he struggled to his feet with Little Crow's help.

The barn door burst open and Mary waded toward them carrying a pail of milk. Her gray hair blew in wisps across the wrinkled face. She stared at Little Crow. "He's the doctor?" Her voice dripped with controlled anger.

"How's Amelia?"

"A lot you care about Amelia! We could all have froze to death in this shack while you was gallivanting around, God knows where." She drew a deep breath. "Who's this—this man?"

"He's Little Crow. I've been at his lodge."

The Indian's face was expressionless. He had heard of this angry old woman who had threatened his friends with a rifle.

"You've been at his lodge? Well, that's nice! While your wife was near death and your old grandmother most scared out of her wits, you don't even go for the doctor. You stay inside out of the storm!"

"Grandmother, I want to know about Amelia!"

The old woman waded toward the cabin, her coat dragging in the snow. "Come!" she commanded. "Come and you'll soon find out what you've done!"

Wilhelm's heart pounded. Did she mean Amelia was dead? He rushed inside followed by Little Crow. Eddie screamed, "Pa!" and ran to his father. He swept him up and with two strides he was at the bedroom door.

Amelia raised her head to lean on an elbow. "Wilhelm! Thank God you're back. I was sure you had frozen to death. Is the doctor with you?"

He kissed her. "I'm so glad you're all right," he whispered. "I got lost and ended up in the Indian camp. Little Crow brought me home. But—but have you had the baby?"

She smiled, a tired, wan smile. "Yes. Grandmother will show you."

"Come, Pa," Eddie chattered. "Come see!"

Wilhelm followed Eddie. Little Crow stood silently staring into a box on the table near the fireplace. Mary poked the fire angrily. "Look!" she sputtered. "Look what you've done! Men!"

Wilhelm gasped in astonishment. For a moment he was speechless. It couldn't be. Finally he stuttered. "Th-th-three!"

"Yah," Mary sighed. "She had a litter. Serves you right, and not a boy among them. You've got three girl babies!"

"Aren't they beautiful?" Amelia called from the bedroom. "We couldn't weigh them but Grandmother thinks they each weigh about four pounds. They're little, but they'll grow."

Wilhelm still stared at the babies in disbelief. He had never known a woman who had three children at one birth.

Mary placed her hands on her hips. "Say something! Don't you wonder what their mother has named them?"

"Yah. Tell me."

"Faith, Hope and Charity."

One of the babies whimpered. A minute later all three were screaming. A faint smile flickered across Little Crow's face. "You be busy." He pulled his blanket across his shoulders and went outside.

Wilhelm was dazed. "Three—three girls," he said softly as he stared at the screaming babies. "Why couldn't they have been boys so I'd have help in a few years?"

Mary snorted. "The good Lord knew what He was doing! He sent girls to help Amelia!" She picked up the nearest baby and rocked it in her arms. "At least I *hope* He knew. Amelia almost died birthing them—and you go off gallivanting with that Indian! And now she's got three babies to raise. You know how much washing three babies make? And there'll be years of cooking and sewing and—and—God only knows how many more babies she'll have! Here, hold this one!" She thrust the baby into Wilhelm's arms and hurriedly picked up the other two.

At last they were quiet. Wilhelm shook his head and silently carried the baby to the bedroom. "I'm sorry,

Amelia," he said. "Can you manage all the work?"

"I'll manage. They're beautiful little girls. We'll get along fine." She smiled and reached for the baby. "I'm glad we have them."

He stooped to kiss her cheek. "I'm glad I have you," he whispered. "Maybe—maybe I'll get used to them."

4.

THE WINTER OF 1850-1851 seemed endless to Amelia, Wilhelm and Mary. Crying, colicky babies, endless laundry drying on lines across the cabin and done by hand in water carried from the river, the constant struggle to keep food on the table and the lack of restful sleep, all combined to cause the adults to exist near the level of exhaustion. Only Eddie seemed to have boundless energy which annoyed Amelia and Mary because he invariably wakened the sleeping triplets.

Amelia nursed the babies but her meager milk supply was supplemented with cow's milk. The children gained weight in spite of their discomfort caused by colic.

Three weeks after the birth of the babies the family was overjoyed to welcome Ernst and Elizabeth who rode over the snow-filled trail on a bobsled pulled by a team of horses belonging to Herman Moltke.

After a happy greeting with her daughter-in-law, Elizabeth held Amelia at arms length and scrutinized her from head to toe. "You've had the baby!" she exclaimed.

"That she has," Mary muttered.

Amelia giggled. "Come and see." She led Elizabeth to Mary's bed where three little girls slept in their box-bassinet.

Elizabeth gasped. "It can't be!" she exclaimed.

"Yah, a litter," Mary laughed as she shuffled to the bed. "But a nice litter."

"I never saw anything like this. Are they boys or girls?"

Amelia beamed. "Three little girls. We named them Faith, Hope and Charity. They were our Christmas present, I tell Wilhelm. Don't you think they look alike?"

"I don't see how you tell them apart."

"We can't. That's why Faith has a red string on her wrist, Hope has a blue one and Charity's is green."

"Yah," Mary said. "We tell 'em by color."

Eddie raced across the rough floor and jumped on the bed beside the bassinet. He touched each baby in turn. "Faith, wed, Hope, boo, Tarity gween!"

Charity's startled jump wakened Hope. A moment later three babies screamed in unison. As the women changed wet diapers they chatted over the children's complaining cries.

Elizabeth asked, "How do you manage to keep the washing done?"

Amelia smiled. "Grandmother helps with everything. I couldn't do it alone. But we don't have enough of anything for three. We're always running out of didies."

"I'll try to borrow some from Sarah Schling. Louise is out of didies now. Sarah'll likely lend you other clothes too." She fastened the safety pin on Hope's triangular diaper and put the crying baby over her shoulder. "There, there," she crooned. "Grandma has you." When the baby was quiet she continued. "The Moltkes are going to Mankato soon, if the weather holds. I'll ask them to bring back some cloth and I'll make didies."

"That would help." Amelia unbuttoned her dress and put Faith to her breast. The baby nursed hungrily. "How is Gretchen getting along?"

"Real good. Her baby is due in March. Besides August, she has Adolph, Frederick and Anna to cook and wash for. It's a good thing she's healthy."

Mary snorted. "How is the old guzzler?"

Elizabeth laughed. "Adolph? Half drunk, as usual. But it's Frederick that we're concerned about. He sits all day by the fireplace cuddling Anna."

"Humph! 'Tain't healthy. You think his mind's all right?" Mary shoved her leather bag under the bed with her foot.

Elizabeth shrugged. "We don't know."

At the barn Wilhelm and his father were catching up on the news. Ernst remarked, "You were lucky you found the Indian camp in that storm."

"Yah. Little Crow brought me home. I don't know who he is, but he speaks English."

"Herman Moltke has mentioned him. He doesn't live at the camp near you. He must have been visiting there and got caught in the storm."

"Where does he live?"

"Farther up the river. He's chief of his band. He's more friendly to the settlers than most of the Indians."

"I asked him where he learned English. He said a name that sounded like 'Prescott'."

"Yah. Herman says Philander Prescott is a middle-aged fur trader who deals with the Indians. They trust him because his wife is a squaw whose daughter is married to Shakopee. He's another Indian with influence in this part of Minnesota."

"Little Crow, Shakopee and Philander Prescott. I'll likely hear of them again."

"Indians often walk through the settlement. Sometimes they stop. One young brave, Shaska, visits Otto and Phidelia Hess."

"Is he sick?"

Ernst laughed. "We think he stops to see Phidelia. She feeds him, teaches him English—and flirts with him."

"Yah? Phidelia flirts with anything that wears pants."

"She's young, a good looker, and I suspect she's bored with Otto. He reads his doctor books by the hour, or sits by the fire and thinks. He's too old for her. They never should have married. I hope she doesn't get too involved with Shaska. It could cause trouble."

5.

THE FIRST WINTER they were in Minnesota seemed endless to Amelia. Unrelenting cold pierced the rough log walls of the cabin and caused a constant chill except when they were near the fireplace. Crying babies demanded attention. Her only respite came as she nursed the infants, one at each breast, to save time.

Wilhelm kept two tubs filled with water in a corner near the fireplace. Wet diapers were immediately rinsed and hung to dry while soiled ones were washed daily in strong soft soap provided by Elizabeth.

There was always food to prepare. Amelia and Mary cooked wild game in every way imaginable. They stewed, fried, and roasted venison, rabbits, raccoons, muskrats and fish. They ate quantities of wild rice which Wilhelm had gathered before winter set in. Bread seemed to disappear like magic and Amelia worried that the rye flour and cornmeal would be gone before spring. Their only fresh fruit was the wild apples they had gathered late in the fall.

Sometimes Amelia reassured herself as she talked to Mary. "I'm thankful that we are well and Eduard is growing like a weed. The girls are beautiful. Father and Mother Winters have been helpful. Father made three nice cradles for the babies and Mother sewed clothes for them and made quilts."

"Yah," Mary agreed as she changed Charity's diaper. "The people at the settlement have been good to us." She put the baby over her shoulder and patted the tiny back until an air bubble was expelled. "I'll be glad when spring comes. Dandelion greens—wouldn't they taste good?"

Amelia smiled as she placed a sleeping baby in the cradle and buttoned her dress. "Adolph likely will make dandelion wine in the spring."

Mary snorted. "The old guzzler." She paused. "But Ernst said he helped make the babies' cradles."

"He's got a soft heart, Grandma."

"And a soft head!"

Wilhelm and Eddie came in from the barn. "Ma!" the boy shouted. "We've got baby pigs!"

"We have? How many?"

"Ten," Wilhelm answered. "Next winter we'll have pork to eat instead of muskrats and raccoons. And there'll be pigs to sell." He sighed. "I figger if we get through this year the others should be easy."

All winter Wilhelm trapped fur-bearing animals. Beavers, mink and muskrats were plentiful. Checking his traps and skinning the catch and stretching them on boards to dry was a time consuming daily chore. He hoped sale of the furs would provide money to carry them through to harvest time.

One spring day the family welcomed Philander Prescott, the fur trader, who came down the river to purchase the winter's catch. Hungry for knowledge of the outside world, Wilhelm questioned Prescott.

The men sat at the table smoking while the women went about their work. Prescott, a bald, clean-shaven man with piercing blue eyes smiled as he noticed the three cradles.

"Big Bear told me about your triplets. The Sioux have never heard of three babies born at one birth. Little Crow also told me about them when I stopped at his camp."

"Yah." Wilhelm paused. "Tell me, are the Indians getting used to having new settlers come here?"

"No. They don't like it. They say hunting and trapping is not as good as it was two years ago. I understand many more families are coming this summer and that will add to the problem." He hesitated. "I'm married to a Sioux woman, so I hear the discussions. The United States government has promised to buy much of the land in southern Minnesota from the Indians."

"When?"

"This year. 1851."

"Where will the Indians go?"

"They're to be given reservation land west of here along the Minnesota River. They're to have two reservations, the Lower Agency, near here, and the Upper Agency, several miles upriver."

"You think the government plan is good?"

"Good for the settlers. The Sioux will have to change the way they've lived for hundreds of years. I don't think they can do it. They have customs the whites cannot understand."

"Like?"

"They have always been a war-like people. The Sioux and Chippewa tribes are enemies—the Chippewas are north of here. Chief Shakopee, a young Indian, recently battled with the Chippewas. He took scalps. The young Sioux men are taught to regard killing as a virtue. In dances and at feasts the braves recite deeds of killing the enemy as a precious thing. It is the ambition of every young brave to secure the "feather" which is his record of having murdered a human. After he gets his first feather his appetite is whetted to increase the number of feathers in his hair. Without these feathers he is regarded as a squaw, usually cannot get a wife and is treated with contempt. The headdress filled with these feathers is called '*wakan,*' which means sacred, and no one other than the owner can touch it."

Wilhelm glanced at Amelia. Her face was drawn. Mary bristled and struggled to her feet. "The varmints better stay away from here! I'll shoot them like—like rats!"

Prescott hastened to say, "These killings happen between the Chippewas and Sioux tribes. I haven't heard of a white settler that was harmed. The Indians have respect—and a fear of the United States government."

"But we live so close to them," Amelia said softly. "Suppose we anger them?"

"When the treaty is signed, they will have their reservation. Gradually, we hope they will become accustomed to white men's ways. My wife, for example, has accepted our customs and religion."

"We have wondered about the custom of putting their dead on scaffolds instead of burying them," Wilhelm said.

Prescott nodded. "It seems weird to us, but it is an old custom of the Sioux. Over the platform of the dead they hang the scalps of slaughtered enemies. Honorable wounds and death are believed to be a sure passport to "the happy hunting grounds." If you look carefully, you will see his weapons beside a dead Indian. His friends often come to visit him and recite his brave deeds."

"Grandma," Amelia said, "the day we found the dead Indian in the fruit orchard, we must have frightened away a friend who came to visit him."

"Yah, the varmints! And those things I thought were pieces of fur on the scaffold must have been scalps."

Amelia shuddered and went into the bedroom.

After dinner Prescott bargained with Wilhelm for his animal hides, packed them in his canoe and proceeded east down the river to the settlement.

When the fur trader had gone, the family discussed his visit. Wilhelm said, "I wonder where Prescott learned to speak German. It was good to be able to learn about the Indians."

Mary said, "I expect he has settlers from several countries that he trades with." She glanced at Amelia. "We'd have been better off if he hadn't told all those weird things about them varmints, though. It don't do us no good to know those things."

Spring came early that year. By mid-April the snow was gone and the ground had settled. The lumber barge again came down the river giving the settlers the opportunity to order seeds and other needed supplies from St. Paul.

During summer Wilhelm worked from daylight to dark. His oxen, deliberate and clumsy, had amazing strength. It was a pretty sight to see them stretch their necks, grip the earth with cloven hoofs, settle their shoulders into the yoke and pull tight the jangling chain. Five words were enough to keep them working. "Getep! Back! Whoa! Gee! Haw!"

Wilhelm plowed around stumps and prepared the ground for wheat, which he sowed broadcast. Later, in early June, corn was planted by hand with a hoe in the fertile seedbed. Near the cabin Amelia stole a few minutes now and then to plant a garden while Eddie and Chief played nearby and Mary watched the babies.

People again traveled the trail. Scarcely a day passed that Indians were not seen. They rarely stopped at the cabin though Big Bear, the Sioux who owned the lodge where Wilhelm had stayed in the storm, sometimes talked briefly with Wilhelm and inquired about the babies. When questioned about Little Crow he motioned toward the northwest. "Live there," he said.

During the summer an influx of settlers arrived from Ulm, Germany to choose unclaimed land near the settlement. The sound of saws and chopping axes resounded through the wilderness as new cabins and barns were erected. Every day now travelers passed the Winters' home on the way to the Upper Agency Sioux Reservation at the junction of the Yellow Medicine and Minnesota Rivers.

The Moltkes led the drive to erect a small Lutheran church at the settlement. Amos and his father worked with the Sioux men and Magdelene spoke with the squaws in an attempt to convert them to Christianity. A few were receptive and attended church on an irregular basis.

Farther to the northwest beyond the Upper Agency Reservation at Lac Que Parle on the Minnesota River, two Presbyterian missionary teams, Dr. and Mrs. Thomas S. Williamson and Reverend and Mrs. Stephen R. Riggs, established missions in the area. Since the mid 1830's the two couples had dedicated their lives to helping the Minnesota Indians. Both men worked to translate the Bible into the Indian language. Occasionally they visited the German settlement, where they were welcomed.

In July of 1851 Amelia received a letter from a cousin in Germany. It had been written February 12, 1851. It contained shocking news. It began:

Dear Cousin Amelia,

I hardly know how to begin this letter, so I will tell you at once why I am writing. Well, Amelia, your parents have both passed away—only a week apart. Your father first, then your mother. We think they had some kind of lung fever. The doctor did all he could but the awful fever and coughing was more than their bodies could stand.

They often talked of you. Your mother asked me to write to you and tell you they loved you and wished you well in America. They are buried in the cemetery near your old home. I will put flowers on the graves in the summer.

I'm sorry to have to send bad news, but they now are at rest.

Your cousin,

Louisa.

Amelia threw herself on the bed and sobbed. Gone. Her parents were dead. Now her ties with Germany were entirely severed.

Wilhelm and Mary consoled Amelia, but for days, she mourned. Life went on and though her heart ached, she had responsibilities to her family which helped her get through the bad days.

During late summer of 1851 a social event of importance occurred. Amos Moltke and Justina Kreiger were united in marriage by Amos' father, Reverend Herman Moltke. Everyone in the settlement was invited: the Indians at the Lower Agency and the Williamson and Riggs missionaries from the Upper Agency, together with the Sioux from that area. A total of seventy-five Indians and whites mingled beneath the trees outside the little

Lutheran church.

Amelia, leaning against the trunk of a large oak, sat on a blanket with her nine-month-old triplets beside her. As she talked with Gretchen Ketchum, who held her young son, Hans, she waged a losing battle to keep the active babies on the blanket. Mary and Elizabeth came to the rescue. The baby girls objected loudly to being confined to their grandmothers' arms.

"You enjoy yourself," Elizabeth said to Amelia. "We'll mind the babies." They walked away to proudly display their grandchildren to any interested guests.

Blanketed Indians with feathers in their hair, wandered about. Most of them spoke some English which they had learned through contact with missionaries and fur traders. As she watched them, Amelia said softly, "They don't seem dangerous—just curious. Still—" She suppressed the thought that each feather in a brave's hair represented a life he had taken.

Gretchen wiped Hans' mouth with a clean diaper. "Yah, they're really curious about your triplets. And they watched and listened during the wedding ceremony."

"It's strange there are no squaws here."

"Perhaps only the men go to affairs like this."

"Two or three of the men have white men's clothes," Amelia noted.

"Yah. Magdelene Moltke told me the missionaries are trying to get the Sioux to change their ways. They're not only working to convert them to Christianity, but they want them to dress like we do, to stop being 'blanket Indians' and to have farms and raise crops to sell."

"Oh? I understand the squaws do the work in the fields."

"Yah." Gretchen brushed a fly from Hans' face. "The men hunt and fish and the women raise corn, potatoes, squash and pumpkins, and they do the cooking and care for the children."

Amelia laughed. "No wonder they couldn't come to the wedding. They're too busy."

"Amos says the men don't have it as easy as they did before the settlers came. Since we have cut down trees and there are so many of us here, the deer have gone."

"Hm-m-m. I heard Wilhelm mention that he hadn't seen as many deer this summer as last year, and I haven't heard wolves howl this summer." She paused. "See that Indian with the black suit? That's Little Crow. He was at our place last winter just after the babies were born."

"Yah. Amos says he sometimes attends church. He has influence with the tribe." Gretchen shifted Hans to her other arm. "Notice that proud-looking brave talking to Dr. Hess?"

"He's almost handsome. He hardly looks Indian in that blue suit. Who is he?"

"Shaska. He visits the settlement often. He always stops at the Hess cabin." Gretchen smirked.

"To see Phidelia?"

"That's what everyone thinks. He's farming like a white man this year—has nice crops, too."

"Does he have a squaw?"

"Yes. I understand they sometimes have more than one."

Amelia smiled. "If Phidelia still is looking for excitement she may get more than she bargained for with him."

Adolph hovered around the beer barrel. Loud and boisterous, he urged drinks on the guests as he walked unsteadily among them. Reverend Moltke and his friends Dr. Williamson and Reverend Riggs approached the old man and guided him to one side.

"Adolph," Herman Moltke began, "We thought you

understood there wasn't to be any beer at this wedding. The Indians can't handle it."

The old man hiccuped. "It'll do 'em good. They're too stiff and cold. They need a few drinks to loosen them up! Hooray! See what it does for me!"

Amos joined the group. "I suggest that you remove that beer barrel from my wedding party. We don't want trouble and the Indians get out of hand when they drink."

"Aw, Amos. The beer is my gift to your party. You hurt my feelings."

"I'm sorry, but we told you there was to be no beer." He turned to Herman. "Pa, help me pull the beer cart back to August's place."

A sudden crash caused everyone to turn. Mary, axe in hand, stood beside the cart containing the smashed beer barrel which spewed the golden liquid in a gush onto the ground. She hit the shattered barrel another whack. "There's only one way to deal with Adolph! Use force! He don't understand ordinary talk!" She leaned the axe against a tree, stooped to pick up little Charity and strode toward the food-laden table.

A twitter ran through the crowd. Ernst chuckled. "You don't fool with Ma," he said. "Look at the Indians. They've seen her in action before. This story will spread like wildfire through the camps."

"She didn't get rid of that beer any too soon," August said. "My father has no sense when he's drinking."

Wilhelm remarked, "That good-looking fellow, Shaska, can't take his eyes off Phidelia, but Otto doesn't seem to mind."

August laughed. "Maybe he's hoping Shaska will take her off his hands." He shaded his eyes against the sun. "Someone's coming."

A horse-pulled wagon with several passengers

emerged from around a bend in the trail. “It’s Joseph Brown and his family,” Herman announced.

“Hm-m-m,” August mused. “Did someone tell me Mrs. Brown is a Sioux?”

“Yah. A full-blood Sioux, Joseph works well with the Indians. They trust him.”

“Where does he live?” Wilhelm asked.

“A few miles upriver between the Upper and Lower Agencies. He has built a fine stone house for his family,” Herman explained as the Brown wagon stopped.

Dr. Williamson called, “The ceremony’s over. We thought you weren’t coming.”

Joseph Brown took an infant from his wife’s arms as she climbed down and lifted a toddler from the wagon. “We couldn’t get away earlier. My wife’s sister is sick and she stopped at the lodge to fix food for the family.”

Mrs. Brown, an attractive young woman, was dressed in the fashion of the day. August thought she looked no more Indian than—than Phidelia with her dark eyes and hair.

Magdelene Moltke greeted Mrs. Brown warmly. “Come join us,” she said. “You know Mrs. Williamson and Mrs. Riggs?”

“Yes. They visit Joseph and me.” The women made their way to the food table.

While Joseph unhitched and tied his team, the men talked of recent happenings. Herman began, “We’ve been wondering if the treaty with the Indians has been signed.”

Joseph Brown answered, “Yes, though it hasn’t been ratified. The Indians are impatient already. Big promises have been made, you know.”

“We haven’t heard much. Tell us about the treaty.”

Joseph ran his hand through his hair. “On July 23 the Upper Sioux, and on August 5 the Lower Sioux, signed treaties giving to the United States most of their land in the southern part of Minnesota Territory. The government is to pay $1,410,000 in cash annuities over the next fifty years to the Lower Sioux and $1,665,000 in cash and annuities to the Upper Sioux."

Wilhelm grinned. "Sounds like more money than I can understand. The Indians will be rich people."

"Yah," August said. "We Germans deal in nothing beyond a few hundred dollars."

Dr. Williamson nodded. "But the treaties left the Indians only two reservations bordering the Minnesota River. That's all the land they have left from this vast territory." He spread his arms wide.

"From talking with the Indians," Joseph Brown continued, "I find the Upper Sioux generally are satisfied with their reservation because it contains the sites of their old camps. However, the Lower Sioux are less happy."

Reverend Stephen Riggs, a slender smiling man, joined the group. "Some of the chiefs believe they have been cheated," he said. "They say the whites tricked them into signing papers they did not understand. It's true the treaty gives traders and half-breeds claims against the Indians for four hundred thousand dollars, which otherwise would have been paid to the tribes in cash. They resent this."

Joseph Brown continued. "I was at the signing of the treaties. Thirty-five chiefs of the Upper Sioux were present on July 23. Though the plan was explained, I'm sure most of them did not understand they were signing away 24,000,000 acres of choice agricultural land. I'm afraid our government has cheated the Indians."

"We can only hope for the best," Herman said softly. "I hear settlers are pouring into Minnesota by the hundreds this summer. Right here in our area more than fifty have arrived since spring."

Amos shouted, "Come on! It's time to eat! Grab a plate and help yourselves!" He rejoined his bride and together they circulated through the crowd.

Amelia sat with Sarah Schling and Justina Wagner. "It's good to see you again," she said. "I'll always remember how you welcomed us last summer when we got off the lumber barge."

Sarah laughed. "Remember how I fainted when the Indians came to the cabin?" She giggled, "and old Mrs. Winters chased them away with the rifle? I'm not afraid of them anymore." Her daughter Louise and Eddie came to stand by their mothers.

"I like Indians," Eddie said. "They wear pretty blankets."

Louise added, "They have pretty feathers in their hair."

Amelia shuddered as she recalled Philander Prescott's remark about each feather representing a killing performed by the wearer.

Justina Wagner studied Amos and his bride. "They're a nice couple," she said. "Josephine is a teacher. Amos says we'll soon build a school. With all the new people that have moved in, we need one."

Sarah asked, "What should we name our settlement? Any ideas?" When no one answered she continued, "Since most of us are from Ulm, Germany, how do you like New Ulm?"

"That's nice," Amelia said, "though we're not from Ulm, I like it. It's a German name."

Justina smiled. "I like it, too. We should suggest that our husbands bring up the idea at the next town meeting. Let's all push for New Ulm."

Frederick Ketchum and Anna sat by themselves watching the activities. Amelia whispered to Gretchen,

"How is Frederick now?"

Gretchen shook her head. "He's not interested in anything or anyone but Anna." She lowered her voice to a whisper. "I wonder if his mind is just right?" She paused. "Maybe Father Adolph's isn't either. August wonders about them, too." She smiled. "We have an unusual family."

6.

THE YEARS PASSED. German and Scandinavian immigrants continued to settle along the Minnesota River as well as near the upper Mississippi. Land was claimed at an amazing rate. Alexander Ramsey was appointed as the first territorial governor.

The little settlement at New Ulm prospered. The industrious German farmers cleared the land, sowed crops and reaped bountiful harvests. By 1858 most of the claimants had made the long trip to the land office at Winona on the Mississippi to purchase their land.

Missionaries and Indian agents worked with the Sioux to convert them to Christianity and to convince them that the whites way of life was superior to their old ways. Little Crow influenced some of the Indians to attend church services, to give up the Sioux manner of dress in exchange for white man's clothing, to live in houses, and to farm the land for a livelihood. But there was unrest on the reservations.

Within five years after the 1851 treaty in which the Sioux first signed away their land to the United States government, white settlers crowded close to the reservation boundaries. They began to clamor for a reduction of the Indians' territory. The result was that in July of 1858, Little Crow and several Sioux chiefs who hoped for increased government annuity payments, accompanied by their agent Joseph Brown, went to Washington, D. C. to sign still another pair of treaties. In the 1858 treaties the Indians agreed to give up their land on the north side of the Minnesota River, an additional million acres, for a price to be set by the United States Senate. By these treaties the 7000 Indians were left with two slivers of land, each about twenty miles wide and seventy miles long, both bordering on the Minnesota River.

The Indians waited. Two years later Congress appropriated thirty cents an acre in payment. However, before they received any money, the traders who owned stores and gave Indians credit, had to be paid. The result was that the Lower Sioux received little cash and the Upper Sioux would get only half the amount voted by the Senate.

Both the 1851 and 1858 treaties contained stipulations that the Indians should be encouraged to become farmers. Some did try the white mans' way but most of them remained "blanket Indians" meaning they wore blankets and followed their old hunting and fishing way of life. They ridiculed the farmer Indians, and called them "cut hairs" and "breeches Indians." They also resented the whites attempt to cause a split in the tribe about their way of life.

A small military post, Fort Ridgley, had been established by the government. It was located some thirteen miles across the river from New Ulm and consisted of a small number of soldiers who had never been in combat. The Commander of the little fort was Captain Marsh.

Changes had come rapidly in southern Minnesota. Many settlements now were scattered through the territory which became the thirty-second state to enter the Union on May 11, 1858. Henry Sibley was the first governor.

New Ulm boasted of their new school, churches, sawmill and trading post. Most necessities of daily living were available to rural residents. The German farmers had prospered.

At the Winters farm a new clapboard house and barn had been built. Amelia now had chairs and a minimum of furniture. A team of horses had replaced Wilhelm's oxen and a herd of dairy cattle pastured in the fertile field near the barn. Undulating waves of oats, wheat, rye and corn rippled across recently cleared land which had produced only a few crops. Daily, Wilhelm proudly scrutinized his prosperous farm. Yah, he thought, My hard work has paid off. It was a lucky day for us when we left Germany.

Amelia, matronly-appearing at age twenty-eight, again was pregnant. Mary, gray and bent, hung a kettle of potatoes from the crane in the fireplace.

"When's Wilhelm going to get us one of them newfangled cook stoves?" she asked.

"Maybe next year, if we have good crops. He wants to buy more tools first."

"Yah. Yah. Men! Their wants always come first. You'd think he could see that life's not all gravy for you!" She slammed a pot down on the kitchen table.

"Grandma, he's ordered me a sewing machine."

A clatter of footsteps raced down the stairs. "Ma!" Hope shouted. "Are we getting a sewing machine?"

Amelia smiled. "Yah."

"Can we sew on it?" Charity asked.

"When you're a little older. Eight years is too young. You'd put the needle through a finger."

"Aw, we're always too young to do things!" Faith

complained.

"You're not too young to set the table. All of you get busy and help Grandma."

Amelia loved her three little girls. She loved Eddie, too, but at almost ten years of age he preferred his father's company to hers. Soon now she'd have another child. The girls would help care for the new baby. Life had been good to her family. She seized the broom and swept two or three grasshoppers outside.

"Pesky bugs," she murmured.

"They're awful thick," Faith said. "When we walk through the grass they jump in our faces and all over us."

Hope shuddered. "I can't stand it when they get caught in my hair."

Mary shuffled to the fireplace. "We have to keep them outside. They eat holes in clothes."

Charity tossed a braid of blonde hair over her shoulder. "They spit—like—like Adolph."

Amelia laughed. "Adolph spits tobacco juice. Grasshoppers don't like to be handled, so they spit something brown. Maybe that is the way they protect themselves."

"When I got a cabbage from the garden, the outside leaves were full of holes. The grasshoppers were eating on everything," Charity said.

At dinner the family's conversation centered around the invasion of grasshoppers. Helping himself to a generous serving of new potatoes, cooked cabbage and German sausage, Wilhelm said, "They're eating the grain crops. It doesn't look good. Another two or three weeks and the wheat and rye would be ready to cut—but—at this rate, there won't be anything left."

Amelia laid her fork on her plate. "Is it that bad?"

"Yah."

Eddie, a strong husky boy, listened intently. "The corn is covered with them, too. They're stripping the leaves down to the stalks. When I was hoeing this morning they jumped around me like—like corn popping."

The adults became silent. Each one realized the seriousness of the situation and the disastrous possibilities of a complete crop failure.

Faith asked, "Are they as thick everywhere as they are here?"

Eddie took another helping of food. "Little Crow came by on his white horse. He stopped to talk. He says the farmer Indians are worried that the grasshoppers will eat all their crops. Do they ever do that, Pa?"

"Huh?"

Eddie laughed. "Do grasshoppers eat everything green?"

"Yah, I've heard such stories." Wilhelm stared out the window.

The next morning when she opened the door, Amelia screamed. The girls came running and Mary, a shawl about her shoulders, shuffled from her room.

"What's wrong? What's wrong?" they asked.

"Look! Look at that!" Amelia dropped into a chair.

Mary slammed the door. Grasshoppers covered everything. The side of the house seemed alive as the crawling, hopping insects searched for food. The porch was a crawling, swirling mass of hungry insects. The grass in the yard was rapidly disappearing before the hungry horde.

"I'm not going out!" Hope exclaimed.

Faith worried, "They're eating everything. Will they eat us?"

Amelia smiled. "No. They don't like us any more than we like them." She went to the window and peered through the squirming insects toward the barn. Wilhelm, his shoulders slumped, stared toward his grain fields; a black cloud of grasshoppers billowed above the bounteous crop which was fast disappearing. The cloud of insects seemed to surge and swell, rising and tossing in an undulating wave.

"We're helpless against them," Amelia whispered as Wilhelm, followed by Eddie, made their way to the house. Brushing the squirming insects from their clothes, they rushed inside and slammed the door.

"It's bad," Amelia said softly as she dropped into a chair.

"Yah."

The children and Mary were silent. The horde of insects made pecking sounds as they slammed against the window. The girls, frightened at the drawn, anxious faces of the adults, clung to Amelia and Mary.

Finally Eddie said, "What will we eat this winter? What will our horses and cows and pigs eat?"

Wilhelm shook his head. "I don't know."

Amelia's thoughts returned to their first fall in Minnesota. She had been pregnant then, too, and food was scarce. They had existed mostly on bread and fish and wild game. They could do it again if they had to.

Mary muttered, "This cursed country. Just when you think you see daylight, something happens. Grasshoppers! We never had anything like this in Germany. Like I've always said—it was a mistake to come here."

No one answered. Finally Amelia got up. "I'd better get some breakfast." As she cooked cornmeal mush, she wondered how long their supply of cornmeal, wheat and rye flour would last. Even if people had money, the trading post wouldn't be able to meet the demand. And prices would be high.

A gloomy family sat down to their meager breakfast.

"Is this all we have to eat?" Eddie asked.

Mary sputtered, "Hush, child! Be thankful you have this! Before spring you'll be glad to have a dish of corn-meal mush!"

By night the grasshoppers had cleaned Wilhelm's land of every green plant. Two days later they moved eastward where they ravished the settlers' crops. Everyone—Indians, settlers and traders—were depressed, for all were affected by the prospects of a long hard winter.

Traders immediately put in large orders for grocery staples. Everyone expected flour to be expensive and in short supply. Families tightened their belts and prepared for the struggle that lay ahead.

There were few deer left in the area. Fishing also was poor. The blanket Sioux were destitute and the farmer Indians were only slightly more fortunate for they owned a few hogs, cows and chickens. They were given small amounts of food on credit at the trading post. The store owner would take his pay from the pittance the government paid the Sioux for their land.

In December Amelia gave birth to a baby boy who was named Herman. The little fellow was the one bright spot for the family in the winter of 1858-1859. Healthy and happy, he alone knew nothing of deprivation.

While the children were in school, Wilhelm trapped, fished and cut wood. The horses, cows and pigs were forced to shift for themselves in the wilderness. The thin, shaggy-coated animals existed by eating tender buds from brush and low branches of trees, while the hogs searched beneath oak trees for acorns.

Amelia experimented with cooking acorns until they were soft. After the brown shell was removed she mashed and seasoned the pulp which was filling, but not very palatable. Wilhelm trapped and saved the fattest of the catch for the family's food.

"We won't eat many hogs," he said. "If they make it through the winter they'll fatten up in the spring and we'll sell them. We'll need every cent we can get. Our money's getting low."

Mary, from her bedroom, eyed Wilhelm. Finally she took her leather bag from its spot on the bedpost and shoved it beneath the bed. Wilhelm watched her through the open door. He grinned. "Are you afraid I'll steal your precious bag, Grandma?"

"You'd better not try!"

"I wouldn't dare. I remember how you 'most shot the Indian who tried. You're a dangerous woman, Grandma!" he roared with laughter.

The children came in from school. "I'm hungry!" Eddie shouted, "and I'm tired of cold rabbit and cold pancakes for lunch!"

"Me too!" each of the girls echoed.

Amelia put Herman in his cradle. "I wish we had something good to send you. Tomorrow I'll put wild honey on your lunch pancake, and the next day I'll spare a little maple syrup."

Eddie became very sober. "When the Indian children come to school, they don't bring lunches. I don't think they have much to eat. Our teacher says we should share with them."

Chief scratched at the door. When Faith opened it he bounded in carrying a freshly killed rabbit which he dropped at Amelia's feet.

Amelia picked up the rabbit. "Good dog," she said as she patted Chief. She turned to the children. "Do you share with the Indians who don't have lunch?"

The girls stared at the floor while Eddie absently scratched Chief's ears. Finally Hope said softly, "We're hungry, too."

Amelia nodded. "Tomorrow I'll send each of you a

bigger pancake and a little more meat. If the Indians aren't at school, bring the food home for Chief."

Charity rocked Herman's cradle. "He's smiling! He's smiling!" she called. The family rushed to see the baby's first smile. He kicked wildly as sudden smiles flashed across his face.

That evening as they ate their meager supper Eddie said, "Pa, do you know where California is?"

"Yah. Out west. There's gold there."

"Mrs. Moltke told us about it today in geography class. She says hundreds of people are going there in covered wagons. Whole families go to find gold. It's a long ways. It takes weeks and weeks to get there. I wish we could go."

"Yah! Let's go!" Faith exclaimed.

Amelia glanced at Wilhelm who was silently studying his plate. "Children, stop such talk!" she exclaimed. "We own our farm here!"

"But, Ma," Eddie argued. "If we had lots of gold we could buy food so we wouldn't be hungry."

Mary glanced at the eager young faces. Wilhelm still stared at his plate. Could he possibly be considering Eddie's wild suggestion?

"Stop such talk!" Mary demanded. "Wilhelm, put a stop to these wild ideas!"

He raised his eyes to stare into the fireplace. "Yah, Ma and Grandma are right. Our land is free and clear. We've only had one bad year in eight. That's pretty good." He paused. "But if we were just arriving from Germany now—well I'd give the California idea some thought."

7.

SETTLERS CONTINUED POURING INTO MINNESOTA by the hundreds. Brown county south of the river contained New Ulm, and Renville County was north of the Minnesota River. These two areas consisted mainly of people of German extraction. By 1860, New Ulm boasted a population of 635 with more settlers arriving monthly. Fort Ridgely, on the north bank of the river, was a few miles east of the Lower Sioux Agency on the south bank. New Ulm, Fort Ridgely and the Lower Agency all were within twenty miles of one another.

The Upper Sioux Agency, approximately thirty miles up-river from the Lower Agency, now was under the direction of Indian Agent, Thomas J. Galbraith, who replaced Joseph Brown. The Sioux resented the new appointment for under Brown's influence over 200 Sioux had become farmers. Likewise, his Sioux wife had been effective in helping the squaws improve sanitary and health conditions on the reservations.

Bishop Henry Whipple, an Episcopal minister, a friend of missionaries Williamson and Riggs, was well-liked by the Sioux. Little Crow, the most influential of the chiefs, claimed to have been converted to Christianity through the influence of Bishop Whipple, whom the Indians called "Straight Tongue."

Bishop Whipple saw evils and dangers in the Indian policies. He called attention to frauds in the treaty system and in a letter to Lincoln, he advocated its replacement by a plan that would make the Indians wards of the government.

Amos Moltke, likewise, was concerned by the Indian situation. As he sat with Bishop Whipple in the Moltke home, Amos said, "I'm glad you have written to President Lincoln. The Sioux, I'm afraid, are being ignored by the government. We have nearly broken up their tribal relations."

Bishop Whipple adjusted his collar. "You're right. They cannot live without law. Indian Agent Galbraith was appointed under a political spoils system. The Sioux are not stupid. They see what is happening. Joseph Brown should not have been removed as Indian Agent."

Amos nodded. "The cash from their land ought to be paid directly to the Indians. As it flows through the traders' hands, too much sticks to their fingers. We both know that Storekeeper Andrew Myrick takes advantage of the Indians. He charges them any amount he wishes for things they're forced to buy on credit."

Bishop Whipple said, "In my letter to Lincoln I suggested that the government replace the present agreement with a plan to provide the Sioux with more goods, seeds, farm implements and schools to make them self-supporting."

"That sounds good, but the government is so involved in the Civil War that I doubt if much attention is given to the Indian problem."

Bishop Whipple sighed. "The North and South have been fighting since last April—almost a year. I'm sure our Indian problem seems of little importance when compared to the struggle to preserve the Union."

"Yah. Last spring when Lincoln called for 75,000 volunteers young Minnesota men by the hundreds signed up. They believed enlisting was a patriotic duty and that if the Union forces were large, they could defeat the Confederates and end the war in one battle. But it hasn't worked that way. I'm afraid the country is in for a long, bloody struggle."

The bishop walked to the window. "Nearly all of our young men under thirty years of age have gone to war. Many of them will not return. I can understand that influential men in Washington are engrossed in plans to save the Union, but I wish they would give a little attention to helping the Indians."

"Yah. I guess the welfare of 7,000 Sioux is not very important when compared to preventing the destruction of the Union."

"That's true, but Amos, some of the chiefs say the Indian people are angry at the treatment they are receiving. John Other Day and his Sioux wife are Christians, as is Little Crow. Shakopee is no friend of the whites though he is married to the daughter of Philander Prescott's Indian wife. There is much unrest, Amos."

"I know. There are bad feelings between the blanket Indians and the ones who have become farmers," Amos mused. "The farmer Indians are ridiculed and tormented by the blanket Indians for living like white men. They are called "dutchmen," thus likening the farmer Indians to us. They consider Germans unwarlike and they don't admire our way of life. Around here the blanket Indians steal pigs and cattle and raid the corn fields of the Sioux farmers. It's a bad situation—a split in the Indian community."

The bishop nodded. "The Indian medicine men, too, are hostile to Christianity. Their attitude and bitterness has great influence on the blanket Indians."

Amos stretched. "I doubt if it will come to violence, but if anything should happen, we're fortunate to have Fort Ridgely nearby."

Outside in the street a crowd gathered about the covered wagon of Peddler John Henning and his wife. The eccentric old man and his domineering mate appeared biannually in many of the settlements. Signs were printed in bold white letters on the sides of his wagon. HENNING'S HEALTH TONIC CURES ILLS, FITS, FEVERS, RHEUMATIZ, DYSENTERY, CATARRH AND CON-

SUMPTION. On the back of the wagon another sign read, BUY A BOTTLE OF HEALTH TONIC AND SEE THE LONGEST BEARD IN THE COUNTRY.

The Saturday afternoon crowd was jovial. Children circulated among the blanket Indians and white settlers who called greetings to the strange old couple as they tied their team to a hitching post.

August Ketchum shouted, "How long is your beard now, John?"

The short old man patted a black cloth sack in which he stored his beard inside his clothes. "Longer than last time I was here! When we get our tent up, I'll show you —if you buy a bottle of tonic."

Pudgy Mrs. Henning repeatedly gave orders to her husband. "Stop gabbing and get the tent out! Here, put it on this side of the wagon! Hurry up, or the farmers will go home 'fore you are ready!"

The crowd snickered and shouted. Wilhelm yelled, "Why don't you get Andrew Myrick to sell your tonic in his store?"

Henning paused to adjust his hat. "Can't do it. I can sell all the tonic I can make myself!" He pounded a tent stake into the ground. Adolph muttered, "Didn't cure me. I still got rheumatiz."

"How many bottles did you use?"

"Two."

" 'Twasn't enough. You have to take it until you're cured. Didn't it help while you was taking it?"

"Yeah. I felt good—kind of happy."

John poked the black bag down inside his trousers. "That's 'cause your body knew you was gettin' help. Better buy a dozen bottles and see what it does."

At last the tent was up and Henning climbed in to stand at the front of the wagon. Mrs. Henning had disappeared inside. "Friends," he began, "My tonic will cure any ills you have. It will make you feel younger. Aches and pains, fevers, tumors, dysentery, upset stomach—they'll all disappear."

"Didn't cure smallpox when my boys had it!" A whiskered settler called. "They was sicker than dogs. Thought they'd die. Gave them the tonic 'till it was gone, but it didn't cure 'em."

"You used it up before they got well?"

"Well—yah."

Henning nodded. "Same old story. You didn't buy enough tonic. But it likely helped 'cause they got well. Many don't, as you know."

He continued. "How many found they felt better—happier—while they was taking the tonic?"

Wilhelm shouted, "My old grandmother was happy as a lark while the medicine lasted. When it was gone she took to finding fault again."

"Yah, it works that way. You need it every day for best results."

Mrs. Henning appeared with a basket of bottles filled with a pale amber fluid. John continued, "My wife will sell you the tonic. It is 25 cents for a large bottle. Buy plenty for we won't be back for some time. Line up at the back of the wagon and she will take your money."

He paused as the crowd shifted. Eleven-year-old Eddie Winters called, "When will we see your beard?"

"Every person who buys tonic can come in the tent. I'll not only show you the longest beard in the country, but we have something new. A performing monkey. He puts on quite a show."

Frederick and Anna Ketchum joined the line behind the wagon. "If I buy the medicine, can my daughter see the monkey?"

"Yah, for one penny. Children with parents who have bought tonic can see the show for one penny." He looked at Anna, a beautiful blonde thirteen-year-old girl. "That your daughter 'side you?"

Frederick smiled broadly as he put his arm about Anna's shoulders. "Yah."

"She don't look like a child, but I'm feeling generous today. Anyone who buys tonic can bring their children to see my beard and the monkey for a penny apiece."

Wilhelm's triplets and Eddie looked expectantly at their father. "Yah. We'll buy some tonic for Grandma and you can see the show. Too bad Hermie's not here. He'd like to see it—'course he's only two. Maybe another time."

The crowd continued to grow as word spread of the Henning's arrival. Shaska, a handsome figure in white man's clothing, made his way to Phidelia Hess' side. Her dark eyes flashed a welcome as he approached.

"Where is Otto?" Shaska asked.

Phidelia tossed her head. "Reading his boring books. Let's each buy a bottle of tonic so we can see the show!" She lowered her voice to a whisper. "Otto says it's no good. He says it makes people happy 'cause it's whisky and water, but I want to see the show!"

Shaska nodded. "Whisky? I'll buy some."

Phidelia giggled like a girl in her teens as she took his arm and guided him to the line behind the wagon.

Elizabeth Winters and Josephine Moltke stood at one side studying the crowd and observing the carnival-like atmosphere. Elizabeth motioned toward Phidelia and Shaska. "They're thicker than thieves."

Josephine nodded. "Otto don't seem to mind. Maybe she's easier to live with when she has an outside interest."

Elizabeth lowered her voice to a whisper. "There's gossip about Frederick and Anna. They act more like a young married couple than father and daughter."

"He built a nice house for her."

"Yah. Ernst thinks when Anna began to develop Frederick wanted to be alone with her—if you know what I mean."

"I know. People here have strict morals. If they were convinced something wrong was going on there, they'd tar and feather Frederick and ride him out of town on a rail."

Elizabeth nodded. "But no one knows for sure, any more than they know about Phidelia and Shaska."

Faith and Hope skipped to Elizabeth's side. "Grandma, we're going to see the monkey and the old man's long beard!" Faith exclaimed.

"That's nice. I'll want to hear about it."

Hope pulled on her sister's arm. "Come on! Pa and Eddie and Charity are going in the tent."

The girls arrived, breathless, to enter the little canvas structure. Wilhelm sent the children to the front where they could see. John Henning stood on a two-foot-high box for better viewing by adults at the back.

He began. "Many years ago I vowed to grow the longest beard in the country. I have succeeded. Those of you who have seen my beard before will notice that today it is longer and fuller than ever." He paused.

Wilhelm shouted, "John, do you use your tonic on it?"

Everyone laughed and the old man chuckled. "I haven't, but I think I'll try. It might even grow hair on bald heads. "Then, slowly and dramatically he pulled the long black sack from his clothes. "This takes time," he explained, " 'cause the end of the sack goes down my pant leg to my shoe top." At last the sack hung to the floor in front of the two-foot-high box.

Still moving slowly for greater effect, the old man gradually stripped the black bag from his beard; then, shaking and fluffing the mass of whiskers, he finally dropped it. The tip of the beard touched the floor.

Adults chuckled and children's eyes were huge as the old peddler kept up the chatter. Finally he said, "Now for the monkey act."

Mrs. Henning, who seemed as broad as she was tall, entered the tent carrying a flashily dressed monkey. As soon as she put him down he tipped his little red hat and held out his hand.

"What does he want?" Eddie asked the old woman.

"Pennies. Give him a penny and he'll thank you."

Children rushed to their fathers for pennies. As each child handed the monkey a coin, he tipped his hat, bowed and dropped the money into a little pouch tied about his waist; he then proceeded to another child. The tent rang with children's laughter.

Finally the show was over. Outside several Indian children looked longingly toward the tent. "Please, Pa," Eddie said. "Could we give them pennies so they can see the monkey?"

"Hm-m-m. Their fathers didn't buy any tonic, but—. I bought two bottles for Grandma. I'll take them in."

The ragged little boys in the manner of the Sioux, did not verbalize their thanks, but the sparkling black eyes plainly expressed their happiness.

And so ended a happy day in New Ulm.

BOOK 4

The Holocaust

1.

THE WINTER OF 1861–1862 was a time of misery and despair in the lodges of the Indians. Because of poor crops the previous year and the failure of the government to provide sufficient relief supplies, the Indians were near starvation. Though they tried to pursue their old hunting and fishing culture during the long hard winter, they were unsuccessful for little wild game remained on the reservations. Stoically they suffered physically while internally seething with resentment at what they regarded as the government's neglect and the white man's attempt to divide the tribe by favors granted the farmer Indians.

In the lodges anger was expressed that several hundred Sioux had been persuaded by the Indian Agent to become farmers. These Indians were rewarded with cooperation and assistance. The blanket Indians contemptuously referred to the farmer Indians as "cut-hairs" and "breeches Indians" because of their change to the white man's style of dress and general appearance. Many of them had accepted Christianity. They also were displeased that Indian Agent Joseph Brown had been replaced by Thomas J. Galbraith, a newcomer to the frontier and a man unfamiliar with Sioux culture.

Another source of displeasure was the fact that the government annuity for their land, when paid, was sent to the traders who deducted any amount they desired for supplies which families had bought on credit. The result was that little if any actual cash was left to be distributed to the destitute Indians.

In the meantime the German settlers happily continued their lives. Their hard work and frugal way of life resulted in the prosperity they had dreamed of when they left Germany. New buildings had replaced the make-shift log cabins and barns of earlier days. Herds of dairy cattle pastured near the remaining woods and horses had replaced the original oxen for farm work.

Wilhelm now owned a McCormick reaping machine which greatly simplified the harvesting of wheat, rye, oats and barley. Though the yield had been cut in half by drought in 1861, his family had not suffered.

The people of New Ulm and the surrounding area no longer feared the Indians who walked the streets as they wandered through the settlement. Always stoic and quiet to the point of unfriendliness the blanket Sioux were accepted as being dirty, lazy and strange, but harmless. On the other hand the farmer Indians were rewarded with the loans of tools and exchange of work.

Little Crow, Traveling Hail, White Dog, Big Eagle, Chief Akepa, John Other Day and Paul Mazakutemani, known as Little Paul, all seemed to prefer the white mans' way of life. These men either were chiefs or leaders among the Sioux. All of them were known to the veteran missionaries Thomas Williamson and Stephen Riggs as well as the Moltke family. Several Indians occasionally attended religious services at one of the area churches. Early in August the Episcopal missionary Reverend Samuel Hinman, whose congregation had just completed a new church at the Lower Agency, warned people at the Upper Agency that he was concerned about unrest on the reservations. Generally, however, the whites were uninterested in the problems of the Indians.

Meanwhile, like a contagious disease, Sioux resentment and anger toward the whites spread from camp to camp throughout the counties of southern Minnesota.

2.

POLITICIAN THOMAS J. GALBRAITH replaced Joseph Brown as the Sioux Indian Agent in 1861. Though he was a man of character and ability he lacked understanding of the Indian culture. Brown sat in the new, government-built stone warehouse at the Lower Agency with Thomas Galbraith. He attempted to prepare Galbraith for his responsibility in a difficult situation.

Brown spoke with knowledge gained through years of association with the Indians. "Tom," he began, "I'm going to be honest with you. Over the years we have made progress in converting the Indians to our way of life. Several hundred men, mostly heads of families, have given up the blanket, had their hair cut, put on white mans' clothes and they've moved onto land allotted to them by the 1858 treaty. At least seven hundred are farmer Indians. They will become useful citizens. We hope in a few years that the farmers will outnumber the blanket Indians.

Galbraith smiled. "You've made great progress with them, Joe." He leaned back in his chair and puffed contentedly on his pipe.

"We've made *some* progress. They have respected my judgment, in part, because my wife is a Sioux."

"I know."

"Jane Williamson is a teacher at the mission school. She says more of the men are working in the fields—the women formerly grew the crops—and the women are learning housekeeping. Many homes now have beds in place of dirty buffalo or deerskin. Instead of a group with wooden bowls and spoons seated around a kettle of stew, the families sit about a table with well-cooked food, sometimes with bread and butter."

Galbraith asked, "But these improvements are found

only among the farmer Indians?"

Brown nodded. "There is great unrest among the blanket Indians. There is much teasing and stealing done by them. They ridicule and torment the ones who are adopting our way of life. The blanket Indians steal pigs, raid corn fields and drive off cattle from the farmer Indians' property. It's a bad situation. The families settled on farms are lonely among the seven thousand still-wild Sioux."

Galbraith rubbed his forehead. "I hadn't realized—it doesn't sound good."

Brown continued. "Then, the medicine men are hostile toward both the missionaries and the Indians who have left the old way of life. They are angry and bitter. They have great influence, Tom."

Galbraith nodded. Brown went on. "The traders, too, are a part of the problem. Generally they are opposed to what they call our 'civilization experiment.' Many of the storekeepers take advantage of the people who are at the mercy of the traders."

"But it is government policy to send their annuity of money and goods to the storekeeper who balances his account with each family before they receive their share."

"That's the way it is. You can understand why the blanket Indians are angry. Then, the payments generally are late. There is one due now, but who knows when it will come? Washington is occupied with the Civil War. I think the Indian problem doesn't concern the government very much."

Galbraith stood up. "As I go about the country I don't see many young white men. They have joined the Union Army."

"That's right. There are very few men under thirty left around here. Getting back to the Indians—I fear for them when winter comes, for the cut-worms have destroyed their corn. As you know, Tom, corn is their chief food."

Galbraith stared from the window. "I'll do what I can. I hope it's enough to keep them from starving."

3.

BECAUSE OF THE DRY WEATHER and the 1861 invasion of cutworms, the Indians' corn crop was a complete failure. By the middle of December the people were starving. Cold, ragged and hungry, the very young and the old and infirm were dying. Agent Tom Galbraith took measures to buy flour and pork on credit to feed the ones most desperately in need of help. From the middle of December 1861 to the following April they depended on assistance without which many more would have died.

With the opening of the new season the Indians planted extensively. Then they waited for payment of the government money.

Near the end of June Agent Galbraith received a delegation of the Upper Agency Indians in his office. Standing with folded arms, the Sioux braves stared into Galbraith's eyes. A few were farmer Indians in white mans' clothes, but most were blanket Indians. Little Crow, the spokesman, stepped forward. In broken English he stated his case.

"The prairie grass is high enough for pasture, so it is time for our payment. Always we wait. Our squaws and children are hungry. We must have food. We have eat all our dogs. There is no game on our land. When we hunt on the white man's land they say, 'Get out! Hunt on reservation!' When do we get our government money?"

Galbraith nervously fingered an arrowhead which lay on his desk. Finally he looked up into the angry eyes facing him. "Soon," he promised. "Have no fear. The Great White Father in Washington will send the payment before July 20."

Little Crow stepped closer to Galbraith's desk. "We are hungry now! July 20 is three weeks. We need food now—there is food in the warehouse!"

"No. No. The provisions and money have not come yet. They will be here July 20. We helped you through the winter. Now the food is gone." Lamely he suggested, "Try to find roots and plants that you can eat."

As one, the group turned and silently strode from the building.

As the summer progressed the caldron simmered, for the Indians' anger and dissent toward the white man continued to ferment as their situation increased in severity. Conditions worsened rapidly after delivery of government provisions was made and the warehouse at the Upper Agency was well stocked. Gradually word spread through the reservations that the Santee Sioux would go in a huge group to Agent Galbraith to demand that the provisions be distributed.

On July 14 when he returned from a visit to the Lower Agency, Galbraith was astounded to discover that five thousand Santee Sioux were camped a short distance from the agency. Bewildered and perplexed by the enormity of the problem he sent for Chiefs Little Crow, Wabasha, Big Eagle and Traveling Hail, all of whom had formerly been cooperative.

Silently the chiefs entered Galbraith's office. He began. "The food has arrived as I'm sure you know, but the money has not come. As in the past, we are not allowed to give out the food until the money arrives. As always, we will pass out both at the same time. Surely it will be here very soon."

Little Crow's face flushed. "Mr. Galbraith," he began, "I am a Santee chief. My father and grandfather were Santee Sioux chiefs. I am sixty years old. I signed both treaties with the Great White Father and agreed, for my people, to live on the reservation. We have done as we promised though we know, now, that we were tricked out of our land and the money promised for the land. I went to Washington to see Great Father, President Buchanan. I gave up wearing breechcloths and blankets for trousers and brass-buttoned jackets. I have joined the Episcopal Church, built a house and started to farm."

He paused and motioned toward the chiefs standing behind him. "We have tried to live in peace with the white man, though he has broken his promise to us. Now five thousand of our people have come to you to ask that you give us food from the warehouse." His dark eyes bored into those of the government agent.

Galbraith nervously fingered the arrowhead on his desk. There was a long period of silence. Finally he said, "I'm sorry. I am not allowed to pass out food until your money comes from Washington so you can pay for it."

Big Eagle stepped forward. "Mr. Galbraith," he began. "Since white men came here and we signed treaties giving up our land, the traders and storekeepers have hovered around like buzzards over a carcass of a deer. We have been cheated out of most of the money for our land. Your white men have abused our women in a certain way. They have disgraced them. You have laughed at us and treated us unkindly. Many of you whites say by your actions, 'I am better than you.' We do not believe any men in the world are better than the Santee Sioux. Now we ask only that you give us provisions to keep us from starving."

Galbraith fidgeted. "But—but the money hasn't come."

Wabasha stepped forward beside Little Crow and Big Eagle. "I have learned to keep accounts," he began. "When the money comes from Washington, the traders claim it and whatever amount they have written in their accounts against us, your government agents pay them. I can figure, Mr. Galbraith. Our records are many dollars less than the traders' accounts.

"Now, Mr. Galbraith, the Santee Sioux have gathered on the Yellow Medicine River," he motioned, "to collect our money so we can exchange it for food. We hear stories that the Great Council (Congress) in Washington has spent all the gold fighting the Civil War and cannot send any money to us. It is because we are starving that we come begging."

Again there was silence.

Traveling Hail had not spoken. Silently he turned and left the room to be followed by Little Crow, Big Eagle and Wabasha.

Filled with frustration and fear, Agent Galbraith sent a rider to Fort Ridgely on the north bank of the Minnesota River thirty miles to the southeast. Frantically he appealed for help.

4.

THE DAY AFTER HIS CONFERENCE with the Indian chiefs, Galbraith reluctantly issued a small amount of food which was delivered to the Indian camp. A short time later a guard of one hundred soldiers under Lieutenant Timothy J. Sheehan arrived from Fort Ridgely. He and Galbraith conferred daily. They heard numerous reports of starvation and misery in the Indian camp. Amos Moltke and his wife Josephine visited the camp and later reported to Agent Galbraith.

"Tom," Amos began, "you have to move or there will be serious trouble. Five thousand people require a lot of food. You sent them only a pittance. The squaws have gathered every edible plant for miles around. There are no more. The men are desperate. A human will take just so much before he rebels. Unless something is done very soon, there will be trouble. Indian men can be cruel and savage when they are pushed too far. I sense that they are turning against all whites. I have grown up with many of these people but they are turning against Josephine and me. Right now I believe they see all whites as enemies."

"What can I do? My orders say no food until the annuity arrives from Washington."

Amos snorted angrily. "For God's sake, Tom! Forget your orders! Feed them! Don't you understand? They are dying of starvation!"

On August 4 the situation came to a head. At daybreak five hundred Sioux, mounted and on foot, surrounded the infantry camp. One hundred soldiers of the Fifth Minnesota Regiment under Lieutenant Sheehan waited in readiness should violence erupt.

While most of the Indians distracted the soldiers as they milled about the perimeter of the infantry camp, a short distance away other young Sioux carried a log to the agency warehouse where they forcefully battered the wooden door until it splintered. Yelling wildly, they poured inside, seized bags of flour and dashed toward their camp. Amid great confusion, many others rushed into the provision-laden warehouse. Shouting, they dashed outside with booty to meet a loaded howitzer aimed at the open door. They stopped.

Lieutenant Sheehan walked boldly through the silent crowd toward the agency warehouse. When he reached the steps he paused to face the crowd. "I am going to talk with Agent Galbraith. If any of you remove more supplies from the warehouse before I return, my men will open fire. I warn you, if there is more stealing, there will be dead men." He disappeared inside as the Indians murmured among themselves.

Pale with fear, Galbraith paced in his office. Lieutenant Sheehan entered. The Indian agent gasped, "They're mad. Can you hold them?"

"No, not without bloodshed. They're desperate. Galbraith, you have no choice. Either you give them food, or there will be violence."

"But my orders—"

"Damn your orders! If you don't give them provisions, they will take everything in the warehouse. They're waiting for me to return. If I go back with your refusal, all hell will break loose." He paused. "And you know who will be the first one they attack."

Galbraith mopped his perspiring brow. "What do you suggest I do?"

"Give them pork and flour so they can have a decent meal. Arrange a conference with the Sioux leaders. I will send for my superior, Captain John Marsh. If we move fast perhaps we can prevent open warfare." The lieutenant paused. "You must face them and tell them of the plan. Do you agree?"

"They'll kill me. You tell them."

Sheehan snorted. "Pull yourself together, man. Indians hate a coward. I'll go out there with you, but you must speak to them."

Galbraith hesitated. Through the open windows the buzz of angry voices grew louder.

Sheehan pushed Galbraith toward the door. A moment later the two men faced the crowd. As the Indian Agent started to speak, the braves became quiet, their angry eyes boring into his face.

"I've—I've decided to give you enough pork and flour so everyone can eat." He paused, expecting a response. When none came, he continued. "I will call a conference with your chiefs for—for tomorrow. We will try to work something out until your government money arrives."

A young brave shouted, "You said it would be here by July 20. Today is August 4!"

Perspiration dripped from Galbraith's face. "I know, but I will give you food now. The money will come. If you will take what I give you and go back to camp, we will try to work something out with your chiefs tomorrow." He turned and went inside, hopeful that a disaster had been averted.

Captain John Marsh rode up from Fort Ridgely two days later. Marsh, Galbraith, Little Crow, Wabasha, Big Eagle, Shakopee and Traveling Hail conferred in the Indian agent's office.

Through the influence of Marsh and the other whites, Galbraith had previously been prevailed upon to be lenient with the rebellious Indians. Now he glanced briefly at each chief—all were again dressed in the clothing of the blanket Indians. His heart thumped. Each feather in their hair indicated a human killing. Though it was a hot day they held their blankets tightly about their shoulders. These men would kill at the drop of a hat. He must be careful.

Shakopee and Big Eagle still wore their hair in braids. In each headband several feathers were worn at a jaunty angle. Chief Wabasha, Traveling Hail and Little

Crow had been regarded as friendly chiefs, but in full Indian dress with the tell-tale feathers in their hair, Galbraith was apprehensive.

"My friends," he began, "we have already given you food. We will give you more at once if you will go back to your villages without further trouble and wait until the money comes."

Chief Wabasha said, "We want peace with the white man."

Big Eagle and Shakopee were silent.

Traveling Hail said, "If you do what you say, we will try to convince our young men to be peaceful. They are angry."

Galbraith glanced at Little Crow who said, "My people from the Lower Agency are not here. You gave us supplies in June. You promised that more food would be given to us, but you have broken your promise. We are hungry. What will you do for us?"

Galbraith coughed nervously. "I will talk to Trader Andrew J. Myrick. I'll try to get him to give you credit until the government money comes."

The old chief glared at Agent Galbraith. "Talk does not feed us! We must have credit!"

"All right. All right. I promise you will be given credit." He studied each sullen face. "Will you agree to go back to your people and tell them what I have said?"

Little Crow, Wabasha and Traveling Hail nodded. Shakopee and Big Eagle silently stared at the perspiring agent.

"Trust me, we will take care of you," he said.

Traveling Hail asked, "When will we get the provisions?"

"At once. Starting today." Galbraith sighed with relief as the group silently left his office.

The situation remained tense during the next three

days while provisions were distributed; then the Indians returned to their homes and all was quiet.

Little Crow waited in his village near the Lower Agency. Finally, ten days later, Galbraith arranged a meeting for August 15. Early that morning Little Crow with a large group of Indians met with four traders, including Andrew J. Myrick. From the beginning every person sensed the tenseness of the situation. Galbraith began. "We are here to discuss the Sioux demands for credit." He directed an explanation to the traders. "We expect the government funds will arrive very soon. Then you will be paid in full. They need food now. What is your answer to them?" He waited.

Then, in turn each trader shouted, "No!" "No!" "No!" "No!"

Angered by yet another broken promise, Little Crow faced Galbraith and spoke for his people. "We have waited a long time. The money is ours, but we cannot get it. We have no food, but here are these stores filled with food. We ask that you, the agent, make some arrangement so that we can get food at the stores, or else we may take our own way to keep ourselves from starving. When men are hungry they help themselves."

Contemptuously Trader Andrew J. Myrick replied, "So far as I am concerned, if they are hungry let them eat grass or their own dung!"

Andrew Myrick's words resulted in an outburst of angry shouts. Then, as one man, they followed Little Crow and stalked outside. Little Crow suggested they go home.

Inwardly furious, to his people the old chief appeared calm. They watched him walk away with a confident step and his head held high.

But Little Crow's mind was in turmoil. For years he had tried to keep the treaties, to follow the advice of the white man and to lead his people to their way of life. But he had lost everything. His people had depended on him to relieve their misery. For some time he had sensed they were turning away from him as though he was responsible for their misfortunes. At a meeting in early summer the Lower Agency Sioux had accused him of betraying them when he had signed away their land by treaties. And—and they had chosen Traveling Hail to be their speaker. If only he could have persuaded Galbraith and the traders to give the people food, they would have respected him again. But he had failed. He was old and no longer could guide his people.

As the old man walked, he absently rubbed his aching arms and wrists which always were covered with long sleeves. His mind went back to his youth when he had received serious wounds while leading his braves in battle. His arms had been left withered and scarred by the badly healed wounds.

Little Crow meditated as he walked. He regularly attended the Episcopal Church where Reverend Samuel Hinman was pastor. Now he was torn between old Indian beliefs and Christianity.

Confused and depressed, the old farmer Indian disappeared into his new brick house.

5.

ON SUNDAY, AUGUST 17, approximately thirty miles north of New Ulm near the settlement of Acton, four Indians who lived far to the southwest of the Minnesota River were on their way home from an unsuccessful hunting trip. About noon they reached the Robinson Jones home which was a combination post office, lodging place and store. The Santees were acquainted with Jones and his wife.

The Indians, Brown Wing, Breaking Up, Killing Ghost and Runs-Against-Something-When-Crawling were hot, tired and hungry. A short distance from the Jones home Brown Wing discovered a hen's nest near a fence. "Eggs!" he called as he took several. "We have something to eat!"

Killing Ghost said, "Put them back. They belong to the white man."

Brown Wing angrily dashed the eggs to the ground. "You are a coward! You are afraid of the white man. Though you are half starved, you are afraid to take even an egg from him!"

Killing Ghost bristled. "I am not a coward! I'm not afraid of the white man, and—and—to show you I'm not afraid—I—I will go to the house and shoot Jones! Do you dare go with me?"

Brown Wing sputtered. "I'll go with you but you won't dare shoot Jones!"

The four Indians made their way to the house. They entered the front room where the store was located. Robinson Jones, a man in his mid-forties greeted them. "What can I do for you?"

Breaking Up said, "We want whisky."

Jones smiled. "I'm sorry. I don't have any. We had a wedding celebration in the neighborhood yesterday, and the whisky's gone."

The Indians did not answer but sullenly lingered about the store waiting for Killing Ghost to make good his threat to shoot Jones. As they loitered Jones' two adopted children, Clara Wilson, age fifteen and her eighteen-month-old brother came into the store.

"Clara," Jones said, "I'll leave you in charge of the store. I have to go to Howard's place to talk with him. Business here is slow. Do you mind?"

The attractive girl smiled. "Of course not. Mother Jones went there earlier. I'll have dinner ready when you both get back."

"Clara will get whatever you need," Jones explained to the Indians as he left. They grunted.

When he was a short distance down the road the breechcloth-clad men followed him. Walking together, they talked as they approached the Howard Baker home.

"Covered wagon in yard. More settlers," Walking Ghost commented.

Jones nodded. "They're the Websters, a young couple from Michigan. They're living in their covered wagon while they look for land."

Breaking Up suddenly asked, "You shoot at target with us?"

Jones smiled. "Sure." He took a paper from his pocket and fastened it to a tree near the Baker home. Then he called Viranus Webster and his son-in-law, Howard Baker. Mrs. Jones and Mrs. Webster watched.

The three white men competed and lost in the contest against the Indians who immediately reloaded their guns. Webster joked, "Next time will be different." He leaned his gun against the wagon beside Jones' and Baker's.

Suddenly the Indians turned on the unarmed men. In a blazing blast of gunfire they instantly killed Mr. and Mrs. Jones, Webster and Baker.

Petrified with fear, Mrs. Webster hid in the covered wagon and was not molested. Mrs. Baker seized her small child and jumped into the cellar. After a time the terrified women left and made their way several miles to the home of another settler. In shock, they gasped out the news of the massacre. Several men from the neighborhood set out for Forest City, nearly twenty miles to the east. There, a group of men immediately started for the Jones house which they reached late at night.

Clara Wilson's body lay in the yard before the store. The little boy was unhurt but hungry. The Indians were gone. Frightened by the enormity of their crime they rode at breakneck speed on four stolen horses toward their village.

These murders committed on August 17 set in motion a series of disastrous events in southern Minnesota.

6.

SUNDAY WAS USUALLY a day for churchgoing and relaxation at the Winters home, but on this day plans were being made for an unusual happening. Wilhelm and Amelia with their twelve-year-old triplets were preparing for a trip to Mankato.

"How long will it take to get there?" Faith asked Wilhelm.

"It's twenty-five or thirty miles and we can't travel fast with a wagon. We'll take our time and come back about Wednesday."

Amelia's smile revealed a missing front tooth. "It will be good to have a change. I want to get into some nice stores again."

"Ma," Charity asked, "Could we each have a store bought dress, just for Sundays?"

"Yah, Ma, could we? We've never had a store bought dress!" Hope added.

Mary limped into the kitchen, grumbling. "All children are the same. It's always 'gimme this' or 'gimme that'." She patted Eddie's shoulder. "Only this one's different. Girls, you don't hear Eddie complaining. He would like to go to Mankato, too, but he and I and Hermie will look after things here while you're gone, won't we boys?"

"Yah, Grandma. I'm fourteen years old. I can do a man's work, can't I Pa?"

"Almost. You're a great help to me. But you can have a vacation while we're gone. Just do the milking, feed the hogs and Ma's chickens. The rest of the time you can fish."

"Can Hermie and I go to New Ulm on Monday? John Henning and his monkey will be there." Eddie laughed. "I want to see if his beard has grown."

"Yah. I'll give you some money. You might buy Grandma a couple bottles of his tonic." Wilhelm grinned. "It sure makes her feel good, don't it Grandma?"

"Humph! Make fun of me if you want, but I know it helps my rheumatiz."

"Children," Amelia broke in, "you must hurry if you're going to church. Pa and I won't go today but Eddie will drive Grandma and the rest of you in the surrey." She guided four-year-old Herman to the sink where she carefully parted and combed his hair. She stepped back to inspect him. "There. You look like a little gentleman."

"Aw, I don't like being dressed up. I can't climb trees, and these shoes hurt my feet."

Fifteen minutes later Wilhelm and Amelia were alone. "The house is so quiet," Amelia remarked. "I can't remember when the two of us have been by ourselves. Do you think Grandma and the boys will miss us?"

Wilhelm laughed. "You sound as though you're

homesick already. Don't you want to get that new cook stove?"

"Yah. I can't wait, but I'll miss the boys and Grandma." She paused. "You know, we can be thankful. We have nice children, a good farm and buildings, and we've never had a death in our family. We've had very sick children with smallpox, scarlet fever and measles, but they all got better."

"Yah." Wilhelm hesitated. "I haven't told you what I heard in New Ulm yesterday."

"Oh?"

"It's Anna and Frederick."

"She's a beautiful girl. She must be about fifteen. With her blonde hair, blue eyes and soft pink complexion, Frederick already must have boys calling at his place to see her."

Wilhelm snorted. "The man's no good!"

Amelia hung her dish towel to dry. "He's strange. He's always been strange since Harriet and Lewis died on that river boat with cholera. The way he's hung onto Anna isn't natural. I hope she doesn't marry someone just to get away from her father."

"Maybe she likes it that way. I've never seen her pay attention to any of the boys. Eddie likes her, but she has eyes only for Frederick."

"Eddie! He's a child!"

"He's only a year younger than she is." Wilhelm continued. "I've waited to tell you until we were alone. Anna is pregnant."

"What? Who?"

"Yah. That's why we haven't seen her this summer. Frederick's kept her inside. She's about nine months along. Frederick's the father of his daughter's child."

Amelia dropped into a rocker. "The poor little girl. Are you sure?"

"People in New Ulm are sure enough so they tarred and feathered both of them before they rode them out of town on a rail!"

"Oh Wilhelm. That poor child. What will happen to her?"

"I don't know. Neither of them had any clothes."

"They're wandering around out there covered with tar and feathers?"

"Yah. Maybe one of the missionaries or ministers will take them in. Personally, I don't care. I think they got what they deserved."

7.

RIDING THEIR STOLEN HORSES at breakneck speed on the evening of August 17, the four Indians who had committed the murders near Acton, dashed into their village at Rice Creek. They immediately went to tell the headman, Red Middle Voice, what had happened.

He listened, his expression somber. Finally he spoke. "You did a foolish thing. You are in deep trouble. You killed white women. Soldiers will come and all of us will be punished for what you have done. They will stop payment of the government money."

The four braves silently stared at the ground as Red Middle Voice continued. "The Lower Sioux will turn against us. Already they say we are 'outsiders' because we, the Upper Sioux, have married Lower Sioux women." He paused, deep in thought.

At last Red Middle Voice said, "We will go downstream to Shakopee's village and tell him what has happened. He's no friend of the white man. We will ask his advice."

Riding down the Minnesota River some eight miles, the five Rice Creek Indians entered Shakopee's camp. Hurriedly, Red Middle Voice explained the situation whereupon Shakopee called his braves together. Again the story of the slaughter at Acton was repeated.

"The white man will make war on all of us," Shakopee said. "What should we do?"

The braves murmured among themselves. Finally a tall young man said, "We should strike first."

Another man spoke. "We must fight the white men. They are not friends of the Sioux."

As the discussion continued, the decision to make war was unanimous. However, young Chief Shakopee realized that two small bands of Indians would quickly be defeated by the white man's soldiers at Fort Ridgely.

After more discussion, Shakopee and Red Middle Voice decided to call a council of chiefs at Little Crow's village which was a few miles farther down the river near the Lower Agency.

Shakopee and Red Middle Voice planned. Shakopee declared, "Little Crow is the only chief who can lead us in an all-out war against the whites."

"But will he do it? He's a farmer Indian and he goes to their churches. He will take the white man's side," Red Middle Voice said.

Shakopee stood up. "It's late, but we must try. We will call the chiefs to a council at Little Crow's house."

It was only a few hours before dawn when several braves rode off to summon chiefs from nearby villages, Later the group of warriors gathered at Little Crow's home. Mankato, Wabasha, Traveling Hail and Big Eagle were included in the group called together by Shakopee and Red Middle Voice.

Awakened from deep sleep, Little Crow sat up. Still angry at having recently been slighted when they selected Traveling Hail to the important position of speaker of the Lower Sioux, he scoffed. "Why do you come to me for advice? Go to the man you elected speaker and let him tell you what to do."

He paused. No one spoke. He continued. "Braves, you are like little children; you don't know what you're doing. You are full of the white man's devil water. (whisky) You are like dogs in the hot moon when they run and snap at their own shadows. We are like little herds of buffalo left scattered; the great herds that once covered the prairies are no more. See! The white men are like locusts when they fly so thick that the whole sky is a snowstorm. You may kill one, two, ten, yes as many as the leaves in the forest yonder, and their brothers will not miss them. Kill one, two, ten and ten times ten will come to kill you. Count your fingers all day long and whitemen with guns in their hands will come faster than you can count."

Shakopee argued, "Are you no longer a great chief? Will you let the whitemen take everything that is ours? They promise food but they give us little. They promise money—next week—next week never comes. Are you going to let them starve us in our own land?"

Wabasha broke in. "It is folly to make war on the whitemen. What Little Crow says is true."

Big Eagle continued. "Wabasha and Little Crow are right. We cannot win such a war."

Red Middle Voice spoke. "The whitemen's young men are far away fighting the Civil War. Only men of forty years or older are left here. Now is the time to strike. We can kill them and the rest will run. Then we will have our land and hunting grounds and we'll be happy as we once were."

Each brave and chief spoke. The young braves and several of the chiefs favored war. The older men stood for peace, but they had little real authority for often in the past the young braves had gone counter to their wishes.

The argument continued. The older men were overruled. The decision was made and those who were reluctant felt they must go along with their people.

Shakopee spoke to Little Crow. "You have our decision. Will you lead us against our enemy? Will you again be the great warrior that you once were—or are you too old, too feeble to fight for your people? Has the once brave Little Crow become a coward?"

Little Crow hesitated. Perhaps, he thought, this was his opportunity to show his military talent and thus regain his lost prestige. He would prove to them he was not a coward.

Red Middle Voice said, "We have not talked about what to do with the cut-hairs."

A brave shouted, "Kill them! Kill them if they won't join us in the fight!"

There was more discussion. Finally Little Crow accepted the responsibility of leading the fight against the whitemen. Firmly he said, "I order an attack tomorrow morning on the Lower Agency. Go back and prepare your people. I will lead you."

The braves whooped and dashed away in preparation for killing the settlers. The fateful decision had been made. The hunter people were determined to drive out the settlers and take back their land. Every white man must die!

8.

MONDAY, AUGUST 18, Wilhelm squinted into the rising sun. "It's going to be another hot day."

"Yah," Amelia replied, "it's good we start early for Mankato while the air is cool."

The horses plodded on toward the settlement of New Ulm. Wilhelm and Amelia sat on a spring seat in the wagon box; the three girls relaxed on a quilt behind their parents.

Charity giggled, "I can't wait 'til we get to the big stores. I'd like a pink dress."

"Ma," Hope said, "we don't have to buy three dresses alike, do we?"

Faith broke in. "I don't want a pink dress. I'd like green. Can't we each have the one we want?"

Amelia smiled. "This time you can each have the color you want."

"Goody!" the girls shouted.

Wilhelm squinted into the brightening sky. "There are two people on horseback coming this way. Hm-m-m. They're riding fast."

As the pair neared the wagon Amelia gasped, "It's Phidelia and Shaska! Where on earth are they going at this hour?"

Wilhelm threw up his hand and shouted, " 'Morning!"

Phidelia waved but Shaska ignored the greeting and urged his horse on.

The girls chattered. "Where are they going? What are they going to do?"

Wilhelm muttered, "I don't like it. She's too thick with that fellow. Maybe she's running away with him."

"Sh-h-h." Amelia whispered. "Little pitchers have big ears."

"Yah. Whatever they're doing, it's none of my business."

Phidelia is a pretty lady," Hope said. "I wish I had black hair and eyes like hers."

Wilhelm laughed. "You wouldn't look as though you belonged to our family. You'd look odd with the rest of us."

"I guess so."

They passed through sleepy New Ulm where only a few people were stirring. They waved and hurried on. At the edge of town they saw Peddler John Henning's wagon and tent. "He's not up yet," Faith said.

They followed the road to the southeast. Farmers were milking or harnessing teams of horses in preparation for the day's work.

Wilhelm mused, "I'm glad our wheat is cut and stacked beside the barn. The threshing machine will be along next week. We will have a good yield this year. At a dollar a bushel we will have more money than we've ever had before. Minnesota has been good to us." He patted Amelia's arm. "Aren't you glad now that we left Germany?"

"Yah. Minnesota is our home." She laughed. "And if we still lived in Germany you wouldn't have had money to buy your reaper and my new cook stove. I'll cook and bake good things when we get back and have the stove set up."

"Yah. Yah."

9.

As WILHELM, AMELIA AND THEIR DAUGHTERS made their way eastward toward Mankato, the Lower Agency, consisting of traders' stores, quarters for Indian Agent Galbraith, shops, barns and other buildings, slowly wakened to the hot humid day.

At 6:30 on the morning of August 18, James Lynd, a clerk in Andrew Myrick's store, unpacked merchandise and placed it on the shelves. Philander Prescott, out for an early morning stroll, stopped to talk. Lynd silently pondered the fact that Prescott the fur trader, was married to a Sioux woman who was Chief Shakopee's mother-in-law.

Lynd pried open a barrel of soda crackers. "You have any trouble with your wife's relatives, Philander?"

Prescott rubbed his hand across his shiny bald head. "No, we get along fine. I've lived among the Sioux for more than forty years. They're my friends."

"Wish I could say that," Lynd remarked. "I've had two Sioux wives. My first wife and I have two children, but—she couldn't give up the old Indian ways. Then I found another Indian girl so I—well—I guess you'd say I deserted my first wife."

"And her relatives are angry?"

Lynd nodded. "To tell the truth, I'm a little afraid of them. Then too, they resent my working for Andrew Myrick. Since he made that statement about them eating grass or dung if they are hungry, the Indians have hated him."

As Lynd and other storekeepers prepared for the business day, a large party of armed, painted Sioux braves silently hid in thickets along the river. At a prearranged signal bursts of gunfire launched the attack.

In the Myrick store Lynd and the owner rushed to

the door. The street was filled with half-naked, screaming Indians intent on revenge toward the whites. Another Myrick employee, George Divoll, ran to the door. A blinding burst of gunfire and James Lynd and Divoll lay dead.

"Myrick!" A painted brave shouted. "Get Myrick!" Three braves dashed into the store and jumped over the bleeding bodies of Lynd and Divoll in pursuit of Myrick who, with Prescott, had disappeared.

Upstairs, Myrick hid beneath a large dry goods box. Shaking uncontrollably, he fought for composure as he listened to gunfire from outside. Silently, in deerskin moccasins, a brave crept upstairs. Cautiously he lifted the edge of the box, then dropped it.

Trembling, Myrick waited. Now it was quiet downstairs. He crawled from beneath the box, stood on it to lift a ceiling trap door into the attic, and climbed through the opening, softly closing the door behind him. Terror-stricken, he waited, wondering why he had not been shot when his hiding place was discovered.

He smelled smoke and heard a crackling sound. Fire! They were going to burn him alive! Rushing to open a small window, he crawled outside and dropped to the roof of a low shed, jumped to the ground and dashed toward the brush on the bank of the river.

At Myrick's appearance war whoops came from all sides. The bloodcurdling cries lent speed to his attempted escape. As he ran, arrows struck his arms and legs. At last he reached the thicket to be met by a shot from a rifle. A convulsive kick of his legs and Myrick was dead.

Whooping Indians gathered about his arrow and bullet riddled body. As a last insult to their enemy, grass and dog dung was stuffed into the gaping mouth of Andrew J. Myrick.

Meanwhile, the massacre at the Lower Agency continued. The surprised whites were easy targets. Many were murdered at other stores. In the street Philander Prescott and a few residents were saved by the ferryman, Charlie Martel, who took them across to the north shore of the river away from the massacre. However, not even the Indians' old friend was allowed to live for Prescott, while making his escape, was killed on the north side of the river.

Some persons at the Lower Agency met death by slow torture. A boy trying to escape was caught and stripped to the skin; then as he was driven along and the Sioux mimicked his cries, he was pierced with knives and sticks while the Indians hooted and laughed until the child died.

Women were tortured. Some with babies in their arms, had their breasts cut off, while others were dragged behind galloping horses until they died.

The Sioux braves were wild with the success of their attack. Many were drunk from whisky they had taken from pillaged stores. Every white was a fair target. They vowed to drive away or to kill every white intruder from their land. This attack was only the beginning.

Dr. Otto Hess, the husband of Phidelia, was murdered while attending a sick man at the Lower Agency. Also killed was his bed-ridden patient.

Always eager for more horses, the raging Indians, intent on stealing the government animals, attacked A. H. Wagner, Superintendent of Farms at the agency and two of his employees. As the dispute raged, Little Crow in full Indian dress with numerous feathers in his hair, approached the group.

"What are you doing?" the chief asked. "Why don't you shoot these men? What are you waiting for?"

The Sioux fired, killing the two employees. Wagner,

who was wounded, died later.

The carnage continued. The nightmare of torture, butchery, burning buildings and looting went on. After killing thirteen people at the Lower Agency, the Sioux turned to looting and plundering which gave the remaining whites an opportunity to flee across the river. The ferryman, Charlie Martel, could have escaped but he remained at his post and doubtless saved many lives.

Finally a group of braves arrived at the crossing. "Kill Martel! Kill him!" a painted brave yelled. "He helped them get away!" One bullet and Ferryman Martel's body lay on the shore. In a sudden wild frenzy they slit his abdomen and disemboweled the torso. Still dissatisfied, the ferryman's head, hands and feet were cut off and thrust into the cavity.

Buildings on every side were burning. Soon only two structures remained at the Lower Agency. From the opposite shore victims who had escaped across the river listened in terror to the mad shouts of the near-naked Sioux as they screamed with merriment at the death throes of their victims. Former friendship and kindness availed nothing.

The first day of the massacre thirteen whites were killed and seven more lost their lives while trying to escape. Ten women and children were captured by the Indians and forty-seven escaped.

The nearest refuge for the victims who managed to cross the river was Fort Ridgely, about thirteen miles to the east. This small military post, the only one in southwestern Minnesota, was ill-prepared for the refugees. Seventy-six men made up the fort's garrison; most of them never had been in combat, but their commander, Captain Marsh, had fought in the Civil War. However he knew nothing about fighting Indians.

Marsh learned the shocking news of the Sioux outbreak about ten o'clock the morning of August 18 when a wagon load of frightened refugees made their way to Fort Ridgely. More fugitives arrived to confirm the news of the massacre.

Marsh was alarmed. He sent a messenger for help. On the previous day a lieutenant with fifty men left the post bound for Fort Ripley on the Mississippi River. They would still be within reach. The urgent message said, "Immediately return with your command to this post. The Indians are raising hell at the Lower Agency. This is urgent."

That day, down the river and on each side below the fort and within six miles of New Ulm and up the river to Yellow Medicine, the massacre continued. Torture, killing, plundering of the Germans' possessions and burning buildings was rampant.

10.

INDIAN AGENT THOMAS J. GALBRAITH was absent at the beginning of the Sioux uprising. The stone warehouse at the Upper Agency and the surrounding stores were doing business as usual on the morning of August 18.

Two weeks earlier there had been disagreement with the Indians and war then looked imminent. However, after Galbraith reluctantly released supplies to the Sioux, he believed the trouble was over. He then decided to throw his efforts into recruiting for the Union.

From employees at the agency and with a number of half-breeds, he recruited a company of Civil War volunteers, and with them Galbraith set out for Fort Snelling on August 13. The Indians thought the whites must be desperate for men to fight the South or they would not come so far out on the frontier and take inexperienced clerks and half-breeds for army life. They saw this as a sign that the northern whites were losing the war.

About noon on the eighteenth rumors of the Indian uprising reached the Upper Agency. Most of the whites refused to believe that anything serious was happening.

Meanwhile Shaska and Phidelia Hess made their way westward. Phidelia was unaware of the violence which had taken place and she kept up a chatter of pleasantries. She flirted coquettishly with the handsome brave, Shaska.

"I'm glad you convinced me to go for a ride with you," she said. "Otto left in the night to see a sick patient, and who knows when he'll be back? Being with you is so much better than sitting home alone."

Shaska urged his horse on. The sound of rapidly approaching hoofbeats caused him to turn. Two Lower Sioux braves dashed up on horses white with lather.

"We want that woman!" a brave yelled as he attempted to seize Phidelia's arm. Alarmed, she pulled away and urged her horse into a gallop. Calling over her shoulder she shouted, "He's riding Otto's horse!"

The whooping Indians streaked ahead followed by Shaska who overtook them as they came abreast of Phidelia's galloping mount.

Shaska exploded, "Don't touch her! She's my woman!"

"She's the doctor's woman," a brave argued, "but he's dead and now she's ours."

Phidelia gasped, "Don't let them touch me, Shaska. I'll go with you."

The second Indian hiccuped, "We'll share her with you!"

"You're drunk with white man's whisky! Have you killed Dr. Hess?"

"Yes. And we'll kill every white we get our hands on. And we'll kill you if you get in our way." He slid to the ground and staggered toward Phidelia.

Shaska sprang from his horse. "The woman is mine. If either of you harm her I'll kill you!" His eyes bored into those of the drunken Indians. Finally they jumped on their horses and rode away toward the Upper Agency.

Phidelia, her face pale, grasped the saddle for support. "I'm weak with fear," she gasped. "They killed Otto?"

"I think so. There's going to be bad trouble around here. That's why I came for you this morning. I'll take you to Little Crow's camp. I think I can protect you there."

Meanwhile a few miles upstream near the Upper Agency about one hundred Indians met to decide whether they should join the Lower Sioux in the war against the whites. A heated debate failed to produce a decision. Among the loyal Christian Indians were John Other Day who had a white wife and child and Chief Akepa who had been educated by the missionaries and was better known as Little Paul, the speaker of the Upper Sioux. These men did not favor war. Privately they planned.

"We must warn the whites," Other Day said.

"I will spread the word," Little Paul promised. "There has been senseless killing between here and New Ulm. I will tell the whites they must leave. Tomorrow may be too late."

"You warn them," Other Day planned, "and after dark I'll get them into the brick warehouse. They'll be safe there tonight. In the morning I'll try to lead them north toward Cedar City and Hutchinson."

Little Paul nodded. "The missionaries are in danger. The Williamsons and Riggs must leave. We have much to do if lives are to be saved. I fear we already are too late." He paused. "We, too, are in danger. Some of our brothers have promised to kill us, the Christian Indians, along with the whites."

"I know. There is not time to go to the missions."

In the early evening of August 18 John Other Day collected most of the whites, a group of sixty-two people, and persuaded them to spend the night in the brick warehouse of the Upper Agency. He and a small band of Christian Indians stood guard.

At daybreak on August 19 several whooping hostile Indians gathered to plunder the traders' stores. During the noise, confusion and wild hilarity of the plundering Indians, John Other Day safely piloted the group of whites across to the north shore of the Minnesota River and out onto the prairie.

Among the group were the wife of the absent Sioux agent Thomas Galbraith and their children as well as John Other Day's white wife and child. The weary people followed their Indian friend on foot; only the feeble old people and small children rode in their three ox wagons and two buggies. John Other Day drove them relentlessly to put distance between them and the rampaging Indians. He hoped they would be safe if he could get them to the town of Hutchinson which was a few miles west of St. Paul.

11.

IN THE AFTERNOON on Monday, August 18, three miles above the Upper Agency at the mission of Dr. Thomas S. Williamson, Antoine Renville, one of the elders from Reverend Stephen Riggs nearby mission, rushed in. Panting with excitement he exclaimed, "The Indians are killing whites!"

Reverend Williamson was calm. "Likely it is only a drunken quarrel with a trader. 'Twill blow over."

Reluctantly the messenger accepted the minister's interpretation and returned to the Riggs' mission. But all afternoon rumors continued; there had been killings at the Lower Agency; entire families had been massacred near New Ulm. Still, most people believed the stories were products of fertile imaginations.

Finally a messenger was sent by Reverend Riggs to the Upper Agency. He later reported that stores had been broken into. Only mildly concerned, the people at the mission went to bed that night to be awakened by violent pounding on the door at midnight.

Reverend Riggs opened the door to Indian friends who demanded the family leave the mission immediately. "But—but—" the old missionary stammered, "we are safe here. They won't harm us."

The young brave was insistent. "Go! Go now! You have three daughters. They will kill you and Mrs. Riggs to get your daughters. Take all your people. No white is safe. They have already killed many times. Hurry! We will help you get away!"

"But—I can't believe this! Are you sure?" The old missionary's hands shook.

"Get the people together now. I will take all of you to an island in the river where I hope you'll be safe."

A few minutes later Reverend and Mrs. Riggs, their

three nearly grown daughters and seventeen other whites from the mission followed the Indian guides through the mosquito-infested tall grass and underbrush along the river. From there they waded hip deep water and were left on an island in the Minnesota River.

As the guides departed Reverend Riggs said confidently, “By tomorrow the danger will be over and we can return to the mission.”

In the forenoon on Tuesday the old missionary went to the Upper Agency village. He was appalled to find the entire area deserted, the stores plundered, and to learn of the escape of the whites under the direction of Other Day. He wasted no time in returning to the island.

Now it was apparent that immediate flight was required. Once more the twenty-one people waded to the north shore. Now every person was convinced that they must immediately leave the area.

Meanwhile, at the Williamsons, though the old doctor was unwilling to believe there was anything more serious than rumors, he decided to send away from the mission the younger members of his family. He, his wife and sister would remain for the present.

12.

GREAT-GRANDMOTHER MARY, Eddie and Hermie waved as Wilhelm, Amelia and the triplets set out for Mankato on August 18. Herman clung to Mary. At age three and a half he had never before been separated for more than a few hours from his parents. Tears quivered in his eyes and spilled down his cheeks.

"I wish I could go," he sobbed.

Eddie swung the little boy to his shoulder. "We'll have fun, you and I. We'll fish, and later today we'll go into town and see Peddler Henning's long beard and his monkey."

Mary wiped the boy's eyes on her apron. "We'll get along fine, just the three of us. Stop crying, Hermie. You're a big boy now."

A smile flickered across the tear-stained face. "Yah. I'm this old." He held up three fingers.

Mary turned and shuffled to the kitchen. "I'll wash the dishes while you finish the chores, Eddie."

"There's not much to do, Grandma. After I turn the cows out to pasture, clean the stable and feed the pigs and chickens, I'll be done until time to do the milking tonight."

"Yah. Yah. It's good you and Hermie can play. We'll have an early dinner so you can get started for town."

A few hours later as they sat at the table their old dog barked furiously. Eddie grinned. "Chief probably sees a woodchuck." He shoveled in more potatoes and sauerkraut. When the barks changed to growls and snarls, Eddie went to the door.

"Oh!" he gasped. "They can't!"

Mary hobbled to the window. "What—what—it's Adolph! The varmints have got Adolph!"

They saw a horrible sight. Coming up the road from the direction of New Ulm were three nearly naked Indians, their faces painted and with feathers in their hair. They were driving Peddler Henning's team and wagon. Ahead of the horses old Adolph staggered while arrows flew from the bows of two whooping braves.

"Dance, old man, dance!" they shouted. An arrow pierced a scrawny arm. The Indians shouted at Adolph's scream. "Dance! Faster, faster!"

More arrows flew. They struck the ground beside the shuffling old feet. "Higher! Step higher, old man! Dance! Dance!"

Another arrow pierced a leg. Adolph screamed in fear. His face was contorted with pain. "Help! Help!" he shouted.

Chief snarled and attacked an Indian who was running beside the wagon. Growling, he sank his teeth into the brave's leg. Hanging on he momentarily slowed the torture, while Adolph screamed, "Mary! Help me!" With each faltering step the arrows waved from his bleeding wounds.

Hermie, terror-stricken, clung to Mary's skirt. Forcefully she removed his hands and went to the bedroom with unusual speed.

"Take Hermie," she ordered, "and go out the back door. Hide in the woods." She returned carrying Wilhelm's rifle. "I'll hold them off 'till you get away."

"But—but—"

"Go! Go! They'll kill you! You must save Hermie!" As she went outside, Mary heard the back door bang.

Screams, shouts, war whoops and Chief's savage growls mingled to form a horrible cacophony of sounds. Adolph staggered toward the house. "Mary, help me," he begged.

She yelled, "Stop, you blasted varmints!" The rifle was leveled at the driver of the team. Mary advanced. "Stop or I'll blow your brains out!" The team pranced nervously.

The driver whooped. "The gun ain't loaded!" He let another arrow fly which struck Adolph in the buttocks. "Jump, old man!" he yelled.

With a moan the victim stumbled and fell, three arrows protruding from his body. Chief still growled and battled the Indian he had attacked. Blood streamed from a wound in the man's thigh and though he kicked, pounded the dog with his bow and shouted, Chief hung on. Amid the confusion Henning's pet monkey appeared atop the covered wagon. Screaming wildly, he repeatedly tipped his little red hat.

"Shut up!" the second brave yelled as his arrow struck the noisy pet silencing him forever. Turning to help his friend who was battling the old dog he quickly ended Chief's life with an arrow through the heart.

Mary still held the rifle on the driver. She shrieked, "Get out of here this minute or I'll drop you!"

"We're goin' to have fun with you old folks. You're gonna dance with the old man!" He yelled to Adolph, "Get up!" Adolph struggled to his feet. "You gotta dance with the old woman!"

Mary, her hand steady and her eyes cold as ice, took aim. The rifle barked. She took a second bullet from her apron pocket and reloaded, observing with satisfaction that the driver had pitched to the ground as the horses broke into a gallop and disappeared toward the west. A five foot long black cloth tube sailed from the wagon seat to the ground.

"Two more to go!" Mary yelled as she drew a bead on the brave who aimed an arrow in her direction. Simultaneously the arrow flew and the rifle barked. Mary and the brave both dropped instantly.

Adolph, on his knees begged piteously. "Please don't kill me. Please. I'm an old man."

The remaining brave, hobbled by his mangled leg silently fitted an arrow into his bow and aimed at Adolph's chest. With a low moan the tortured old German breathed his last.

13.

TERRIFIED, EDDIE AND HERMIE watched the carnage from a thick clump of hazelnut bushes.

"What are they doing? What are they doing?" the little boy whispered.

"Sh-h-h. We must be quiet so they don't find us. Keep your head down," Eddie warned. His heart pounded at the horrible sight of his great-grandmother's and Adolph's bodies lying in the yard. They must be dead; they hadn't moved. Neither had Chief or the monkey or the two Indians.

Eddie's mind was dazed. This gruesome thing couldn't be happening. Was the whole incident a nightmarish dream? No. Grandmother and Adolph were dead. So were the Indians and faithful old Chief.

Hermie pulled on his brother's sleeve. "Can we go back to the house now?"

"Sh-h-h. Be quiet," he whispered. "We can't go back. He would hurt us."

The one remaining wounded Indian limped toward the barn. A minute or two later smoke drifted from the doorway. In spite of his mangled leg, the revenge-filled brave dragged the slight bodies of Mary and Adolph to the barn where he threw them into the burning building. As he retreated from the excessive heat, the stacks of dry wheat bundles on either side of the open barn doors erupted in a giant conflagration. Flames and black smoke rose straight up for a hundred feet in the still air.

Eddie swallowed the lump in his throat. Gone—Grandmother Mary, old Adolph, Chief, his father's new barn, their wheat crop, the reaper. Only the house was left and the cattle and pigs in the pasture.

The war-painted brave picked up Wilhelm's rifle and went into the house. Eddie and Hermie waited. Would he burn their home too?

After a time the Sioux came out carrying the rifle and one of Grandmother's crazy quilts which was rolled into a bundle filled with plundered items. Stopping for a quick glance at his dead friends, he picked up his bow, threw the bundle over his shoulder and limped toward the west.

Hermie whispered, "Will he come back?"

"I don't know. We'll stay here and watch."

The barn burned rapidly. In minutes the roof collapsed with a roar amid a firestorm of flying sparks and leaping flames.

Hermie whispered, "I'm scared."

"Yah."

"When can we go back to the house?"

"Sh-sh. Someone's coming." A pair of horses pulling a surrey slowed as they neared the burning barn. Eddie gasped. "Indians with Amos Moltke's team!"

"Why have they got paint on their faces?" Hermie said softly. "They scare me. The others threw Grandma and Adolph in the fire."

"Yah. We'll keep out of sight. We must be quiet."

The two half-naked braves jumped out and stood over the bodies of the Sioux. Then, together they lifted the dead braves into the back seat of the surrey and tied the team to the hitching post. With a whoop they dashed into the house. A few minutes later they carried the family's household items to the buggy—pots and pans, dishes and clothing were piled inside the surrey.

As the boys watched three of Wilhelm's cows moseyed along the riverbank to a shallow spot where they often drank. The Indians talked. Then one ran to the backyard and cut down Amelia's clothesline with a knife he carried in his belt. Cautiously they approached the cattle. The tame animals allowed the braves to put ropes around their necks and lead them away where they were tied to the back of the buggy.

As they drove away Eddie muttered, "The thieves! They've stolen our cows and the things from the house. They're murderers and thieves! If only I had Pa's rifle, but they took that too!"

Hermie sobbed, "I'm scared. Will they kill us?"

Eddie clenched his teeth. "Not if I can help it." He put his arm about the little boy's shoulders. "I'll take care of you. Pa and Ma and the girls will be back in a day or two."

Tears ran down Hermie's face. "But they shot Grandma and Adolph and Chief and the monkey. Maybe they'll shoot us."

"They'll have to find us first."

The heat from the August sun beat down on the thicket where the boys lay. They crawled a few yards until they were shaded by a white pine.

Time passed slowly. Dark clouds gathered in the western sky. Hermie slept as Eddie pondered their situation. He was puzzled by the vicious attack of the Indians. They must have killed Amos Moltke or he would not have given them his team. They were murdering the people and stealing their possessions. The Indians had gone crazy.

Several more Sioux, most of them loaded with plunder, passed the house going west toward the reservation. At first Eddie wondered why there were no whites on the trail, but as he considered the situation, he decided either they were hiding—or dead.

Flies buzzed about in the sultry air. Eddie kept them off Hermie's face as he wondered what they should do. There was a distant rumble of thunder. Hermie sat up. "I'm hungry," he said.

"Yah. If you'll promise to stay here, I'll try to get to

the house to find some food. Will you stay here and wait for me?"

"Yah."

"I'll be back soon, but you must stay right here. Understand?"

"Yah."

Eddie glanced both ways. No one was on the road. Running at top speed he raced to the back door and went inside. The entire house had been pillaged. Papers, books, towels and even curtains littered the floor.

He hurried to the bread box. Empty. So was the cookie crock. Grandmother had baked a ham on Sunday —he'd take that. The cupboard was empty. Nothing edible remained in the house, not even a soda cracker.

They hadn't taken the furniture. Eddie stood before Grandmother Mary's bed. His eye fell on a strap which protruded from beneath the bed. Grandmother's leather bag. He pulled it out and threw it over his shoulder. An old quilt remained on a chair. He took it. Since their coats had been stolen, he and Hermie would cover themselves with the quilt. Glancing out the front door he spied a long black bundle on the ground. He dashed out, gathered it up and raced back to the woods where he found his brother crying. "I'm scared. It's going to storm. Can't we go to the house?" Hermie whined.

"Sh-h-h. Listen." A moment later Eddie said, "Two of them are coming with Mr. Henning's team and wagon."

Again the Indians stopped before the house and went inside to repeatedly appear with chairs, the dining room table and other pieces of the family's furniture which was loaded into the wagon.

Eddie sighed. "They've taken everything. When she gets back Ma's new cookstove won't do her much good."

On their last trip into the house the Sioux returned emptyhanded. As they drove toward the reservation, black smoke began to drift from the door.

A lump rose in Eddie's throat. Their beautiful new house was on fire. The villains had left them nothing. Hatred filled his heart. His family had never harmed the Indians. Why were they doing this to them?

Flames raced through the tinder dry wood of their home as the horrified boys watched. Hermie sobbed, "Where will we live?"

Eddie, his arm about his brother's shoulders whispered, "I'll take care of you."

The fire snapped as it climbed to the second story. A few minutes later flames shot from doors, windows and along the edge of the roof. Suddenly the roof collapsed in an inferno of spurting flames and a shower of sparks.

The storm was coming closer. The forest was still. No birds chirped. No insects sang. No leaves rattled. It was as though nature mourned the destruction of the Winters' home. Only the snapping of the fire broke the stillness of the sultry afternoon.

The air had been hot all day, but now in late afternoon it was heavy. It hung over the trees and pressed on the tense shoulders of the boys. Eddie glanced to the southwest. Clouds were piling on one another to form a ridge of mammoth white columns rearing high against the darkening sky. Lightning flashed and the rumble of thunder was close.

Soon black clouds covered the late afternoon sun. A sudden gust of wind stirred the branches of nearby trees and sent dry leaves scurrying toward the east. Thunder rumbled nearby.

Hermie said, "It's going to rain. Where will we go?"

"Right here. We'll cover up with our quilt." Eddie put it over them. "See? This is our tent."

The first drops of rain were huge. Leaves shuddered under their weight before rebounding to dump their load of water. The rhythm of the raindrops quickened. Lightning struck a tree nearby. Hermie shrieked at the crack of thunder. The next bolt raised the hair on the back of Eddie's neck. The rain now became a torrent which found its way through the old quilt and dripped on the frightened children. The rising wind wildly tossed the tree branches. In the distance a tree crashed to the ground.

Hermie sobbed as he clung to Eddie who peered from beneath the edge of the quilt. He could see only a short distance in the downpour. Suddenly hailstones thumped against the quilt over their heads. They bounced against the ground and splashed in puddles.

Gradually the storm began to pass and the sky brightened. Water still dripped from the trees on the saturated quilt. When it stopped Eddie spread the quilt over a hazelnut bush. "Maybe it'll dry by night," he said.

"We going to sleep here?" Hermie asked.

"Yah. Right here."

"I'm hungry, Eddie."

"After dark I'll go to our garden and get some potatoes and carrots. There's nothing else—not even milk, 'cause they took our cows."

"How will we cook potatoes and carrots?"

"We'll eat them raw."

Hermie shivered. "I'm cold. My clothes are wet." His teeth chattered.

Eddie tried to warm his little brother by holding him closely. Silently he studied the smoking remains of the Winters family's house and barn. He shifted his position and his hand touched Grandmother's leather bag; the purse and quilt were all that remained from their home. He touched the damp black bag which he had picked up in the road. He didn't recall having seen it in the house. The Indians must have dropped it. Opening the end, he peered inside. Hair, long gray hair.

Reaching inside he removed about a yard of coarse hair. His hand touched something cold. Looking closely he shuddered as he recognized the horrible thing. He was holding Peddler Henning's long beard with chin and facial flesh attached.

Nearby the weird, unearthly cry of a loon drifted up from the river. Eddie shivered and held Hermie closer.

14.

THE SIOUX UPRISING BEGAN on Sunday August 17 near Acton in Meeker County when starving, angry Indians took their revenge for the white mans' broken promises. The first massacre of innocent whites was the spark which ignited the explosion that was felt throughout Minnesota.

On August 18, 1862, the day when Little Crow's band attacked and murdered German settlers at the Lower Agency, $70,000 in gold arrived at nearby Fort Ridgely; this money was the overdue payment for the Sioux tribes of western Minnesota. But it was one day too late for already the Indians had begun to take their claim in settlers' blood. The money was never distributed.

At a hotel in Mankato Wilhelm and his family learned of the uprising on Monday night. In the dining room horrible stories were told of murders, scalpings, burning and pillaging of the whites' possessions.

Scarcely able to believe the frightening news, Wilhelm and Amelia talked. Amelia said, "We must go home at once. If things are so bad we have to be there to help." Softly she added, "And Hermie, Eddie and Grandma are alone."

"Don't go," a man at the next table advised. "I got my family out and we'll stay here until it's safe."

Wilhelm scratched his head. "We have to go. We have children and other relatives near New Ulm."

"But your three daughters," the man added motioning toward the triplets. He whispered to Wilhelm. "The villains rape young white girls and women. Leave your wife and daughters here."

Wilhelm nodded. "Yah. It's better that way."

But Amelia had other ideas. Later that evening in their room she announced firmly that she would not be left behind. The girls—yes. Since the stove and other items had not yet been purchased the money would pay the hotel owner for the triplets' board and lodging until she and Wilhelm could return for them after the Indians quieted down.

Because Faith, Hope and Charity did not fully realize the seriousness of the situation, they were happy to remain in Mankato. Hurried arrangements were made with the hotel owner, John Moore, who suggested the girls could work out part of their expenses in the hotel kitchen and dining room.

After bidding the triplets good-bye Wilhelm and Amelia were back in the wagon and headed for New Ulm by ten o'clock that evening. Frightened by the horrendous reports they had heard at the hotel, they were filled with dread at what they might find at home.

It was raining gently but to the west the night sky was red from burning buildings. Silently they watched as Wilhelm hurried the team along.

Finally Amelia said, "If—if—our buildings are gone, where will we go?"

"Our friends or relatives will take us in."

"But—if the buildings are gone, where—how—" she sobbed, "how will we find Eddie and Hermie and Grandma?"

Wilhelm patted her shoulder. "Don't think the worst. Things may not be as bad as they said at the hotel."

Most of the night they rode without talking, but their minds were filled with the possibilities of gruesome discoveries ahead.

15.

COLD, WET AND MISERABLE, Eddie shielded Hermie from the constant rain. "Try to sleep," he whispered.

"I can't." The little boy shivered. "I'm cold."

"As soon as it's daylight we'll get some potatoes and carrots from the garden."

"I wish Pa and Ma was here. They'd know what to do." His teeth chattered.

"Yah." In a moment Eddie added, "Some day when we're old men we will laugh about the time we slept under a pine tree in the rain."

"I—I—don't think it's funny. My feet are so cold."

"So are mine, but we can stand it." Later, when the sky lightened, Eddie said, "Let's have breakfast."

After rolling up the wet quilt and throwing Mary's leather bag over his shoulder Eddie, followed by Hermie, went to the garden. They pulled carrots and dug potatoes. As they munched the sandy vegetables Eddie stuffed several carrots into his pockets. "We'll eat these later," he said.

They started down the road to the east. Hermie's short legs pumped fast to keep up with his brother. "There's Chief and the monkey," he said.

"I wish we could bury them, but we have to keep moving. We'll try to get to Grandpa and Grandma Winters' place."

"Will the Indians come back?"

"I hope not." He broke into a trot. "If we run we'll warm up."

Hermie puffed along behind his brother. They passed two farms where the burned out buildings still smoldered. Eddie wondered about the people, the Schmidt and Mendel families. Had they escaped? They ran on. Finally Hermie gasped, "I can't run anymore."

"All right. We'll walk." After a time Eddie said, "I wonder where all the people are. Some of the buildings aren't burned, but no one is around. Over there—see the cows are waiting to be milked." A sudden thought struck him. "Let's get some milk!"

"Yah!"

The boys ran to a cow near the barn. Eddie squatted beside her and motioned for Hermie. "Get closer and open your mouth. I'll squirt milk into it."

The little boy swallowed rapidly. Finally he said, "I'm full."

Eddie milked into his own mouth. When he could swallow no more he remarked, "These cows weren't milked last night. See how their udders hang down?"

"Uh-huh. Can we go to the house?"

"Uh—wait here. I'll take a quick look." He ran up the steps and peered through the open door. His heart leaped at the sight before him. On the floor a man lay in a dried puddle of blood. Next to him was a small child. Both of their heads and faces were bloody. Quickly his eyes swept the room. The mother, her face on her arms, still sat at the table. A bloody gash in the back of her head told something of the gory happenings. Feeling ill, Eddie ran back to Hermie.

"Let's get out of here! There's no one home!" Unmindful of his brother's short legs, Eddie ran at top speed, his mind seething. The villains had killed these people like—like they were animals in a trap. They had split their heads open with tomahawks.

"Eddie! Wait for me!"

Silently he waited as his eyes swept the countryside. The next farm had been ravaged. The buildings still smoldered from being torched the previous day. Something lay in the tall grass beside the road. Hermie still was puffing along toward him as Eddie stepped aside to investigate. He recoiled in horror. Felix Meuller! The fiends had scalped him! Turning quickly he ran on so Hermie wouldn't see the awful sight.

Hermie panted, "Why—why do we have to hurry so —so fast?"

"We want to get to Grandpa Winters' house as soon as we can. There's Amos and Josephine Moltke's place ahead. We'll stop there to rest."

Running up the steps Eddie was relieved to see Josephine and Amos at the table with Anna and Frederick Ketchum.

"Come in," Amos called. "Are you folks all right out there?"

"Ma and Pa and the girls went to Mankato yesterday morning." Eddie swallowed, unable to go on.

"Then they're likely all right. The Indians took my team, but they didn't hurt us. After all, I've grown up with them," Amos said.

Eddie nodded and glanced at Anna and her father. He hadn't seen Anna all summer but she was so big she looked as though she was pregnant. He took a deep breath. “They—the Indians burned our buildings, and—and—” he sobbed, “They killed Grandma Mary and Adolph.”

The room suddenly was silent except for a large black fly that buzzed at the window. Anna’s face was colorless. Her father stared into the woods. They seemed numb at the news of Adolph’s death—their father and grandfather.

Josephine got up. “You and Hermie can stay here until—until your parents are back. Anna and Frederick are living with us too.”

“Thank you, Mrs. Moeltke.” Then, through tear-filled eyes Eddie saw the Indians in the road. They seemed to be arguing. “Indians,” he said softly. “They’re coming in.”

Amos jumped up. “All of you get out the back door. Hurry!” He stepped outside.

“’Morning Pete! ’Morning Joe!” he called.

The Sioux grunted. Amos met them halfway to the road. He noted the war paint and the eagle feathers in their hair. Five feathers. These men already had killed five times. They carried rifles.

Amos asked, “Do you need food?”

Again the braves grunted.

Trying to buy time for the others to escape Amos continued talking. “We have been friends for many years. I’ll help you now. What do you need?”

“We need to kill every white man on our land. You say you’re our friends but you steal our hunting grounds so that we starve.” Without warning he raised his rifle and fired point blank. Amos dropped.

At the back of the house Eddie and Hermie raced toward the tall prairie grass at the edge of the Moeltke cornfield. Diving headfirst into the grass the boys lay flat on the ground.

Anna, large with child, clumsily made her way down the steps. Josephine and Frederick each grasped an arm to rush her along.

"Hurry! Hurry!" Josephine urged. "We'll go to the hen house!"

But it was too late. Three quick shots and it was over. Anna, her father Frederick Ketchum and their friend Josephine Moeltke had been slain within a matter of seconds.

Eddie and Hermie lay side by side in the tall grass. "Don't move," Eddie whispered as he threw his arm across the boy's shoulders. "Keep your head down."

Hermie whispered, "My foot hurts." Eddie didn't answer.

Though Eddie was horrified at the slaughter he had witnessed his eyes were drawn to the scene at the back of the house.

The knife-carrying Indians bent over the bodies of Anna and Josephine. Then with quick rotations of the wrist, they straightened and held up two things—one blonde and one dark. One of the men bent over Anna's huge abdomen, made a sudden move with his knife and held up something that squirmed. Anna's baby! Another slash of the knife and the squirming stopped. The brave tossed the baby onto Anna's bleeding abdomen.

Eddie was nauseated. He must not make a sound. He gulped to keep from vomiting, watching with horror, as the Sioux held up the scalps of Josephine and Anna, while they admired the beautiful long hair.

Anxiously Eddie glanced at Hermie. The little fellow's head was turned toward the cornfield. One of the braves now held Frederick's scalp. Without a backward glance at the blood-spattered bodies, the Indians went into the house carrying their trophies.

"Are they gone?" Hermie whispered.

"No. Be still. Don't move."

"Eddie, my foot hurts."

"You're all right."

Half an hour later the Indians headed east toward New Ulm. Then the boys cautiously crawled the few feet to the cornfield where they worked their way deep into the five-foot-high forest of corn plants.

Eddie's mind was in turmoil. Because the Indians had gone toward New Ulm, they couldn't go to their grandparents' place. For now they were safe in the cornfield. Taking Mary's leather bag from about his neck he placed it on the ground for a pillow. He had to think. Where would they be safe?

The Fort. But Fort Ridgely was on the north side of the river and it was several miles upstream.

"Eddie, my foot hurts and it's bleeding."

The older boy sat up to inspect the injured foot. "Hm-m-m. You have a deep cut on the bottom of your heel. How did it happen?"

"When we was running I stepped on something sharp. It hurts bad."

"I wish we could wash the dirt away but we can't go to the river now. Maybe after dark tonight."

"The Indians shot Amos and Mrs. Moltke and Anna and Frederick, didn't they?"

"Yah."

"Eddie, I'm scared. What are we going to do?"

"I don't know. I'll think of something. Put your head on Grandma's bag and try to sleep. I'll watch."

The sun beat down on the cornfield. Not a breath of air stirred at ground level. Gophers eyed the boys suspiciously. Finally Hermie slept.

Eddie shuddered at the recollection of the gory sights he had seen. He must put these thoughts from his mind. They had to get away. He must plan.

Suddenly he remembered that Amos had a canoe on the bank of the river. Maybe, if they waited until night, they could get across to the north shore. Then, by walking in darkness to the west, perhaps they could reach the safety of Fort Ridgely.

Eddie sighed. Tonight they would cross the river. It was the best plan he could think of.

16.

AFTER THE SIOUX OUTBREAK AND MASSACRE at the Myrick store at the Lower Agency, the nearest refuge for those who managed to escape across the river with the help of the ferryman was Fort Ridgely. Though it wasn't much of a fort, it was the only military post in southwestern Minnesota.

Captain Marsh, commander of the post, had fought in the Civil War but he knew little about fighting Indians. He first learned the news of the outbreak about ten o'clock the morning of August 18 from J. C. Dickinson, the boardinghouse operator at the Lower Agency who had escaped via the ferry with his family. With other panic-stricken refugees, the Dickinsons made their way to the fort in a wagon.

Soon more fugitives arrived, all telling stories of rape, murder and thievery. Leaving nineteen-year-old Lieutenant Thomas Gere with twenty-nine men to hold the fort, Marsh with forty-five enlisted men started for the Lower Agency. The commander was mounted on a mule and the other men rode in wagons. Along the way the soldiers met many excited settlers, among them Reverend Samuel Hinman, the Episcopal missionary whose sermon Little Crow had heard the previous evening.

Reverend Hinman motioned for Captain Marsh to stop. "Sir," he began. "I must warn you that the Indian situation is dangerous. You have very few men. Where do you plan to go?"

"To the Redwood Ferry and across to the Lower Agency."

"Turn back. I doubt you will get that far, but if you do, you surely will be outnumbered."

Marsh threw up his hand. "Thank you, Reverend, but my men can handle a skirmish with a few Indians." The soldiers moved on.

Several times refugees warned Marsh and suggested that he turn back, but the warnings were ignored in spite of evidence of murder and destruction. The soldiers passed farm buildings in flames and saw several corpses along the road, one of them being Philander Prescott, the old fur trader and supposed friend of the Indians who had been murdered after he crossed to the north shore of the river.

A short distance from the ferry the soldiers left the wagons and walked in single file. At the landing there was a heavy growth of hazel and willow brush which provided fine cover along both sides of the river.

Scores of Indians lying in ambush waited for the soldiers. With guns ready, they hid in the brush as the troops approached the ferry.

The flat-bottomed ferryboat was moored at the north shore as if waiting to take them over. Across the river on the south shore a "cut-hair" Indian named White Dog waved. In broken English he called, "Friends, come over for a council."

Marsh and his men, however, were reluctant and made no move to cross. Suddenly a single shot rang out and immediately Indians sprang from among trees and bushes and fired. During the confusion and pandemonium, thirteen soldiers were killed. Captain Marsh's mule was shot from under him but he rallied his men for a volley at the Indians who had taken over the ferry-house behind him.

Realizing that he was cut off on three sides, Marsh led his remaining men through a thicket that ran westward along the north shore for two miles. Here, there was shelter from the Indian guns. As the afternoon wore on they slowly made their way to the end of the brush.

Marsh conferred with some of his men. They decided to cross the river and go down the south side to the Lower Agency. A strong swimmer, Captain Marsh started to lead the soldiers. When only part way across a cramp seized him. In spite of all efforts to save him, the captain drowned.

A young nineteen-year-old sergeant, John Bishop, now took over the command. He led the fifteen survivors, including five wounded men, back to Fort Ridgely. They reached the post after nightfall. Eight more men later straggled in.

The results of the day were disastrous for the little fort. Twenty-four men were lost including the commander.

Only one Indian was killed. The skirmish at Redwood Ferry caused great hilarity among the Sioux. They celebrated boisterously for they now boasted, "We can kill the white men like sheep."

17.

LIEUTENANT GERE sent an urgent message to Governor Ramsey which said, "Captain Marsh and most of his men were killed at the Lower Agency. Little Crow and six hundred Sioux warriors are approaching the fort and likely will attack us. We have two hundred fifty refugees at the fort. The Indians are killing men, women and children. We need immediate relief."

Private William Sturgis, one of the eight survivors of the Redwood Ferry massacre, set out in the darkness to carry the urgent message one hundred twenty-five miles to Fort Snelling. Earlier in the day on August 18, Fort Ridgely had been surrounded by Sioux, but about midnight, aided by darkness, the young soldier managed to slip from the fort with his horse. He rode toward the east down the Minnesota Valley. To his right, the river guided him.

The fertile valley led through the most beautiful regions of Indian country; great lush forests, broad meadows, broken clearings where prosperous settlers had built homes—everything spoke of great abundance in a fruitful land.

William Sturgis thought of the urgent message he carried, a dispatch telling of death and fire, of blood and cruelty. Behind him the dark sky was streaked with flames that lighted the sultry August night for fires were rampant as flames rose from settlers' homes and barns.

Private Sturgis had enlisted a few months earlier at the age of nineteen. The previous day had been the first time he had taken enemy life. His company had been sent out from Fort Ridgely to meet the rebelling Sioux. Chief Shakopee's band were murdering, plundering and burning settlers' homes far and near.

As he rode the young man relived the previous day.

At Red Wood Ferry his band of forty-five had been surprised by Chief Shakopee. He had seen Captain Marsh drown while trying to cross the river, and many of his fellow soldiers fell the victims of Indian bullets. He had been one of the group of eight fortunate survivors. Fort Ridgley's defense now rested with twenty-nine soldiers under the command of Lieutenant Gere.

"Relief immediately!" The words pounded in the mind of William Sturgis. His horse galloped on through the roadless country, along unfamiliar paths and around fallen trees. He often glanced over his shoulder at the fire-red sky. He must hurry—there were lives to be saved—he must pound on doors and warn those who still might escape the murderous Indians.

It was the harvest season. Exhausted from the work in the fields, many farmers slept soundly only to be rudely awakened by thundering horse's hoofs, a rider banging on their door, a frightening call: "The Sioux are on the warpath! They're headed this way! They are murdering all whites—men, women and children! Send women and children away! Hide in haystacks, cellars, woods! Shakopee is coming this way! Hurry! Hide! They're burning everything!"

Dazed with sleep, the people rushed to the door but the rider already was on the way to another house. They wondered if they had been dreaming—but everyone in the house had heard the call. "The Sioux are killing whites! Hide! Hide!"

The settlers looked to the west. There were yellow-red flames. The rider had said, "They're burning everything!"

William Sturgis rode on. Did they believe him or were they saying such things don't happen in quiet Minsota? But he had seen horrible murders with his own eyes. Shakopee and his band had spread out along the north side of the Minnesota River. The chieftain already had taken many scalps. William had seen him and his band the previous day as they swung their tomahawks in brain-spattering killings.

Some images would remain in William's mind until death. A man leaning against a board barnyard fence as though he might be resting. But he was nailed to the boards with arrows stabbed through his inner groin. The man still lived. He screamed wildly. His eye sockets were empty and the gouged-out eyes were lying in pools of blood beside him. William had pulled out the arrows from his groins and the man fell to the ground. He stopped screaming. He lay dead beside his barnyard fence.

Later William had come upon the body of a boy about four years old, the forehead crushed by a tomahawk blow. Not far away a dead woman lay in the tall grass. Her abdomen had been slashed and the intestines removed. William's horrified mind had taken in the scene. The woman had been pregnant. He could see parts of a cut-up baby which had been returned to her abdominal cavity. He thought the dead boy likely was the woman's son.

As William had been fleeing to the fort from the Red Wood massacre, he had hidden in tall grass beside a wheat field where two settlers were shocking wheat. Chief Shakopee and his band dashed up on their horses. They wasted no time in their orgy of killing for within two minutes the settlers' heads were crushed by Sioux tomahawks. Methodically the braves opened the dead men's trousers and swiftly cut off the genitals and lay them on the crushed skulls.

Other images from the previous day flashed through William's mind as he sped through the night. An old man was leaning against the trunk of an apple tree as though he might be sleeping. But when he came closer he was horrified to see the old settler had been scalped and that both arms were cut off.

On that horrible day, August 18, on the way from Red Wood Ferry to the fort, William had seen only two living settlers, one of them being a little girl perhaps nine years old. He had heard a whimper from the branches of an oak tree. Looking up he saw the frightened child. Reluctantly she came down from her hiding place, so petrified with fear that for a time she couldn't speak. She whimpered like a frightened puppy, sobbed with dry eyes and hiccuped for breath. He spoke kindly to her and at last she gasped out her story.

She told William that on the previous day four Indians with feathers in their hair had come to her parents' home about noon. The family were at dinner. Before her eyes they tomahawked her parents and tied her sister's hands; then all four raped the thirteen-year-old sister. While the mayhem was going on the younger girl climbed out a bedroom window and hid in the oak tree. She had been there more than twenty hours. She was sure her parents and sister were dead before the Indians torched the buildings.

William had taken the girl with him. A short distance from the fort they came upon a distraught woman who raced wildly from one haystack to another in a field where there were half a dozen haystacks. "My children!" she screamed. "I can't find my children!" With hair flying she dashed madly from haystack to haystack, almost insane with fear.

After a time William managed to calm her. She said she had hidden her children in a haystack when she learned the Indians were coming. She had run to the woods and hidden in a marsh. When she returned, buildings were burned and every field seemed to have haystacks. She didn't know where she had put her children. She continued to sob and scream, "Where are my little ones? Where is the haystack? Maybe the Indians have killed them!"

William had suggested that she go to Fort Ridgely with him and the little girl, but the woman refused. He left her as he had found her, screaming and rushing from haystack to haystack.

William shuddered. It seemed he could still hear her screams. His horse thundered on through the night as he spread the alarm. "Hide your children! Hide! Hide!"

Private Sturgis changed horses at St. Peter about 3:30 A.M. Twelve hours later on Tuesday, August 19, he rode into Fort Snelling where he delivered his message to Governor Ramsey. He had spread the alarm through the countryside and covered one hundred miles in fifteen hours.

18.

MILFORD TOWNSHIP IN BROWN COUNTY bordered the eastern edge of the Lower Agency Sioux Reservation and in the Indian uprising the township had the highest death rate of any in the state. On August 18 Indians from nearby villages viciously attacked unsuspecting neighbors, killing more than fifty during the day.

On that Monday afternoon while two of Joseph Brown's children, Samuel and Ellen were at the Upper Agency, an old Indian woman told them there was going to be trouble. She stressed that they should get away.

At four the next morning the family was awakened

and told to escape at once. There was no time to catch horses on the prairie; three yoke of oxen were hitched to wagons and twenty-six people started for the fort.

Mrs. Joseph Brown, wife of the former Sioux agent, was determined to lead her family of thirteen children and several neighbors to the safety of Fort Ridgely. Joseph was absent from home when his Sioux wife and her family left their attractive stone home on the north side of the Minnesota River.

With the wagons loaded to capacity, Mrs. Brown set out in the first vehicle behind a pair of oxen. For several miles there were no problems. Then, without warning, they were ambushed by a large group of Indians including Chiefs Cut Nose and Shakopee.

Cut Nose, a repulsive-looking man, so named because of a split in his battle-scarred nose, jumped from his horse to be followed by Shakopee. The chiefs, fresh from an encounter with a party of settlers who were attempting to flee to Fort Ridgely, again were bent on murder. Only a short time before a party of defenseless whites, men, women and children, had huddled in their wagons, prayerfully bending down their heads as they waited for death. In the murderous episode, while braves held the horses, Cut Nose had jumped into the first wagon that contained eleven people, many of them children. Deliberately and in cold blood he tomahawked them all—split open the head of each while the others, stupefied with horror and frozen with fear, listened to the heavy dull blows crash through flesh and bones as they waited their turn.

Fresh with victory, the band of Indians now anticipated another massacre as they confronted Mrs. Brown and her party. Breechcloth-clad Cut Nose was frightful-appearing in war paint with tomahawk in hand. He shouted, "Get out of the wagon!"

Mrs. Brown bristled. "I demand that you let us pass!"

Shakopee lingered with the braves. He likely recognized Mrs. Brown who now urged the oxen on.

Cut Nose raised his tomahawk. "Every person in these wagons will be killed!" The braves watched.

Shaking her fist at Cut Nose the fiery lady shouted in Indian language, "I am Joseph Brown's wife! Like you, I am a Sioux! Chief Akepa is my relative. If you harm any of these friends of mine you will answer to Chief Akepa and his tribe. Now let us pass!"

Cut Nose motioned for Shakopee and the braves to come forward. For several minutes they argued. When the council finally was over Shakopee reluctantly said, "Your men can go. Women and children will be captives at Little Crow's camp. He can do with you what he will."

The Indians then took the women and children to Little Crow's house. The old chief sat on a couch in his brick house. They were escorted inside by Shakopee who explained the situation. When Mrs. Brown entered the room Little Crow got up to greet her. He handed her a cup of cold water before he hurried the group upstairs.

"You must be quiet," he warned. "I will get blankets for you."

"Thank you," Mrs. Brown murmured, knowing quite well that Little Crow realized the necessity for keeping the friendship of the Indians from the Upper Agency. She had good reason to believe he would protect them.

Meanwhile, Eddie and Hermie Winters lay hidden in a thicket several miles east of Fort Ridgely. They had crossed the river the night before in Amos Moltke's canoe and had walked westward until dawn. Because of Hermie's sore foot, progress had been slow. Now, from their hiding place, they saw panic-stricken settlers fleeing their homes, some going east, but most seemed to be traveling toward the fort.

Hermie asked, "Why don't we ask them for a ride?"

"No. Many of them will be caught by the Indians. We'll wait here until night, then we'll walk."

Tears stood in Hermie's eyes. "I don't think I can walk. My foot hurts bad."

Eddie brushed sand from the feverish, dirt-encrusted wound. Red streaks showed halfway to the knee. "When we get to the fort there will be medicine to make it better."

"But—but—I can't walk. It hurts bad."

"Then I'll carry you. We'll make it someway."

19.

AT THE TIME OF THE SIOUX UPRISING New Ulm was the largest settlement near the reservation. Located near the junction of the Cottonwood and Minnesota Rivers, the mostly German settlers numbered nine hundred people by 1862. Because of its nearness to the reservation the young braves were eager to collect the loot it promised.

Another reason New Ulm was an attractive target to the Indians was that most of the young German men had gone to serve in the Union army. They also knew that few of the people owned guns and ammunition. Another factor in the Indians' favor was that the terrain on which the town stood would make defense difficult for the land rose two hundred feet in two huge steps from the Minnesota River to the high bluff behind the settlement. In addition, woods which ran along the crest of the bluff behind the town offered ample cover for the attackers.

August 18, when Wilhelm and his family passed

through New Ulm on the way to Mankato, was planned to be a festive day in town. The people intended to give a noisy sendoff to a recruiting party heading west over the prairie to enlist Civil War volunteers from among the farmers. But the group was ambushed in Milford Township. The survivors rushed back to New Ulm bringing word of the Indian outbreak. Shortly afterward families began to stream into town with terrifying news.

Panic seized many of the people, but finally some defense measures came out of the confusion. The Brown County sheriff, Charles Roos, had military experience. He organized a group of about forty men with guns into military units. Others were armed with pitchforks and similar crude weapons. All went to work erecting barricades around three blocks where there were brick buildings that could be defended.

Women and children were packed into the Dacotah House Hotel and other nearby brick structures. Because of the fashionable hoop skirts of the time each woman required much space. In spite of their anxiety the ladies smiled as they discarded their hoop skirts to make room for new arrivals to crowd into the hotel.

Messengers were sent to secure help from neighboring settlements and others led parties into the nearby countryside to bring in farmers unaware of the danger. Some of the people chose to remain on their farms, among them Amos Moltke and Ernst Winters. Peddler Henning and his wife likewise decided to remain camped outside New Ulm.

That day, several people near the reservation were murdered, including Mary Winters, Adolph Ketchum and Peddler Henning and his wife. Though looting and burning were widespread, in the town of New Ulm Monday passed without incidents. That night, however, the townspeople slept uneasily.

Before dawn on Tuesday, Wilhelm and Amelia returned to New Ulm. Worried, bedraggled and exhausted they were stopped by a guard at the east edge of town who emphatically told them they would not be allowed to return to their farm.

Wilhelm exclaimed, "But my boys and my grandmother and my parents are out there!"

"You are needed here. Go to the Dacotah Hotel. Your wife will be safe there and someone will give you instructions as to how you can help. New Ulm may be attacked at any time."

"Have people been killed west of here?"

"Several—but we don't have names—only reports of corpses in yards and along the road, and many burned and plundered buildings."

Wilhelm's voice rose. "I have to find my family! You have no right to stop me!"

"I understand you're worried. There are many refugees inside the barricade. Your relatives may be safe here. It would be foolhardy to go out there. Wait."

Silent, anxious and dejected, Wilhelm and Amelia rode to Dacotah House. It was impossible to secure authentic information. All morning they searched and questioned neighbors but none had seen any of the Winters family.

Wilhelm whispered to Amelia, "Maybe later today I can sneak out to our place." Swallowing a lump in her throat, Amelia nodded.

In nearby towns groups of citizen-soldiers gathered arms and ammunition in preparation for the march to New Ulm. Charles E. Flandrau, an attorney and judge who was highly respected by the German settlers, commanded the volunteer forces. All day Tuesday small squads of volunteers reached New Ulm.

Throughout the day the people worked to strengthen

the town's defenses. Confusion was rampant as refugees continued to pour in.

The first assault on New Ulm came about 3:00 P.M. on Tuesday, August 19. One hundred Sioux began firing from the wooded bluff behind the settlement. The men who had guns returned the fire which kept the attackers at bay. A few men made a run for a house outside the barricade and they helped drive the Sioux back. Meanwhile, at the upriver end of town several houses burned.

It seemed strange, but the Indians had no leader. No chiefs were present. Suddenly a late afternoon thunderstorm struck which slowed the fighting.

Within the barricaded buildings women and children crouched in terror. Thirteen-year-old Emilie Pauli became hysterical and attempted to dash across the street to the building where her mother hid. Fighting was heavy and the child was the first casualty. In this onslaught five others lost their lives and several more were wounded.

By ten o'clock that night Judge Flandrau arrived with one hundred twenty-five Frontier Guards and two physicians. Dr. Charles Mayo and Dr. William McMahan set up a hospital in a front room of the Dacotah House. Two other physicians did likewise in a basement store across the street.

During the night Flandrau's forces strengthened the town's defenses by gathering barrels, wagons and other items to fortify the street barricades.

The following day Flandrau's command was enlarged by the arrival of one hundred men from Mankato. This group brought the number of poorly-armed citizen-soldiers to about three hundred.

After the first battle at New Ulm, tension mounted, especially among the women, children and unarmed men. More than a thousand people were crowded into the small barricaded area of the settlement's main street. Every available space was filled with anxious, short-tempered humans.

Though Wilhelm and Amelia continued to inquire and search, no one could recall having seen Eddie, Hermie or Mary. Likewise Wilhelm's parents, Ernst and Elizabeth Winters were unaccounted for.

Amos Moltke's parents, Herman and Magdelene, also feared that Amos and Josephine had been killed since they were not among the refugees. August and Gretchen Ketchum and their children were safe within the barricade, but old Adolph had not been seen since early the morning of August 18. Since Frederick and Anna had been disgraced by being tarred and feathered and forcefully removed from town, their whereabouts were unknown.

Nearly everyone was worried about the welfare of a relative, neighbor or friend. Wilhelm and August Ketchum discussed the problem.

"I'm going out to my place," Wilhelm said. "I have to know what has happened."

"Commander Flandrau will stop you."

"Not if he doesn't know I've gone."

August scratched his head. Finally he said, "I'll go with you." He cleared his throat. "I think we'd better take a shovel." He hesitated. "Of course many of these missing people may be safe at Fort Ridgely."

Wilhelm didn't answer. For the time being there was no sign of Sioux in the area. The people knew, however, that the nearby thickets might be cover for numerous braves ready to attack.

After Wilhelm and August told Amelia and Gretchen of their plan, the men went behind the village and for a time they worked to strengthen the barricade. Eventually they slipped unnoticed into the woods on the bluff and headed west.

At the outskirts of the settlement they came across the mangled bodies of Peddler Henning and his wife. Wilhelm shook his head. "The fiends killed the old people and took John's greatest pride and moneymaker—his long beard."

"We'd better go on," August said. "If there's time we'll bury them on the way back."

Silently they walked on. The next farm was that of Ernst and Elizabeth Winters. When they still were far down the road Wilhelm exclaimed, "The buildings are burned!" They broke into a run.

Nothing remained of the neat house and barn but a pile of charred rubble. "Maybe your folks got away," August said.

Wilhelm hurried to search around the razed buildings. He found the bodies lying face down with arrows in their backs. Staring at the bloated, fly-covered corpses of his parents, he murmured, "Why? Why did this happen? They never harmed the Indians." With tear-filled eyes he said, "I'm afraid to go on—but I have to know."

At the next farm the buildings were intact but the farmer, his wife and two children had been murdered and their bodies lay in the barnyard.

Sorrowful and depressed the men pressed on toward the Amos Moltke farm. "The buildings are gone," August said.

"Amos grew up with the young braves," Wilhelm said. "Surely they wouldn't harm him and Josephine."

"They're vindictive villains! They have decided to kill every white person for we are the enemy who took their hunting grounds!" In the back yard behind the burned house the two men recoiled in horror.

"My God!" August exclaimed. "Frederick and Anna, her baby, Josephine and Amos—all brutally murdered—

and scalped!" He turned away and covered his eyes to shut out the horrible sight of the mutilated, decomposing bodies.

Wilhelm muttered, "They're monsters! The devils even cut that poor girl open and killed her baby! They'll stop at nothing."

August shook his head. "Frederick and Anna deserved to be punished, but—not this!" He looked around. "Anyway, Pa isn't here."

Wilhelm turned to pick up a large pile of cloth in the middle of the yard. It was wet from the downpour of the previous evening. Frantically he turned it over. "No! No!" he exclaimed.

"What is it?"

"Grandma's crazy quilt! See that piece of cloth? That was from an old shirt of mine. And this blue woolen piece? That was from one of Pa's old jackets."

"Maybe you're mistaken."

"No! I'd know this quilt anywhere! I recognize most every piece of cloth." He broke off suddenly. "But if it's here, who brought it?" He started toward his farm on the run, still carrying the old quilt.

August sprinted behind him. After passing two or three deserted and burned out sets of buildings, they slowed to a walk.

Finally Wilhelm groaned. "My buildings are gone," he said dully. "I could see them from here." Again he broke into a run. "I pray my boys and Grandma are all right."

They searched. Finally August said, "We may as well go. They're not here. At least you can have hope that they escaped."

"Humph! Two little boys and an old lady? What chance would they have against those fiends? You know as well as I do, they're dead. My boys, my mother and father and Grandma. My buildings are gone. Nothing's left but this cursed Indian land. They can have it! I never want to see the damned place again!" He carefully folded his Grandmother's crazy quilt and put it under his arm. "This quilt is all I have left from my home."

They started back toward New Ulm. August carried the shovel over his shoulder. For a long time they didn't speak. Finally Wilhelm said, "How will I tell Amelia?"

"But you don't know. The boys and Mary might have escaped—some way."

"Yah. They escaped like my Pa and Ma and like Frederick and Anna and all the others. This cursed state. Why in God's name did I come here? Why didn't I listen to Amelia and Grandma back there in Germany? They knew we should stay there. It's all my fault."

"Your three girls are safe in Mankato."

"Yah. And I don't have a way to support them."

Without more conversation they hurried on to the Moltke place. August spoke first. "Let's put all five of them in one big grave here in the cornfield."

When they were finished they hurried to the Ernst Winter homestead where they silently buried Wilhelm's parents. The bodies, like all the others, were engulfed by a black cloud of buzzing flies. They gathered and hung over the dead from daylight to dark. Wilhelm knew he would forever be haunted by the awful sight of his parents' decomposing bodies engulfed in a cloud of buzzing, whirring flies.

As they smoothed the damp soil over the grave, Wilhelm whispered, " 'Bye Ma, 'Bye Pa. I'm sorry I brought you to this." Wiping away a tear the men returned to New Ulm.

Back at the settlement, tension was high as the settlers waited for the next attack. Wilhelm and August dreaded the ordeal of informing relatives and friends of the sad news of their loved ones.

Stoically Amelia received the word about the absence of Eddie, Hermie and Mary and the death of Wilhelm's parents and the destruction of their buildings. When she hadn't spoken for several minutes Wilhelm stared at her in disbelief. "Did you hear what I said?"

Her mouth was set in a tight line. "Yah."

"I don't know what we'll do," Wilhelm said softly. "There's nothing left but the land. Two of our children and Grandma—and Ma and Pa—gone. All that's left is this old quilt of Grandma's."

"We still have our girls. We can start over."

Wilhelm exploded. "Never! I'll leave this cursed place! I don't know where we'll go but—" his voice caught. Amelia put her hand over his.

Herman and Magdelene Moltke accepted their son's death as God's will. Herman wiped away a tear. "He and Josephine lived good lives. In their last day they were protecting Frederick and Anna when no one else would help them. God has called them home."

One by one the neighbors were accounted for. Dr. Otto Hess was presumed to be dead since he had not returned from the Lower Agency where he was visiting a patient at the time of the August 18 attack. His wife, Phidelia, was gone, but Wilhelm and Amelia believed she might be somewhere with Shaska. The other immediate acquaintances were accounted for through August's and Wilhelm's reports. In the meantime, the people waited for the next Sioux attack.

20.

DRAMATIC INDIAN RAIDS occurred over all of southwestern Minnesota. Rural inhabitants of twenty-three counties fled eastward leaving a vast stretch of the southern part of the state depopulated. The settlers' panic was increased by the fear that the Winnebago Indians living on a reservation a few miles south of Mankato, and the Chippewas in the northern part of the state, would combine with the Sioux in an attempt to drive the white man from the area. Fleeing refugees swelled the population of every city in southern and eastern Minnesota. Many settlers never would return to their land. Others, at least temporarily, found havens in New Ulm and Fort Ridgely.

In darkness and rain Eddie and Hermie struggled along the road toward the fort. The children were wet, cold, hungry and tired. Hermie limped badly on his infected heel. "I—I can't walk anymore," he sobbed.

"Don't step on your heel. Walk on your toes."

"I can't. My whole foot hurts." He sniffed and wiped his nose on his sleeve. "Eddie, I can't go any farther."

"We have to go on. Now that we're on the north side of the river, the fort can't be many miles away." Eddie shifted his grandmother's leather bag to his right shoulder. "I'll carry you." He squatted until Hermie was on his back. "Put your arms around my neck." Grasping one of the little boy's legs under each arm, he struggled to stand.

"Here we go," he said softly. By bending forward Hermie's weight was more evenly distributed. Silently he forced himself to push on, one step after another. Occasionally they rested but rain and fog caused their wet clothing to feel uncomfortably cold. The night seemed endless.

At last it was morning. The boys hid in a small pig pen near the road. A wagon loaded with people went west. Eddie was tempted to ask for a ride but fear of being overtaken by Indians stopped him. A few moments later he was thankful he hadn't asked, for four armed Indians on horseback galloped up to the wagon.

Screaming wildly with bloodcurdling Sioux war whoops they shot the panic-stricken people one by one. Frightened, Hermie cried softly.

"Don't look," Eddie whispered.

In less than five minutes the massacre was over. The braves tossed bodies from the wagon and tying two of their horses behind it they drove away with the team and wagon.

Eddie's heart pounded. He could see five bodies on the ground. Two of them were children. The wind blew softly ruffling the rich prairie grass. In the distance a cow bawled. Everything seemed peaceful, yet Death lurked in wait for anyone who ventured on the road.

"Eddie, my leg aches and I'm awful hot. A while ago I was cold."

Reluctantly the older boy bent to examine his brother's swollen, inflamed foot. Red streaks were halfway to the knee. He didn't know what to do. Maybe they should go back and try to get to New Ulm where there was a doctor. But they didn't dare walk the roads in the daytime. Again the cow bawled from nearby woods. She wasn't far away and they needed food.

"Get on my back. We're going to get some milk," Eddie said. Running hunched because of Hermie's weight, he made his way to the edge of the woods where he put his brother under a tree. He scanned the road. No Indians.

"There's the cow!" The friendly animal came toward them. Her enormous milk-filled udder nearly dragged on the ground. She stood quietly, welcoming the relief of having milk drawn from her udder.

Soon Hermie said, "I'm not very hungry."

"Try to swallow a little more."

Finally they leaned back against a maple tree and the cow wandered away. Eddie jumped up. "There's some blackberries! I'll get them for you."

As he picked the juicy purple fruit, Eddie planned. They couldn't have come far last night in the darkness. They likely were closer to New Ulm than to Fort Ridgely. If they made their way back to Amos Moltke's canoe, they could cross to the south side of the river; then they would be close to Grandpa Winters' home just outside of New Ulm. But they had to travel today; Hermie's foot needed attention.

Soon Eddie again got his brother on his back. "Hang on tight. We have to hurry," he said.

"Where are we going?"

"Back. Back to Amos Moltke's canoe."

"But—but—why?"

"Just trust me and hang on."

Trotting east through the woods parallel to the road, the boys made good time. When there were no woods they hurried across fields, keeping a wary eye on the road. If they saw wagons or other traffic they hid in the tall grass. On and on they plodded. Though Eddie was exhausted he pushed himself to reach the point on the river where they had left the canoe. They would cross over in darkness and head for Grandpa Winters' house.

At last from across the field Eddie saw the charred remains of the farm buildings where they had crossed the river. "I think that's the place," he said.

"How can you tell?"

"'Cause there was a windmill beside the burned barn and a long chicken house in the field. There they are.

We'll wait here in the grass until dark."

Hermie, feverish and miserable slept fitfully as Eddie kept watch, his mind in turmoil. Had he done the right thing to return? Suppose the canoe was gone. He could swim, but Hermie couldn't and he had known several children who had drowned in the river.

As soon as twilight had deepened to darkness, Eddie with his brother on his back struggled across the road to the riverbank. Anxiously he peered to the right where he had pulled the canoe into some bushes. He couldn't see it. Putting Hermie down he searched. At last his bare foot touched something. He felt with his hands.

"I've found it," he whispered. Five minutes later they were paddling across to the south shore.

When they were on land and Hermie again was loaded on his back, Eddie said, "Soon now we'll be at Grandpa Winters'." But in the back of his mind was the awful thought that something might have happened to his grandparents.

Hermie whined, "My foot hurts bad. I hope Grandma can fix it."

"Yah." He thought his brother must have a high fever for he felt burning hot against his back. "Sh-h-h. We must be quiet. Someone might be on the road."

Half an hour later they rounded a curve. "We're almost there," he whispered. He should be able now to see the outline of the buildings. He could smell charred wood. Without speaking he walked to the place where the house should be. There was nothing but a pile of rubble. "Oh-h-h. The house is gone."

Hermie whimpered. "Where will we go? Where are they?"

Wearily Eddie hitched Hermie higher on his back. His arms and legs ached. He had walked in a bent-over position so long he wondered if he could straighten up.

"We'll go on to New Ulm. Maybe we'll find them there." The awful thought crossed his mind that perhaps the Indians had killed everyone in the settlement.

"Eddie, when will Ma and Pa be back?"

"I don't know. Soon, I hope. Now be still." They plodded on. After a time he whispered, "We'll soon be at the edge of town." Suddenly a shout raised the hair on the back of his neck.

"Who goes there?"

The voice didn't sound like an Indian's but he hesitated to answer. Should they dive into the bushes beside the road?

Again the call came. "Who goes there? Answer or I'll shoot!"

His voice trembled. "Ed—Eddie Winters and my—my brother!"

"What is your father's name?"

"Wilhelm. Wilhelm Winters."

The tone of the voice changed. "Welcome. Your parents will be happy you're here. We thought you were dead."

The boys went on until they stood beside the shadowy figure. "Who are you, sir?" Eddie's voice trembled.

"Charles Schling."

"Yah, I know. My parents told me we stayed at your place when we first came to Minnesota. Where can I find my parents?"

"At the Dacotah House. Your mother is there. Your father's on guard duty. Can you find it?"

"Yah."

"Guards will stop you in the dark. Tell them who you are real fast." Charles patted Eddie's shoulder. "I'm glad you and your brother are safe."

"Thanks." Ten minutes later the boys were admitted to Dacotah House where they joyfully joined Amelia.

21.

THROUGH THE DAY AND INTO THE NIGHT refugees poured into Fort Ridgely. Some of the two hundred fugitives were wounded which taxed the post's limited hospital capacity. A majority of the people were women and children. Dr. and Mrs. Alfred Muller cared for wounded refugees as they arrived. Several women fugitives acted as nurses, made bandages and prepared meals.

The little post was poorly situated to repulse an attack. Deep ravines to the north, east and southwest offered easy approaches. The prairie stretched to the northwest.

The fort had no stockade; the post was merely a collection of unfortified and detached buildings. Stables for the horses lay to the south and ammunition magazines stood on the prairie two hundred yards northwest of the fort.

No well had ever been dug. The men filled tubs, barrels and other containers with water from a spring below the bluff.

The belated arrival of the Sioux annuity money at noon on August 18—$71,000 in gold—which might have prevented the uprising, now became an added burden for young Lieutenant Thomas Gere. The kegs of money were hidden in one of the buildings until they could be returned to St. Paul.

Hours passed and more refugees arrived with reports of savage attacks upon the settlers. Lieutenant Gere, who was ill with mumps, became extremely anxious and his urgent message to Governor Ramsey for help was carried to Fort Snelling by Private William Sturgis.

Though it was unknown to Lieutenant Gere, while he wrote his urgent message the Indians were celebrating their victory. They were not yet ready to attack the fort.

It is likely that if they had struck Monday night or Tuesday morning they could have captured Fort Ridgely which would have opened a clear route to the Mississippi.

However, young Lieutenant Gere and his small force took what precautions they could. Expecting an attack at any minute, he ordered the women and children to crowd into the stone barracks. Pickets were posted around the fort. Some were civilians who were issued muskets from the post's limited supply. In spite of the fear of an attack, the night passed quietly.

The next morning, August 19, as the fort's lookout watched through a telescope, Indians on foot and on horseback met on the prairie west of the fort. Big Eagle and Mankato wished to attack Ridgely at once but they were overruled by the younger braves who argued for an attack on New Ulm where there were stores to loot and girls to be captured. The gathering broke up and moved off toward New Ulm.

During the day, reinforcements arrived until by evening more than one hundred eighty men were at hand to defend the fort. Thus prepared, they waited.

Early in the afternoon of August 20, (Wednesday) Little Crow with four hundred warriors made a distracting demonstration on the west side of the fort; meanwhile the main body of Indians crept up from the east in a ravine. They struck and gained a few buildings.

Lieutenant Sheehan, who took over command from Lieutenant Gere, told his men to take cover and fire at will. They had two twelve pound howitzers which were aimed at the approaching Indians. The fire of the howitzers plus the discharge of muskets, drove the Sioux back into the ravine.

After the first rush failed the Indians continued firing for five hours. In the evening, they withdrew. This was their first encounter with artillery, and it frightened them. They were afraid of the howitzer shells which they called "rotten balls" because they flew into pieces when fired.

A heavy rain fell all night on August 20. Things were quiet at the fort until the Sioux returned on Friday, August 22, when Little Crow with eight hundred warriors launched a strong attack.

To cover their movements the Sioux camouflaged their headbands with prairie grass and branches. They attempted to set fire to roofs with blazing arrows but because of the recent rain, the effort failed. The few small fires that were started were quickly extinguished with water.

So the onslaught was unsuccessful, but the Sioux were then prepared to try hand to hand combat. They gained possession of the stables to the south, but well placed artillery shells set the building on fire.

After hours of see-saw shelling and maniacal Indian yells, Mankato took over the attack from the southwest because Little Crow had been wounded. Strong artillery fire sent the warriors fleeing in disorder and the defense of Ridgely held, but at a cost in lives. Sioux casualties were thought to be a hundred, while three whites lost their lives and thirteen were wounded.

Soldiers and citizens alike expected more attacks. Governor Ramsey gave his friend Henry Sibley a colonel's commission and asked him to put down the outbreak. Sibley knew the Sioux, their customs, language and country. Formerly an American Fur Company's representative, he had traded with them for twenty-eight years; he also had been Minnesota's first governor.

Colonel Sibley realized the seriousness of the situation and waited until supplies arrived at St. Peter. Finally on August 26 he advanced with fourteen hundred soldiers and arrived at the post the following day. On August 29 many of the refugees were moved to St. Paul in the wagons that had brought supplies.

Later, Chief Big Eagle who fought the whites at Fort Ridgely remarked that the Indians thought the fort was the door to the valley as far as St. Paul, and that if they were able to capture it, nothing could stop them. He said, "But they defended the fort. They were very brave and they kept the door shut."

22.

IN THE DAYS FOLLOWING the first attack on New Ulm, tension increased among the more than a thousand men without guns and women and children who were crowded into the small barricaded area on the main street. Most of them were in the cramped quarters of Dacotah House and the Erd Building.

On Saturday, August 23, lookouts spied smoke rising in the direction of Fort Ridgely. Commander Flandrau was deceived into the belief that the fort had fallen and the Sioux were about to attack New Ulm from across the river. So sure was Flandrau that this was the plan that he sent an officer with seventy-five men across to meet the attackers; they were cut off and forced to retreat toward St. Peter with the result they did not get back to New Ulm until the following day. This left Flandrau with only two hundred twenty-five guns as the Indians were ready to attack. Because Little Crow had been injured at Fort Ridgely, Chiefs Mankato, Big Eagle and Wabasha led the six hundred fifty Sioux in the second attack on New Ulm.

At 9:30 A.M. the Indians emerged from the woods onto the prairie where they formed a long curved line. Flandrau directed his men to meet the attack outside the barricade.

Wilhelm and August had been issued muskets. They listened as the lookout with a telescope reported. "They're advancing in a long line about a mile and a half away and the line is expanding like a fan. They're running!"

When the Sioux were about double rifle shots away the warriors screamed blood-curdling yells and dashed toward Flandrau's men.

Unaccustomed to Indian warfare, the yells unsettled the men and they broke for the rear. The Indians immediately seized the unoccupied houses until Flandrau rallied his men and they regained some of the buildings. Firing from both sides was sharp and rapid—a true Indian skirmish in which every man fought in his own way.

Two groups of Flandrau's men, about forty in all, occupied a large wooden windmill and the post office. Their sharp sniping prevented the Indians from storming the barricades.

The battle continued. Because of their superior numbers, the Sioux gained ground until they gradually enveloped the town. Many buildings burned leaving open spaces across which they did not advance; this fact slightly slowed their progress. The Indians then concentrated near the river where they set buildings on fire and advanced behind the smoke.

About 3 P.M. Flandrau and his men faced a charge of sixty mounted and foot warriors. In the counter charge the New Ulm defenders were aided by a volley from the barricades. Yelling like savages, the settlers routed the Sioux. Though there was fighting until dark, this was the turning point of the battle.

That night Flandrau ordered that the forty buildings still standing outside the barricade be burned. A total of one hundred ninety structures were destroyed in New Ulm; only those within the barriers were left standing.

Early on the morning of Sunday, August 24, the Indians again appeared. They made a feeble attack in which they fired long range shots, attempted to drive off some cattle, and then withdrew. Later that day Flandrau held a council with his officers and the physicians. Soberly they discussed their precarious position.

Dr. William Mayo was concerned about the health of the noncombatants who had huddled for five days in cellars and small rooms. "There is danger in these conditions," he began. "Epidemics of disease flourish where people are crowded like sheep in a cattle car. They have insufficient food and sanitary conditions are poor. We have ill and wounded who need medicine and attention which we are unable to give here. I have a child patient with blood poisoning in his foot, several men with gun shot wounds, pregnant women and others with contagious dysentery."

There was much discussion as to whether they should stay and fight for what was left of New Ulm with their limited amount of ammunition, or whether the town should be evacuated. A vote was taken and it was decided to evacuate.

Huddled in a corner of Dacotah House, Wilhelm and Amelia whispered. "You think Hermie is better?" Eddie interrupted.

Amelia answered, "He seems easier since Dr. Mayo lanced his foot, but he has a high fever. They're doing all they can to keep him comfortable. Gretchen is sitting with him."

Wilhelm muttered, "I'm glad we're leaving this cursed place tomorrow. I never want to see it again."

Eddie whispered, "Pa, won't the Indians attack us on the road to Mankato? I've seen them murder whole wagon loads of people."

Wilhelm's voice was expressionless. "It's possible they will give us a bad time, but we have to do something. If we stay here they'll kill all of us when the ammunition is gone."

Eddie took Mary's leather bag from about his neck. "I found Grandma's leather bag. I remember she told me once that when she died you and Grandpa Winters were to have it. What do you suppose is in it?"

Wilhelm stared at the worn old bag. "Nothing worth much. Just Grandma's keepsakes, I expect. You look after it, will you?"

"Yah. But when we get to Mankato I'm going to file the lock open. I've always wanted to see what she kept in it."

Wilhelm still stared at the bag. "A crazy quilt and an old leather bag—that's all we have to show for twelve years of hard work."

Amelia stood up. "I'm going back to Hermie now. But Wilhelm, you're forgetting something. We have our five children—that's the important thing. I'm sorry about Grandma Mary and your parents, but we are lucky our children were spared."

"They have been this far but who knows what the fiends will do when we're on the road to Mankato?"

The following morning one hundred-fifty-three wagons loaded with women and children, sick and wounded, plus many refugees on foot, began the departure from New Ulm. Their destination was Mankato, thirty miles to the east.

It was a sad spectacle to see these people leaving their homes. Only a few days before they had been happy and prosperous; now they were destitute and starting on a journey through hostile country where at any moment an attack was possible.

Wilhelm's wagon carried his family and several of the wounded. Hermie seemed brighter and his fever was almost gone. Eddie and Amelia constantly scanned the countryside for Indians.

"We'll see the girls when we get to Mankato," Amelia said as she watched Hermie who was sleeping at her feet in the wagon box. He looked pale.

"Yah." Wilhelm, bitter and depressed, was uncommunicative. Eddie absent mindedly fingered the lock on his grandmother's leather pouch but his thoughts were of the horrors he had witnessed. He tried to remember—how many humans had he seen murdered? Twelve? Thirteen? He shuddered.

Amelia wondered what would happen to her family. Five children, no home or money, no property except acres of land that was worthless because no one dared to live on it. If they safely made the journey to Mankato, then what? They owned the team and wagon and the clothes on their backs—that was all. They had lived in Minnesota for twelve years and they were leaving the land as it was except for a few cleared fields. They hadn't even left their footprints in Minnesota. They came with nothing and they were leaving with nothing. Only then, they were young. Now she and Wilhelm were approaching middle age. She turned to glance at the wounded men lying behind her. Stoically they met her gaze.

The silent, melancholy procession went on, hour after hour. Commander Flandrau accompanied the wagon train with one hundred fifty well-armed men. His thoughts went back to the battle at New Ulm. He had lost thirty-four men and sixty were wounded. Some of them would die. He wondered how many Indians had been killed. Flandrau knew his troops and the inexperienced German settlers had put up a heroic fight to save their town against a greatly superior force of enraged savages who were determined to capture New Ulm and to plunder and take scalps. He felt that possibly future historians would say they had saved towns further down the river from attack. But, he reminded himself, this was wishful thinking. Surely the Sioux would attack again—somewhere.

After a long, uncomfortable, anxious journey, the weary procession safely arrived at Mankato late in the evening of August 25, 1862.

23.

AFTER THE JOYFUL REUNION of the Winters family the previous evening, there was much to talk about the following day. For the first time Wilhelm and Amelia had an opportunity to hear from Eddie in detail the terrible experiences he and Hermie had endured. Tears were shed as the family heard of Grandmother Mary's bravery in confronting the Sioux.

"She saved Hermie's and my life. She sent us to hide while she held them off. She tried to save Adolph," Eddie said, "and so did Chief, but the Indians were like crazy men."

Faith wiped her eyes. "It makes me feel bad that they threw her into the fire—and Adolph, too."

"You don't know how they killed Grandpa and Grandma Winters, do you?" Charity asked.

Wilhelm answered, "They were shot with arrows."

For a time no one spoke. Then Hope said, "We only have our family now. All the other relatives are gone." Tears ran down her cheeks.

Wilhelm walked to the window and stared into the street. Amelia said, "It's hard, but, thanks to Grandma Mary, our family is safe. We should be thankful. And Hermie is going to be all right."

Hope said, "I don't know how you carried him so far on your back, Eddie."

The boy grinned. "I had to. He couldn't walk."

Hermie raised up in bed. "Will the Indians get us here?" His eyes showed the fear he felt.

Amelia patted his shoulder. "We're safe now."

"Pa," Eddie said, "Do you think the killing will go on out there?" He motioned to the west.

"They've taken women and children prisoners. I don't know what they'll do with them. And I understand from the hotel owner, John Moore, that they're still killing, plundering and burning in the country."

Amelia said, "Girls, shouldn't you be helping Mrs. Moore?"

The triplets got up. "We're going. There are breakfast dishes to wash," Faith said.

"The Moores are nice people," Hope said. "Mrs. Moore has showed us how to do a lot of things."

When they were gone Wilhelm said, "We have to decide what we're going to do. This morning while Eddie and I fed and watered the team, John Moore was cleaning the stable and we helped him. He says he can't keep the work up at the stable and the hotel, too. He asked if Eddie and I would work for him while we're here. I said we would. It's a break for us. We can earn our keep until we know what we're going to do." He paused. "And he said Mrs. Moore would like the girls to stay on with her too. She also suggested that she could use you, too, Amelia."

"I don't know much about hotel work, but I expect I could learn." She laughed. "We'd all be working except Hermie."

Wilhelm planned. "We could lay up a little money." He glanced about the room. "We will be crowded, it won't be like our house was. John said because the hotel has such a demand for rooms now, we could have only one room. He said he'd put another bed in this room."

"Three beds. One for the boys, one for the girls and one for us. We can manage! Let's do it!"

Wilhelm got up. "That takes care of us for now, but we will have to give some thought to the future."

"Maybe we can stay here," Eddie said.

"Never! The sooner we can leave this cursed state, the better! But we have to have money first."

24.

WITH THE SUCCESSFUL DEFENSE of Fort Ridgely and New Ulm, the first phase of the Sioux uprising ended. The second aspect was an organized military effort to defeat and punish the Indians and to force the release of captives.

Many of Colonel Henry Sibley's volunteers were of doubtful military value. Because they were volunteers, they had not enlisted for any set period of time and many of them soon decided to take their horses and return home. Thus Sibley was left with the nearly impossible task of locating the mounted Sioux.

The foot soldiers also were ineffective. Colonel Sibley was forced to check several times each night to see that his pickets were awake. The arms provided him were a miscellaneous collection for most of Minnesota's good firearms had gone with earlier regiments to the Civil War and Sibley was left with old firearms, many of foreign manufacture, so that often ammunition did not fit them. The colonel sent repeated pleas to the state officials for mounted troops and Springfield rifles.

Training and equipping his soldiers was but one of Sibley's tasks. Relatives and friends of murdered settlers reminded the colonel that bodies lay where they had fallen days earlier. Finally on August 31, after scouts reported that no large group of Sioux lurked nearby, Colonel Sibley sent out a burial party from Fort Ridgely—teamsters, wagons and a detail of soldiers and settlers, about one hundred seventy in all. Agent Galbraith was among the group.

Major Joseph R. Brown, former Indian agent, commanded the burial party. Brown was instructed to find out where the Indians had gone and what their plans were. He had a special interest in this information for he believed his Sioux wife and their thirteen children were captives.

The burial party stopped from time to time to bury sixteen bodies. The poor condition of the corpses was due to having lain in the hot sun for nearly two weeks. Clouds of huge black flies swarmed around the bodies. There were many signs of mutilation.

The next morning the force divided. Brown crossed the river. At the Lower Agency the group found several corpses, among them the storekeeper Andrew J. Myrick who had been murdered on August 18.

Slowly they worked their way toward Little Crow's village which was abandoned. Brown, experienced in Indian ways, felt that no Sioux had been about for several days. He thought they might have gone to the Upper Agency.

On the north side of the river the second part of the burial party worked throughout the day. They found a woman, Mrs. Justina Kreiger, who had been wounded and left for dead on August 19. For days she had wandered about the area. A bed was fixed for her in one of the wagons.

Near sunset Brown's party recrossed the river and the two groups set up camp. Together, they had buried fifty-four settlers during the day. Neither group had seen any Indians.

However, Little Crow had partially recovered from his wounds and his raiding party was lurking nearby. On September 1, the day Brown was at Little Crow's abandoned village, the old warrior had led one hundred ten braves to a rendezvous with Chief Gray Bird and three hundred fifty warriors. Indian scouts followed Brown's party and learned the location of the soldiers' campsite. They planned to surround the camp at night and destroy the entire party the following day.

Always cautious and keenly aware of Indian ways, Brown set up camp in the accepted manner with wagons parked around the outer edge with the team horses still fastened to them. The enclosure within the circle of wagons was less than a hundred yards in diameter. Tents were set up inside the fortification. Although Brown did not expect trouble, ten pickets were stationed around the camp.

While the soldiers slept, two hundred warriors led by Big Eagle and Mankato joined Little Crow and Gray Bird. Some of them occupied Birch Coulee to the east of

Brown's camp; others gathered on a knoll to the west. On the north, Gray Bird's braves crawled toward the wagons through the tall prairie grass while still others were divided between the coulee and a swale to the south.

Just before daybreak on September 2, the camp cook noticed that the horses were uneasy. He reported the matter and as he and a guard watched, Indians were seen moving in the grass. They fired a single shot and raised the alarm.

The Indians responded with blood-curdling yells as they poured a deadly barrage into the sleepy camp. Thirty men were wounded within a matter of minutes. Others tried to take cover behind wagons. Since most of the horses were killed in the first onslaught, the men used the carcasses as barricades.

Heavy fighting lasted for an hour. Brown's party suffered casualties. Agent Galbraith and Major Brown were wounded. When the Indian fire slackened, the men with only four shovels, their bayonets, knives and tin plates, dug shallow rifle pits. As the day wore on the attack lessened in ferocity; however, the siege continued.

Fort Ridgely, sixteen miles downriver, learned of the battle. Colonel Sibley promptly sent a relief party of two hundred forty men under the leadership of Colonel Samuel McPhail. Not far from where the battle raged, McPhail was met by a group of Indians. He pulled back, and thinking he was surrounded, hurriedly sent a messenger back to Fort Ridgely for reinforcements.

Sibley immediately left the fort with his entire remaining force of six companies. He reached McPhails bivouac about midnight. At daybreak the force moved on toward the besieged camp, shelling the area as they went. The artillery fire and their superior numbers scattered the Sioux and Colonel Sibley rode into Brown's camp before noon on September 3.

Sibley found a gruesome sight. Thirteen men and ninety horses lay dead, forty-seven men were seriously wounded, and many more were hurt less seriously. Decaying bodies caused a nauseating stench. The survivors were weak and exhausted from a thirty-one hour siege in the heat with little food or water. Debris littered the camp and tents were shredded from bullets. Through the long battle Mrs. Kreiger had remained in her wagon, the only one that remained upright. There were two hundred bullet holes in the blankets and robes around her, yet miraculously she escaped serious injury. However she was so frightened and exhausted from the ordeal that for a time she was unable to speak.

The dead were buried near where they had fallen while the wounded were placed in wagons and taken back to Fort Ridgely.

The heaviest casualties of the war were suffered in this battle at Birch Coulee. Events there taught the whites it was extremely unwise to attempt to move in hostile Indian territory without a well-trained, large army.

As the days passed skirmishes were reported throughout southwestern Minnesota. Little Crow and his braves made their way toward Acton where the Sioux uprising had started two weeks before. The younger warriors still were bent on the murder of settlers and the plunder of homes and towns.

Groups of soldiers were scattered throughout the rural area prepared to meet Indian violence. One such group was camped within two miles of Little Crow and his braves near Acton. When the company of soldiers came upon Little Crow's camp, a running battle occurred in which six soldiers were killed and fifteen were wounded.

Skirmishes such as this caused more settlers to hurriedly leave the Acton-Forest City area. Other settlements north of the Minnesota River threw up fortifications.

South of the river defense measures also were under way. Governor Ramsey authorized Colonel Flandrau to command all troops along the states southern and southwestern frontiers. On September 3 he set up defense lines with forts at close intervals from the Iowa border to New Ulm. These quickly made, rude defenses were effective in deterring roving bands of Indians.

After a few more battles in September, the backbone of the Sioux uprising was broken. Flandrau and Sibley were ordered to carry out a plan designed by Governor Ramsey. Flandrau was to hold the frontier with its new chain of forts while Sibley moved against the Indians. Ramsey had two objectives in his plan; first, to free the captives; the second, as expressed by the governor, was that "The Sioux must be exterminated or driven forever beyond the borders of the state." Everywhere throughout the state the people demanded, "Death to the murderous Sioux—exterminate the fiends."

However before the Minnesota military forces could seize the initiative, Sibley must move his troops upriver from Fort Ridgely where they were headquartered. Preparations proceeded so slowly that Sibley was criticized by citizens and newspaper editors. Though he was stung by the criticism, Sibley refused to be stampeded into moving before he had soldiers and supplies necessary to handle any Indian forces he might meet.

The task of securing men, arms, ammunition and supplies fell largely to Governor Ramsey and the adjutant general who bombarded the war department in Washington, President Lincoln and the governors of other states, with requests for help.

At this time the Civil War was going badly for the Union and Lincoln had asked governors of northern states to send more men. Governor Ramsey protested that Minnesota could not meet its quota, to which Lincoln replied, "Attend to the Indians."

By September 5 the Minnesota governor's pleas to Washington for help still were ignored. On September 6 Ramsey dispatched a telegram to President Lincoln. He said: "Indian outrages continue. Secretary Edwin Stanton refuses our request for five hundred horses. This is not our war, it is a national war. Answer me at once. More than five hundred whites have been murdered by the Indians."

At last Ramsey got action. He received a letter written on September 17 instructing Sibley to push on and exterminate the Indians. But he still had a shortage of horses due to the loss of ninety animals at Birch Coulee; he had only twenty-five mounted men and he was bogged down by a lack of disciplined soldiers and experienced officers.

Colonel Sibley was deeply concerned and aware that delay made more difficult the situation for whites and half-breeds who were held prisoner by the Indians. He also knew if he made a mistake in dealing with the Sioux, the captives would be killed.

Sibley thought Little Crow might be weary of war and ready for negotiations. By a note to the old chief, the colonel suggested that they negotiate and that the prisoners be returned under a truce flag. However, Little Crow refused to give up the prisoners and Sibley was adamant that his demand be met before he would consider proposals for peace.

Unknown to Little Crow was the fact that there was division in his ranks. The half-breed who carried Little Crow's letters to Sibley also carried one from Mankato in which he asked how his men could be taken under Sibley's protection. Colonel Sibley replied that soon his troops would be moving and the Sioux who wished protection should gather with their captives on the prairie with a white flag plainly displayed.

Though he was cheered by evidence of a division in Indian ranks, Sibley was convinced that Little Crow still controlled the main body of braves. Daily drills soon whipped Sibley's inexperienced soldiers into an effective force. A consignment of ammunition arrived as well as clothing and provisions. On September 13 Sibley also received two hundred seventy experienced infantrymen of the Third Minnesota Regiment who had seen action in the Civil War.

Again Sibley made plans to move, and again he was delayed—this time by heavy rains that turned the prairie into a muddy quagmire. At last on September 19 he left Fort Ridgely to begin his march up the valley with an army of 1619 men. The old missionary, Reverend Riggs, went along as interpreter and chaplain, and the friendly Indian, John Other Day, who had alerted and planned the escape of Upper Agency whites weeks earlier, acted as scout.

Four days of marching toward the Upper Agency brought Sibley's troops to Wood Lake where they camped. Again the colonel was deceived into believing the Indians were farther up the valley; actually, they were only a few miles away. The following morning the Sioux attacked and after two hours of fighting, they withdrew. During the battle Chief Mankato was killed. His body was carried away but fourteen other Indians were left on the battlefield. Some of these warriors were scalped by the soldiers who had been told that Indian scalps were selling for $200 in St. Paul. Sibley sternly expressed his disapproval and promised extreme punishment to any men who repeated the act of scalping Indians.

The battle of Wood Lake was a decisive victory for Sibley's troops, though seven men were killed and thirty-three wounded. The colonel declared that the Indians would not dare to make another stand. He was right for the victory of the whites marked the end of organized warfare by the Sioux in Minnesota.

25.

COLONEL SIBLEY REMAINED at the Wood Lake camp for two days to work out his strategy. He hesitated to chase the hostile Indians because he feared that if they were cornered, they would kill the prisoners. It later was proven that Sibley was correct in his decision, for Little Crow did threaten to kill the captives after returning from Wood Lake. By then, however, the old chief again had lost much of his power and the warriors did not carry out the threat.

Now there was a serious split in the Sioux ranks. Many wanted to make peace. Little Paul, who had been educated by Missionaries Riggs and Williamson, was speaker of the Upper Sioux. In more than one council he had boldly suggested that they should release the prisoners and end the war. Though it was unknown to the whites, many Christian Indians and other "friendlies" had been protecting white captives brought into Indian camps.

While Little Crow and his warriors were fighting at Wood Lake with Shakopee, Red Middle Voice and others, friendly Indians took the captives to their own camp near Missionary Riggs' deserted Hazelwood Mission. When the Indians were defeated, the "friendlies" and prisoners watched in astonishment as several of the chiefs gathered their families and possessions and headed for the open prairie; others, including Little Crow ran to Canada out of the reach of Sibley's army.

On September 25 the troops set up their camp near the friendly tents where the captives were quartered. Many Indians who never had favored war, and Lower Sioux who were tired of fighting, now were ready to surrender.

On September 26 Sibley and an escort of troops, all unmounted, entered the camp. With drums beating and colors flying, Colonel Sibley spoke to the Indians and half-breeds. "We are glad to be here to talk with you. We are sorry for all the deaths on both sides that this war has caused; like you, we are weary of fighting. However I am determined to carry out orders from Governor Ramsey to pursue and overtake the guilty parties. I demand that all captives be delivered to me immediately, that I may take them to my camp."

That same day the friendly Indians released ninety one whites and one hundred fifty half breeds. Within the next few days additional captives were freed—two hundred sixty-nine in all. Most of the whites rescued were women and children.

Among those released were Mrs. Joseph Brown and her thirteen children, and Phidelia Hess. Phidelia, however, chose to return to Shasta's lodge where she was accepted as one of the wives of the handsome young Indian. The grateful captives were taken to Camp Release, as Sibley's encampment was called.

Mrs. Joseph Brown, with tears running down her face said, "We have watched for your coming for days.

Look at us! When some of the women and children were captured, they were half-dressed. They have been nearly naked for the whole time. There never was enough food or clothing. We were always hungry. We have roamed about as captives for weeks, expecting any day that we might be killed."

The soldiers did what they could to relieve the discomfort of the freed captives. The following day most of the women and orphaned children went in wagons to Fort Ridgely; others were sent to various settlements.

When Colonel Sibley took over the friendly camp about 1,200 Indians were taken into custody. Daily the numbers rose as small groups of starving Sioux continued to surrender. Finally a separate camp was set up nearby until eventually the number grew to two thousand.

Feeding the Indians was a problem. In early October Sibley sent 1,250 Sioux, under guard, to gather corn and potatoes from fields near the ruined Upper Agency. In the meantime soldiers searched the region for more captives.

The fighting was over, but punishment of the Sioux remained to be decided by a military commission.

26.

ON SEPTEMBER 28, a five-man military commission convened at Camp Release to try the Sioux prisoners. A few weeks later Sibley moved his army and the prisoners to the Lower Agency where trials were resumed early in October.

Residents of Minnesota followed court proceedings in the newspapers. In Mankato, as in every other southern city of the state, farmer refugees took whatever work they could find to provide food for their families. Many who had money left the state never to return.

Wilhelm and his family were comfortable at the Moore Hotel where they were employed. At the end of each day they gathered in their room where Eddie and the triplets took turns reading aloud from the *Minnesota Pioneer* newspaper the stories of the trial and the experiences of people who had been captives of the Sioux.

On November 5, Eddie, holding the newspaper, sat beside the dresser where a kerosene oil lamp flickered. "It says here," he began, "that the trial commission has finished its work at the Lower Agency. They have tried 392 prisoners, sentenced 303 to death and given prison terms to 16."

"Humph!" Wilhelm snorted. "Only 303 got the death penalty? I'd have liked to have been on that commission! I'd have voted for the death penalty for every one of the fiends! And there was a hell of a lot more than 392 of the villains. What are they going to do with the others? They're getting off easy! Three hundred three to get the death sentence and they killed 500 Minnesotans! Yah, and they let Little Crow get away! He was in charge of the whole attack!"

"Where did he go?" Amelia asked.

"John Moore says several of the chiefs escaped to Canada, and some went west."

Eddie skimmed the page. "Pa, it says here many Indians who expected to be treated as prisoners of war were sentenced to death just for being present at the battles."

"Serves 'em right! The murderous savages don't

deserve to live!"

Eddie continued. "Colonel Sibley would like to execute the condemned ones right away, but he thinks he doesn't have the authority."

"Hang 'em now and argue later! That's what I'd do."

"Sibley is going to send the list of condemned with their records to President Lincoln."

"You think he might pardon them?" Amelia asked.

Wilhelm jumped up. "Hell, I hope not! Minnesota don't need them villains and neither does any other place in the United States! Get rid of 'em! Kill them like they killed our people! Don't the Bible say an eye for an eye and a tooth for a tooth?"

Hope asked, "What will they do with the squaws and children? They didn't kill people."

Wilhelm nodded. "We'll have to take care of them—feed and clothe them. But you know the old saying—'Nits make lice'."

Eddie turned a page and scanned a few paragraphs. "Here's an interesting story about a white woman that was captured."

Faith reached for the paper. "Let me read it. It's about a woman named Mrs. Justina Kreiger. Her trouble started the day we went with Ma and Pa to Mankato. It says on August 18 settlers from thirteen families in Renville County learned the Indians were on the warpath. They gathered at the home of one of the German farmers and made plans to escape the area. They travelled all night in eleven ox-drawn carts on their way to Fort Ridgely. By sunrise they were half way to the fort when a party of Sioux warriors overtook them.

"The Indians knew one of the farmers, a man named Paul Kitzman. According to Mrs. Kreiger, the Indians said it was the Chippewas who were killing whites, not the Sioux. They convinced the farmers to return to their homes, even offering to accompany them so they would arrive safely.

"However, when the settlers reached their homes the treacherous Sioux suddenly turned on them, killing the men and some of the women and children—twenty-five in all."

Wilhelm jumped up. "The beasts!" He paced. "They're not human!"

Faith resumed reading. "Mrs. Kreiger was wounded and left for dead. She had seen her husband and two children butchered. Four of her children were spared because they pretended they were dead. Her own back was filled with wounds from buckshot.

"For three weeks Mrs. Kreiger and her children lived in a swamp. Their only food was wild plums and nuts. They suffered from cold as fierce rains and chilly night air added to their misery. One day while she was scouting for food her children disappeared. She wandered nights and hid during the days. Constant fear, worry and exhaustion made her like a wild woman."

Hermie exclaimed, "Just like Eddie and me!"

Faith continued. "Colonel Sibley's men rescued her before the Birch Coulee battle. For thirty-six hours, this poor woman hid in a wagon box protected only by a tent canvas as the battle raged. Two hundred balls passed through the wagon box and her blankets and the canvas. Miraculously, she was not hit."

Charity asked, "Does the paper say what happened to the children?"

"Yah. Some soldiers rescued them and took them to Fort Ridgely where Mrs. Kreiger found them."

Amelia nodded. "That's nice—but her husband and two children were killed the first day."

Faith scanned the paper. "Here's something about Mrs. Joseph Brown. I remember her. She's a Sioux."

"Yah," Eddie commented. "I heard she was a captive and so were all thirteen of her children."

Charity reached for the newspaper. "It's my turn to read now." Rapidly she skimmed the news items. "It says Mrs. Brown, her family and some other people from the Upper Agency were captured on their way to Fort Ridgely. Since she was a Sioux, she threatened them with revenge from her Indian relatives if her group was harmed. The warriors took them to Little Crow's village. For days they wandered with the old chief's band, never knowing when they might be killed. They were freed at Camp release. None of her group were harmed."

Amelia rubbed her forehead. "There are a few happy endings to these terrible events." For several moments no one spoke. Then Amelia said, "I'm thankful we're safe and together. We miss Grandma Mary and Grandma and Grandpa Winters, and all the others, but they're at rest now and we have to go on with our lives." She glanced at Wilhelm. His facial expression frightened her. What was he thinking?

27.

FOR SOME TIME Lincoln's representatives in Washington reviewed the trial records. Meanwhile Sibley decided to transfer the 1,700 uncondemned Indian captives who had surrendered at Camp Release to Fort Snelling near St. Paul. The transfer was necessary because of the difficulty to secure food for the large group at Fort Ridgely.

On November 7 the Indians set out on the long trek to Fort Snelling, a distance of approximately 130 miles.

The procession of men, women and children was four miles long. In a daze the slovenly, dirty Sioux shuffled slowly along. Depressed, they stared at the ground or the feet of the captive ahead of them. They no longer were proud Sioux; now they were hated Indians who had no hunting grounds or lodges to call home. They were at the mercy of the angry white men.

Days passed before they came to Henderson, a village north of Mankato and southwest of St. Paul. White citizens filled with rage at the sight of their hated enemies attacked the prisoners with stones, clubs, knives and guns. It was bedlam as guards tried to restrain the yelling, revengeful whites. Many Indians were hurt before the soldiers could restrain the angry citizens and again get the Sioux back into a procession. Finally on November 13, after a miserable journey, the captives reached Fort Snelling where they were put into a fenced camp of tepees on the north bank of the Minnesota River.

Cold and weary the prisoners settled in for a wretched winter during which many died as they waited for a decision from the government about plans for their future.

Meanwhile the 303 Indians who had been condemned to death were moved from the Lower Agency to Camp Lincoln. The shackled, condemned men were closely guarded, but the soldiers were unprepared for the vicious attacks of the enraged citizens of New Ulm. The procession of condemned men arrived at the time when the Germans who had remained in the area were burying their dead.

Armed with stones, bricks, clubs, axes and knives, the whites attacked the shackled Sioux. For a time mayhem reigned as the captives were beaten. Because many of the white men were absent, women led the assault.

The soldiers tried to protect their prisoners but the infuriated mob wielded axes, hatchets, knives, sticks and stones so effectively that about fifteen of the prisoners were injured. One woman split the jaw of an Indian with a hatchet, and another fractured a skull so that the victim died a few days later. Finally Sibley's soldiers drove the crowd back with a bayonet charge. Some of the guards also were seriously injured.

In Mankato, as in every part of the state, anger at the Sioux was at the boiling point. Men plotted how they could dispose of the 303 condemned men at Camp Lincoln. Quietly they armed themselves with knives, clubs and a few guns. On the night of December 4 they marched toward the camp, intent on murdering the Indians. But alert guards stopped the group, and the following day the condemned men were moved to a well-fortified log building at Mankato.

From the press, Governor Ramsey, generals in the army, and other prominent citizens, appeals came to President Lincoln for the immediate execution of the entire list of convicted Indians. Only one voice was raised in protest, that of Episcopal Bishop Henry B. Whipple who visited President Lincoln soon after the Sioux uprising ended; Bishop Whipple alone braved the mob spirit of the citizens to intercede for the condemned Indians.

For weeks the main topic of conversation throughout the state was what the decision would be from Lincoln about the number and names of Sioux to be executed. On December 6 the Minnesota Pioneer announced in two-inch headlines, "Only 38 Sioux To Die."

Wilhelm, Amelia and their children poured over the newspaper. Wilhelm exploded, "I can't believe it! Only thirty-eight of 303 convicted murderers! Lincoln should have been here! If his parents had been killed, he'd feel as I do! Hang 'em all!"

Amelia nodded. "Bishop Whipple talked to him. He's very—very—"

"Persuasive," Eddie volunteered.

"Yah. Whipple should have stayed out of it." Wilhelm got up. "I'm more sorry now than ever that we didn't get to the villains two nights ago before the president's decision. We could have finished them off for good. Only thirty eight! I can't believe it!"

"Will they let the others go?" Eddie asked.

"I don't know. Who can tell what Lincoln will do?"

The triplets listened, wide-eyed. "When will they kill them?" Charity asked.

Eddie managed a sickly grin. "December 26. It's a late Christmas present."

"How will they do it?"

"The paper says by hanging on the gallows in Mankato's public square."

"I'll be there," Wilhelm muttered.

Lincoln's list of condemned men was given to Major Joseph Brown, and to him fell the responsibility of identifying those who were to be executed. It was an agonizing task since the old Indian agent was acquainted with many of the men. Finally the condemned Sioux were separated from the rest of the prisoners and securely chained.

In the time remaining before the execution, the missionaries, Williamson, Riggs and Father Augustin Ravoux, spent much time with the convicts. Many of them were converted to Christianity and baptized. On December 24 and on Christmas Day, relatives of the condemned were allowed to visit them. According to reporters some broke down during these last visits, while others, true to the Sioux custom, faced death stoically.

The doomed Sioux asked permission to dance their

death dance in the prison yard just prior to the hanging. This request was refused.

Early the morning of December 26 people in the street listened as the condemned men inside the prison stockade began chanting their death songs. Over and over the slow, monotonous "Hi—yi—yi" of the weird Sioux song echoed through the December air. The eerie wail continued while Joseph Brown and his assistants prepared the victims for the gallows. Some listened to the priest while others painted their faces for their meeting with Death. After their chains were removed, their arms were bound with cords. The slow, solemn dirge stopped as a white cap was placed on each head. The cap would be rolled down over the face before the execution.

The doomed men objected to wearing the caps because they felt it was humiliating. Finally they crouched, subdued and waiting.

Long before the hour for the execution arrived, curious, vengeful citizens crowded the square for glimpses of the condemned. Rooftops were covered with onlookers and every window framed eager faces.

In the public square Eddie, Wilhelm and August Ketchum crowded close to the line of mounted soldiers. Behind them the citizens craned their necks. In front of the mounted men a double line of uniformed armed soldiers, their bayonets gleaming, strengthened the human barricade; as an added measure of security, still another line of armed men in uniform faced the ten-foot-high square gallows. In all 1300 soldiers were on hand to keep order.

Smoke poured from nearby chimneys to instantly be whipped away by the wind. The flag snapped from atop the tall flagpole. The crowd was hushed as they waited expectedly for the mass execution.

At 10:00 A.M. the thirty-eight prisoners marched from the prison to the wooden scaffold. As soon as they were in the yard they saw the gallows with the huge iron ring to which thirty-eight attached ropes swung wildly in the wind.

Again the unearthly Sioux death song began causing chills to race up the spines of many citizens. "Hi—yi—yi, hi—yi—yi, hi—yi—yi." They sang the deliberate, measured beat in unison as they mounted the gallows steps. The white caps were pulled over their faces and a noose was placed around each neck. The death song ended. The silence was intense.

Major Brown began a slow measured drumbeat. At the third roll, the executioner stepped forward and cut the rope. The platform fell and thirty-seven kicking, wriggling bodies were left blowing in the chill December wind. One rope had broken and the body was on the ground. Horrified, the spectators watched as the body again was suspended. After a few minutes the ropes hung straight with their victims.

A low prolonged cheer came from soldiers and citizens alike. Then everything was quiet. The crowd had witnessed America's greatest mass execution.

The dead were buried in a single grave near the river they loved. Rumor says that that night several doctors dug up the bodies to be used as subjects for anatomical study; Dr. William Mayo drew the corpse of Chief Cut Nose, and later his doctor sons learned osteology from the Sioux skeleton.

However, most of the chiefs in the uprising escaped execution. Many, including Little Crow, Shakopee, and Medicine Bottle escaped to the Dakota Territory when they realized they could not win the war against the whites. Eventually most of them made their way across the border into Canada.

The army unsuccessfully pursued Shakopee and Medicine Bottle into the Dakota Territory, but the chiefs ran to Canada where they were kidnapped in 1864 by government agents and brought back to Fort Snelling and sentenced to death. They were executed November 11, 1865. According to a legend, as Shakopee mounted the steps to the gallows he heard one of the early steam locomotives. Pointing to the train he said, "As the white man comes in, the Indian goes out."

The death song of the thirty-eight on that December morning in Mankato was the death song of the Minnesota Indians. They had made their last major attempt to drive the white intruders from their land.

28.

THE WINTERS FAMILY relaxed in their room in Moore's Hotel on a bright Sunday afternoon in January. Eddie went to the wooden peg on the wall behind the door which served to keep the family's few clothes in one place. He took down his coat, cap and a shirt. Then he slid the strap of Great-grandmother Mary's brown leather bag from the peg.

"What you doin'?" Hermie asked.

Eddie replaced his clothes on the peg. "I'm going to file this lock open."

Faith objected. "Grandma wouldn't like it. She never let anyone see inside that bag."

"Yah, I know. But it's all right now, ain't it, Pa?"

Wilhelm nodded. "Go ahead." He returned to study a

column of numbers on a paper before him.

Amelia sat beside the window mending Wilhelm's socks. The girls and Hermie gathered around to watch Eddie, who sat on the bed holding the bag between his knees. He drew the file back and forth against the shackle of the padlock. It grated and squeaked against the hard metal.

Hope put her hands over her ears. "I can't stand that noise! It sets my teeth on edge!"

Eddie grinned and filed faster. "Sure is hard metal," he remarked. At last the shackle fell apart and he removed the padlock and peered inside.

"Let me see! Let me see!" the girls and Hermie cried together as they gathered around the boy. Wilhelm and Amelia watched and listened.

"Get back!" Eddie complained. He pulled out a pair of once-white, age-yellowed knitted baby's bootees. Inside one little bootee there was a scrap of paper in writing which he handed to his father. "It's in German, Pa. Read it."

Wilhelm nodded. "Just as I thought. Grandma's keepsakes. It says, *November 1805. Ernst's first bootees.*"

Charity asked, "Are those Grandpa Winters' baby boots?"

"Yah. What have you got?" Wilhelm asked as Eddie studied a paper yellow with age.

"Grandpa Winters' baptismal paper." He reached in the bag and pulled out a folded paper. "Hm-m-m. This one was yours, Pa. It is a note you wrote. It's in German." He handed it to his father.

Wilhelm smiled as he translated. "It says, *June 1835. Dear Grandma and Grandpa, I want you to see how well I can write. I am seven years old. Wilhelm.*"

"What else is there?" Faith asked.

Eddie continued through several more keepsakes of

the Winters family. Finally he pulled out a heavy cloth sack from inside the bag. He peeped inside. "Whew!" he exclaimed. "You'd better do this one, Pa. No wonder Grandma's bag was so heavy!"

The girls and Hermie gathered around Wilhelm as he opened the drawstring. "Money!" they exclaimed.

Amelia came to look over Wilhelm's shoulder. "Well, I'll be—" he muttered as he reached inside the bag and pulled out a handful of silver dollars. "Where did she get this—and in United States money?" He dumped it on the bed.

Wilhelm opened a small folded paper. "Here's a note to Pa. It says, *Ernst: Jacob and I saved our money in Germany—all our life we saved. In New York I had it changed to United States dollars. They wanted me to take paper money, but I wanted silver.*

I would like Wilhelm to have half of the dollars and so would Jacob if he was here. Your mother, Mary."

The triplets and Eddie were counting. Finally Eddie announced, "Four hundred dollars! We're rich!"

Wilhelm shook his head. "I don't know how they saved that much. Grandma always was—well—stingy. And all the time she was saving for us."

"Can we have some new clothes, Pa?" Charity asked.

"Yah, can we?" Faith and Hope chimed.

"We'll see. The money, with what I got when I sold the team and wagon, will make a nice little nest egg for us to get started again. We can't spend it foolishly."

Eddie said, "We could go back to our land and start farming."

Wilhelm jumped up. "Never! I never want to see that cursed place again! Twelve years of sweat and work from daylight to dark and those Indian fiends destroyed it in minutes! They took my relatives and my buildings; without them, the land is nothing. The damned savages can have it!"

Amelia nodded. "A lot of settlers feel that way. I'd be afraid to go back out there. They say hundreds of settlers already have left Minnesota. But where should we go?"

Hope said, "I like Mankato. There's a school for girls here. It would be nice if we could go this fall."

"There are 1,700 Indians in the camp at Fort Snelling," Eddie said, "but they're supposed to be 'good Indians,' and they're guarded. Someday I'm going to get a pass and go see that camp."

"Humph!" Wilhelm snorted. "There's no such thing as a good Indian—unless he's dead!" He stared at the pile of silver on the bed. "I think we'd better stay here, work for the Moores and save our money until we know what we want to do. By then we'll have a nice little sum to start something new."

29.

ABOUT SEVENTEEN HUNDRED "good Indians," men, women, children and half-breeds, were quartered at Fort Snelling on the banks of the Minnesota River during the winter of 1862–1863. The Indian camp was enclosed by a high board fence around hundreds of tepees. Armed soldiers guarded and paraded inside and outside the quarters. For this large undertaking the United States government outlay for the Indians' support was less than $2,000 per month.

Hundreds of widows and orphans were mainly dependent for food and clothing on their own efforts, or on those of a sympathetic public. Visitors thronged the enclosure with passes from the post commander.

Early in January Wilhelm and Eddie visited the camp. They were shocked at the deplorable conditions. As they left the office of the post commander, a filthy sight was revealed. The streets between rows of tepees were covered with offal, human waste, rubbish, intestines and other internal organs of butchered animals. Even in January, the stench was overwhelming. For several minutes father and son silently studied the appalling sight before them.

Finally Eddie said, "How can they live like this?"

Wilhelm shook his head in disbelief. "Our hogs had better quarters," he muttered.

Barefooted women and children splashed around in the filthy muddy slush, seemingly unaware of discomfort. Their ragged, dirty clothing was small protection against the January weather. The sound of violent coughing came from every side.

"It's likely many of these people have lung fever and will die," Wilhelm said softly.

"Yah. What will the government do with more than 1700 people?"

"I don't know. There's talk that in May they'll be sent to reservations in the Dakota Territory."

Wilhelm and Eddie gingerly picked their way through the filthy streets. "There's not many men," Eddie remarked.

"No. They're mostly squaws and children. Some of their men are condemned captives who were pardoned by Lincoln. They're still in Mankato and I've heard they'll be sent to Davenport, Iowa, in April."

"Maybe some of them are the husbands and fathers of these poor people. They'll still be separated."

"Yah, but don't start feeling sorry for them. Don't forget what their men did. They murdered nearly a thousand settlers in cold blood, they burned our buildings and crops and they've driven ten thousand Minnesotans from their homes. They carried a hundred of our women and girls into captivity and some of them were treated with fiendish brutality—tortured and raped." Wilhelm's voice was rising.

"Yah, Pa. I read in the paper they murdered five hundred people—not a thousand."

"Who knows how many? Every news story gives a different number."

Silently they walked on. Haggard, stoic faces with hollow eyes met their glances. Eddie whispered, "I wish I could help them. There's a boy about Hermie's age."

Wilhelm turned on his heel. "Let's get out of here."

They hurried toward the gate. "Pa," Eddie said. "There are the missionaries, Reverend Williamson and Reverend Riggs. Let's talk to them."

After exchanging greetings the aged men looked out over the camp. "Pitiful sight, isn't it?" Williamson said.

"Yah, but Reverend, they brought it on themselves. Their men murdered, burned and plundered. Now their wives and children are punished for what their men did. It's too bad, but I wish the government would get them out of here."

Reverend Riggs bristled. "Wilhelm, it's true the devil took possession of the Indians, but he also possessed some of the whites. Maybe you didn't know multitudes of white men and women turned plunderers. As the people fled a town, the inhabitants of the town and country beyond, who were fleeing, came in and plundered the houses after the panic had subsided. The whites went through the deserted districts and gathered up wagon loads of property which the Indians had left. Farming tools as well as household goods were stolen."

Wilhelm scratched his head thoughtfully. "I hadn't

heard that."

Reverend Williamson broke in. "The newspapers print only one side of the story. You hear about Indians taking scalps. It's true, some did, but whites also took Indian scalps and sold them in St. Paul for large sums of money. The white plunderers and the army finished what the savages had spared."

"The whole thing is a dirty business," Wilhelm said softly. "I'd like to leave Minnesota, but I don't know where to go."

Reverend Williamson glanced at Reverend Riggs. "We have much work to do here in trying to reduce some of the misery and to convert these people to Christianity. My son, John, also is working with the prisoners."

Missionary Riggs nodded. "As you know the 265 condemned men who President Lincoln pardoned are in the prison in Mankato. They're more fortunate than these poor people," he motioned, "for the prison is one great school. Groups of ten or so gather about the ones who attended our mission schools. We've had spelling books made for them. They're learning to write. Soon they will write letters to their families here at Fort Snelling. Wilhelm, they learn fast. They are making great progress."

Wilhelm grunted. Reverend Williamson continued. "My son, John, and I work with the men, too. I preach to them on Sunday and we pray and sing with them in evening meetings. Many are becoming Christians. Soon now we will have a baptismal service."

Wilhelm stared at a barefooted, ragged squaw with a baby strapped to her back. Her eyes met his. She walked on, but she saw the disapproval and disgust in his expression.

Reverend Riggs went on. "We're going to start classes

here for the ones who want to learn to read, and we preach and pray with them often."

"Humph," Wilhelm grumbled. "It looks to me they might better spend time cleaning up this filthy camp."

Reverend Williamson commented, "It's true there is much to be done. Bishop Whipple, Reverend Hinman and Father Ravoux are working with us on helping these people. We cannot accept Governor Ramsey's statement that they be regarded and treated as outlaws."

Wilhelm turned. "I agree with Ramsey. I'll be glad to see them gone from Minnesota. I don't care where they send them, but I'd like to go where I'd never see another Indian. They're untrustworthy and irresponsible and should be treated no better than the states treat lunatics. Frankly, I'd like to see all of them exterminated!" He turned to Eddie. "Let's get out of this place."

30.

EDDIE AND HIS FATHER labored at cleaning the stables of the barn at Moore's Hotel. "Pa," the boy began, "have you decided where we're going when we leave Minnesota?"

Wilhelm tossed a forkful of straw and manure to the manure pile outside the stable. "No. I just know I don't want to farm again."

"Why don't we go west to the gold fields in Colorado or California?"

"Hm-m-m. I'd like that. I think with the money Grandma left us, we'd have enough cash to make the trip." He hesitated. "But your Ma and the girls wouldn't want to go. They like living in Mankato."

Eddie leaned on the handle of his pitchfork. "You're the head of the family, Pa. You make the important decisions."

"Yah, but I was the one that decided we would come to America. I was wrong. It was the worst mistake I've ever made. I don't want to make another like that."

"You want to stay here and be a stable hand the rest of your life?"

Wilhelm scratched his head. "Hell no, but—going west would be quite an undertaking. We'd have to have a team, covered wagon and supplies. And I don't know where we'd start from to go west."

"We can find out. Think about it, Pa."

"Yah, I will. I've always wanted to go out there since I heard about the gold rush in New York in 1850."

A few days later while Amelia darned socks, the girls read and Hermie played with blocks on the floor, Wilhelm brought up the subject of future family plans.

Amelia glanced at Wilhelm and Eddie who sat bolt upright in their chairs near the window of the hotel room. "You two look uncomfortable. What's the matter?"

Wilhelm squirmed and looked at Eddie. The boy urged, "Tell them, Pa."

Reluctantly he began. "We need to decide what we're going to do. I don't want to be a stable hand the rest of my life."

Amelia dropped her darning. Her blue eyes were clouded. "Why not? We're comfortable here, we're laying up money and soon we can build a house and live like a family again."

"Well—Eddie and me, we'd like to go west."

"Why? We have everything here that we need."

"I want to leave this cursed state. And we might make it big in the gold fields."

There was dead silence in the room. The girls and Amelia, their eyes huge and disapproving, stared at him. His face reddened.

Eddie broke the silence. "It would be an adventure! We'd travel in a wagon train in a covered wagon with a lot of other people. It would be exciting! And we'd probably find lots of gold! We'd all camp together at night—it would be fun!"

"Do we have to go, Ma?" Charity asked. "Faith, Hope and I could stay here and go to school and work for Mrs. Moore."

Amelia's face was drawn and tired-looking. "Whatever we do, we'll stay together as a family." She picked up her darning.

"We don't have to make up our mind now," Wilhelm said softly. "Think about it."

Amelia brushed back a lock of gray-streaked blonde hair. "I know from the past—when you're set on doing something, you'll do it come hell or high water. And Eddie is just like you. The Winters men want to wander the earth. Yah, girls, we will all go west to look for gold." Her voice was low and resigned. "We'll traipse along with your father and brother while they look for the pot of gold at the end of the rainbow. Our family is like those Indians on the gallows. This Indian war left them and all of the settlers just—just blowing in the wind. No home, no nothing."

Wilhelm caught Eddie's eye. He winked triumphantly.

EPILOGUE

ON FEBRUARY 16, 1863, Congress cancelled all treaties with the Sioux. Now they truly were homeless. An act of March 3, 1863 provided that Indians in custody of the government should be removed from Minnesota. President Lincoln decided to locate them on the Missouri River near Fort Randall. The removal was the responsibility of Clark W. Thompson, the Superintendent of Indian Affairs for the northern area, including Minnesota.

Superintendent Thompson was authorized to make necessary purchases and to select a reservation on the northeast bank of the Missouri River about 80 miles above Fort Randall and 600 miles northwest of St. Louis.

Preparations were made to ship the exiled Sioux like so many cattle, to the assigned tract of land. On May 4 the steamer *Davenport* took on 770 Indians. At the loading on the levee in St. Paul white citizens hooted and threw stones at the defenseless Indians, but none were seriously hurt.

Reverend Samuel Hinman accompanied this party. The following day 540 Sioux were put on board the steamboat *Northerner*. John P. Williamson, a son of the old missionary, traveled with this group. He reported that they shoved off at dusk. In a short time from all parts of the boat the Indians sang hymns, soft sweet music "like the murmur of many waters." Prayers were said between hymns. Finally they drew their blankets about them and fell asleep.

This party was transferred to railway cars at Hannibal, Missouri and transported to St. Joseph, Missouri where they waited several days for the arrival of the *Davenport* with its large group of Indians. On to this steamer was crowded the whole body of exiles. Because there was so little room, they were forced to sleep in relays, since all of them were unable to lie down at one time. The weather was hot and rations of hardtack and pork were musty. The steamer labored against the powerful current of the Missouri and did not reach its destination until the end of May. Because of the heat and unhealthful conditions, many of the Indians died before they reached the end of the trip at Crow Creek.

But their problems were not over. Because of the Santee Sioux arrival date, it was too late to plant potatoes and too dry for corn to grow well. They were, in a sense, prisoners of war so they were not allowed to search the country for edible berries and plants to supplement their rations. It was evident the government would have to furnish food for the winter of 1864 not only for the Sioux but also for the Winnebagos who had also been removed from Minnesota and placed on a reservation near that of the Sioux.

Provisions were sent by wagon train from St. Paul and Mankato. The trip took twenty days. The food was of poor quality and insufficient quantity to feed the more than 3,000 Indians. Eventually permission was given the desperate people to go to the Indian agency near Fort Randall to beg for food and fuel.

So once again there was hunger and threatened starvation in the bark lodges. John Williamson remained with the Indians. In mid-winter of 1864 a Sioux hunter, who had a hidden gun, escaped from a guard. He returned to tell Williamson that there were buffalo on the plains and that he could kill enough animals to keep the people alive.

Williamson secured reluctant permission for a buffalo hunt. He accompanied the fifty men, who with their families made a group of nearly five hundred. They had half a dozen guns and ammunition, rations of flour and pork and two horses, one of them Williamson's. They traveled one hundred miles up the James River and camped north of Redfield, South Dakota. The desperate people found vast herds of fat buffalo so that their food supply, for the present, was assured.

John Williamson remained throughout the excursion with the Indians, who called him their "Saint John." Each morning and evening, in the snow, he met with the Christian Indians to read the Scriptures, pray and sing hymns.

Finally, after three years, the Santee Sioux were moved from the miserable Crow Creek reservation to one near the mouth of the Niobrara River in northern Nebraska.

In later years Williamson wrote of the Santee Sioux, "They are without doubt the most advanced in civilization of any of the Sioux nation."

Returning to the fate of the Indian convicts in the Mankato prison, we find that on April 22, 1863 they were shipped down the Mississippi River to Davenport, Iowa, where there were government barracks. Here wide liberty was allowed, for some of them worked on farms or about the city.

Finally by 1866, John Williamson had succeeded in securing pardons from the president for the men. Shortly thereafter they returned to their families on the Niobrara River.

Little Crow, the Sioux leader in the uprising of 1862, was conspicuously absent from the trials and punishment of the Indians. He first fled to the Dakota prairies and in early 1863 he spent time near Fort Garry in Canada. He returned to Minnesota in June with a squaw, a sixteen-year-old son, Wowinapa, and sixteen Indian followers. Little Crow and his men planned a horse stealing raid.

During June and early July six murders were committed in the area where Little Crow's party was operating. Whether Little Crow's braves were responsible is not positively known, but feelings ran high against the Indians.

On the evening of July 3, the old chief and his son were picking berries a few miles northwest of Hutchinson. At the same time two white residents of the area, Nathan Lamson and his son, Chauncey, were hunting. They saw the Indians, but did not know who they were.

Believing any Indian was fair game, the Lamsons crept behind a tree close to the berry patch and shot Little Crow above the hip. The old chief returned the fire, slightly wounding the elder Lamson in the shoulder. The farmer crawled out of the line of fire and tried to reload his rifle. At the same time Chauncey Lamson and Little Crow exchanged shots. The Sioux chief fell, fatally wounded by a shot to the chest.

The younger Lamson thought his father was dead, and believing other Indians were nearby, he hurried to Hutchinson for help.

At daylight the following morning, citizens and soldiers from the fort found the body of an Indian, neatly laid out with a pair of new moccasins and wearing the coat of one of the six men murdered a few days previous.

Nathan Lamson had disappeared, leaving behind his white shirt. When the group returned from Hutchinson, he greeted them explaining he had waited quietly until the Indians' moaning and talking had stopped, and then he had gone into town at night.

The dead Indian was taken to Hutchinson where the scalp was removed and the corpse horribly mutilated before it was buried in a pile of offal.

Though several people who saw the body declared that it was that of Little Crow, the death was not positively confirmed until twenty-six days later when the half-starved sixteen-year-old son, Wowinapa was captured. The boy told how the white men had killed his father.

Wowinapa was tried and found guilty of taking part in the 1862 uprising, of attempted murder and horse stealing. Though sentenced to be hanged, eventually he was pardoned and released.

Later in life Wowinapa became a Christian and took the name of Thomas Wakeman. He is known as the founder of the YMCA among the Sioux.

In 1864 Nathan Lamson received a reward of five hundred dollars from the state for killing Little Crow. Chauncey Lamson, who actually fired the fatal shot, collected a bounty on Little Crow's scalp.

A state monument erected in 1929 marks the spot where the old chief died.

For many years Indian bandits created panic along the Minnesota frontier. As civilization moved westward, other Sioux tribes challenged the white man. While Little Crow and the Minnesota uprising still were fresh in the nation's memory it learned of other Indian leaders —Red Cloud, Sitting Bull and Crazy Horse. Bloody battles were fought and finally in 1890 the Wounded Knee incident brought an end to the Indian warfare which had been set in motion twenty-eight years earlier at Acton, Minnesota in August, 1862.

HISTORICAL CHARACTERS

Akepa — Sioux chief

Baker, Howard — Son-in-law of Howard Jones

Big Eagle — Sioux chief

Bishop, John — Sergeant at Fort Ridgely

Breaking Up — An Indian brave

Brown, Joseph and wife — Government Indian agent

Brown Wing — An Indian chief

Crazy Horse — An Indian chief

Cut Nose — Sioux chief

Dickinson, J. C. — A white refugee

Divoll, George — An employee at Myrick's store

Flandrau, Charles E. — An attorney, judge and military man

Galbraith, Thomas J. — A government Indian agent

Gere, Thomas — A lieutenant at Fort Ridgely

Gray Bird — An Indian chief

Hinman, Samuel — An Episcopal minister and missionary

Jones, Robinson — Storekeeper and innkeeper

Killing Ghost — An Indian brave

Kitzman, Paul — A German settler

Kreiger, Justina — A German settler

Lamson, Chauncey — A Minnesota farmer

Lamson, Nathan — Chauncey Lamson's father

Lincoln, Abraham — United States President

Little Crow — A Sioux chief

Little Paul (Paul Mazakutemani) — A friendly Indian

Lynd, James — A clerk at Myrick's store

Mankato — A Sioux chief

Marsh, John — A captain at Fort Ridgely

Martel, Charles — The ferryman at the Lower Agency

Mayo, Charles — A doctor at the emergency hospital at New Ulm

McMahun, William — A doctor at the emergency hospital at New Ulm

McPhail, Samuel — A colonel at Fort Ridgely

Muller, Alfred — A doctor at Fort Ridgely

Myrick, Andrew J. — Storekeeper and trader

Other Day, John — A Christian Indian

Pauli, Emilie — A thirteen-year-old victim of the war

Pokagon — A Potawatomi Indian from Michigan

Prescott, Philander — A fur trader

Ramsey, Alexander — The first territorial governor

Ravoux, Augustin — A Catholic priest

Red Cloud — An Indian chief

Red Middle Voice — A Sioux chief

Renville, Antoine — An elder at the Riggs mission

Roos, Charles — Sheriff of Brown County

Runs-Against-Something-When-Crawling — An Indian brave

Shakopee — A Sioux chief

Sheehan, Timothy J. — A lieutenant at Fort Ridgely

Sibley, Henry — First governor of Minnesota

Sitting Bull — An Indian chief

Stanton, Edwin — Secretary of State under President Abraham Lincoln

Sturgis, William — A private at Fort Ridgely

Thompson, Clark W. — Superintendent of Indian Affairs

Traveling Hail — A Sioux chief

Wabasha — A Sioux chief

Wakeman, Thomas — The white man's name taken by Wowinapa

Webster, Viranus — A settler from Michigan

Wilson, Clara — The adopted daughter of Robinson Jones

Williamson, John P. — A missionary

Williamson, Thomas S. — A missionary

Whipple, Henry — An Episcopal bishop and minister

White Dog — A Sioux chief

Wowinapa — A son of Little Crow

BIBLIOGRAPHY

Brown, Dee. *Bury My Heart At Wounded Knee*. Simon and Shuster – Pocket Books, 1981.

Carley, Kenneth. *The Sioux Uprising of 1862*. Minnesota Historical Society, 1961.

Folwell, William Watts. *A History of Minnesota II*. Minnesota Historical Society, 1924.

Heard, Isaac V. D. *History of the Sioux War*. Harper and Brothers, 1865.

Kirtland, Caroline. *Our New Home in the West*. G. P. Putnam's Sons, 1953.

May and Brinks. *A Michigan Reader*. William B. Eerdmans, 1974.

McConkey, Harriet Bishop. *Dakota War Whoop*. R. R. Donnelly and Sons, 1965.

Michener, James A. *Centennial*. Fawcett Crest, 1974.

Moberg, Vilhelm. *The Emigrants I, II, III, IV*. Popular Library, 1978.

Schlissel, Lillian. *Women's Diaries of the Westward Journey*. Schocken Books, 1982.

World Book Encyclopedia: C Book – Canals; I Book – Indian Wars; Map, p. 57, Ill. and Miss. Canal (abandoned).

Please Cut Along This Line

Wilderness Adventure Books
320 Garden Lane P. O. Box 968
Fowlerville, MI 48836

Please send me:

__________ copies of *BLOWING IN THE WIND* at $11.95

(Postage and sales tax will be paid by the publisher.)
Send check or money order — no cash or C.O.D.   I am enclosing $__________.

*Mr./Mrs./Ms.*______________________________

*Street*______________________________

*City*______________ *State/Province*______________ *ZIP*__________